Between Two Flags

BETWEEN
TWO FLAGS

The Life of
Baron Sir Rudolf von Slatin Pasha,
GCVO, KCMG, CB

by
GORDON BROOK-SHEPHERD

FOUNDED 1838

GPPS

G. P. PUTNAM'S SONS
NEW YORK

FIRST AMERICAN EDITION 1973

To my old friend
Fritz P. Molden
whose idea this was

CONTENTS

ILLUSTRATIONS

Following page 174.

1 A 'beau sabreur' already, when barely six years old. Rudolf (left) with his two brothers, Adolf and Heinrich. (c) *Sammlung Paul Slatin, Wien*
2 Mohammed Ahmed – The Mahdi (a contemporary sketch). *The Mansell Collection*
3 Gordon's head brought to Slatin Pasha: 'Is this not the head of your uncle, the unbeliever?' *William Gordon Davis*
4 The Khalifa's house in Omdurman. The corner where Slatin Pasha sat when a prisoner of the Khalifa. *Durham Archives*
5 The Khalifa's harem (the only two-storied building in Omdurman), in which one of his wives was killed by a shell. *Durham Archives*
6 'The Prussian Oak' that never bent – the German Charles Neufeld (fellow-prisoner of Slatin's), with his wife and children. *Durham Archives*
7 General Charles William Gordon (Pasha) – Slatin's first British hero and commander. *William Gordon Davis*
8 The Gallows: A crowd gathers round the body of the last man hanged by the Khalifa. *Durham Archives*
9 The victorious General Kitchener leaves the field after the Battle of Omdurman. *Durham Archives*
10 The Union Jack being hoisted again over the ruins of General Gordon's Palace in Khartoum, after the victory at Omdurman. *Durham Archives*
11 The Mahdi's banner, captured at McNeill's Zeriba and presented to Queen Victoria. *Radio Times Hulton Picture Library*

FOREWORD

A hundred years ago, a young Austrian boy, Jewish by blood but Catholic by faith, set off on a whim from Imperial Vienna to seek fame and fortune in what was then the very dark continent of Africa. His name was Rudolf Slatin and the impulse to leave his home and the boundaries of the Habsburg Monarchy for the first time in his life was nothing more than the hope of finding a job with a Cairo bookseller. It was an amazing start to an amazing life.

This lad, with no money and nothing but the commercial instincts of his forebears in his veins became, not a trader in Egypt, but a soldier in the unruly Sudan to the south. Indeed he was soon one of General Gordon's key commanders in the struggle against the Mahdi, and the last one to hold out. Unlike Gordon, he survived defeat in that battle, but only to be held a captive for eleven years in the Mahdist camp.

Then the great escape across hundreds of miles of desert to the British Army lines which made his name a European byword overnight; the triumphant return to Omdurman with the Anglo-Egyptian expedition which smashed the Mahdist regime for good; and after that, fourteen years as Inspector-General of what was, in fact though not in law, a British protectorate. And all this without ever ceasing to be an Austrian citizen and a loyal subject of His Apostolic Majesty the Emperor Franz Joseph.

There is enough that is extraordinary and exciting even in

that one section and one aspect of his life to make him a figure of interest. But Rudolf Slatin was much more than a desert adventurer. For twenty summer seasons in Europe he was also a bright star in the firmament of the old social order, welcome in half a dozen of its royal courts and in scores of its great houses. The breastful of international decorations he accumulated included two British knighthoods. He became a great personal favourite of the old Queen Victoria and, later, a constant companion of Edward vii, her son and successor. This is a second interest of Slatin's career. Through his eyes we get a parvenu's inside picture of that great Edwardian age which, for all its surface glitter, seemed as solid as granite underneath.

Then everything, the glitter as well as the granite, went up sky-high at Sarajevo. In some ways Slatin's life now becomes more fascinating, as well as more difficult to follow. The Great War destroyed his world, as it did that of millions of others. But in his case there was something else. Lieutenant-General Baron Sir Rudolf von Slatin Pasha, GCVO, KCMG, CB (as he then was), was made up of two equal and separate halves that could only remain stuck together with the cosmopolitan glue of peacetime Europe. Now, he was cruelly chopped in two. In August 1914, the two halves fell apart – Slatin the subject of Austria and Slatin the servant of Britain. He was crushed by merely having to face this (to him) unthinkable dilemma. Trying to find a way round it in the dreadful war years that followed almost destroyed him. The memory of it, and the legacy of it, recorded implacably in the secret archives of both London and Vienna, pursued him forever afterwards – at the Peace Conference at Versailles (which he attended for the new Austrian Republic) and even as a peacetime pilgrim back to his beloved England.

There is a love-story to lighten these agonizing years, involving a very remarkable woman whom Slatin married only four days before war broke out. This too is touched with tragedy. She had entered his life too late and was to leave it too early.

But it is this inner dilemma of his, even more than his romances and his career on the battlefields and in the ball-rooms, which makes Slatin such an archetypal figure. For, at heart, his was the problem of roots, the problem of personal identification. In our time, much more than in his, this is one of the critical problems of society. The millions of refugees, displaced persons, émigrés or even sun-seeking expatriates who dot our globe all have Slatin's dilemma somewhere inside them.

Where, they may well ask themselves, as he did, do we belong: to the country of our birth or the country of our adoption? Where do our real loyalties lie? Which is our natural culture? Where, ideally, would we like to live; or, more important, to die?

As well as the excitement and glamour of his life, it was the mystery of human roots which attracted me to writing this first full-scale biography of Rudolf Slatin (and only the second work in any language ever to appear on him). As he himself published only an account of his African adventures (and that incomplete) his story has had to be reconstructed piece by piece out of his personal diaries; out of the letters which have survived (fortunately hundreds of them) to and from his many friends; out of governmental and royal archives in England and Austria; and, last but not least, out of the recollections of a handful of Europeans who knew him and who are still alive today.

These living eyewitnesses are as varied as was Slatin's own life. They range from the last Empress of Austria-Hungary, in exile in Switzerland, to an inn-keeper's daughter in Styria; and, on the English side, from a Knight of the British Empire retired in Bournemouth to a Major who commanded the Sudan Camel Corps more than sixty years ago, and who now lives just off Piccadilly. All of them are in their 80s and several well into their 90s.

Nor of course are they confined to Europe. When I was in Cairo in the spring of 1971, thinking my research was over, I happened to mention the name of Rudolf Slatin to a very distinguished old lady living in a cavernous villa in Zamalek. She disappeared without a word and returned a few minutes later to her drawing-room carrying a shoe-box bursting with envelopes. Inside were scores of personal letters written to her by the great man early this century. She had not re-read them for years and handed them to me on one promise. I had to destroy them when I had made whatever tactful use of them I chose. 'Il est temps de brûler mon passé. Aidez-moi donc.'

A few days before writing this Foreword (which is, of course, the last thing to be written in a book), I duly burnt those heavily-embossed scraps of her past, and of Slatin's. It reminded me yet again how fascinating his life had been, and what pleasure it had given me to try and re-create it.

ACKNOWLEDGEMENTS

Any list must begin with the name of Richard Hill, who pioneered research into Slatin Pasha with his book of that name, the first on the subject in any language. This is only a short (152 pp.) volume and the only section of Slatin's life dealt with fully is the period he spent as an Anglo-Egyptian official in the Sudan, a country where Mr Hill himself later served.

Perhaps more important than the book is the work the author did as archivist at the University Library, Durham where all Slatin's papers, and many associated documents, were deposited. Mr Hill's painstaking work of cataloguing is a boon to any subsequent researcher. While on the subject of Durham, I would like to thank Sir John Richmond KCMG, a former ambassador to the Sudan and now a lecturer at the University, for his help; also Mr Foster, the Keeper of Oriental Books and his staff for their unfailing courtesy.

As for the Austrian end of the operation, I am indebted, as Mr Hill was, to the Haus, Hof und Staatsarchiv and to the two researchers who worked there on my behalf, Drs Anton Staudinger and Karl Stuhlpfarrer. Generalleutnant von Bornemann very generously provided me with the results of all his research into Slatin's war-time activities, as shown in other Vienna archives, much of which had never been previously published.

The list of other people in Austria who each contributed something of their own to the Slatin story is too long to give in full. I would like to single out Paul Slatin, a great-nephew, who produced dozens of most valuable family letters and other material; my friend Prince Alois Auersperg, who kindly put me in touch with Count Wilzcek, a descendant on his mother's side from Slatin's great patrons, the Kinskys; Dr Kurt Kamniker, whose father was a colleague of Slatin's at the 1919 peace negotiations at St Germain; another old friend, Dr Julius Meinl, who seems to know something about everything; and two long-standing collaborators, Anneliese Schulz and Dr Karl Zrounek.

In England I must thank above all Sir Ronald Wingate Bt. (son of Slatin's greatest friend and most influential colleague) for the many hours of his time he has given me. Sir Michael Adeane, Private Secretary to the Queen while this book was being written, provided some youthful memories of his own of Slatin at the Court of St James and kindly arranged a family luncheon so that I could meet and talk to his aunt Lady Stamfordham, who met Slatin at the same court much more often.

Arthur Dodds-Parker MP introduced me to his nonogenarian uncle Major Alec Wise, who provided some interesting sidelights on Slatin in the Sudan sixty years ago. Several even more revealing anecdotes were provided by Sir Mervyn Wheatley KBE, a Sudan Government colleague of Slatin's who lived for some years in the very next house to the Pasha in Khartoum. Another surviving old Sudan hand and colleague who has helped me is Sir Angus Gillan.

One old English lady who knew Slatin in Egypt in her youth is Mrs Esmé Nicoll of Honiton, and I am most obliged to her (and to her nephew Sir James Bowker KCMG) for arranging to let me see and use references to Slatin in her diaries of the early 1900s.

I must also thank Miss Beatrice Griffiths of the British Embassy in Cairo for helping me to trace several of Slatin's surviving friends and acquaintances in Egypt, and for introducing me to one or two of them.

All the above people had not previously been contacted over Slatin and the material they provided is thus quite new.

The most massive sources of new material however have been found in archives in this country quite unconnected with the Slatin Papers at Durham. The Public Records Office provided many fresh details of his official life, (and quite a few about his personal life) especially in the 1914–18 and post-war periods.

Above all there has been the hitherto unpublished material on Slatin in the Royal Archives, references to which are very frequent from the middle chapters onwards. My thanks are again due to the Queen's Librarian, Robert Mackworth-Young, and to Miss Jane Langton and other members of his staff for all their help, some of it, as the military citations have it, 'beyond the normal call of duty'. I am by now accustomed to regard this most august of Britain's archives as also being, in my experience, the most efficient. It is nonetheless worthwhile saying so.

Part One

Africa in the 1870's showing the rival thrusts of the Great Powers

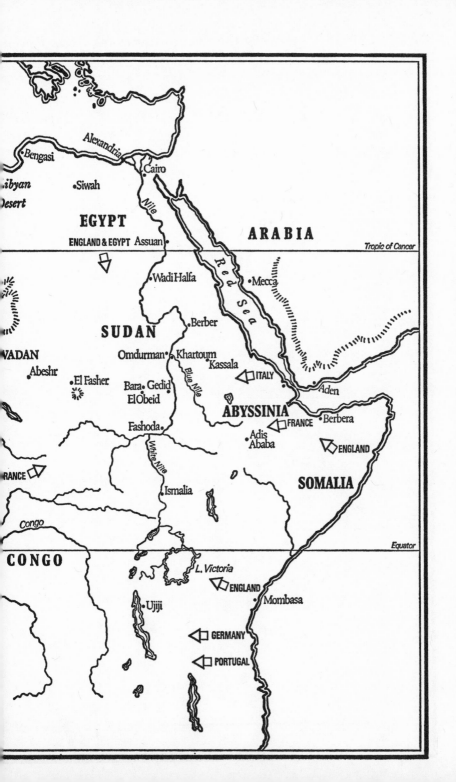

Chapter One

THE BOY FROM VIENNA

It was a strangely unilluminated beginning to a life that was to be lived in the constant public glare of two continents. In the one book Rudolf Slatin ever wrote, which deals with his adventures in the Sudan of the Mahdi, he tells us absolutely nothing about his origins and first years in Vienna. The subject never crops up in any of the scores of lectures he gave nor in the hundreds of private letters of his which have survived. There is not one childhood story in all the family correspondence still preserved by his Austrian descendants. We do not even know whether there was a cat on the hearth-rug or a Christmas turkey on the table. Two old ladies still alive today* who, as young girls at the turn of the century, both admired him and grew fond of him, cannot recall a single sentence from his lips about the years before he leapt to fame. The same is true of the son† of his lifelong English protector and friend, a son who grew to manhood with Slatin as a regular part of his own family background. It is as though Baron Sir Rudolf von Slatin Pasha, GCVO, KCMG, CB, soldier-of-fortune and darling of the old European courts, wanted to begin his life as he ended it, cushioned so grandly between all those titles and decorations. The plain Rudolf Slatin in the middle he was content to leave in the shadows.

However, the Vienna of the Emperor Franz Joseph into

---

* Frau Ermina Köchert (see pp. 237) and 'Miss Emily' (see p. 236).
  Sir Ronald Wingate (see pp. 211-12).

which he was born was a highly-documented capital, where each citizen was officially registered not only according to his religious faith but also according to his *Stand* or personal and professional status. So the church registries of the early and middle nineteenth century yield up a few family details. The present-day descendants of the great aristocratic house of Kinsky, patrons of the Slatins, have supplied a few more. Scanty though these facts are, they none the less give clues to Rudolf's life and character.

The Slatins originally came from Bohemia. Their native village of Herzmann Miestitz (Herˇmanuˇv Mĕstec in Czech) was on the main Kinsky estate of that name and it is possible that, for generations back, they had served the local grandees in one capacity or another. Exactly how it is impossible to say. Markus Slatin, who was Rudolf's grandfather, is entered in the local records simply as a merchant or trader of the place. His son Michael, who was born at Herzmann Miestitz on 24 July 1811, is described almost as vaguely as a *Commissionär*.

There is much more precision about their racial origin. All these early Slatins were Jews who married Jewish women, and all of them down to and including Markus and his wife Theresia also practised the Jewish faith. Thus it is no surprise, when they moved down to Vienna in the 1820s or '30s to try their luck in the Imperial capital, to find them living in the Leopoldstad, a district in the flat and swampy area east of the Danube which had once been the official Jewish ghetto and which still housed most of the city's Jewish inhabitants.

However, Michael Slatin proceeded to introduce some drastic changes in the family chronicle, both as regards how they worshipped and where they lived. On 25 March 1938, when he was in his twenty-seventh year, he was baptized a Roman Catholic at Saint Augustin's Church in Vienna's First District or 'Inner City'. It was not everybody who could be baptized in the famous and fashionable *Augustinerkirche*; and it was quite exceptional at that time for a young Jew of no name or standing in the capital to be accorded the privilege. This is borne out by a note made in the church registry to the effect that Michael's baptism had been specially authorized 'by high government sanction No. 69202 of 5 December 1837'. Quite possibly, the

Kinskys had already extended their patronage to Michael Slatin in Vienna, as they were to do later with all his sons.

We can, of course, only speculate as to his own motives for abandoning his religious creed; but for anyone bent on making his mark in the capital, the advantages were obvious enough. To be a Jew by religious faith as well as by blood in the Austria-Hungary of 1838, meant that one could not yet move freely throughout all the domains of the Monarchy and that permits were still needed to settle in a particular area or to take up any of the professions. (These archaic restrictions were not finally abolished until ten years later, as part of the aftermath of the 1848 Revolution.) But if the Jew by race became a Roman Catholic by faith, then nearly all doors were open to him in theory, though he would find that a lot of them moved very stiffly in practice.

In short, if someone like young Michael Slatin wanted to climb up the social ladder of his day, he could only do so by stepping over the faith of his ancestors. Michael evidently did want to move up, and, thanks in part to that Catholic baptism, he succeeded. The registries show that he married twice, and each time in the best Catholic churches. His first wedding was celebrated on 9 June 1844 in St Stephen's Cathedral itself. The bride was one Anna Bichler, who died in 1848, after having borne him apparently only one child, a son called Ferdinand. His second marriage took place on 29 June 1851 at the Benedictine *Schottenkirche*, also in the Inner City. The bride this time was a Maria Anna Feuerstein. As the name indicates, she was the exact counterpart of Michael, Jewish by origin but Roman Catholic by faith. She was suitable in other ways too. She came from Galicia, the northernmost province of the Empire, and her father had been in government service. He was only a lowly figure, it is true, an *Accessist* or supernumerary clerk. But it was a step away from the purely Jewish 'ambience' of commerce, a step Michael clearly wanted to take and which he tried to encourage his sons to take after him.

This is the family we are concerned with. Soon after their marriage, Michael and Maria Anna moved out to the very fashionable suburb of Ober Sankt Veit, in what was then a peaceful wooded area west of Schönbrunn Palace. It was here, at Wolfrathplatz 1, a pleasant though not a pretentious house, that most if not all of their six children were born. First, in 1852, came twin girls who, aptly, were each given half of their mother's name and were called Anna and Maria respectively. A son, Heinrich, followed in 1855 and another, Adolf, in 1861. A third daughter, Leopoldine, came in 1864. Between Heinrich and Adolf came Rudolf Anton Slatin, who was born on 7 June 1857. (For some reason the Anton was later dropped and Carl used in its place.)

Before starting with him, however, we should just finish with his father. Michael must have made a certain amount of money in order to have moved out to Ober Sankt Veit. But it is something of a mystery how much he made, and even more how he earned it. A search made among Vienna's trade and industrial registries of the 1850s and '60s has failed to reveal any Michael Slatin, nor is there anywhere even the formal police registration which was by then becoming obligatory.* The few documents with references to Michael Slatin which have survived give a different description of him almost every time. Thus on Rudolf's own birth certificate, the father is entered as a 'licensed silk-dyer'. But Rudolf's school records ten years later describe his father's occupation at that time as 'fruit-dealer'. The family fortunes seem to have declined with the change, for the parental home is now given as Neustiftgasse in the Neubau, a much less attractive and less expensive district. Elsewhere, he appears as an 'ice-dealer'. By the time Rudolf is doing his military service, however, the father is described simply by the anonymous but respectable term of 'house-owner'. That was, and has remained, the badge of the Viennese bourgeoisie.

Whatever Michael Slatin did for a living and however many occupations he had, two things are clear. The first is that he built up no family business which could be handed over lock, stock and barrel to his children. The second is that though, at times, he commanded a good income, he was never a man of real substance, that is a man of capital or property. He was himself the family's greatest asset, and the asset died with him. This is shown in one passing reference, as usual without any details, which in later years Rudolf made to his father's death.

* I am indebted in particular to Dr Karl Zrounek of Vienna for making these and other investigations and for securing attested photo-copies of all the birth, marriage and baptism records which are extant on the Slatins.

In a letter to the fiancée of his brother Heinrich, sent from the Sudan in 1881 to welcome her into the family, he writes:

You know that, after the death of our Papa, we lived in circumstances which were far from grand. Indeed we brothers and sisters had to help each other out and could only carry on by sticking together and so enable each one of us to create an individual existence which, though not brilliant, was honourable and held prospects for the future.

The lack of any established family business was one reason why all Michael Slatin's sons eventually branched out into fields far removed from the Jewish home ground of commerce. Another probable reason was the very natural desire of the parents to give their children more of the security and social status they had themselves come to Vienna to find. At this point we are on sure ground in believing that the Kinskys took this family from their own Bohemian domains under their wing in Vienna, for a living descendant of those Kinskys still remembers the circumstances well.*

The eldest of the Slatin sons, Heinrich, was given a post as private tutor in the Vienna palace of the Kinskys while he was still a student. Prince Karl Kinsky, the head of the house (and immortalized in English sporting history by winning the Grand National on Zeodone in 1883), then launched the young tutor on a coveted career. The Marshal of Horse at the Imperial Court was a childless uncle of the Kinskys, Prince Rudolf Liechtenstein, and Kinsky persuaded him to take the industrious and well-mannered Heinrich on as a trainee clerk. Heinrich seized the golden opportunity with both hands.

Luck had it that, while he was still only a junior official in the office, he was given the daunting and delicate task of going down to Mayerling in January of 1889 to help investigate the double suicide of Archduke Rudolf, heir to the throne, and his teen-age mistress, Baroness Marie Vetsera. Heinrich, whose report on the tragedy exists today, acquitted himself well at that Habsburg shooting-lodge – invaded by crowds of rumour-mongers and sensation-seekers – which, for a few days, was the focus of all European eyes. There were some influential people

---

* Count Ferdinand Wilczeck. His mother, Elisabeth, was one of the Kinsky children who had Heinrich Slatin as house-tutor. Count Wilczeck, father-in-law of the reigning Prince of Liechtenstein, is the oldest living offspring of the Kinsky family.

9

around who lost their heads over the affair and others desperately anxious not to lose their standing. Heinrich firmly recorded the facts as he saw them, but just as firmly kept his mouth shut. Such a blend of honesty and discretion was not all that common in Imperial Vienna, and the Mayerling tragedy became a stepping-stone in his career. Heinrich could never hope to achieve the honour of Marshal of Horse itself, which was a titular post filled only by the upper aristocracy. But he got as high as he could have done in the Vienna of his day and ended up as effective Director of the Department, with the Civil Service rank of Under-Secretary and, ultimately, with a minor title from the Emperor.

Adolf, the youngest of the three Slatin sons, never aspired to those heights and does not seem to have had the talents. He became a lawyer and worked for many years in the management of the great Kinsky estates, first as a member of the administration office and ultimately as its 'Central Director', in which capacity he had the complete trust and confidence of the head of the house. He outlived both his brothers and died in 1942, in the middle of the Second World War.

What, meanwhile, of Rudolf? At first, all seems to go normally enough for a child of his background. He was sent for three years to a state secondary school, the Ober-Realschule am Schottenfeld, and, according to his first year's report there (for 1867), he was a very average pupil. The only high marks he got for any subject was one 'excellent' for arithmetic. Otherwise it was a case of 'satisfactory' and 'adequate' all round. There was one 'unsatisfactory' and that was for handwriting. It is a verdict that anyone who, a century later, has had to decipher the tiny German scribble of his diaries would heartily endorse.

While on the school bench, Rudolf was not dreaming of adventure in far-away continents; or, if he was, he kept his dreams very much to himself.* The future vocation which he chose at the time was that of 'builder', yet in the autumn of 1871 we find his name on the books of Vienna's Intermediate School for Commerce. This seemed to suggest that one at least of the three Slatin boys was after all planning to be a trader of some sort like his father and grandfather before him. He

* Only one portrait of Slatin by a school contemporary has survived and this, printed in the *Neues Wiener Journal* for 4 April 1920, is too banal to be worth quoting.

ploughed on, again without particular distinction, through two years of this intermediate course and the records of the institution show that in 1873–4 he started off on the higher commercial course.

Then something startling happened. His entire life was transformed by hearing of a Cairo bookseller who was seeking for his shop a young assistant with languages and some commercial training. Rudolf Slatin dropped everything, scratched together the fare, and left for Egypt to take up the post. Seen against his own background and that of the time, it was a remarkable leap into the unknown. He was barely 17 years old and had never been abroad in his life. He had no international family connections and no great name which would assure him of any entrée in a foreign capital. He had no fortune to lean back on and, being a very unacademic person, almost the only books he had ever read were school textbooks, and those with reluctance. Furthermore, for people like the Slatins, hovering uncertaintly between middle-class and lower middle-class status as the father's commercial ventures fluctuated, this was simply not the age of travel, not even to the neighbouring Alps of Switzerland. As for Cairo, apart from diplomats, scientists, explorers and the like, it was only the aristocracy who went to such exotic places. What made this teen-age boy do it?

A partial explanation lies precisely in those fluctuations of the family's situation. His father died on 31 March 1873 and, as we have seen from his own pen in later years, Michael Slatin's death had left the widow hard-pressed. The twin girls were 21 by that time and presumably earning something. Heinrich was a student of 18 and this is probably the time that the Kinskys took him on to help pay for his studies. But Adolf was still only 12 and Leopoldine a little girl of 9. It was up to someone to restore the family fortunes, especially if, in the meantime, it meant abandoning a long commercial training course which was only costing money. Rudolf seems to have decided that the someone was himself.

Yet sudden family hardship was not the only reason. To see another and deeper motive we only need to look at a photograph taken of the three Slatin boys when still very small (facing p. 14). Baby Adolf in the middle is too young for us to notice anything much about him, and he has not helped by stirring slightly just as the shutter was clicked, so that his features are anyway a little blurred. The eldest brother, Heinrich, stands at the right of the picture, his arm protectively around the baby. It is a good face, calm and steady, and everything speaks of the solid family man and loyal government servant of the future.

The contrast with Rudolf on the left leaps to the eye. He must have been about five or six years old when that picture was taken. Yet, already, he is striking the pose of the *beau sabreur* he was to follow all his life – legs crossed, arm placed swaggeringly on the hip, the little head thrown back, and the gaze thrown defiantly at the photographer as though he were taking on the world even before taking on his first schoolmaster. Rudolf Slatin evidently wanted to make a splash from the word Go, and he wanted to make it quickly. Not for him the hard slog at the law books or long apprentice years at the high desk of an office clerk. He had to find somewhere where he could hope to be accepted from the start as an equal, somewhere far removed from the implacable social divisions of Imperial Vienna. Though Michael Slatin had helped his sons to a career by bringing them up in the Catholic faith, the fact that they had been born nobodies still meant that they had to fight their own way up every hard inch of the way into the circles that mattered. For the sort of rapid progress Rudolf was interested in, the hidebound social life of the Monarchy was not the best spring-board. So off and away he went.

Africa proved exactly the land of exciting opportunity he was seeking, the land of the unexpected. Who should walk into the Cairo bookshop within a few weeks of Slatin's arrival there but Theodor von Heuglin, a well-known German explorer.* Heuglin was about to leave on a scientific expedition for the Red Sea coast and agreed to take this eager Viennese youth with him. When Heuglin's trip fell through, Slatin decided to make the journey anyway with a local German businessman and consular official, Herr Rosset, who appears to have put up at least part of the money.

For over a year – from the autumn of 1874 to the end of 1875 – Slatin tacked himself on to that restless cosmopolitan

---

* Heuglin was particularly noted in his day as an ornithologist. He died in 1876, only two years after this chance meeting with Slatin.

group of merchants, surveyors, engineers, scientists and soldier-adventurers who wandered around these turbulent deserts of the Sudan, which had then been occupied for up to fifty uneasy years by the Khedives of Egypt.* Quite what he did and how he managed for money is something of a mystery. He tells us himself that on his first journey he got as far south as the Nuba mountains. He would have gone further afield into the Darfur province, a name that was soon to play a great role in his life, had he not been refused a travel permit on security grounds (the area had only recently been occupied by the Egyptian Army). All we know is that he stayed for a while with the Austrian Catholic mission at Delen and from there was exploring the Kadero mountains when the local Arabs rose in revolt against their new Egyptian masters. It was no place for civilian travellers and Slatin gave up.

Back in Khartoum, he was straight away on the look-out for other horizons. He made friends in the Sudanese capital with another German explorer, Eduard Schnitzer, who had entered the Khedive's service for the administration of the Sudan and who, as Emin Pasha, was to rise to high office in it. Emin was on his way to visit another of the Khedive's band of international administrators, the Englishman, General Gordon, at that time Governor of the southernmost Equatorial province of the Sudan, with his headquarters in Lado. Slatin promptly asked if he could go as well; but by the time, two months later, his permit from Lado came through, a letter had arrived from his family in Vienna, summoning him back home. He would be nineteen years old in June of the following year and the first preliminary notice had been issued for his compulsory service in the Austro-Hungarian Army.

It was a summons no young Austrian dared ignore. Rudolf Slatin's Sudanese jaunt was over for the moment and he packed his bags. Before leaving Khartoum, however, he asked his new friend Schnitzer-Emin to put in a word for him with the great General Gordon, who was already famous for his exploits against the Boxer rebels in China. Perhaps, one day, there might be a niche in this improvised edifice of the Egyptian

* Egypt's quasi-Empire in the Sudan had begun in 1820 when Mohammed Aly conquered the northern part and founded the capital of Khartoum. Kassala province to the east of Khartoum was taken in 1840 and the Red Sea port of Suakin in 1865.

Khedive's Sudan which he, Rudolf Slatin, could fill? The eighteen-year-old youth who then reluctantly set off for his native Vienna, his mind full of the Nile and the desert, could not have dreamt what that request would soon bring.

First, however, his own Emperor claimed him for a couple of years. From 25 September 1876, when Slatin joined the 12th Feldjäger Battalion as an ordinary recruit, the romantic wanderer around Africa becomes just another tiny and insignificant cog in the great military machine of an eleven-nation Empire. Insignificant, but not inefficient. His personal military file has survived among the Imperial War Ministry archives in Vienna. From this we see that he passed his training course in the ranks 'with excellent success' and on 29 December 1877 was commissioned as a subaltern of the reserve in the 19th Infantry Regiment, one of the units of which the Crown Prince, Archduke Rudolf, was the nominal commander. The personal details entered on his commission papers were surely supplied by Slatin. He describes himself as 'single, of independent means, and by profession an explorer of the wild'. It is a brave description of the penniless youth whose first and only trip outside the confines of the Monarchy had been 12 months of adventure that had started in a Cairo bookshop. He is still very much the little boy in the photograph, positively willing his dreams into reality.

In view of what lay ahead, it is worth while looking at the purely military qualifications and experience of this newly-commissioned second lieutenant. His report for 1877 says of him: 'Commands a platoon and a company well. Leads his platoon carefully. Very useful in the field and on patrol duty and properly discharges in every way the tasks given him.'

But all this referred only to war games. Indeed, though Slatin did part of his service as an officer with the forces sent down to garrison Bosnia-Herzegovina (the two Balkan provinces which Austria occupied during the Near Eastern crisis of 1875–8), his record sheet for that episode notes: 'Not involved in any engagement.' Thus, when the call to real action on a distant war front came, Slatin answered it having never fired a single shot in anger.

The summons he had dreamed of but scarcely dared to expect arrived in July of 1878 when Slatin was sitting with his regiment on the Bosnian frontier. It must have caused quite a stir in the little officers' mess, for it was from General Gordon, now Governor-General of the Egyptian Sudan, offering Slatin a post on his staff. Emin had kept his promise and had evidently put in an exceptionally good word for his young Austrian friend. That was all Gordon wanted. Indeed, it was all he had time for in finding the Europeans he so urgently needed to help him run the Sudan. There was no point in holding examinations or even in arranging for preliminary interviews in Khartoum. His men had to be picked on a hunch or a recommendation and then taken on trust.

Slatin seems not to have hesitated for a second in accepting, despite the upheaval this would obviously bring about. The lack of roots in Vienna and the lack of prospects there had helped to drive him away from his native city two years before. Becoming another of the thousands of the Emperor's lieutenants of the reserve had done nothing to alter this. A glittering career as a regular officer in his own Empire in peacetime was out of the question. It was the same old story of Slatin's background and, far more important, his social obscurity barring him from the highest posts and, in this case, the best regiments as well.*

But if the Austro-Hungarian Army had no particular use for Rudolf Slatin, it would not give him an immediate release. He had to go through the bureaucratic machine in leaving it just as he had done in joining it. Not until December, when his regiment had been transferred back to Pressburg (now Bratislava), was he demobilized. He had just eight rushed days in Vienna to put the whole of his old life behind him and launch himself into the new one. There was an anguished farewell from his mother, who had a presentiment there and then that she would never see this restless son of hers again. On 21 December 1878 he caught the train for Trieste, from where he sailed for Cairo.

He was then aged twenty-one, and unknown. He was not to see Trieste or any part of his homeland again until he was a middle-aged man of forty, and famous.

---

* Though this was possibly on technical grounds, his final report notes that he was 'not suited' even for further promotion in the Army reserve due to 'current regulations'.

Chapter Two

THE WASTE OF THORNS

To Europeans, the land to which Rudolf Slatin had come to make his name lay like a vacuum in the heart of Africa – unknown, untouched and forbidding. Its barrenness compounded its huge size, and kept all but a handful of white outsiders away. In its million square miles of rocky desert, sand-dunes, savanna and swamp, there was not a city worthy of the name and not a single mile of railway track or metalled road. One of the few Western travellers to cross it at this time, Ewart S. Grogan, described it in words which still quiver with repugnance nearly a century afterwards:

In the course of a chequered career, I have seen many unwholesome spots; but for God-forsaken, dry-sucked, fly-blown wilderness, commend me to the Upper Nile. A desolation of desolations, an infernal region, a howling waste of weed, mosquitoes, flies and fever, backed by a groaning waste of thorns and stones—waterless and waterlogged. I have passed through it, and have now no fear for the hereafter.

Even if the Sudan had struck the stray traveller as a paradise, and not a hell on earth, it was still a difficult place to get at. True, its eastern flank lay on the Red Sea, with the ancient Ottoman ports of Suakin and Massawa. But the Red Sea Hills and the wild Beja tribes (Kipling's 'Fuzzie-Wuzzies') who inhabited them did much to seal Sudan's interior off from this, its one coastline. The other approaches were all as gaunt as

16

the Sudan itself. To the north and west, the great Sahara Desert stretched between it and the Mediterranean and Atlantic coasts. Its south-west fringes (it had nothing that could be called a frontier here) sank slowly into the jungles of the Congo. To the south-east lay the mountains of Abyssinia. It was a wilderness enclosed by a wilderness. For centuries, the world had passed it by, glad to leave it to struggle with itself. Yet however remote the place was, all paths were now leading to it. The Sudan was the central cross-roads on the emerging African map, and the great European powers were already set on their different marches towards that cross-roads. They were coming from all points of the compass and from each of Africa's shores.

The so-called 'scramble for Africa' was not in full swing when Slatin arrived. But the colonial powers had all staked out their coastal claims to the continent and there was only one direction in which these enclaves could expand – inwards. To the north stood Egypt and her powerful creditors and protectors, France and England. Three years after Slatin's arrival on the Nile, England reluctantly became something more than Egypt's protector, when, to suppress a bloody mutiny against the Khedive, British troops in 1882 occupied Cairo. From the north-west and west, France pressed into the Sahara from her semi-circle of foot-holds which stretched from Tunisia in the Mediterranean round to Guinea in the Atlantic. England was also established in the Gulf of Guinea and so, in the Cameroons, was Bismarck's Germany. From the south-west, Belgium and Portugal were pushing inland, up through the Congo and Angola. Away to the south-east, from Zanzibar and the coast of the Indian Ocean, Portugal was again jostling for territory, this time with Germany and England as competitors. Finally, even closer to the east, in Abyssinia and the Horn of Africa, Italy was leading France in the race for spoils, with England a fairly passive third. Some of these many rival thrusts might stop short of the Sudan. Other might bypass it. But most were bound to meet headlong in Grogan's 'groaning waste of thorns and stones'. The Sudan could hardly go on eluding the outside world for much longer. Without knowing it, Slatin had timed his arrival well.

Not that any of the European powers had any clear idea as to what this prize in the heart of their African arena really

17

amounted to. Its people were as complex as its frontiers were vague. It is estimated that the Sudan of those days (and, for that matter, of today) contained anything up to 600 separate tribes, of all colours from light brown to deepest black, and talking between them over a hundred different languages and dialects. Some were sedentary cultivators, others cattle-nomads. Some, like the powerful Baggara Arabs of Kordofan, were warriors who lived on the booty of their fighting and above all from slave raids. Others, like the Bongo of the south, were passive peoples, whose traditional role seemed to be to suffer, and provide the stock of slaves. Some tribes had deep roots in history, claims to sultanates or kingdoms that stretched back to the Middle or even the Dark Ages. Others had left nothing behind them in the sands but their bones. There was no common past, no common identity, no common culture. The Sudan was not even a nation, let alone a state.

This extraordinary jumble of peoples then numbered between two and three million. Only two things gave it any meaning. The first was that, taken all together, these tribes formed the link in Africa between the Moslem Arab north of the continent and its pagan negroid centre. This accident of geography was, and has remained, the Sudan's vital but unhappy function in Africa's history.

The second thing which gave even the primitive Sudan some identity was, of course, the Nile. Indeed, the further back one goes – the further away from modern irrigation and fertilizers, from airlines, railways and roads – the bigger the Nile looms. In Slatin's day, the Nile *was* the Sudan (and, for that matter, Egypt as well). Both the Niles, the main White Nile and the Blue, rise south of the Sudan. But the thousands of serpentine miles which they and their tributaries trace through the Sudanese plain give the land both its water and its food: in short, its life. Three-quarters of the length of the main river flows through the Sudan, and the country's ancient name of Nalsa applied only to this riverain region, as though existence away from the great watercourse was unthinkable.

Anyone who, even today, has flown down from Cairo over the desert wastes to Khartoum, can see what the ancients meant, better than they themselves could have seen. The river valley, with its muddy arms and islands, forms a twisting green ribbon of cultivation and habitation. Away from its banks, where the green drains slowly into the brown, life seems to drain away as well. The same contrast can be seen from the air at night. The lights of towns and villages hug the river. To left and right, it is inky black.

A hundred years ago, the Nile was something more for the Sudan, its only real road and railway combined. There were the old caravan routes across the desert, of course. The most important were the East-West axis, running from Suakin on the Red Sea right across to the Sultanate of Darfur; and the North-South route which led up from Sennar into Egypt. But for the passage of bulk goods, as opposed to cargoes of slaves, who could walk, the river was irreplaceable. Navigation was complicated by cataracts and especially the six big ones, which all lay downstream of Khartoum, the Sudanese capital. An even bigger obstacle was in the south. This was the so-called 'Sudd', a dense floating carpet of weed and papyrus which choked three hundred miles of the upper Nile, turning it into a kind of inland Saragossa Sea. It was not until the white man brought his powerful steamers to the water that the 'Sudd' was beaten. Before that, it had to be endured, as so much else in the Sudan, as part of the price for existing at all.

Such was the land to which the young Viennese Rudolf Slatin joined his fortunes when, on 15 January 1879, he arrived at Khartoum to take up his duties. His own position was as strange as his surroundings. Technically, he was a servant of the Khedive of Egypt who ruled the Sudan (or, if you like, a servant of the Sultan of Turkey who, in a shadowy way, still 'ruled' Egypt). In practice, he was an international civil servant under the command of an Englishman, General Gordon, who was in the Sudan as the Khedive's agent. Yet in law he was an Austrian subject and a lieutenant of the Reserve in the army of His Apostolic Majesty, the Emperor Franz Joseph. The arrangement sounded much more impractical than it was for the Sudan of the 1870s.

Certainly, no attempt to change it was made by Gordon when he was formally appointed Governor-General of the Sudan by the Khedive in 1877. The specific task given him by Cairo was to put down slave trading in the country. His real job was far wider: to bring some semblance of order to this vast and seemingly ungovernable territory, a task which the Khedive had long since despaired of finding any Egyptian or Turk able or honest enough to discharge.

It was a daunting enough mission, even for someone of Gordon's religious fervour and physical drive. To maintain law and order in this million square miles now under his control, he had only some 30,000 regular troops of the Egyptian Army, backed up by locally-raised black infantry battalions and the notorious *bashi-bazooks*, an unruly force of mounted Sudanese gendarmerie. If the military machine was inadequate, the administrative one was almost non-existent. In theory, a chain of civil command ran from Gordon's palace in Khartoum to the Governors of the various provinces and regions and so right down to the headmen of the villages. But it was a paper chain. There was, in fact, no administration worthy of the name. Taxes were arbitrarily assessed and brutally collected, usually by the *bashi-bazooks*, who settled any dispute with their 'kurbash' or hippopotamus-hide whip. It was all hit-or-miss, with the accent very much on hit.

All Gordon could do with this clumsy and creaking apparatus was to staff it at key points with his 'Foreign Legion' of European officials in the hope that their personal ambition, coupled with their relative incorruptibility, would supply the leadership that neither the Egyptians nor the Sudanese themselves could provide. His motley band of adventurers were soon dispersed in strategic provinces all over the Sudan. A German-speaking Swiss, Werner Munzinger, was made Governor of Massawa on the Red Sea. Bahr Al-Ghazal in the extreme south was put under an Italian, Romolo Gessi, who was to be succeeded by the ill-fated Englishman Frank Lupton. Another Italian, Messedaglia, governed the far western province of Darfur; one of his lieutenants was a certain Emiliani dei Danziger, a Venetian of Austrian origin. And in Khartoum, as deputy to Gordon himself, sat one Giegler Pasha, a telegraph engineer of German origin. By the end of the seventies, the new rulers of the Sudan were becoming as polyglot as the native tribes themselves, and almost as quarrelsome.

For these Europeans, the pay was poor, the future was uncertain and the present unhealthy and dangerous (most were to be killed in battle or to die of one of the Sudan's generous choice of diseases, which ranged from yellow fever, dysentery and malaria to leprosy and cholera). Such was the hardy band that Slatin had joined. As a native of Imperial Vienna, which ruled over eleven different peoples, he could at least feel much that was familiar and even comforting about the cosmopolitan air of Gordon's Khartoum.

Slatin found a house and servants already placed at his disposal, and seems, from the first, to have taken to his new life like a duck to water. Gordon had a soft spot for the Austrians, dating from the time he had served with them on the Danube Commission. He was amiability itself to his young new recruit and received him every day to size him up and put him in the picture.

The Governor-General's first orders were not, however, to Slatin's liking. Early in February, less than three weeks after his arrival, Gordon appointed him Inspector of Finances, with a brief to tour the country and report on defects in the taxation system. Considering that the system was virtually all defects, most of them deeply-rooted, it was a thankless task. Slatin went on his travels and wrote his report. This told Gordon little he did not know. The rich could escape taxation altogether by bribes thrust in a few palms. Most of the local government officials claimed exemption anyway because of their 'special services'. The burden thus fell cruelly and unfairly on the small man, who was too poor to bribe the *bashi-bazooks* when they arrived on their tax-gathering missions, and too weak to defend himself against them.

Slatin did what he could to dispense justice on his journey; he even arrested several of the delinquent Sudanese officials and forced them to pay up their arrears. But the complexity of the problem utterly defeated him. At Mesallamia, for example, an important trading centre between the White and the Blue Niles, he found an immense collection of young female slaves, owned by the most respected merchants of the town. These worthies either sold or hired out the women as concubines or else ran brothels with them. That the business was lucrative was obvious. But how on earth was it to be taxed, and would it not be wrong to recognize it by taxation?

Slatin declared himself so beaten by these problems, and so lacking in financial experience of any sort to guide him, that he sent in his resignation with the same post as his report. Frustration was doubtless one reason behind this step – a little drastic for one so new to Gordon's service. But shrewd calculation probably played its part as well. Slatin felt himself better cut out for a direct command rather than an administrative role, and he knew that there were many such commands to fill and precious few Europeans to fill them with.

He was right. Gordon was at the time touring the province of Darfur, which was torn by fighting. Not long after getting Slatin's message, he sent a telegram back appointing him *Mudir* or District Governor of Dara, the south-west region of Darfur. Slatin was to start out as soon as possible and be ready to conduct military operations against Harun, the son of a former Sultan of Fur, who was trying to take back his country from its Egyptian conquerors by force of arms.

The bulk of the province, and nearly all the main towns, were held by Egyptian troops, in uneasy partnership with the private army of a redoubtable slave dealer named al-Zubayr who had in fact routed the Fur army and killed the old Sultan seven years before. But Harun and his Fur warriors held out in the Marra mountains of the south, in the area of Slatin's new command. This was a task after his heart: action, adventure, danger, and direct responsibility – the things he had come from his cosy Vienna to seek in this remote corner of Africa. Rudolf Slatin's climb up the ladder had begun.

On the first stage of his 500-mile ride Slatin was summoned to a rendezvous with Gordon, who was now returning to Khartoum and wanted to bring his freshly-appointed *Mudir* up to date with the tangled situation in Darfur. The meeting took place on Gordon's steamer, at anchor in the White Nile. For hours the two men sat alone in the stern, discussing the situation. Slatin's English was fairly primitive at this stage of his career and so they conversed mainly in French. It was in this language that, past ten o'clock at night, the Governor-General bade his young official farewell as he saw him into the rowing-boat: 'Goodbye, my dear Slatin, and God bless you. I am sure you will do your best under any circumstances. I am perhaps returning to England and, if so, I hope we may meet there.'

It may have been just politeness, it may also have been a

presentiment that made Slatin stand for an hour on the river bank, waiting for the steamer to weigh anchor and slide downstream towards Khartoum. For there was no pleasant meeting ahead for them in England, but only a bloody and irrevocable separation in the Sudan. Those, in fact, were the last words Slatin was ever to hear Gordon speak, and this the last time he was ever to see the legendary Englishman alive.

The next morning, Slatin began his long journey west. He was mounted on a pony Gordon had given him and which was to carry him through all sorts of perils almost every day for the next four years. At El Obeid, capital of the Province of Kordofan, and nearly half-way along his desert route, he teamed up with the Sanitary Inspector of the Sudan, Dr Zurbuchen (yet another European) who was also bound for Darfur. They assembled their baggage camels and, early in July 1879, set out from El Obeid together.

Slatin had not been riding long before he realized what it meant to hold power in this land. Though he was not yet in his own district of Dara, petitioners flocked to him at every stop, drawn partly by the rumour that he was 'Gordon's nephew' (a story probably inspired by his blue eyes and clean-shaven face). He could not resist intervening in one case – though, strictly speaking, it was no business of his – because it fascinated him too much to leave alone. A nineteen-year-old youth, recently arrived in the neighbourhood, had been tempestuously wooed by a rich old woman, who was smitten with an apparently ungovernable passion for him. Though engaged already to a much prettier but much poorer cousin in Khartoum, the young man had given in and married his wealthy admirer. Now the broken-hearted fiancée was demanding her rights.

Slatin saw the youth, persuaded him to seek a divorce, and then retired to his little brick hut for an afternoon rest from the heat. His peace was soon shattered by the infuriated old wife who, disregarding all the rules of Arab etiquette, burst in upon him. Slatin found himself confronted by an appalling harridan with a wrinkled yellowish face, three tribal slits down her cheeks, greying hair twisted coquettishly into dozens of greasy little ringlets, and a voice like a frantic parrot.

Moreover, when Slatin tried to remonstrate with her for marrying a lad young enough to have been her grandson, the apparition lost all control, tore off her veil and raised her hands as though she was about to strangle the Commissioner-designate of Dara. Fortunately his orderly, who was listening outside, rushed in and removed the screaming woman by force. Her behaviour seems to have resolved the last doubts in her husband's mind, for he left post-haste the very next day to rejoin his sweetheart. (The story had a happy ending. Some years later, Slatin met the young man in Khartoum, happily married to his first fiancée, already the father of a family, and profusely grateful for everything.)

Another incident, which happened a day or two later, was less pleasant. Slatin and his party had halted for the night to stay with Sheikh Hassan, who had been given the Egyptian rank of Bey by Gordon for his great loyalty to the government. Hassan was fat, with a perpetual smile and a huge appetite; in fact, he had struck Slatin on sight as 'the Falstaff of the Sudan'. The supper he prepared was certainly worthy of the title. They sat down to an entire sheep baked on charcoal, with quantities of roast fowl and *asida* (a sort of Sudanese *polenta*), and, to wash it all down, red wine and jars of *marissa*, or Sudanese beer.

At sunrise, when Slatin and Dr Zurbuchen got up to say goodbye, they discovered that someone on their baggage caravan, which Slatin had ordered to go on ahead, had carried off one of their host's finest rugs. Slatin dispatched his orderly to overtake the caravan and investigate, while he sat down with his aggrieved friends to wait. A few hours later the orderly returned with the stolen rug across his camel and the culprit, one of the eight black soldiers of the escort, tied on behind. Slatin had the man flogged on the spot and then sent him back a prisoner to the nearest military post. It was the first punishment he had had to administer. He did so to set an example and to squash any idea spreading about that 'as is the servant, so the master'.

After a brief stay at El Fasher, the capital of Darfur, where he was cordially received by his immediate superior, the Italian Governor of the province, Messedaglia, Slatin rode out again, this time southwards, on the final stage of his journey, to his own district of Dara. What he did next was typical of the guile that was to stand him in such good stead in the years to come. His companion, the Swiss Sanitary Inspector of the Sudan, was anyway a few years older than Slatin and, with his long black beard and spectacles, looked old enough to be Slatin's father. Indeed, he had often been taken already for the new Governor of Dara. Slatin now decided to profit by the confusion. He rode on in front of Dr Zurbuchen and reached the last village before Dara well ahead of him. Here he found villagers busily preparing to greet the approaching party, sweeping out the houses, and laying down straw mats and carpets for the local sheikh's reception.

Slatin dismounted from his camel, declared himself to be simply 'one of the new Governor's escort', and then proceeded to ply the villagers with questions about the situation in Dara and the loyalty of various officials there. He had got some frank and useful answers by the time the bearded doctor and the rest of the caravan arrived. A bewildering few minutes followed for the Sanitary Inspector as the sheikh and other notables, grouped in a semi-circle, began their fulsome speeches of welcome, praising his virtues and describing the joy of the people at his arrival. Just as the poor Doctor, whose grasp of Arabic was very poor, was beginning to realize what had gone wrong, Slatin stepped out of the crowd and identified himself. Profuse apologies, and laughter all round, then followed. Slatin had got more out of it than amusement and information. He had gained the reputation of cunning which he knew he needed to offset his boyish looks.

The next day, to a salute of seven guns from the fort on top of the city's sand-hill, Slatin entered Dara and formally took over command of Southern Darfur. It was an unprepossessing place. But the great fort – a rectangle of stones five hundred yards long, three hundreds yards deep and twelve feet high – was the military key of the whole region. And even the town below, which was mainly a collection of mud and straw huts, was of considerable importance as a trading centre. Including the garrison, Dara at that time numbered between seven and eight thousand souls.

It was still the month of Ramadan, the great Arab fast, when they arrived and so it was not until the gun boomed again at sunset that the officials emerged from their prayers to greet their new master. They were probably glad of a respectable excuse to fill their empty stomachs. At all events, the meal they now offered Slatin was the full-scale Sudanese banquet of mutton, chicken, rice, milk and honey, a feast which made up in quantity for what it lacked in delicacy.

He did not get much time to enjoy it in peace. Barely had he started tearing off pieces from the roast sheep (with his fingers, like everyone else) than there was a great commotion and two men pushed themselves into the circle. They turned out to be messengers from the small garrison of Bir Gowi, three days' march to the south-west. Sultan Harun, the young pretender to the crown of Fur, was about to attack them and, as they would be heavily outnumbered, they proposed to evacuate the post unless Dara could send immediate reinforcements.

Though he had only left the saddle a few hours before, Slatin jumped up at once and announced that he would himself lead the relief force. By midnight, he was off again on a new mount (Gordon's pony was too tired) with two hundred black Sudanese infantrymen and twenty Turkish and Egyptian horsemen behind him. At sunset two days later, after an uneventful but tiring march through dense scrubland, they reached Bir Gowi. It must have brought home to Slatin how precarious the outer defences of his district were. The military post was nothing more than a *zariba*, or square barricade of thorn bushes, piled six feet high and twelve feet deep. Along the outside of the square a ditch had been dug and, inside this, an earth platform had been raised so that the soldiers could fire out over the thorns.

The total garrison was some one hundred and twenty men, and the welcome they gave to Slatin and his relief force left little doubt about their delight. As he rode up to them, their copper war-drums and skin-drums were beaten, bugles and antelope horns were blown, and those who had neither signified their joy by rattling pebbles in leather gourds. To top the fanfare off, rifles were fired into the air.

Slatin went to bed exhausted and with a splitting headache. The next morning he woke up feeling really wretched. It was just as well that there was no sign of hostile troops, for he would have been in poor shape to engage them. He spent the day dozing and submitting to various local 'headache cures'. One of these consisted of the Sheikh's physician pressing Slatin's temples between his thumbs, muttering a few verses of Arabic, by way of incantation, and then suddenly spitting in his face. Slatin had knocked the man down in rage before the wretch could explain that this treatment was precisely what the Koran and diverse holy men prescribed for such maladies. The mortified Sheikh next offered Slatin one of his favourite girl slaves, saying that she was not only young and pretty, but a trained nurse, wise in all the ailments of the country. Slatin, in no mood for any further special cherishing, even from such attractive hands, declined with thanks. The next morning, in any case, he arose feeling fully restored and the Sheikh's physician was promptly restored to favour.

Still there was no news of Harun and his army and Slatin whiled away the time as best he could like a tourist. He visited the sulphur springs nearby and the local market, which displayed a wide variety of merchandise from female slaves to cotton cloth and sulphur. He invested modestly in a few palm mats. Finally, after two more days of idle waiting, a messenger came in with the news that Harun, alarmed by accounts of the relief army, had dispersed his men in the hills and withdrawn. Slatin had no choice but to return to Dara a disappointed man.

He was not kept waiting long for his first real action in the Sudan. A few weeks after getting back to Dara, he received a letter in French from the Provincial Governor at El Fasher announcing a joint plan to smoke and stamp out the rebels for good. Slatin was ordered to march secretly on Niurnia in the Marra Hills, about one hundred and fifty miles north-east of Dara, where the Sultan Harun had his headquarters. Messedaglia would send another force out from El Fasher to rendezvous with Slatin's men and join in the attack.

This first real campaign was not to be as straightforward as he had hoped, however. It took his column four days' hard slog over the Marra Hills to reach the valley which was his objective, and when he finally got there, it was only to find that the elusive Harun had once again fled. The town was empty. A strange game of hide-and-seek now followed. Early the next morning, part of the troops advancing to join him from El Fasher met up with Slatin's men – or rather, clashed with them, for in the dawn they were mistaken for the enemy. A regular battle ensued and before Slatin, who was in the thick of it, could end the confusion with 'cease-fire' bugle calls, seven men had been killed. Slatin himself had a narrow escape when one bullet struck his horse and another passed clean through his cloak.

After this curious baptism of fire, Slatin led the combined forces back over the hills again and so down into the plain he had crossed the week before. Here he learnt that Harun, so far from waiting to do battle with him at Niurnia, had slipped out days before and had actually marched east on Slatin's own headquarters at Dara, hoping that, with so many of the garrison away chasing him, he could take the fort by surprise. He had only failed by a hair's breadth in a night attack which killed many of the town's people. Harun had then retired again towards his native hills, burning the villages along his route and seizing the women as slaves.

It was on a grassy slope in these 'small hills' at the foot of the Marra range that Slatin finally caught up with his wily opponent. Slatin, with just over three hundred men in his combined force, was outnumbered more than two to one. But on this occasion, as on others to come, even the limited tactical experience of a reserve lieutenant in the Austrian Army was too much for the primitive enemy. Slatin led the frontal assault on the camp himself, dismounting and marching ahead at the double when his horse grew too restive. (This, incidentally, was a great gesture in the eyes of the ordinary Sudanese infantryman, for when a commander left his precious horse to go into battle on foot it was proof that he intended to fight and die with his men if need be.) At six hundred yards, Slatin loosed off the first volley, and so did a force of eighty-five men he had stationed on the flank. Caught in the cross-fire, Harun retreated and Slatin turned the retreat into a rout by attacking now on the other flank with his small reserve. The Sultan's horse was shot dead from under him but Harun himself escaped across the Marra Hills at nightfall. Both his army and his prestige had been broken, however, by this engagement and soon afterwards he was tracked down, killed, and his hand cut off and sent to El Fasher. Slatin had restored peace to his district and he could now return to Dara to set about administering it.

This was every bit as formidable a task as pacifying it and, as usual, the chaotic taxation system was the root of the trouble. The district was divided into five *kisms* or divisions, each of which was supposed to pay a certain sum. Slatin discovered that this fixed levy system was simply being passed on down the line, with each tribe paying a regular tax which the head Sheikh raised by making arbitrary levies in turn on the sub-tribes. In this way, many individual merchants and land-owners were escaping practically scot-free.

Though he had balked at the task of putting the whole of the Sudan's finances in order for Gordon, Slatin lost no time in tackling it in the district which was now his own responsibility. He ordered each division to submit lists of the men of wealth or property in every village, so that the taxes could henceforth be assessed on a personal basis. When the lists were in, he set out on a long tour of inspection to make sure that they were fairly drawn up and, at the same time, to meet every village headman and tribal sub-sheikh in his area. He found that, almost everywhere, taxes were paid not in gold or silver coin, but in kind – principally camels, cattle, or a native cotton fabric called *takia*. By fixing a basic scale for these contributions and converting their value into Egyptian piastres, which was the currency of the Sudan, he managed to bring some sort of order into the finances of Dara, and to iron out many injustices in the process.

The year 1880 was now ending, and Slatin had every reason to look back with satisfaction. In less than eighteen months, he had quelled the military revolt of Sultan Harun which threatened to tear Dara apart, and had then given his district the foundations of a just and stable administration. He knew that Khartoum was pleased with him. But even Slatin was unprepared for what came next. Shortly before Christmas, Messedaglia, his Italian superior at El Fasher, committed an almost unbelievable blunder by sending one of his own senior officials back to the capital in chains on a charge of cruelty. It would have been a stupid way to deal with such a case even had the charge been justified. But as the accusation proved unfounded as well, Khartoum decided that Messedaglia was simply unfit to command. On 14 December he was recalled and dismissed. Less than three months later, early in April 1881, Slatin received a telegram from His Highness the Khedive of Egypt in far-away Cairo appointing him Messedaglia's successor as Governor of the whole Darfur Province.

Slatin had been in the Sudan for precisely twenty-seven months. Yet he was now to rule, virtually with powers of life and death, over a vast expanse of Africa some four hundred miles square, set in a strategic position between the Sahara and the Congo at a time when all the great European powers (excepting his own native Austrian Empire) were edging towards it. And all at the age of twenty-four.

This was the sort of prize he had travelled so far to seek. In terms of age balanced against responsibility, only that élite of young British officials who ruled India in their Queen's name could compare with him. Yet there were at least three respects in which his task was far harder than theirs. First, he had no highly developed civilian administration to sustain him. Second, he had no formidable army, backed by the reserves of the greatest empire on earth, to fall back on. And third, the Sudan, with Slatin now one of its key commanders, was on the brink of a native explosion of such prolonged savagery that the Indian Mutiny of the Raj became a mere flash of violence by comparison. The great Mahdi revolt, which was to plunge the Sudan into bloodshed and terror for seventeen years, and cut it off entirely from the outside world for twelve of these, erupted only three months after the new Governor of Darfur took up his post. Young Slatin was now heading for more adventure than even he had wished for; yet, at the same time, for greater fame than he had ever dreamt of.

Chapter Three

THE MAHDI

It was inevitable that, when the explosion came in the Sudan, it should have been a religious spark that set it off. No mere palace *coup* in Khartoum against the Europeanized regime of the Egyptian Khedive could have produced a broad shift of power. There was no Sudanese crown and therefore no banished pretender who could be produced to the people as a rallying-point against foreign occupation. The country was, in any case, too vast and too decentralized to be harnessed to any revolt in its capital, especially as that capital was an Egyptian city resented by the provinces. Nor was the army – which, later on in Africa's history, was to throw up so many revolutionary leaders in so many states – a possible vehicle for opposition in the Sudan of Slatin's day. The native Sudanese soldiers in its ranks were docile, politically unformed and powerless under their Egyptian and European commanders.

As for those hundreds of tribes which were the muscle and bone of the country, they were far too numerous and divided against each other to join together in any secular cause; and no single sheikh or emir existed among them mighty enough to impose his will upon the rest. There was only one fuse which, once it started to splutter, could run from tribe to tribe, village to village and province to province of this patchwork land, and that was the fuse of the *jihad*, the Moslem holy war against the infidel.

It could do this again, because it had done it so often before.

It was a fact of history in Northern Africa, as well as an article of faith that, whenever Islam was threatened, a messiah would arise to speak with the divine voice of Mohammed the Prophet, destroy the corrupt order of things and rebuild on the ashes a purified theocracy in his name. Such messiahs had always been known as 'Mahdis' or 'Guided Ones', apparitions from the past come to redeem the present. In the Middle Ages, two had redeemed their present to such effect that they had carved out great kingdoms for themselves and their successors. One of the later and lesser of this line of messiahs had confronted Napoleon in Egypt less than ninety years before Slatin's time. Bonaparte's troops had made short shrift of that particular claimant. But there was no such army and no such general on hand now to deal with the newest and most terrible Mahdi of them all.

This one, Mohammed Ahmed, had sprung literally from the mud-banks of the Nile, for he was born a boat-builder's son in or around 1844 on an island of the river near Dongola, which lies in the Northern Sudan between the Third and Fourth Cataracts. Twenty-five years later, after religious studies in Khartoum, he was already making a name for himself as a wandering preacher whose severe asceticism had become too much even for his tutors. A description we have of him at this time is of a tall, lean but muscular young man with pleasant features, large eyes, and the *falja* or gap between the two front teeth which passed as a special mark of divine favour. With a passion that inflamed and enslaved his audiences, he would inveigh against the cruelties and injustice of the foreign oppression that lay upon the land and hint – less and less darkly as his following grew – that a miraculous salvation was at hand. After such tours he would return to Abba Island on the White Nile where he had made his home with his brothers. But even here, doing nothing, his fame grew. Whereas they lived in normal dwellings, he inhabited a cave on the river bank, with the native *angareb* or low hide bed as his only furnishing and a crude thatch of palm leaves as his only shelter from the sun. Before long the government steamers slowed down in salute to him as they passed the island.

The vibrant expectancy of these months is well and romantically caught in the account given by an English officer, Major (later General) Reginald Wingate, who was to become the dominant force for good in the life both of Rudolf Slatin and of the Sudan. He writes of the popular mood at the turn of the year 1880–81:

> The Lord would send a deliverer who should sweep away the veil before their eyes, clear the madness from the brain; the hideous dream would be broken for ever and, strong in the faith of their divine leader, these new-made men, with clear-seeing vision and well-laid plans before them, should go forth and possess the land ... With the coming of the Mahdi the right should triumph and all oppression should have an end. When would this Mahdi come? What wonder that every hut and every thicket echoed the longing for the promised Saviour? The hot wind roamed from desert to plain of withered grass, from mountain range to sandy valley and whispered 'Madhi' as it blew ... All nature joined in ... The women found eggs inscribed with 'Jesus', 'Mohammed' and 'Mahdi'. The very leaves rustled down to the ground and in their fall received the imprint of the sacred names ...

On 29 June 1881, Mohammed Ahmed finally reached out for his crown. Before an assembly of notables specially summoned to Abba Island, he formally proclaimed himself to be the new Mahdi and he called on the faithful everywhere to rally to him. For the Sudan, and everyone living in it or concerned with it, nothing was ever going to be the same again from this day forward.

The new Mahdi did not pick his moment because of some sudden flash of divine guidance. The time of the proclamation had been shrewdly chosen and the approach to it well prepared. Nor was this preparation by any means all religious. As Slatin had found by his own experiences, resentment against the cruel and arbitrary taxation system had produced a constant ground swell of anger against the foreign 'Turk', especially among the poorer masses. It was a ground swell on which any agitator could ride. A narrower but even more powerful cause for grievance had been Gordon's campaign, on instructions from the Khedive in Cairo, to put down slave-trading in the Sudan. The Baggara tribes, who dominated the area of Central Sudan where Mohammed Ahmed had always been most active, were among the principal slave-traders who stood to lose everything if this aspect of the 'Turk's' administration succeeded. What more natural than an alliance of interests with the new popular leader? After all, it was only the equivalent, in the Sudan of the 1880s, to that marriage of convenience which, fifty years later in Germany, the Ruhr barons were to make with that even greater daemon and demagogue, Adolf Hitler, just before he made his bid for power.

Though many of the Baggara sheikhs supported the new leader out of calculation, at least one of them, Abdallahi, seems to have become his devoted disciple out of religious conviction (and was later on to become his natural successor). Such support, in the very province of Kordofan where he operated, gave Mohammed Ahmed the 'power-base' he required, and probably decided him to make his bid. It is, in any case, significant that in March of 1881, three months before the public proclamation on Abba Island, he first told a few close followers, including Abdallahi, of his 'divine mission' in secret.

· General circumstances were as favourable as local ones for the new Mahdi to come forward when he did. The old Khedive Ismail, who had first appointed Gordon to the Sudan, had been deposed in 1879. Egypt was now in a state of incipient revolt from an under-paid army, the turmoil that was soon to lead to British military occupation. Finally, Gordon himself had temporarily left the Sudan after Ismail's fall. His successor as the new Khedive's Governor-General in Khartoum was Mohammed Rauf, a man of part Nubian, part Abyssinian blood, who had none of the great Englishman's charisma and little of his drive. The latest of the Mahdis had not planned any of this. But he can hardly be blamed for receiving it all as a hefty nudge from the Prophet to get down to business.

Despite all these practical political advantages, however, the black flag of revolt which he now raised could only be hoisted and kept flying as the religious banner of a redeemer. And a redeemer, as opposed to a mere rebel, was the only thing that any Governor-General in Khartoum feared in the way of native resistance. Rauf Pasha first tried diplomacy. On 7 August 1881, an emissary of his landed on Abba Island to try and persuade the self-proclaimed Mahdi to come voluntarily to the capital. The summons was haughtily rejected. The two companies of regular Egyptian troops which landed on Abba Island five nights later, with orders to bring the rebels back in chains, fared even worse. Though the Mahdi's followers lying in wait for them were totally untrained and armed only with swords, spears and even bare sticks, their own fanaticism, added to the blunders of their enemies, more than made up the difference. The leader of the expedition made chaos inevitable by promising promotion to whichever of the two company commanders should capture the Mahdi. The wretched troops landed, split into two groups, and wandered aimlessly around in the darkness until the dervishes poured on them from an ambush. Six officers and 120 men were slaughtered for the loss of twelve of the Mahdi's followers. Scores more of the soldiers were captured. Only a handful managed to find their way to the water's edge and swim back to the steamer.

In conventional campaigns, it is the last battle that counts. A self-proclaimed messiah must however win the first, to set the seal of success upon his own magic. This the Mahdi had now done. None of his delirious followers can have doubted, as they paraded their prisoners in front of bonfires, that it was the Prophet himself who had befuddled their enemies' minds and led them through the night straight on to the spears of their captors.

The Mahdi shared their joy and also, doubtless, their reasoning. But he was prudent enough to realize that there were limits to what even Allah could achieve in the military field; and one of these was to go on protecting for ever an isolated island in the Nile from invasion by the infidel. Abba was as insecure as it was sacred, and far too close for comfort to Khartoum, with its fleet of armed steamers. So, having placed his affairs in the surrounding district in the hands of reliable lieutenants, he left the holy island, crossed to the left bank of the river, and led his followers westward to Kordofan and the safety of the Nuba mountains. This move combined strategy with hallowed tradition. What he had now embarked on was not merely a military retreat but a hegira, a religious flight like that made from Mecca to Medina by the Prophet himself.

Straggling across the scrub and desert, their only fire-arms the captured rifles they hardly knew how to use, the Mahdi's little band were as vulnerable as they had been on their island. But, helped again by Egyptian army incompetence, they escaped any serious clashes on the way. On 31 October, they reached their mountain sanctuary of Jebel Gedir, where they were welcomed by the local sheikh. With a characteristic stroke of show-manship, the Mahdi promptly declared this was really Masa, the mountain in the Atlas range of Morocco from where, legend had it, the Redeemer would come. None of his followers had ever seen Morocco and they would have believed their master had he declared their new home to be the Great Pyramid of Gizeh itself. This new vision of his was accordingly acclaimed with joy.

Here, at the re-christened Jebel Gedir, the Mahdi made his base for the critical months ahead. With every one of those months that passed, his numbers grew as new recruits from the whole of Central Sudan trekked to his camp. Religious zealots or malcontents; criminals on the run or merchants on the make; army deserters or escaped slaves – all were welcomed as new *Ansars* or followers,* provided they swore total obedience to the Mahdi and total submission to the strict code of conduct he was now evolving.

There was one more serious challenge before the year was out, and this he again overcame triumphantly. Jebel was at the southern tip of Kordofan, near its frontier with Fashoda. The Governor of this latter province, Rashid Bey, ignored an order from Khartoum to bide his time, and decided to win glory by annihilating this ragged band of rebels with local troops. But though he collected four hundred regulars and some thousand Shilluk tribesmen for his march on Jebel, he was annihilated himself, together with most of his men, on 9 December. Warned of the approaching danger by a woman who had walked throughout the night with the news, the Mahdi was able to ambush the force that was hoping to surprise him. Even more important than the hundreds of extra fire-arms he now collected was the renewed boost to his claims. Surely this must indeed be the Chosen One of the Prophet whose spearmen could so easily wipe out the well-equipped soldiers of the Egyptians – first on the sacred island of the Nile and now on this sacred mountain of the desert?

So the year 1881 ended. The self-proclaimed Mahdi of the summer had, in little more than five months, set the whole Sudan buzzing. He had inflicted two total defeats on govern-

---

* Another religious-historical touch. *Ansars* or 'Helpers' was the name given by the Prophet to his followers at Medina.

ment forces in the field. He had extended his political alliance to include most of the powerful Baggara emirs. For the first time, the government in Khartoum, seriously alarmed, sent out warnings to all its key officials. Among these was Rudolf Slatin, the recently-appointed Governor of Darfur, whose provincial capital of El Fasher lay some four hundred miles north-east of the Mahdi's mountain headquarters at Jebel. It is to Slatin that we must now return, and view what followed through his eyes. The paths of the boat-builder's son from Dongola and the silk-dyer's son from Vienna were soon to cross.

The first official news Slatin heard of the Mahdi's revolt reached him a few days after the latter's victory at Jebel on 9 December. Slatin was on tour across the Marra hills and beyond Kebkebia (the area where he had chased the rebel army of Sultan Harun) when, early one morning, mounted messengers from the east overtook them. They handed him a cipher message in French which had been relayed by telegraph and horsemen from the Governor-General in Khartoum. It read: 'A Dervish named Mohammed Ahmed has, without just cause, attacked Rashid Bey near Gedir. Rashid Bey and his troops have been annihilated. Take the necessary steps to prevent malcontents in your province from joining this Dervish.'

Slatin had already heard vague reports about a religious sheikh from Central Sudan who was giving the government trouble but so far he had attached little importance to them. This message put a different light altogether on the affair. It also put Slatin in an immediate quandary. On the one hand, he was clearly needed back in his provincial capital with all possible speed. On the other hand, he had come all this way from El Fasher to receive the formal homage of the local Bedayat tribes, and this now seemed more important than ever to secure. He compromised by sending an immediate signal of compliance back to Khartoum and by winding up his mission as rapidly as he could.

Everything in the Sudan takes time, however, and before the Bedayat sheikhs could be assembled, Slatin had the chance to travel around for another day or two; to admire the great beauty of the women of these free Arab tribes with their long flowing hair, and to learn much about their customs. One of the quaintest of these concerned the rights of inheritance and succession. When the head of a Bedayat family died, Slatin was told, all the relatives went out with the body to the cemetery, which was normally a mile or two from the village. When the burial ceremony was over, a signal was given and, at that, all the sons in the party raced each other back to the house of the deceased. The one who got there first and fixed his spear or arrow in the dwelling, became the acknowledged heir, inheriting at a stroke all his father's cattle and all his wives and other women, with the exception of the principal wife now widowed. Apparently, this system of the right of the swiftest worked quite happily.

It was over a week before the preliminary negotiations could be ended and the four Bedayat sheikhs were ready to swear their oath of fidelity to the Governor of Darfur. An impatient Slatin found some consolation in the picturesqueness of the ceremony. As he describes it:

A horse and saddle was brought and placed in the midst of the assembly and on this was laid a large earthenware dish filled with burning charcoal. A lance was then fixed to the saddle, and the head-Sheikhs with their attendants now came forward and, stretching out their hands over the lance and burning charcoal they recited the following words with great solemnity: 'May my leg never touch the saddle, may my body be smitten by the lance that kills; and may I be consumed by the burning fire if ever I break the solemn oath of fidelity which I now make to you'.

There was no time to linger among these handsome and appealing people. That same afternoon, Slatin gave the order to start back to El Fasher, where he could get some first-hand news about 'the Dervish, Mohammed Ahmed'. The news he heard was grave, and was soon to get worse. Rauf Pasha had been made the scapegoat for bungling the initial moves to bring the Mahdi to heel, and in March 1882 had been recalled from Khartoum by the Egyptian Government. His interim replacement as Governor-General was none other than Giegler Pasha, the German who had started his career in the Sudan as a telegraph engineer. Giegler instantly set about raising the largest expeditionary force he could muster to crush the revolt once and for all. A contingent of some 4,000 men, many of them regulars, was dispatched from Khartoum down to Kordofan, and at El

Obeid, the provincial capital, these were eventually joined by 2,000 more. This combined force of 6,000 men, under the command of an experienced soldier, Yussef Pasha, then set out to march the three hundred miles further south to Fashoda.

Everything went wrong from the start. At the farewell parade at El Obeid, the great war drum of one of the contingent commanders crashed from its camel to the ground. Even the immediate slaughtering of a bull to dispel the evil omen failed to lift the general feeling of gloom. Shortage of water on the long march did nothing to improve matters, and the soldiers' morale was further shaken by the behaviour of two Mahdist spies denounced and turned over to them. Hoping to make an impressive public example, Yussef Pasha ordered the two men to be put slowly to death in the most barbaric manner before his assembled troops. But their bravery put his cruelty to naught. As their arms and legs were hacked off one at a time they shouted defiance and finally died with the Mahdi's name on their lips.

Yussef himself got a personal taste of his opponent's calibre when he summoned him, in a haughty personal letter, to submit before the approaching battle was joined. The Mahdi's reply, dated 22 May 1882, radiated a calm confidence:

You say that our only followers are the Baggara, the ignorant, the nomads, the idolaters. Know then that the followers of the prophets before Us and of our Lord Mohammed *were* the weak and the ignorant and the idolaters, who worshipped rocks and trees ... Our going is only by the command of the Apostle of God, in the time that God will. We are not under your command but you and your superiors are under Our command ... For there is nothing between Us and you save the sword ...

Having tasted the mettle both of the Mahdi himself and his followers, the arrogant negligence which Yussef Pasha displayed now the two little armies drew near for battle was unbelievable. On the last stage of the march towards the rebel stronghold, he camped for the night of 6 June at Mesat, not far from the enemy's 'sacred mountain'. Yussef did not even bother to construct the usual *zariba* of thorn bushes around his camp, which was essential for protection in the open. Instead he allowed his men to lie down behind low heaps of ordinary scrub. At dawn on 7 June, the Mahdi's men broke through on the sleeping soldiers and within minutes slaughtered them almost to a man. Yussef Pasha was killed in his nightshirt at the door of his tent. One of the camp concubines was among the few to take any toll of the attackers. She shot two of the dervishes dead with a revolver before dropping dead at her master's feet with a spear through her body.

It mattered little that, once again, the sheer incompetence of his opponents had proved the Mahdi's strongest weapon. To him and his followers, this victory, by far their greatest so far, was further proof of his invincibility and of his divine mission. He had now routed not just a local force, but the biggest expedition that Khartoum could dispatch against him. Great quantities of arms and booty had fallen into his hands, and new recruits by the hundreds flocked to his standard. This half-hour battle had put the whole of Southern Kordofan under his control. With letters to the sheikhs in the north and to the merchants of El Obeid, the provincial capital, he now reached out for the rest of the province. One such message read simply: 'I am the Mahdi, the Successor of the Prophet of God. Cease to pay taxes to the infidel Turks and let everyone who finds a Turk kill him, for the Turks are infidels.'

It was plain, pungent stuff. No programme was announced; not even a promise. Neither was necessary. After his latest triumph, the Mahdi could afford to assume this tone of calm infallibility. As for his two brief instructions, the order to withhold all taxes answered the deepest economic and social grievance of the day; the order to kill all foreigners on sight as unbelievers stirred the bloodlust and xenophobia of a primitive people and gave them absolution for any slaughter in advance.

For a while the Mahdi bided his time at Jebel Gedir while his lieutenants, clearing the path for their master's attack, subdued or harassed the minor garrisons of Kordofan. And not only of Kordofan. In June 1882 he ordered the Emir Madibbo, a Baggara chief who had been dismissed by the government earlier that year and who had promptly joined the Mahdi to seek revenge, to march on his old stronghold of Shakka and retake it. Shakka was the principal town and garrison in the southern sector of Darfur, Slatin's province. From this point on, he too was engulfed.

Slatin's first problem when the revolt reached him was communications. Most of the main roads were by now cut or unsafe and the official postal system was as good as destroyed. He was forced to send any message outside his province sewn up in the clothes of his bearers, stuck between the soles of their sandals, or hidden in the hollow staves of their lances. Ammunition was short, mainly because the extra supplies he had ordered from Khartoum had first been held up through negligence and finally dispatched from the capital in the charge of one of the crookedest merchants in the Sudan. This gentleman lived up to his reputation by deserting to the Mahdist forces *en route* with the entire munitions convoy. Trained soldiers were also none too plentiful. When he saw the fighting moving towards him, Slatin had urgently asked Khartoum for reinforcements of regular cavalry. A contingent of four hundred, mostly Turkish and Egyptian, set out; but only a hundred got through to him at Darfur. He thus began the fight thrown back on his own resources and already largely isolated in his remote eastern province.

His only course was to attack before Madibbo could rally all the tribes of Southern Darfur around the 'victory flag accompanied by invisible angels', which the Mahdi had given him for the expedition. Slatin accordingly moved south and set up his temporary headquarters at Darra, about 130 miles north of the threatened Shakka. In the next few weeks, with a force of two hundred infantry and seventy-five cavalry, he inflicted a series of stinging tactical defeats on Madibbo's little army, and once managed to surprise and overrun the enemy's camp. But these were peripheral successes against peripheral challenges. The immediate fate of the southern Sudan hinged on the movement of the Mahdi's own forces. In the heat of mid-summer, he finally stirred. On 28 July 1882, he left his mountain retreat and marched north on El Obeid, provincial capital of Kordofan. For the Mahdi, the days of retreating and mauling his pursuers were over. He was now on the attack himself, seeking the prize of his first major city.

At the beginning of September, after a month's unopposed march, he arrived within sight of the walls of El Obeid, and set up his vast camp only six miles to the south-west. Inside the town, morale was already low. Those who could leave, like the Christian merchants, had slipped back to the imagined safety of Khartoum. Fear had divided those who remained. The Egyptian governor, Mohammed Said Pasha, was a resolute man; but when he decided to abandon the town proper and concentrate both soldiers and citizens in the fortified cantonment, many of the leading families stayed outside, and soon drifted over to the Mahdi's camp. Here, by contrast, all was confidence and unity as preparations for the mass assault were made.

Yet, despite this contrast in morale, when the Mahdist army delivered its first frontal attack on 8 September it suffered a defeat so bloody as to be almost mortal. At daybreak, wave after wave of horsemen, at first obscured to the defenders by the clouds of dust they raised, galloped in two converging columns on the fortifications. But the dervishes carried only their traditional swords and spears and though they managed to break through the outer ditch and ramparts, their fanaticism proved no match for the Remington rifles and cannon of the garrison, which poured shot into them from almost point-blank range. By afternoon, the Mahdi, who was watching the slaughter of his followers from a safe distance, gave the order to retreat. According to one estimate, he left ten thousand of his thirty thousand warriors dead on the field, including two of his own brothers.

Had Mohammed Said made an immediate sortie in pursuit of the shattered dervish columns, he might have turned the retreat into a rout. As it was, this so-called 'Friday Battle' put a severe damper on the Mahdists' spirits, and there were some who even advised a general withdrawal. It was a critical moment. But the Mahdi finally decided to stick it out. After what he had just witnessed, he also quietly resolved to rely less in future on the 'angels' banners' and rather more on military common sense. The rifles and other captured weapons which had hitherto been spurned as mere tools of the infidel were now brought out of storage and distributed among black Sudanese army prisoners who knew how to use them. The black captives had little choice but to consent. Henceforth, the Mahdist army always had this hard core of non-Arab regular soldiers, trained by the Egyptian and firing his arms, which could be used to stiffen the disorganized bravery of the spearmen.

As for El Obeid itself, the Mahdi did what besiegers have done since time immemorial after a frontal assault has failed. He sat in his camp outside the beleagured town and let starvation do his work for him. It proved more deadly than his dervishes. Father Josef Ohrwalder, an Austrian Catholic priest captured by the Mahdi at the beginning of the siege together with several other priests and nuns of his mission, watched the life drain out of El Obeid as autumn passed slowly into winter.

At first, items such as camel-meat, millet, chicken and eggs could still be bought at inflated prices and only the poorest were literally starved. But soon there was little or no normal food to be had for any money. To begin with, when regular meat supplies ran out, the townspeople fell back on the familiar siege diet of donkeys, dogs and mice. Then, when these grew scarce, they turned to insects. Crickets were eaten and cockroaches, which were prized as a delicacy. White ants were also much sought after and the ground was frantically dug up for their nests which contained minute heaps of food which the ants had stored for the coming winter. By now, both the streets inside the cantonment and the defence ditch which ran outside were choked with the decaying bodies of hundreds of the emaciated dead. The air over El Obeid was pestilential and black with carrion crows which feasted on the corpses. From his melancholy observation post in the Mahdi's lines, Ohrwalder saw how these birds became so bloated with their constant gorging that they could no longer fly. The soldiers of the garrison shot them as they waddled on the ground – and then devoured them greedily. Finally, when all living things – animal, bird or insect – ran short, the people boiled and ate their leather sandals, or else fed on gum, and died of that.

All the while the dervishes just outside the walls taunted the garrison with their own plenty. The Mahdi, with the surrounding countryside in ecstatic submission to him, had food in abundance. His main camp was probably too far off for the wretched townspeople to catch the smell of wholesome roasts. But, every night, the feasting was literally spread out before their eyes as the dark plain turned into a sea of thousands of tiny cooking fires, twinkling away under the stars. Indeed, some of the Mahdi's men even managed for a while to turn a vast profit by smuggling food into the town and selling it to the highest bidder. He put an abrupt stop to this by cutting off the hands of the offenders, and parading them as examples through the camp, the amputated stumps of their arms tied to their necks.

By the New Year of 1883, it was clear that the agony of El Obeid could not be stretched any further. Discipline had collapsed altogether under the scramble for food, and the garrison was anyway becoming so weakened physically as to be of little military value. The soldiers barely had the strength left to raise their rifles. On 5 January, Bara, about eighty miles to the north, and the only other government stronghold in Kordofan still holding out against the Mahdi, capitulated. The Mahdi celebrated the event with repeated salvoes of guns, and the wretched people of El Obeid at first took this to be the fire of an approaching relief column. Their gloom when the truth was known was the last psychological straw which broke Mohammed Said's stubborn resistance. At first he considered blowing himself up with the garrison powder magazine rather than submit personally. Then his officers persuaded him to accept a new surrender demand sent across by the Mahdi on 15 January, provided that the lives of the defenders would be spared. Four days later, on 19 January, the Mahdi made his triumphal entry.

During the next fortnight, the inhabitants of El Obeid went through a nightmare even worse than their four months of slow starvation. Even to the Mahdi and his sheikhs, the town was an exciting prize, with about £100,000 in its provincial treasury and all the private hoards of its officials and merchants on top of that. To the primitive dervishes, it was an Aladdin's Cave of treasure. A reign of terror began which made the familiar excesses of the government tax-collectors mild by comparison. Every building was plundered from top to bottom. Anyone suspected of possessing and hiding even a few trinkets was flogged continually until he disclosed their whereabouts.

Said Pasha, resolute to the last, refused to reveal the hiding-place of his treasure; but his concubine and his servants were tortured until the secret was revealed. For this refusal – and for attempting to smuggle an official report on the surrender back to Khartoum – the Governor paid with his life. The Mahdi had him literally hacked to death with axes. He then obligingly announced that, in a vision, he had been able to persuade the

44

Prophet to send Mohammed Said to paradise instead of to hell.

Thus already, the Mahdi's pronouncements were taking on a distinctly tailor-made look. A certain scepticism may be called for in judging another declaration he now made, condemning the wild plundering of El Obeid. This read:

> If you have no better example to follow than that of the Turks, it is not sufficient for you ... After taking what they formerly possessed, you have begun to follow in their footsteps; consequently, you will be destroyed as they were ... Repent, obey my orders, and return the loot you have taken ... The Prophet has told me that after I have killed the infidels and captured this province I must return and punish those who refuse to obey me. Such punishment will be death.

It could be argued that this reflects a genuine concern over the cruelty of his own followers and the sufferings of his enemies. But in view of the systematic bloodbath into which the Mahdi was to plunge the whole Sudan, it is more likely that it reflected anxiety in case valuable plunder should be diverted from his own hands or from the State Treasury which he now began to build up.

There can be no argument over the political effects of this latest and greatest victory of his. He was no longer an obscure rebel; no longer even just a troublesome one. He was now the master of a whole province. And from Kordofan, his shadow fell darkly across all of southern and central Sudan and even touched Khartoum itself. One of the many messages he distributed from El Obeid contained the words: 'On the arrival of this my letter, assemble all those in whom you can trust, join and fight with him wherever he goes and lay siege to Khartoum. . . .'

What, meanwhile, of Slatin?

Chapter Four

DEFEAT AND SURRENDER

While the Mahdi was starving El Obeid into submission, Slatin continued the running fight some four hundred miles to the east against his wily lieutenant Madibbo for the mastery of Darfur. Slatin had scoured the province for reinforcements to his garrisons, bringing in all the tribesmen who were still loyal to the Government, and begging, borrowing or hiring all the armed *bazingers* or black slave troops that he could find. By the end of the summer he had mustered a campaign force of 2,150 rifles (550 of whom were regular soldiers armed with Remingtons) plus about 7,000 spearmen and 400 horses from the friendly tribes. For artillery, he had a single muzzle-loading mountain gun operated by a crew of thirteen.

In October of 1882 he left Dara and led this miniature army southwards on Madibbo's trail. Slatin placed all the camels in the central square of his column, together with the ammunition train and the one precious gun. This square he covered on each side with Egyptian regulars or black troops, with three groups of two thousand spearmen on either flank and in the rear, and finally an outer screen of horsemen beyond these. For a few days all went well. They overran a village recently built by the enemy and captured quantities of grain. The scouts found sufficient water ahead along the 150-mile road to Shakka, Slatin's immediate objective, and reported that Madibbo had fled even further south than that. The truth was very different.

In fact, Madibbo was not two hundred miles ahead of them

but right on their tail and, at a place called Om Waragat, half-way on the march, he struck. As Slatin's column was crossing a stretch of boggy moorland, with most of the men in the centre busy pulling the animals out of the mire, a force of several thousand half-naked dervishes pounced out from cover on the rear guard. This barely had time to loose off one volley before it was pressed back by sheer weight of numbers into the main square itself. In a matter of seconds, the square in turn became a mêlée of panic-stricken camels and disorganized soldiers who had not even had the time to fix their bayonets and fight off the attacking spearmen at close range. Slatin, who was suffering from a heavy bout of fever at the time, shook himself into action as the first shots were fired and galloped back to the scene.

For a man running a high temperature he showed a remarkably cool grasp of the situation. Realizing that his only hope lay in separating as many of his own men as he could from the enemy he ordered the bugler to sound the 'lie down' call and then poured fire on to those still standing up. By this drastic means, the day was saved and all the attackers who had broken into the square were eventually dispersed or killed. But they were not the only victims. Slatin's Egyptian regulars, who had obeyed the order to lie flat, escaped relatively unscathed. But the untrained *bazingers*, most of whom had no idea what the bugle call meant, had been mown down together with the dervishes, while the camels, who had even less idea about military signals, had also been decimated.

The entire action lasted less than twenty minutes. They had been enough to break Slatin's confident little army as an offensive force. When he called the roll, he found that no fewer than ten of his fourteen infantry officers had been killed, while an eleventh was wounded. Of his thirteen artillerymen, only one was left alive. Five of his sheikhs had fallen and the bands of loyal tribesmen had been almost completely wiped out, either massacred on the moor or hunted down in the surrounding forest. Some trickled back during the day but when he counted heads again that evening Slatin found that he had only nine hundred men left out of the force of nine thousand he had led out of Dara the week before. Of the four hundred horsemen, thirty had survived. There was no question now of

47

pursuing Madibbo. Slatin knew he would be lucky if he could beat off further attacks and limp back to Dara alive.

For the first time indeed, chill fears about his own survival now struck him. He wrote farewell notes to his mother, his brothers and his sisters in far-off Austria and gave them to a messenger, together with a report on the battle, ordering him to break through Madibbo's lines on horseback at all costs and make for Dara. He scribbled another note to his English colleague, Lupton, Governor of the Bahr al-Ghazal province which bordered on the Congo, urging him to mount a diversionary attack on the Mahdi's forces from the south. This message Slatin concealed in a dry pumpkin gourd and handed to two trusted *bazingers* to deliver. Once the messengers had left there was nothing for it but to fortify their corpse-strewn camp with the usual *zariba* of thorn bushes and await Madibbo's next blow.

For five days they remained there, attacked once if not twice a day. Then, as food was running desperately short, Slatin decided to make a break for it and head back for Dara. It was a sad-looking band which set out at sunrise, exactly one week to the hour after the disaster. There were only two camels left to draw the mountain gun in the centre of the column. Also inside the marching square were 160 wounded. Some of these could hobble along but others were so badly hurt that they had to be piled two or three at a time on to the backs of the few remaining horses. As for mounted scouts, all Slatin could spare now were a couple of Arab horsemen to patrol each flank.

But though vulnerable, Slatin's nine hundred survivors were determined. Knowing Madibbo's ways, he sensed that if he could only beat him off decisively once or twice, the enemy would gradually tire of the pursuit. So it proved. The first attack came when they had been barely an hour on the march and it was again launched from the rear. Rushing in with great lances in their right hands and bundles of smaller throwing spears in their left, Madibbo's men tried to repeat their overrunning manoeuvre of Om Waragat. This time Slatin was ready. He had placed the gun right at the back of the column, with a group of lightly-wounded men holding shells and cartridges for instant re-loading. This single artillery piece, helped by the volleys of Slatin's riflemen (and as they had weapons

48

galore to go round, nearly everyone loosed off a shot), decided
the skirmish. They were attacked again during the retreat –
notably when some of the column, half-crazed with thirst,
rushed waist-deep into a water pool where an ambush had been
set. But the enemy's actions were growing weaker all the time
and eventually the column limped back into Dara to lick its
wounds.

Slatin's own injuries were far from trifling. A bullet had
shattered his right hand and the ring-finger had to be amputated. Another bullet had struck his leg, causing the bone to
stick out. There was a lance wound in his right knee. Thanks
to that phenomenal constitution which was to stand him in
such good stead in the years to come, he seems to have needed
nothing more than a few days' rest before returning to action.

The sinking morale of his troops took more restoring. As
Slatin tried to build up his forces over the next few weeks,
there were several signs that the tide of popular fear or sympathy was flowing steadily the Mahdi's way. A caravan that
Slatin sent north to his own provincial capital of El Fasher, for
example, with an urgent request for ammunition and regular
troop reinforcements, eventually arrived back with the ammunition but with excuses, instead of soldiers, for the reinforcements.
Then, in the third week of January 1883, the news of the fall of
El Obeid came in from the east.

Immediately, poor morale became not just a problem for
Slatin but a grave danger. His best intelligence agents operating
among his own troops were the prostitutes of Dara, who plied
the soldiers with *marissa* or native beer on their visits to the
town brothels, and thus got them to loosen their tongues as
well as their clothing. He had known for some time by these
means that a few malcontents were grumbling against him personally as an 'infidel' and muttering that the days of 'Turkish
power' in the Sudan were now over. After the fall of El Obeid,
the talk got tougher and open sedition was plotted in the
brothels, with a plan for mass desertion to the Mahdi's forces.
Slatin had no difficulty in identifying the six ring-leaders and
getting them to confess their guilt before a court martial. There
was also no opposition – apart from a painful struggle within
himself – when he ordered the death sentence to be carried out.
The six men were shot in public by their open graves. But

Slatin knew in his heart that the trouble could not be contained by firing-squads, for the Mahdi held a more powerful weapon than all the rifles in the Sudan.

Slatin's own officers brought it into the open that same evening. The troops, they told him through a senior spokesman, accepted his severe discipline because it was fairly meted out. They were grateful for their regular pay and for their share in any plunder. Furthermore, they knew they were commanded by a man who always fought in their midst and who asked nothing of them that he would not do himself. But the conviction was spreading that this was, after all, a religious war. Slatin Bey was a foreigner and a Christian, and, as such, he could never win it; his bravery could only postpone the hour of their own deaths, and of his. Slatin dismissed the spokesman and pondered. If he could do nothing on the spot to change his nationality, there was plenty he could do about his faith. His reasoning is best given in his own disarmingly frank words:

... After a few minutes deliberation, I resolved to present myself to the troops the following morning as a Mohammedan. I was perfectly well aware that in taking this step I should be placing myself in a curious position which could not fail to be condemned by some. However, I made up my mind to do it, knowing that I should thereby cut the ground from under the feet of these intriguers and should have a better chance of preserving the province with which the Government had entrusted me. In my early youth, my religious ideas were somewhat lax; but at the same time I believed myself to be by conviction as well as by education a good Christian, though I was always inclined to let people find their own path to salvation. The simple fact was that I had not been sent to the Sudan as a missionary but as an official of the Egyptian Government.

Having taken his decision, Slatin sensibly decided to go the whole hog and extract the maximum psychological dividends from it. At sunrise, he had all the troops paraded in a square and rode into the midst of them on horseback. After briefly extolling their bravery and loyalty, he uttered the crucial words: 'I am not an unbeliever. I am as much a believer as you. I bear witness that there is no God but God and that Mohammed is His Prophet.' As he finished speaking there was much joyful shouting and brandishing of lances in approval, and it was some time before order was restored and the parade

50

could be dismissed. Then Slatin issued his first order as a Moslem commander. It was to distribute twenty oxen among the troops as *karama* or sacrificial offerings, with one extra ox apiece for each officer.

For an Austrian of the 1880s, when the Catholic religion was one of the pillars of his social and political life, it was a grave decision, even if he was in Dara and not back on the banks of the Danube. Though temporarily a servant of the Egyptian Khedive, he remained a subject of His Apostolic Majesty, the Emperor Franz Joseph, and a proud if lowly officer on his Army Reserve. For these reasons, there were some, like General Gordon, who neither understood nor ever forgave Slatin's action. Indeed, for the great hero and martyr-to-be of the Sudan – who was to die, as he had lived, by his Bible – this young Austrian governor he had personally raised up had, by his apostasy, put himself beyond the moral, as well as the Christian, pale. Gordon simply wrote Slatin off. There may well have been others who, without condemning him so ruthlessly, would always wonder, after this nimble religious somersault, what trust could be placed in any of Slatin's professions of loyalty, once the heat was really on. It is likely that Slatin himself, even during those years of glory that were to follow his years of suffering, never quite overcame a feeling of uneasiness about his performance at this dawn parade at Dara.

That explanation of his only tells part of the truth. In it, he merely proclaims himself a pragmatist, not indifferent to ideals, but not averse to dropping them when they got too heavy to carry. But the real reason why, all his life, he could change his soil so easily – whether that soil was religious or political – was simply that he had no roots to pull up. The Austro-Germans of the old Habsburg Empire were hazy in themselves when it came to a sense of corporate identity. They could never make up their minds whether they were in fact a separate nation, like the Magyars, the Poles, the Czechs and the other peoples of the Empire, or whether they were simply the German-speaking stewards of the dynasty, who had swapped their own profile for the perquisites of power. And within this loosely-anchored Austrian community were the Viennese; a race to themselves, or rather, a people so mixed in blood and so cosmopolitan in outlook as to be no race at all.

51

Slatin was one of them, sharing their virtues and their faults. In addition, he was of Jewish descent even if no orthodox Jew by faith. There was precious little in all this to tug at his coat tails and hold him back when, faced with a desperate plight alone and far from his own homeland, another formal change of religion seemed to offer some prospects of survival. Survival was the key word. It is a racial instinct of the Jews and a political speciality of the Viennese, both having developed naturally and understandably over the centuries. Rudolf Slatin was of the breed and he was to prove worthy of it.

For a few months, he was able to draw profit from his drastic decision. The soldiers followed their newly-declared Moslem chief into battle with all the enthusiasm of their early campaigning days together, and throughout the summer of 1883 Slatin was able to conduct effective sorties from Dara. On more than one occasion they routed Mahdist bands who easily outnumbered them, and Slatin's men duly attributed these successes to the fact that their commander now regularly took his Friday prayers kneeling with them. This was not his only concession to his new faith. According to one of his European contemporaries in the Sudan, Slatin, in these last months as Governor-General of Darfur, not only had himself circumcised but also formally took a native wife, one Hassanieh, of the royal Darfurian family. He was thus living like a true Moslem, as well as fighting like one.

This curious interlude did not last long. Slatin's last bout of military defiance was, indeed, just as unrealistic as his new mode of life. With every day that passed, the tide was flowing more strongly in the Mahdi's favour. In the autumn of 1883 the torrent engulfed and destroyed another and even larger expeditionary force, now under British command, which was sent out from Khartoum to stem it. This was the tragedy of Major-General Hicks Pasha, which sealed Slatin's fate, and virtually that of the whole Sudan as well.

It is a doleful story of muddle, squabbling and hesitancy. The hesitance began with the British Government who, though refusing to back the Egyptian Khedive with British or Indian troops in his renewed attempt to suppress the Sudan revolt, none the less raised no objection to British officers serving on the expedition. Hicks, the ill-fated commander whom the Egyptians found, was a retired Indian Army officer with no knowledge at all of Sudan campaigning, let alone of the remote province of Kordofan he was now called upon to subdue. Though entirely responsible to the Egyptian Government, he was also in direct touch by telegraph with the British Agent in Cairo, Sir Edward Malet. The cipher-books he used for encoding his secret messages were those of a serving British officer, Lieutenant-Colonel Stewart, who had been sent down to Khartoum as early as November 1882 to investigate the Sudan imbroglio without actually intervening in it. Of the ten European officers the Egyptians recruited to serve under Hicks, five were British, including the Chief of Staff, Colonel Arthur Farquhar.

This policy of strictly limited and strictly unofficial support for the 1883 Sudan expedition, though reasonable in itself at the time, ended by giving the British Government the worst of both worlds. The disaster that lay ahead was a blow to British military prestige though not a single British soldier was involved. The fighting force that finally paraded under General Hicks at Omdurman on 8 September 1883, before marching south to meet the Mahdi consisted, in fact, of 7,000 regular Egyptian Army infantry, 500 Egyptian cavalry and 400 *bashi-bazooks* as mounted irregulars. Among the non-martial elements which marched out with it was a transport train of no fewer than 5,500 camels and an estimated 2,000 camp followers, ranging from merchants to prostitutes. This flabby and vulnerable appendage was not the least of the commander's worries.

A far worse one was the squabbling. Hicks had had quite a struggle to get himself clearly nominated the Commander-in-Chief in the first place; but his mission was still complicated by the fact that Ala ed Din Pasha, the newly-appointed Governor-General of the Sudan, accompanied the expedition as its principal political and administrative officer. Of the repeated quarrels that arose, the most fateful was over the route to be taken from their forward base at Duem on the White Nile to the Mahdi's stronghold at El Obeid. Hicks, though he knew not a foot of this inhospitable country, wanted to take the northern trail, via Bara, for the obvious reasons that it was shorter, quite open, and passed through tribal territory that was neutral or even friendly. All this would have greatly reduced the weight of that enormous baggage train that dragged at his soldiers' feet with every step they took.

But Ala ed Din, afraid there might be too little water along this trail, argued for the roundabout southern route via Al Rahad. This was far longer; much of the region was covered with dense scrub and tall grass, thus immensely increasing the danger of ambush; and almost the entire line of march lay through hostile tribal areas. But water was the magic word in this parched land and Ala ed Din could speak louder on such matters than the total stranger Hicks. The Egyptian was emphatic that, apart from wells, a seasonal watercourse which straggled across the area, forming three shallow lakes as it went, would give them all the drinking water they needed. The rainy season, which ran from June to September, was only just ending. So, after much debate, south it was. On 27 September Hicks led his main column out of Duem, having sent advance parties ahead to seize the first wells.

The perils of the route they had taken soon became apparent. They found village after village deserted as they entered it; the tribesmen had fled, taking all food and stores with them. Local reinforcements that the guides had promised never turned up when the rendezvous was reached. The guides themselves became suspect. Even the water supply, though adequate on the first stage, began to look more questionable the further south they went as, with every day of the intense October heat, the rain pools dried out further.

Asked how he felt before leaving the safety of Duem, Hicks had quietly replied: 'I feel like Jesus Christ surrounded by the Jews.' Despite the presence of the dashing Colonel Farquhar, who had made several sorties at enemy scouts, and the handful of other European officers at his side, this feeling of utter desolation must have mounted with every mile they now pushed on into this scorching wilderness. The few diaries and dispatches which have survived* already breathe a doom-laden air before the final tragedy struck.

The huge square dragged itself forward in the heat like a tortoise without even its hard protective shell. The horde of

---

* Notably the diary of an Austrian officer on Hicks's staff, Major Herlth; Hicks's own dispatches and those of Mr O'Donovan, correspondent of the London *Daily News*; all authenticated by several verbal accounts given by survivors.

camels, who formed instead its very soft centre, could not be allowed out to graze in the dense hostile countryside around, and were forced to feed on anything they could pick up on the trampled line of march. Eventually they had to be fed the straw from their own saddle pads and the bare wood that was left rubbed deep wounds into their haunches. Scores died every day, their loads being piled on to the backs of the animals still alive. Most of the horses, too, were dead before they were ever ridden into battle.

The plight of the eight thousand soldiers who formed the four sides of the square, with Hicks and his little staff group in the van, was not much better as the October days went by. The men were listless due to lack of any real action and wearied by the long marches. The officers were divided by the continued disputes between Hicks and his Egyptian colleagues.

The Mahdi, waiting with his hordes at El Obeid, was kept well informed of all these troubles by his spies. He played the obvious waiting game of drawing the enemy as far forward as he could into the wastes, knowing that its strength would only be drained further with each mile of its advance. For the time being, he merely ordered strong *Ansar* reconnaissance bands to harass the column, picking off any stragglers who fell behind, and filling up any wells that lay ahead. The rest he left to Allah and to the sun.

His confidence was only strengthened when Gustav Klootz, originally an orderly to one of the German officers on Hicks's staff, deserted and made his way to the Mahdist forces. The white captive was brought in triumph to the giant Adansonia tree outside El Obeid where the Mahdi held his court and his daily parades, and was questioned closely about the state of the approaching column. Klootz, who was mistaken, because of his blond hair, for an English officer, gave pleasingly frank answers: though Hicks's army would certainly fight rather than submit, he said, it was weakened and divided among itself and no one serving in it really believed in victory any more. The German was rewarded for this news not only with his life but with pieces of fried meat picked off a plate and given him by the Mahdi's own hand, a rare mark of favour.

So great was the Mahdi's delight indeed that he now had hundreds of proclamations written out and distributed in villages along Hicks's path, calling on him to surrender. They were in the serenely confident language of all the Mahdi's summonses. One read in part:

Every intelligent person must be aware that God rules and his authority cannot be shared by muskets, cannons or bombs and no one has any strength except he whom Almighty God strengthens ... If ye have light, ye will believe in God, in his Prophet ... and will accept the truth of our mission as Mahdi, and will come out to us surrendering yourselves. He who surrenders shall be saved. But if ye refuse and persist in denying my divine calling, and trust in guns and power, ye are to be killed, even as the Prophet foretold many other deaths before you.

Hicks received this letter on 29 October at Aluba, less than 20 miles south of El Obeid. Two days later, on 1 November, the Mahdi struck camp himself and moved out to meet the approaching column. Every man, woman and child of the town streamed out behind Mohammed Ahmed's forces, eager to see and share in the expected victory. They were not to be disappointed.

For the last stage of his advance, Hicks had chosen to march through a thickly wooded valley which gave the Mahdi the ambush cover he wanted for his *coup de grâce*. He stationed strong forces in the forests on either flank of the valley and hid a few men in a wooded dip in the centre of the valley floor, right in the path of the oncoming marchers. The dervishes had already taken terrible toll of Hicks's men on 3 November, as they struggled through a gorge approaching the valley. Fire was poured from either side on to this weary mass of men and camels who were so closely packed that scarcely a bullet could fail to find some sort of living target.

But it was at Shakyan, where the ground was already broadening out a little and where Hicks must have hoped he had survived the worst, that, on 5 November 1883, the final trap was sprung. In a rather belated attempt to make his force less vulnerable, Hicks had now split it up into three smaller squares, each with its own transport and ammunition at the centre. He and his staff led the first square. The other two followed it at left and right to the rear, keeping three hundred paces behind and the same distance from each other, so that the whole procession resembled a giant equilateral triangle on the move. At about ten-thirty in the morning, when they had been going half an hour, the leading group walked straight on to the dervishes hidden in the wooden dip. When these leapt up at them – literally, it seemed, from the ground – the first square broke apart in a few seconds in startled confusion. Their comrades on the flanks fired wildly inwards to support them but, as all those in the centre were by now locked in hand to hand fighting with the enemy, these fusillades killed as many Egyptians as Arabs.

At this point, the main forces of the Mahdi poured out from the forests on either side of the valley and the entire heaving triangle of men and animals was completely encircled. All three squares were broken; the guns had no time to open up; a wholesale massacre took place. In fifteen minutes, the Egyptian expeditionary force under the command of General W. Hicks Pasha became little more than a mound of corpses. All the bickering there had been between English and Egyptian officers was dissolved in the bravery of their last stand together. Ala ed Din was killed trying to make his way from the right-hand square to help Hicks at the centre. Hicks, meanwhile, had cut his way on horseback with his staff across to the left of the valley where a few large trees provided a rallying point. Here he fought to the end, first emptying his revolver into the attackers and then, as his horse was brought down underneath him, charging on foot alone with his sword, scattering a whole group of Arabs in his path. At last, pierced by several spears, he fell. He was the last European to die and his gallantry became a legend even in this country so inured to sacrifice and blood and fanaticism. The Baggara tribesmen he had taken on, almost single-handed, at the end, were nicknamed in an Arabic play on words 'Baggar Hicks', or 'the cows driven by Hicks'.

This was a tribute for posterity. But on the day itself, by 11 a.m. on 5 November, his body, and those of his staff officers, lay beheaded or mutilated where they had fallen, with every passing Arab dipping the tip of his spear in their remains. Out of his whole expeditionary force, only about three hundred men were left alive, and most of these were wounded captives. When the dervishes, on the other hand, collected their dead and laid them out in line, they counted barely five hundred bodies. They had won this battle not by sheer weight of numbers, but by greater unity, better intelligence, higher morale and surprise.

Ever since his repulse of that first landing on Abba Island, the Mahdi's victories had followed one another by geometrical progression, the scale of each success doubling the size of the one before. The triumph of Shakyan outstripped even this scale. Both its military importance and its psychological impact were immeasurably greater than anything the Mahdi had yet achieved. So far, he had successively routed his pursuers, subdued garrisons and captured one provincial capital. But always, as in the case of the previous expedition sent from Khartoum to suppress him, he had been dealing solely with the Egyptian occupation army and its local levies. Now he had annihilated Egyptian troops commanded by an English general with an English Chief of Staff and with several of its units led by other English or European officers. To the faithful or the credulous, that meant that Mohammed Ahmed's magic stretched even beyond their own known world of the Nile Valley. His prestige expanded accordingly. After Shakyan, emissaries arrived not only from Tunis and Morocco but even from India to hear the teaching of this remarkable Sudanese holy man turned warrior. The Mahdi had made his entrance on to the international stage. He and his successors were to haunt it with their presence right down to our own times.

Within the central Sudan itself, his reputation as the true redeemer became well-nigh impregnable, and everything was done to put the victory in this light. While the Mahdi remained with his forces near the battlefield, mainly to sort out the loot, his agents secretly set light to some of the bodies of the enemy dead, to promote the idea that, as unbelievers and foes of the Messiah, they were being consumed by hell-fire. And when a week later, the Mahdi returned to El Obeid – riding on a white camel at the rear of a huge triumphal procession which included a few naked survivors from Hicks's army – it was as though the Prophet himself were entering the town walls. Father Ohrwalder, who was in El Obeid, noted that the Mahdi's personal servants now took to distributing the dirty water in which their master had washed himself among the faithful, who drank it eagerly as a cure for all ills.

In a practical military sense, the battle of Shakyan ended all the Government's hopes of taking the initiative against the Mahdi. There were to be no more punitive expeditions paraded in Khartoum and marched off south to subdue him. Henceforth, the Egyptian authorities had to concentrate on holding what they still had of the Sudan. Above all, they had to think about defending Khartoum itself against the now inevitable attack.

Inevitable, but not immediate. Moving, as ever, like an animal through a treacherous jungle, the Mahdi first wanted to make sure of the ground under his feet before leaping ahead again after his prey. And that meant subduing to the east of him the province of Darfur, with its resourceful young European Governor. We must now turn to the catastrophic effect of the Shakyan battle on Rudolf Slatin.

Though he had received no direct news from Khartoum for nearly a year, Slatin learned of the departure of the Hicks expedition in the early autumn of 1883. Fortunately for his own morale, he seems to have known nothing then of the quarrels which divided it nor of the dubious line of march it had chosen. He realized that his own future, and perhaps his own life, was now strapped on the backs of Hicks's camels. All he could do was to play for time, while showing that his own spirit was not yet broken.

To continue any sort of fight was becoming increasingly difficult. By the summer, his ammunition stocks at Dara were down to a few rounds per man, with shortage of lead the main problem. He tried to meet it by melting down some of his precious lead bullets for use in the percussion rifles and making copper bullets instead from the bracelets and anklets he bought off the black women and melted down. There was a similar desperate improvisation about his attempts to smuggle messages through the Mahdist lines, who, by now, were wise to all the usual tricks. One morning, he noticed that a donkey in the fort was having its skin tightened, to cure a lame foreleg, by small incisions in the shoulder. He repeated the operation on a healthy donkey in the privacy of his house, sewing a tiny military report into the cut which he dressed with natron powder and tied up with silk thread. The message got through.

He even managed to deal another stinging blow at his old enemy Madibbo, who had now encircled Dara and was also awaiting events. Leading a party of two hundred picked men out of the fort by night, Slatin made a surprise attack on

Madibbo's camp at dawn and seized everything there, including the Arab chief's famous copper war-drums. Madibbo barely escaped with his own life by riding off bare-backed on a horse after his men. Yet, as Slatin himself realized, these successes were by now like brushing flies off the meat. They would only settle again.

The real question was how to persuade the Mahdi to delay an all-out attack against Dara until the fate of Hicks's expedition was known. This Slatin solved with a mixture of native Viennese subtlety and acquired Arab guile. His own Sub-Governor at Dara, Mohammed Khaled, happened to be a cousin of the Mahdi's and therefore highly suspect from the Sudan Government's point of view, despite his continued protestations of loyalty. Slatin both got him out of the way and established a preliminary peace feeler with the enemy camp by persuading him to go on a peace mission to the Mahdi at El Obeid. Then, as the siege closed in more tightly on Dara, with more and more local tribes joining in, and all of them demanding his surrender, Slatin hit on a new ruse.

Calling the tribal chiefs to parley under the inevitable Adansonia tree (there was a suitably large one a few hundred yards from the fort), he persuaded them to call a truce on the condition that he wrote a formal note of submission. This was not to be addressed to his besiegers at Dara, however, but to the Mahdi, or any relative the Mahdi might appoint, in El Obeid. All the emirs except the suspicious Madibbo (who stayed away from the talks) agreed, and Slatin duly wrote his letter. It read:

In the name of the Most Merciful God. From the slave of his God Abdel Kader Slatin to Sayed Mohammed el Mahdi. May God protect him and confound his enemies! Amen!

For a long time I have been defending the province which the Government confided to my care, but God's will cannot be fought against. I therefore hereby declare that I submit to it and to you, on the condition that you send one of your relatives with the necessary authority to rule this country, and to whom I shall hand it over. I demand a pledge from you that all men, women and children with the fort shall be spared. Everything else I leave to your generosity.

If Hicks won, Slatin could forget the letter. Meanwhile, however, it had won him a breathing space.

If Hicks won. . . . Throughout September and October, Slatin waited, going to the market place every day in the hope of finding a traveller with some scrap of information. But, strangely, the bad news of Shakyan moved very slowly the four hundred miles to Dara. It was not until the end of November 1883, three weeks after the event, that the first rumours reached Slatin of the annihilation of Hicks's forces. Still he clung to the hope that they might be exaggerated. Then, on 20 December, a messenger arrived at the fort bringing not only his own eyewitness account of the disaster, but bearing also a summons to Dara from the Mahdi's camp to surrender.

It was the end of the road, and Slatin knew it. At the beginning of the year, after the fall of El Obeid, and when there was still a chance of an ultimate Government victory, he had been able to buy months of time by turning Moslem. But even the last few weeks of respite had only been won by a paper pledge of surrender, and now that pledge had to be redeemed. Slatin had no tricks, and no cards left to play. Darfur could certainly not be held after this. Indeed, it looked doubtful whether the whole of the Sudan could be saved. Of that, in any case, he knew nothing. He was completely isolated, more than six hundred miles from a capital that was now concerned only with its own survival. His officers, whom he consulted that evening, were all of the same opinion. As if to drive home the point, when he awoke next morning it was to learn that all the black troops of the garrison had deserted the town. The chief merchant of Dara had also fled with his family. It was more than the rats who were leaving the sinking ship. The crew were going as well. Slatin, who had made up his mind anyway overnight, now sent word of his surrender back to El Obeid.

After three days of parleys out in the plains, Slatin prepared to hand over to the new Governor of Darfur. It was, of course, to be none other than his own former subordinate, Mohammed Khaled, cousin of the new all-powerful Mahdi. The last night of his liberty Slatin passed without closing his eyes, camped in the open outside Dara. Ironically, it was Christmas Eve. He describes those still hours as the saddest of his life. He kept on thinking of home and of that *Heiliger Abend* all his countrymen in far-away Austria would be celebrating – the Christmas trees in every home, bright with tinsel and candles, with presents heaped up around them; the special services being held every-

where from St Stephen's Cathedral in Vienna to the tiniest
Alpine church in the Tyrol; the crisp air and the snow; the
peace and prosperity that was the Austro-Hungarian Empire of
the 1880s. Almost impossible to believe that those were the
same stars shining above him now in this desert sky as he, the
Khedive's Austrian Governor-General of Darfur, was preparing
to hand over his province and his own fate into the hands of a
Sudanese fanatic in the heart of Africa. Those thoughts of
Christmas reminded him painfully of something else: his
formal abandonment of his Christian faith and the consequences this would now bear. As he wrote afterwards:

> Moreover I was well aware that my surrender would place me
> absolutely and entirely in the hands of this mock-religious reformer
> and that not only would I have to behave like a Moslem in the
> ordinary sense of the word but, to carry out the role surrender
> would entail for me ... I must become a devotee, and henceforth
> show myself to be a Mahdist in heart and soul!

It is little wonder he got no sleep.

The next morning Slatin rode back into his old headquarters
at Dara, now completely garrisoned by dervish troops. He
watched his own men hand over their arms, company by company, and then went formally to present himself to Mohammed
Khaled, his successor and the servant of his new master.

Just before leaving his house for the last time to do this, he
had a reconciliation there with Madibbo, his wily and elusive
adversary in the past two years of campaigning in Darfur. The
two men had been worthy opponents and each, in his fashion,
had grown to respect the other. They soon made their personal
peace now. Slatin returned to the Arab warrior his precious
war-drums, captured from him in the night raid of that same
summer and, taking a sword down from the wall, laid that on
them for good measure. Madibbo attempted to give Slatin his
horse, which was the finest animal owned by his tribe.

Slatin refused this, but did accept some last words of advice:

'I am only an Arab,' Madibbo said, 'but listen to me. Be
obedient now and be patient. Practise this virtue, for it is
written, "God is with the patient".'

For long years to come, Slatin was to provide the patience
in the hope that God would provide the reward.

Chapter Five

KHARTOUM

During the first weeks of 1884, Slatin was held under loose guard in Khaled's camp, a helpless spectator of the mopping-up of the province that had once been his to rule. After Dara had been taken over, El Fasher, the most northerly garrison of Darfur, and the only one still to hold out, was stormed despite brave resistance by the defenders.

Cruelty, as Slatin knew, was as much a part of the Sudan scene as the sand and the sun. Yet the tortures the Mahdi's men now inflicted before his eyes on any captive believed to be withholding hidden treasure seemed to him to set a new mark of calculated ferocity. At Dara, suspected hoarders were hung by their legs down the well-shafts until the rush of blood to their heads rendered them unconscious. At El Fasher, one Egyptian major who defied Khaled to his face was given the almost unbelievable punishment of one thousand lashes a day for three consecutive days in an attempt to draw from him the hiding-place of his gold. The major held out under his ordeal like a block of stone, but it was too much for Slatin to watch. He went to Khaled and pleaded for the officer to be set free. Khaled agreed, if Slatin would prostrate himself in front of him. In the Sudan, this was the ultimate humiliation but Slatin went through with it, and, as a reward, was allowed to carry the major's mangled body back to his house. Here the poor wretch died, four days later. In his last moments, he tried to murmur in gratitude to his rescuer the spot where his

63

money was hidden. Slatin firmly forbade him, and soon buried the Egyptian in the same earth as his gold.

Such was Slatin's introduction to the Mahdi's methods. In June 1884, six months after his capture, he was finally introduced to the Mahdi himself. The meeting took place at Rahad, a day's march south-east of El Obeid, in an open-air camp which Slatin describes as 'a sea of straw huts stretching as far as the eye could see'. His servants had made him a new *jibba* (the shirt-like robe of the dervishes) for the occasion. They had stitched on the obligatory patches with such regularity that, in his own words, he looked 'exactly like a lady in a fancy bathing-costume'. There any parallel with far-off Europe ceased abruptly. Slatin met his new master not merely as a white captive but as Abdel Kader, the Moslem. He kissed the great man's hands when he emerged from prayers and then knelt on the edge of his sheepskin to repeat after him the *Beia*, or solemn oath of allegiance. With these few Arab words, the Austro-Hungarian officer from Vienna swore, among other things, never to disobey the Mahdi 'in his goodness', and not to flee from his religious war. Hours of sermons and communal prayers followed, stretching throughout the day until dusk, so that when Slatin was finally allowed to rise from his motionless squatting posture and leave the presence he could scarcely unwind his cramped legs and hobble back to his hut. Everything from the sheepskin oath to the aching limbs was part of the price he was now paying, and would have to go on paying, for that lightning conversion of his to Mohammedanism at Dara eighteen months before.

As for the Mahdi, there was good reason why he should summon his fair-skinned captive and convert at this juncture. Slatin's friend and former commander, General Gordon, was back in Khartoum for the last time. The great Moslem fanatic of the Sudan was coming face to face with its great Christian fanatic. Mohammed Ahmed knew that, for his magic, and therefore his power, the supreme test had come. This Abdel Kader, who had been one of Gordon's Governors, who knew the Englishman's mind, might be helpful even to the successor of the Prophet in interpreting the likely course of events.

The tale of Gordon's final and, for him, fatal mission has been told too often and too well to need repeating in any detail here. We have only to view the familiar tragedy through the eyes of Rudolf Slatin, watching the defeat and death of his hero as a captive in the enemy camp.

Gordon's reappointment to service in the Sudan had come about at the beginning of the year. It was another of those odd crab-like steps by which the British Government was being pulled, against its own will, into the Sudanese furnace. Mr Gladstone's Cabinet was still opposed to any direct military commitment against the Mahdi, which seemed as thankless and as limitless a task as taking on the Devil himself. But the Government stood almost alone in its reluctance. England's prestige had been struck a stinging, if indirect, blow by the massacre of General Hicks and his army, and a public demand for action of some sort was mounting. It grew into a clamour when the British press, led by the *Pall Mall Gazette*, demanded that Gordon should be sent back to the Sudan to deal with the emergency. Queen Victoria shared her people's ignorance about the Sudan. She also shared their romantic faith that, despite this remoteness, it was already in some mysterious way part of the white man's burden. As she wrote to Gladstone during the great debate:

We must not let this fine and fruitful country, with its peaceful inhabitants, be left a prey to murder and rapine and utter confusion. It would be a *disgrace* to the British name, and the country will NOT stand it.

Apart from those rosy adjectives applied to the Sudan, she was, of course, quite right.

By the time the sovereign penned that letter on 8 February 1884, however, a typically English compromise had been reached. Gladstone stuck to his guns in insisting that Egyptian troops should evacuate the untenable Sudan, and that the British Army should for the time being keep clear of it. But as a proposal had already been aired that a British officer should be sent to Khartoum to supervise this evacuation, the solution was obvious. Gordon found himself swept into this appointment on a wave of public agitation.

Where chaotic solutions are soluble, a compromise can sometimes help, by buying time to solve them. The story of the British Empire was indeed full of such triumphs by temporization. But there are other compromises that only compound chaos because they carry the seeds of further muddle in themselves. Gordon's last mission for his Queen was one of these.

He arrived in Khartoum via Cairo on 18 February 1884, having been formally re-appointed Governor-General of the Sudan *en route*. But if his title was now clear, his functions were still hazy. His central task, as laid down in his official instructions, was purely advisory and administrative: 'to consider the best mode of evacuating the interior of the Sudan'. But by the time he took up his post he had already talked his dubious superiors into a plan for replacing the doomed Egyptian regime in Khartoum by restoring the ancient Sudanese ruling families to office. In other words, he had embarked on what was an outright political challenge to the Mahdi's power. From here to a military confrontation with the Mahdi was but one small and unavoidable step. Yet the one thing vital to secure this second step – the dispatch of an Anglo-Egyptian army to back up Gordon's challenge with force – was first denied and then delayed until the cause was anyway lost. What exactly drove Gordon to leap so far ahead of his Government – the vanity of a Messiah complex; a secret wish for martyrdom; or the feeling that he, rather than Gladstone, embodied the real hopes and wishes of the British people – will always remain obscure. The one certain thing is that his personal commitment to a showdown with the Mahdi pulled England in after him; and its humiliating failure made a British occupation of the Sudan sooner or later inevitable.

Of much of this Rudolf Slatin, his deposed lieutenant, was at the time unaware. Like all who opposed the Mahdi, Slatin had drawn new hope from the news of Gordon's return. This hope grew as, during the spring and early summer of 1884, Gordon managed to deal some sharp blows in sorties against the *Ansars*, using only the eight thousand troops of the Khartoum garrison. All the time, however, the rough noose that the Mahdi was throwing around the capital's neck was growing tighter. This was the situation, full of uncertainty and confusion, yet still not without cheer, that faced Slatin when he swore allegiance on the sheepskin rug at Rahad and became automatically one of the Mahdi's *mulazemin* or servant-courtiers.

For a few weeks, the Mahdi remained at Rahad. He held immense military parades every Friday in which his three divisions of the Blue, Green and Red Flags, each bright with the banners of its attendant emirs, formed up in a vast open-ended square of some forty thousand men for the Mahdi to bless and inspect. Then, on 22 August 1884, they broke camp and headed in three separate columns north-west towards Khartoum. Slatin travelled with the main and central column, in the suite of the Mahdi's oldest ally, the Khalifa Abdallahi, to whom he had been assigned.

Before they had been moving many days, a bizarre interlude occurred. Rumours spread about that a mysterious European Christian had arrived in their rear at El Obeid and was making for the Mahdi's camp. Some said he was a close relative of the Queen of England. Others declared he was the Emperor of France in person. At length the traveller arrived and the Khalifa sent for Slatin to perform the first of his many services as interpreter.

Slatin found a tall fair-bearded man in his thirties who could barely speak a word of Arabic. He was neither an Emperor nor the kinsman of an Emperor, but a young French adventurer named Olivier Pain. The stranger declared that he had left his wife and two children and come all the way from Paris just to help the Mahdi in the fight against Gordon and the accursed English. It was a small but significant forerunner of those chauvinistic rivalries between England and France in the Upper Nile which were to culminate in the famous Fashoda incident of 1898.* The Mahdi had no knowledge of these growing rivalries and Slatin did not enlighten him. As far as Mohammed Ahmed was concerned, this new arrival at his camp was an obscure and probably mad foreigner with no official position behind him and no troops to contribute. He was dismissed and left to his own devices. A few weeks later, Olivier Pain died of typhus. He was buried in the Sudanese sand he had dreamt of conquering for the tricolour.

By this time, the Mahdi's army, so swollen by the thousands of newcomers that it resembled a walking town, had reached the White Nile and had moved to within a day's march of the beleaguered Khartoum. Slatin had seen Gordon's steamers

---

* In the summer of that year, a tiny French force under Captain Marchand reached Fashoda on the Upper Nile and laid claim to the whole region for France. There was a bloodless confrontation with the British on 19 September, but not until November, after a serious diplomatic crisis in Europe, were the French troops withdrawn.

moving up and down the river in the distance. They did not fire one shot at this vast procession, but moved slowly down the left bank alongside them. They were there only to observe and report.

At this point, sometime in the second week of October 1884, the Mahdi decided to bring his most precious prisoner into the game. He sent for Slatin and told him to write a letter to Gordon calling upon him, in the Mahdi's name, to surrender, since he was outnumbered and had no prospect of victory. Slatin solemnly agreed, went back to his threadbare tent, and did exactly the reverse. He wrote, in fact, three letters under the open sky that night, the texts of which have survived. The first was a brief covering note to Gordon in appalling French saying that his main letter was written in German because his captors 'had burnt his French dictionary, thinking it was a Christian prayer book'. The second was a note to the Austrian Consul in Khartoum, Hansall, telling the garrison that they had nothing to fear from the Mahdi's army and begging Gordon not to surrender anyway because in that case he (Slatin) would be tortured and killed by the Arabs.

The third, and most extraordinary document of all, was the German letter addressed to Gordon himself. Apart from outlining a scheme to get Slatin through the lines and into Khartoum in the guise of an intermediary, this contains not a word about the Mahdi or the coming battle. It is one long apologia to the Governor-General for Slatin's conversion to Mohammedanism in the summer of 1883 and for his eventual surrender at Dara the following Christmas. On the first point, Slatin wrote, as though to his confessor:

Whether by my conversion I took a dishonourable step is a matter of opinion—it was made easier for me because, perhaps unhappily, I had not received a strict religious upbringing at home.

And, on the second issue, Slatin told his former Commander-in-Chief:

Officers and men demanded capitulation and I, standing there alone and a European, was compelled to follow the majority. Does Your Excellency believe that to me, as an Austrian officer, the surrender was easy? It was one of the hardest days of my life.

The letter ended with an offer of his 'feeble services' which, he stressed, was not made out of any desire for 'a higher post of honour'. This might have been an appeal written in the complete safety of Europe by a shame-faced subaltern trying to secure his future with an angry general after a blunder in some Balkan skirmish. In fact, it came from the captive of a Sudanese fanatic, preparing to do battle across the Nile with a British pro-consul in what was to become one of the most traumatic slaughters of the century. To any Englishman in such a plight – and especially to a man of Gordon's uncompromising stamp – the Austrian's obsession at this hour with self-justification and with his own career simply made no sense. 'Never apologize; never explain' was a motto always beyond Slatin's comprehension. He was constantly doing both when he thought it would do the slightest good. It did not help him here.

Gordon simply wrote in his Journal:

October 16. The letters of Slatin have arrived. I have no remarks to make on them and cannot make out why he wrote them.

And in a later entry that day, commenting on Slatin's plea for his own life in his letter to Hansall:

He (Slatin) evidently is not a Spartan ... If he gets away I shall take him to the Congo with me; he will want some *quarantine*; one feels sorry for him.

This little exchange was the first sample of what was to become one of the patterns of Slatin's whole life: the emotional yearning of the Viennese for full acceptance by the English he loved, and the affection tinged with faint amusement with which some of the lordly English of that age met his longing. But in 1884 there was, of course, no holiday jaunt to the Congo ahead with an indulgent and forgiving General Gordon. Indeed, Slatin was not to see his hero alive again, though he did contrive to send one more message to Khartoum in the same pleading vein, on the pretext of acting as the Mahdi's intermediary. The languages Slatin used – French and German – seemed to him almost as safe as two sets of ciphers in this unlettered Arab camp. Yet somebody must have either broken one of the codes, or at least suspected that Slatin was playing a double game. Late at night on 17 October, when he was impatiently awaiting permission to cross the lines, he was summoned instead to an unsmiling group of the Mahdi's henchmen, accused of conspiring with the enemy, and cast without further ado into heavy chains. This was the Sudanese equivalent of close arrest, and there is no doubt that, even by European standards of warfare, Slatin had invited it. By the Mahdi's standards of ferocity, Slatin had indeed been lucky to escape a brutal and lingering death. Here, after all, was a *mulazem* who had sworn the solemn Moslem oath of loyalty actually betraying to the great Christian infidel the cause of the 'holy war'.

Slatin may have survived because the Mahdi was uncertain of the facts and anyway wanted him alive as a hostage. Perhaps it was his value as an interpreter and go-between in any future parleys with Gordon that counted most. Perhaps the fact that, though a Moslem convert, he was still a European 'guest' at an Arab court saved Slatin's skin on this, as on future tense occasions. He can be forgiven for not rejoicing unduly at his relative good fortune. His plight, as an Austro-Hungarian officer feeling chains around his limbs for the first time, was bad enough.

This is how he describes the scene when, at dawn two days later, the great war-drums boomed out and the Mahdi marched on the capital:

Tents were struck, baggage packed and loaded on camels, and the whole camp was in movement. The weight of iron on my feet prevented me from walking, so they brought me a donkey. I had amused myself by counting the number of figure-of-eight links in my long neck chain. They added up to eighty-three, each about a span in length. In this iron casing I was hoisted on to the donkey and then had to be held there in position by a man on each side, otherwise the weight would have made me overbalance and fall. Several of my old friends passed by on the march but dared do nothing but pity me in silence. In the afternoon, we halted on some rising ground and from here I could see the palm trees of Khartoum. How I longed to join, as one of the garrison, in its defence!

In fact, had he but known it, Slatin was better off where he was, trussed up like a ship's anchor in hundred-weights of iron chain on one of the Mahdi's donkeys. For though he was merely in temporary trouble and discomfort, Khartoum and its defenders were doomed. Again, the familiar tragedy need only be re-told as it touched on Slatin personally.

On 23 October the Mahdi pitched his final camp just south of Omdurman, on the opposite bank of the Nile to the Egyptian-built capital. The long siege began, and for weeks at a time Slatin was left alone with his guards, his chains, and his own mournful thoughts. Only twice during this whole period does the Mahdi seem to have thought of his captive and have tried to use his services. Both times, Slatin managed to wriggle out of it. On the first occasion, the Mahdi's 'earnest wish' was conveyed to Slatin that he should take charge of one of the field guns which the Arabs had brought up to pound the Khartoum fortifications. He was even promised his liberty if he obeyed. Slatin almost certainly distrusted the promise. None the less, the answer he gave – that he was too ill and weak and had no idea how guns worked anyway – amounted to open defiance, and the result was yet another set of iron rings forged on to his ankles. But as he philosophically commented: 'An iron more or less did not make much difference.'

The Mahdi's second approach was even trickier. Towards the end of December, when the siege had been on for two months, a message which Gordon was trying to smuggle to the outside world was intercepted. It was in French, and the Mahdi, who could only make out a word or two, had it sent to Slatin for full translation. Roused out of his sleep in the middle of the night, Slatin held the tiny scrap of paper to a lantern and immediately recognized the handwriting and signature in black ink as that of his former chief. There were four sentences, all of them somewhat cryptic except the first, which was brutally clear. It read:

I have about 10,000 men; can hold Khartoum at the outside till the end of January.

To have passed this one sentence on to the Mahdi would have meant betraying the crux of Gordon's plight. Slatin talked his way round it, pretending that the words were written in old English ciphers which even he could not understand. Considering that his own letters to Gordon in German and French were already under suspicion, as the chains wound about him

71

showed, this was a plucky piece of bluff. But it worked, and there were no reprisals.

That one sentence was anyway punishment enough for Slatin. Now he knew the bitter truth, whereas the Mahdi only suspected it. Khartoum had a month at the most to live, unless the much-rumoured relief column got down from Cairo in time.

Though Slatin could not have known it, this rescue expedition had actually been sanctioned in London five months before, after the ever-reluctant Gladstone government had been goaded into action at last by an anguished British press and public. But it was not until 5 October 1884 that the famous Desert Column, under the command of Lord Wolseley, left Cairo on the 1,600 mile march south; and it was not until the end of December that Slatin, in his prisoner's tent outside Omdurman, heard any reliable news of it. All England was asking the question he put to himself: who would win the race, the redcoats or the dervishes?

As the new year came, Slatin saw the contest go first one way, then the other, and, though he could hardly move an inch in his chains, he lived through all the ups and downs of those tense weeks. On 5 January (Slatin mistakenly writes 15 January) he saw the fall of the Omdurman fort, after heroic resistance by the commander of the Egyptian garrison, Faragalla Pasha. Yet, only six days later, Slatin, to his astonishment, heard the rejoicing in the Mahdi's camp suddenly give way to loud weeping and wailing. His sentries, as curious as himself, went to inquire the cause, and brought him back the startling news that a great Mahdist army had been annihilated by the English advance guard at Abu Klea, only some 150 miles away to the north. The stories that the Mahdi's men had fallen 'in their thousands' at this battle proved greatly exaggerated. Yet clearly, this had been a severe set-back for the dervishes and Slatin's secret delight was only matched by the public lamentations of his captors.

His joy was to be short-lived. On Sunday, 25 January 1885 – 'a day I shall never forget as long as I live' – the Madhi, convinced he must now risk everything, crossed the Nile himself as darkness fell, to direct the final assault on Khartoum. Having sat up anxiously all night, Slatin was just dropping off to sleep when, at early dawn, he was aroused 'by the deafening discharge of thousands of guns and rifles' on the far bank. The din lasted only for a few minutes and then, apart from an occasional shot, all was quiet again. It was eerie. What Slatin had heard, though he could not yet believe it, was the sudden overwhelming of Khartoum. The proof was brought to him soon after sunrise. As he relates:

I crawled out of my tent and scanned the camp, a great crowd had collected before the quarters of the Mahdi and the Khalifa, which were not far distant. Then there was a movement in the direction of my tent and I could see plainly that they were coming towards me. Three black soldiers marched in front. One, named Shatta . . . carried in his hands a blood-stained cloth in which something was wrapped. Behind him followed a crowd of weeping people. The slaves had now reached my tent and stood before me with insulting gestures. Shatta unwound the cloth—and showed me the head of General Gordon!

The blood rushed to my temples and my heart seemed to stop beating; but, with a tremendous effort of self-control, I managed to gaze in silence at this ghastly spectacle. His blue eyes were half-opened; the mouth was perfectly natural; his short whiskers were almost completely white.

'Is this not the head of your uncle* the unbeliever?' said Shatta, holding the head up in front of me.

'What of it?' I replied quietly. 'A brave soldier who fell at his post. Happy is he to have fallen; his sufferings are over.'

The procession moved on with its grisly trophy. Slatin crept back to his tent where he could safely give vent to his misery and his recriminations against the tardy British Government. Like many other contemporary observers, he was perhaps deceived by the appearance of the first steamer-loads of relief troops off Khartoum only 48 hours after its fall into believing that this tiny advance party of 20 British and 200 black soldiers could have turned the tide. It could never have done so physically, though the effect on the morale of the Khartoum garrison had it arrived a few days earlier would doubtless have been considerable. As it was, the two steamers, seeing that the Egyptian flag had been hauled down over the capital, had no

---

* It was a widespread belief among the Arabs that Slatin was related to Gordon. This may have been an additional reason that the Mahdi prized him so much as a hostage or intermediary.

option but to put about and retreat smartly down-stream under
a fusillade of Mahdist fire from the banks. It was really a case
of too little all along as well as too late in the day. As a modern
authority has pointed out, all the force under Lord Wolseley's
command might well have proved inadequate to save Khartoum
from the Mahdi.

The British people, and Queen Victoria herself, reacted to
the disaster as though it were fabulous India, that 'brightest
jewel', that had been lost and not the capital of a million square
miles of arid African desert that they had never, in fact, possessed. The public poured their anger and frustration like hot
coals over Gladstone's head. For weeks, he was jeered at in
Downing Street. On the stages of London's music-halls, the
Grand Old Man had his popular initials reversed so that he
became MOG, or 'Murderer of Gordon'. The sovereign, who
had been crying calamity for months past over the Sudan, was
just as intemperate in her own regal style now that the calamity
had arrived. She dressed in black at Osborne to announce the
news of Gordon's death. Then, in order both to give vent to
her feelings and to make sure that the whole kingdom knew
what these were, she sent the following telegram *en clair* to
Gladstone, Lord Granville and Lord Hartington:

These news from Khartoum are frightful and to think that all this
might have been prevented and many precious lives saved by earlier
action is too frightful.

The Queen, who was repeating her adjectives in her agitation,
thus administered an open rebuke through the Post Office to her
Prime Minister, her Foreign Secretary and her War Minister
respectively. For a constitutional monarch, it was almost unpardonable behaviour. Her only excuse was that, like royalty
itself, 'Anger hath a privilege'. The truth was that neither the
press, the people nor the sovereign could behave rationally
about the Sudan. And this despite the fact that when it came
down to it, they, unlike the Government, were feeling rationally about it. They already sensed what the next decade was to
demonstrate: once England had become effective master of
Egypt, she could not shake off responsibility for Egypt's unruly
southern province, any more than she could cut the Nile waters
that linked them together.

Slatin, of course, knew nothing of all this commotion in a far-off London he had never seen. It is mentioned here because, though it did not touch him at the moment, it was to help transform his whole life later on. From this day forward, both England and her sovereign nursed a guilt complex and a revenge complex towards the Sudan of the Mahdi. When it was Slatin's turn to rise to fame, this sense of English outrage was one of the currents that bore him up.

But the present looked bleak and desperate indeed for him. For five days, he languished neglected in his tent while the dervishes re-enacted, in the streets of Khartoum, those scenes of atrocity they had staged almost exactly two years before at El Obeid. There was an orgy of torture, murder, rape, arson and looting. Almost the only inhabitants to escape unscathed were the better-looking women and girls. The Mahdi took his pick of them, to swell his already huge harem, on the actual day of the conquest. His Khalifas had first choice of the rejects, followed in turn by the emirs and the lesser sheikhs. This winnowing of the youth and beauty of Khartoum went on for several weeks. The chaff that was finally left was thrown on to the open slave-markets for disposal.

On the fifth day after the fall of the city, when the first fruits of conquest had been devoured and it was clear that the English were not returning to dispute them, the Mahdi turned his thoughts back to his captive across the river in the Omdurman camp. Slatin suddenly found himself plucked from his tattered tent and carted off on a donkey to the general prison. There yet a third iron bar with rings was hammered on to his ankles. The newcomer, nicknamed by the gaolers the *hajji fatma*, weighed eighteen pounds and was, he learnt, reserved for only the most dangerous or most infamous of the prisoners. Eventually he discovered why he had been placed in this unenviable category. Letters written by General Gordon to some of the Khartoum outposts had been captured, in which Slatin's secret messages about weakness and dissension in the Mahdist camp had been relayed to boost the garrisons' morale. This was proof positive of what, in the Mahdi's eyes, constituted outright treachery by a sworn adherent. Slatin, as he later admitted himself, was lucky to get away with eighteen extra pounds of iron. In the gloom of the prison enclosure, he recognized Lupton, the young Englishman who, until last year, had governed the Bahr Al-Ghazal province south of Darfur and was now, like himself, one of the Mahdi's prize captives.

This was the lowest point in Slatin's fortunes, but it did not last for long. His food improved after a week or two, and there was a great moment when, on the way to the river one day for the communal prisoners' wash, he picked up the lining of an old donkey saddle. This replaced the stone he had been using for a head-rest and, in his words, 'that night I slept like a king on a pillow of down'. After a while, he was also allowed to converse with Lupton, whose hair and beard had turned almost completely white, though he was barely thirty. It was noticeable that these two European ex-Governors of Gordon's were the only prisoners exempted from manual work.

Then, after some five months, Slatin managed to talk the pair of them out of their chains. To the Khalifa Abdulla, who came one day on an inspection visit, he delivered a long-prepared speech stressing that he belonged 'to a foreign tribe' and thus sought protection; that he had sinned and now regretted all his misdeeds; and that he now lay 'patiently on the bare ground awaiting the hour of pardon'. Lupton, well-rehearsed, seconded these sentiments. Off came the irons for both of them and the Khalifa (in Slatin's own words, 'thoroughly taken in by our mendacity'), then brought them to the Mahdi to receive his forgiveness in turn. This Slatin won with a paraphrase of the Prophet's wisdom: 'Sire, the man who does not love you more than himself, how can his love proceed truly from his heart?'

The flattering conundrum pleased the Mahdi so much that he made Slatin repeat it. Then he and Lupton knelt to take a second oath of allegiance (having, as the Mahdi rightly pointed out, broken the first). They kissed the great man's hand and were dismissed. Lupton was allowed to rejoin his native wife and family in the camp. Slatin was assigned, at his own request, to be a personal attendant of the Khalifa's.

He had shaken off his chains by a mixture of guile, glibness and flattery. These, together with patience, were the same weapons he was to go on using against all the hardships and dangers ahead. Not many men commanded these qualities as thoroughly as Slatin. Of the few who did, not all could have swallowed their pride so completely as to employ them in this way. In his will to survive and his ability to survive, Slatin was pre-eminent, even in the Mahdi's hard school.

In material terms, the tactics paid off immediately. He was allotted a piece of ground six hundred yards from the Khalifa's house, on which to build a residence of three huts for himself and the servants allotted to him as a member – even if a captive member – of the ruler's entourage. The money and valuables taken off him on his imprisonment – £40 in cash, some sequins and gold nose rings – were returned. He was given the clothes and the French Koran of the hapless Olivier Pain to make up for the other belongings that had been stolen from him. It was, in the circumstances, a very fair deal. The Khalifa even promised him some wives, declaring that 'A man without offspring is like a thorn-tree without fruit'. But that is another story.

Excitement now suddenly concentrated on the Mahdi himself. When receiving his pardon, Slatin had noticed that Mohammed Ahmed had become so fat that he was hardly recognizable as the lithe and virile warrior of a year or two before. For some time, debauchery had been taking a steady toll of his strength, and the end of the fighting removed the last constraints of self-discipline. On 14 June, shortly after Slatin's release, the Mahdi fell ill. According to one contemporary version, one of his countless women victims had managed that night to revenge herself by administering him a deadly poison. Less romantically, but rather more probably, Slatin says it was typhus. Whatever the cause, six days later the Mahdi died. With one of his last breaths, he reaffirmed the Khalifa Abdallahi, Slatin's master, as his successor.

This is not the place to analyse the Mahdi's achievements, except to suggest that the truth lies somewhere between those who only sang his praises or only condemned his excesses. His reign had been brief and brutal. It never extended beyond the Southern and Central Sudan and it never closed those gaps between Arab and negroid or between Khartoum and countryside which are still visible in the Sudan today. Yet he did give the ethnic and tribal jumble of his followers some fleeting experience of a common identity, and, for this reason, was understandably hailed by later generations of Sudanese as the great father-figure of their nationalism.

Perhaps equally understandably, this misses what is surely the main point. The real significance of the Mahdi for his people was not that he defeated the foreign infidel. It was rather that, by this defeat, he made it certain that the infidel – especially in the shape of the Englishman – would return, vanquish his successor and then occupy his country for more than fifty years. Sooner or later, the English would have gone into the Sudan in some fashion anyway, dragged inexorably southwards from their new seat of power at Cairo. The challenge of the Mahdi made sure that the strike would be sooner, and that the grip would be complete.

Chapter Six

THE KHALIFA'S CAPTIVE

Before the Mahdi's body was cold, the Khalifa Abdallahi stepped into the sandals of the Expected One and set about tying them firmly to his own feet. Those around the death-bed, who included most of the Mahdi's principal adherents and relatives, were the first to swear fidelity to the new ruler. Then the *mulazemin*, including Slatin, were called in to follow suit. Finally, the Khalifa moved to the door of the mosque and, mounting the Mahdi's pulpit for the first time, took the allegiance of the masses, who were torn between wailing for their late master and shouting for his successor. The enormous crowd came forward in groups to take the oath. Throughout the day and then after dusk, the ceremony went on. Slatin noticed that, at the beginning, the Khalifa seemed almost humble, with tears rolling down his cheeks and a tremor in his voice. But the tears dried up as the hours went by, and he became so elated by the adulation of his subjects that, at midnight, he had to be gently dragged away, exhausted, from the rostrum. The absolute corruption of absolute power had already begun its work.

So the man who was Slatin's master became also the master of the Mahdist state. For the next eleven years, Slatin was to be the prisoner of both, a captive in a double sense. Not only was he bound to the Khalifa's household at Omdurman, a city which the new ruler made peculiarly his own, and which he rarely left. The Madhi's Sudan itself now dropped out of civilization as though the African sands had swallowed it up. Almost

79

the only points of contact were sporadic campaigns or skirmishes at the fringes: to the north with the Egyptian army, which, after the disaster of Khartoum, had pulled right back across the Nubian desert together with the British expedition sent out to save it; with the Italians based on the Red Sea littoral to the east; with the Abyssinians to the south-east; with the emergent Belgian Congo to the south-west.

Yet all this friction at the edges served only to emphasize the isolation of the Sudan rather than to penetrate it. For a while, the outside world seemed glad to ignore the savage realm of the Khalifa and he seemed grateful to be forgotten. Without as much as a watch, a diary, or a calendar, let alone a supply of European books or newspapers, Rudolf Slatin was imprisoned by a tyrant who was himself imprisoned within a vacuum of history.

When later Slatin tried to write the story of those eleven years of captivity from memory, time moved backwards and forwards in his narrative like a shuttlecock, for all his attempts to keep a chronological sequence. There is thus no point in trying to construct a strict sequence of events here. The story is best grouped around the main preoccupations of his life. These were: his perpetual battle of wits with the Khalifa to survive complicated by the Khalifa's own fight to maintain supremacy; his struggle to carve a comfortable niche for himself in the bizarre Mahdist regime that grew up around him – a severe regime in which the only permissible creature comfort allowed to all and sundry, Slatin included, was an inexhaustible supply of women; his contacts with the other European captives held by the Mahdi, none of them half as important as himself but at least one of them twice as defiant; the tenuous links that slowly developed as the years went by with Cairo and even with far off Vienna; and finally, arising out of these, the saga of his desert escape on which his fame and fortune were to rest.

Slatin describes the Khalifa at the time of his accession as a well-built but very agile man in his late thirties with fine dark eyes and hair, the very image of the warrior-virility of his native Baggara tribe. The image quickly faded as indulgence, lack of exercise and the constant intrigues for power took their toll, so that the man Slatin finally escaped from was fat, heavy on his feet and almost white in his beard. But the main traits of his character as his prisoner saw them – suspicion, malice, brutality and a hot temper – were not transformed; they only deepened as time went on. Happily, this process was accompanied by an ever-increasing vanity and susceptibility to flattery. Through these broad chinks Slatin could always find a space to penetrate the Khalifa's armour of distrust.

In this way, the young Viennese, with his wit and charm and glibness which all came across even in his unpolished Arabic, gradually worked his way up into a position of relative well-being and even privilege. The improvements that came were erratic and could at any instant be wiped out – as indeed could his own life – by one uncontrollable tantrum of the Khalifa's. The eleven-year ordeal that Slatin now entered on lasted more than twice as long and, in pure psychological terms, was probably twice as demanding as any ordinary captivity suffered by the millions of prisoners-of-war in World War I. Indeed, for a parallel to the constant stress and fear and degradation he had to go through and the daily horrors he had to witness (though without being subjected to them himself) we can look only to the plight of his fellow-Jews in Hitler's concentration camps. Slatin lived permanently on a volcano, whose slightest rumbles he had to detect and soothe away into silence before they could erupt. But, considering that this was the Mahdist Sudan and that he was its prisoner, it became a remarkably comfortable volcano.

After only a few months of his captivity had passed, for example, the Khalifa allowed him to accompany an expedition he was dispatching to Wad el Abbas, some 250 miles south of Omdurman on the Blue Nile. The commander of the expedition, Yunes, was an old friend of Slatin's as well as a relative of the Khalifa's, and though Slatin was kept under constant surveillance during the journey, in case he might try to escape, he was never actually under guard. Indeed, he seems to have functioned as a sort of Quartermaster-General to the Khalifa's forces and to have travelled in style. A request he put to the Khalifa before setting out shows how far he had already come since the days he had slept fitfully in his bed of chains in Omdurman jail. Slatin's 'household' by this time already consisted of four male servants with their wives, and he had asked to take three of the men with him. Not unreasonably, the

Khalifa refused, but ordered other arrangements to be made for Slatin's comfort during the journey.

The next glimpse we have of Slatin's progress is an incident that occurred some eighteen months later, in June of 1887. The Khalifa was riding out of Omdurman to inspect a new encampment and Slatin, as was usual on such inspections, walked behind. He cut his foot, which started to bleed freely. Slatin, who had great physical endurance to match all his gayer gifts, limped on without saying a word. The Khalifa dismounted at the next house, praised Slatin for his fortitude and then presented him on the spot with a fine steed, authorizing him in future to ride out in attendance. Slatin's walking days, which had often brought him to the brink of collapse, were over.*

By now, less than two years after the chains had been struck from his limbs, Slatin had become a sort of aide-de-camp to the Khalifa, without of course ceasing to be his captive. Indeed, at 'manoeuvres' (the mock battles which the Khalifa staged from time to time between his own troops and those of the Omdurman garrison), Slatin literally functioned as such, trying to bring some sort of order in the monumental confusion created when thirty thousand dervishes tried to play at military science. It was tasks like this which fed the early rumours in the outside world that Slatin was 'commanding the Mahdist cavalry'. He was never in fact given anything to command, for the Khalifa could obviously not bring himself to place that degree of trust in this former Governor of Gordon's. He knew, despite all Slatin's protestations of perfect loyalty and contentment, that his prisoner's heart was with the white infidels away to the north and that his mind was always set on escape.

When that escape finally took place, the Khalifa was doubtless exaggerating for effect when he angrily declared in public that he had treated Slatin 'like a son' and had 'never taken any step without his advice and guidance'. But if he never gave Slatin – or anyone else for that matter – his complete trust, he was forced to take him into his confidence. Slatin was the only European officer and high official he had, the only man in his vast retinue who knew anything of modern war and modern

---

* After his escape, he told a British colleague Major Wheatley (later Colonel Sir Mervyn Wheatley) that the greatest hardship of his whole captivity had been this walking or running behind the Khalifa's horse. The hard outer skin of his heels split open, he said, and he used to bind them together with string to give some protection from the hot sand.

government, the only man who spoke the languages and knew the ways of the Anglo-Egyptian army that was licking its wounds resentfully down the Nile. Not only was the Khalifa flattered to have as a personal prisoner the man who had once ruled the great province of Darfur, including his own Baggara tribe. It was vital to him to have, always at hand, one representative of the world he was fighting, to help him interpret its ways and foretell its moves.

And eventually, as the years passed, it is likely that the Khalifa developed an affection, however grudging and suspicious, for his captive. It was difficult for anyone to dislike Rudolf Slatin, much less be bored in his company. For all the Khalifa's terrible temper, notorious ferocity and absolute power of life and death, there is something also of the cantankerous old couple about their relationship as time went by. Though almost every day in each other's company, there was no predicting the mood five minutes in advance. One night the Khalifa would have Slatin to dine with him, and for hours they would discuss amicably the problems of this world and the consolations of the next. Then, at a whim or a chance word, the Khalifa would disappear under a dark cloud, and days of frowns and silence would follow. Yet whether friendly or hostile, the Khalifa seems to have got attached to Slatin's presence. Indeed, as blood-bath succeeded blood-bath in his reign, and his rivals were eliminated in succession, Abdel Kader's became one of the very few familiar faces left from the palmy days of the storming of Khartoum.

The certain sign of Slatin's steady rise to favour and to a form of personal security was the steady improvement in both the quantity and quality of the women he was allowed to keep. As indicated, sexual indulgence was the only pleasure of the flesh which the Mahdi had permitted his followers. Chewing tobacco and drinking, both virtually ineradicable in the Sudan, were none the less savagely punished whenever detected. Even for drinking the *marissa* beer, for example, the culprit would first be paraded round the market place, showered with mud and dust, and then, the marissa bowl broken over his head, dragged before the *Kaedi* or judge. Eighty lashes was the minimum sentence imposed. Nor could the Khalifa's subjects give vent to their feelings by swearing. Eighty lashes for each profane word uttered was also the punishment for that.

The one outlet not only sanctioned by law but encouraged by law was sex. Into this outlet the Khalifa's subjects poured all the frustrations of a life that was not only denied the other passions of the flesh but also the distractions of a normal social life or culture. Slatin describes how the Khalifa made it easier to acquire four legal wives – the number authorized by the Koran – by reducing the dowry for a girl from ten to five dollars, and how he also simplified the financial arrangements for divorce, an automatic procedure itself under Moslem law. As a result, there were many men in Omdurman whom Slatin saw marrying forty or fifty times during the eleven years of his stay. The number of concubines was limited only by the individual's appetite and the depth of his pocket. Homosexuality and buggery (what Slatin coyly describes as 'unnatural love') were also rife despite initial attempts by the Khalifa to control them by banishing the offenders. Whatever else it was deprived of, the world around Slatin was deluged with authorized, even sanctified, sex.

The extent to which Slatin himself wallowed in this flood is something over which he drew a discreet veil. His book, *Fire and Sword,* was written for the prurient audience of the Victorian era; an audience, furthermore, which regarded intercourse between a civilized European and a native woman with the disgust of the Anglo-Indian 'mem-sahib'. But whether Slatin wallowed or not, there is little reason to doubt that he regularly indulged. He was in every way married to Hassanieh, the Darfurian wife of royal blood he had taken while still Governor-General of the province to consummate his conversion to the Moslem faith; and she remained the head of his household in Omdurman. A fellow European prisoner there tells us that after Slatin's escape, Desta, an Abyssinian wife of his, gave birth to a child of his within a few days of his flight. She had been treated roughly and reduced to the status of a slave after her master's defection. Perhaps because of this, the baby boy survived only a few weeks.

Wives and female slaves were of course a mark of status as well as libido; but whichever impulse was uppermost, Slatin collected his full complement of both, as befitted a virile man and a 'confidant' of the Khalifa's. Abdallahi's own contributions to Slatin's female household were significant in both senses of the word. Slatin may have started off with a few dirty crumbs from his master's banqueting table, but he ended up with some choice titbits. Nor was there any chance of Slatin, once he had accepted the women, simply using them as servants in his household. He once told the same colleague already quoted, Major Wheatley, that the Khalifa regularly questioned the women he had given to his captive, to make quite sure that Slatin really was cohabiting with them.

The first offering came during the siege of Khartoum, soon after Slatin had been released from jail and allocated to the Khalifa's retinue. The night he was moving in to the three huts erected for him, a closely-wrapped female slave was sent over as a gift. Slatin, looking at her as she stood on her palm mat, decided that her deep voice 'did not presage well for the future'; yet she proceeded, invitingly enough, to remove the scented white drapery from her head and expose her shoulders and part of her bosom. It was dark, and Slatin motioned his servant to bring the lantern nearer. His own description brings the lady to life even today:

I had to summon all my self-control in order not to fall off my 'Angareb' for fright. Two little eyes peered out of her ugly black face. She had a great flat nose and, below it, two enormous blubber-shaped lips which stretched out so wide when she laughed that they threatened to touch her ears. Her head was joined to her grossly fat body by a neck like a bull-dog's. And this creature actually had the audacity to call herself Maryan (Mary)!

It was a sardonic offering for a first gift. Having noted, however, the next day, how well Slatin took it, the Khalifa himself selected 'a young and somewhat less ugly girl' and sent her over as well.

From then on, the 'largesse' got bigger and better. When Slatin set out to accompany the expedition to Sennar, for example, in 1885, the Khalifa offered him one of his own wives for the trip 'so that, in case of indisposition or illness, you may have someone to look after you'. He unveiled a woman, who, Slatin admitted, 'was really very pretty, in spite of her dark colour'. On this occasion, fearing the responsibility and the encumbrance, Slatin begged to be excused, cleverly pointing out that he, the servant, could not presume to take the wife of his master. The Khalifa was so delighted by this apparent humility that he gave Slatin instead one of his white *jibbas* to wear, a garment which had been specially blessed by the Mahdi. It was a gift for which many a Mahdist fanatic would have given his right hand. Slatin laconically remarked that it was 'an excellent exchange'.

The Khalifa's subsequent offerings were mostly accepted, for Slatin soon had a household capable of absorbing them. In 1888, after one of his lieutenants had conducted a triumphant raid into Abyssinia, Abdallahi presented Slatin with one of the choice girls sent back to Omdurman with the booty. (She was not the Desta of 1895, for Slatin records that this Abyssinian slave pined to death before long.) A little later, after an angry exchange with Slatin in which the Khalifa lost his temper, he tried to 'make it up' by sending a very special gift – an Egyptian lady who had been born at Khartoum and who, because of her relatively fair skin, was a great female prize. Slatin's comment that the Khalifa, instead of giving him a steady salary, kept presenting him like this with wives 'who were a source of considerable expense' sounds a trifle churlish, though it is true that in this case he did have to cope the next day with 'a decrepit old Abyssinian lady who presented herself as my future mother-in-law'.

At all events, the Khalifa's bounty never dried up. After one lot of manoeuvres outside Omdurman, where Slatin had valiantly battled with his usual hopeless task of aide-de-camp, he received 'two black young ladies' as proof of his master's goodwill. And the climax came in 1894, towards the end of Slatin's captivity, when the Khalifa, beset by troublesome campaigns on his eastern and southern borders, tried to bind Slatin closer to him by offering him one of his own cousins for a wife. Slatin, suspecting that on this occasion the Khalifa sought only to plant a reliable spy on his pillow, managed to decline. Again he sought refuge in feigned humility. How could he, the Khalifa's servant, subject one of his master's relatives, descended like the Khalifa from the Prophet, to petty domestic quarrels? This time, the silver words did not quite do the trick. The Khalifa, who, whatever the motive, had offered Slatin kinship – 'as one of us, as my friend and faithful adherent' – was somewhat piqued, and he showed it.

Slatin was right in observing that in any case his master could well afford to be generous with his gifts. The Khalifa had gradually accumulated a harem containing no fewer than four hundred damsels, mostly derived from the war booty of his various campaigns. Their skins were of every shade from the lightest brown to the deepest black. Almost every tribe of the Sudan, as well as the bordering countries, was represented in their heavily oiled and perfumed ranks. They were divided into groups of fifteen to twenty, each under a head woman, and every two or three groups together were placed under the orders of a concubine specially appointed by the Khalifa. They were guarded by adult eunuchs and summoned to their master's couch by one of the fifteen boy eunuchs who formed part of his personal retinue. It is not hard to see why the Khalifa so rarely left Omdurman.

His daily life in that city changed but little, and set the monotonous pattern of Slatin's own existence during these eleven years. The Khalifa's only regular public duties were the taking of the five daily prayers in the main mosque: at dawn, at two and four o'clock in the afternoon, at sunset, and finally three hours later at night. His family, his *kadis* and *mulazemin* (Slatin always included, unless he was specially excused because of illness), his emirs and, behind them, thousands of his people, attended every session to repeat the prayers in unison after their chief. These regular mass gatherings served a functional as well as a devotional purpose. Through the open iron-work of his *mihrab*, the Khalifa could literally keep an eye on all the principal men of his capital and make sure they were not up to mischief. (He always discouraged them, Slatin tells us, from meeting in each other's houses or indeed from any social activity, in order to minimize the risk of criticism or subversion.)

In the spaces between these prayer sessions, which were placed like fixed columns across the day, the Khalifa would deal with his correspondence. This consisted of reports and letters brought to him from all parts of his realm by his 'postmen', who were in fact selected informants as well as messengers, with sixty to eighty riding camels permanently at their disposal. The Khalifa could neither read nor write. He dictated replies to the written messages after their contents had been read out to him. Often, there were visiting emirs to be received, while at irregular intervals he would hold sessions with his *kadis*. These meetings passed for the equivalent of 'Councils of State', though in fact there was rarely any discussion and never any argument.

Then, in addition to the 'manoeuvres' already mentioned, there were the regular military reviews, originally held every Friday but later extended to three-day jamborees staged only four times a year. They must have been colourful affairs. Slatin tells how, long before sunrise, the various emirs, with their banners aloft and their followers behind them, would assemble on the flat stony plain outside Omdurman. As dawn broke, the Khalifa would make his appearance facing the main flag, an immense piece of black cloth, and then the entire army would wheel in the early sunshine and pass in front of him. The foot soldiers would wear fresh *jibbas* and turbans, while the cavalry would don for the ceremony bartered or captured coats of mail of European or Asiatic origin, with multi-coloured cotton caps surmounted by heavy iron helmets on their heads. Clanking past in their armour, on horses clothed in padded patchwork quilts, they must have looked more like a phantasmagoric parade of medieval knights than an army of late nineteenth-century Arab horsemen.

. Finally there would be the occasional excursions of the Khalifa's, nearly always limited to the country immediately surrounding his capital. They were purely ceremonial affairs and no theatrical device was neglected. The roll of war-drums and the low moan of the *ombeiya* (horns made from elephant tusks) would announce the ruler's departure. Then, from the large square behind the mosque, the cavalcade would stream out. Six men blowing the horn went immediately before the resplendent mounted figure of the Khalifa. At his side walked an immensely powerful Arab who had the honour of lifting his master in and out of the saddle. Immediately behind came the buglers, to sound halt or advance at his command. The column would be encased by a solid square of soldiers and attendants containing, somewhere inside it, a musical band of fifty black slaves playing African tunes on antelope horns accompanied by drums fashioned from hollow tree trunks.

As one of the Khalifa's chosen *mulazemin*, Slatin had to turn out for all the parades and excursions as well as for the manoeuvres and the eternal sessions cross-legged at the mosque. But he was only rarely summoned to the Khalifa's administrative sessions usually when there was a foreign document to be translated or some affair concerning the outside world to be discussed. Otherwise he was free at these times to walk around the city and pursue such social life as he could.

The main sight of Omdurman (apart from the mosque and the Mahdi's tomb, with both of which Slatin must have got thoroughly fed up) was the slave market. Though he always had to get special permission to visit it, on the pretext of wanting to buy or exchange slaves himself, he managed to pass many fascinated hours here. This is the picture he gives:

Round the walls of a mud-brick house, the women and girls stand or sit. They vary from the decrepit and aged half-clad slaves of the working-class to the gaily-clad 'surya' or concubine. As the trade is regarded as a perfectly legal and natural business, those put up for sale are examined from head to foot without the slightest restriction, just as if they were animals. The mouth is opened to see if the teeth are in good condition. The upper part of the body and the back are laid bare and the arms carefully examined. They are then told to take a few steps backwards or forwards so that their movements and gait may be studied. A series of questions are put to them to test their knowledge of Arabic ...

When the intending purchaser has completed his scrutiny, he then refers to the dealer, asks him what he paid for her, or if he has any any better wares for sale. He will probably complain that her face is not pretty enough, that her body is not sufficiently developed, that she does not speak Arabic and so on, in order to reduce the price as much as possible. Among the various hidden defects which oblige the dealer to reduce his price are snoring and bad qualities of character such as thieving. But when at last the bargain is struck, the sale deed is drawn up and signed, the money paid over and the slave becomes the property of her new master.

As befits a Viennese merchant's son, Slatin carefully noted the standard rates, which ran from a minimum of fifty local dollars for an aged working slave up to seven hundred dollars for a really beautiful and talented concubine; and he observed that the rates fluctuated according to market value or a special demand for one particular race.

Such were the few distractions that relieved the weary boredom of Slatin's daily life. Most of the other excitements were caused by the series of plots, real or supposed, against the Khalifa's supremacy, plots which ran like a blood-stained thread through Slatin's captivity at Omdurman. He dreaded these periodic upheavals, not merely because any tension in the Khalifa's camp made his own position more precarious but also because of the sickening butchery in which they usually ended.

Those who tried to defy Abdallahi ranged from a group of mutinous black soldiers who, as early as 1885, tried to establish a miniature pro-Egyptian 'republic' in the Nuba mountains, to various ideological rebels. These latter included a postman who declared himself to be 'Isa' or Jesus Christ in person, and a *Fiki* who had the audacity to proclaim in Omdurman itself that, though he was a good Mohammedan and indeed the 'Light of the Prophet', he was not a follower of the Mahdi. The mutineers were wiped out in battle almost to a man. The religious rivals were hung from public scaffolds. The Khalifa's Sudan was rarely at peace. Individual tribes and sometimes whole provinces (like Slatin's former realm of Darfur in 1887–8) tried to defy Abdallahi's writ. But the most immediate threat to his power was undoubtedly the revolt of the so-called 'Ashraf', or kinsmen of the late Mahdi, in Omdurman itself in 1891.

This came as the climax to the most dismal phase of the Khalifa's reign. The years from 1887 onwards had brought poor harvests and increasing food shortages and by 1889 famine stalked the land. Slatin describes two vivid street scenes in Omdurman at the time. On one occasion he saw a starving man snatch up a piece of tallow and cram it into his mouth. The owner leapt at his throat and squeezed it until the man's eyes bulged. But the thief refused to disgorge his precious 'food' and ultimately collapsed, still with his mouth tightly shut. The other spectacle met him as he was walking home one night under a full moon:

I saw three almost naked women, with long tangled hair hanging about their shoulders. They were squatting around a young donkey which was lying on the ground, having either strayed from its mother or been stolen by them. They had torn open its body with their teeth and were devouring its intestines while the poor animal was still breathing ... The wretched women, crazed by hunger, gazed at me like maniacs and then the beggars who had been following me fell on them to try and seize their prey. I fled from this uncanny scene.

And every day, Slatin noted, the waters of the Blue and White Niles that swept past Omdurman carried past hundreds of bodies of the peasants who had died from starvation along their banks.

The famine seems to have been one reason for an attempt which the Khalifa now made to invade Egypt. It was a desperate lunge and it ended in total disaster. On 3 August 1889, Anglo-Egyptian forces under Grenfell Pasha, the British Commander-in-Chief in Egypt, gave battle to the invading column from the Sudan at Toski, a village on the west bank of the Nile some fifty miles south of the great Abu Simbel monuments. The Khalifa's army, which had set out hoping to bring him food, gold and white-skinned slaves galore from the treasure-house of Cairo, was wiped out as a fighting force. Some five thousand prisoners and refugees were taken into the Anglo-Egyptian camp. When the news of the defeat reached the Khalifa, he was so distraught, Slatin observed, that he did not go near his harem for three days.

It was against this recent background of economic unrest and military set-backs that the Ashraf, who had staged one unsuccessful trial of strength with Abdallahi as early as 1886, now launched their armed uprising in his capital. Many of the Mahdi's relatives, including two of his sons, were involved in the plot, which was fed by the usual Sudanese mixture of family feuds battening on to broader taxation grievances. Typical also was the betrayal. For when, in November 1891, after months of preparation, the rebels finally gathered near the Mahdi's tomb and handed out their secret weapons – about one hundred Remington rifles and a few elephant guns – the Khalifa, who had a spy in their ranks all along, was quietly preparing his counter-moves from his own house a stone's throw away. At dawn the mutineers found themselves surrounded by strong forces of riflemen and cavalry. None the less they curtly rejected the Khalifa's peace appeal and some desultory street fighting broke out.

Slatin was agog with excitement. Rebellions far away across the desert could help him but little. But if the capital itself were to be set alight by feuding and looting he might make a dash for freedom amidst all the hubbub. His dismay may be imagined when, after two days of parleys interspersed with firing, a compromise was reached: the Mahdi's relatives got back their honours and their pensions in return for surrendering their arms. The Khalifa lost no time in dishonouring the third part of the bargain, which was a general pardon for all who had supported the distinguished rebels. Barely three weeks after the cease-fire, several of their principal sympathizers were arrested, taken up-river by steamer to Fashoda and there beaten to death with freshly-cut thorn-sticks. To justify this barbarous duplicity, Abdallahi invoked the authority of the Mahdi, who, he declared, had appeared to him in a vision, calling for severity. Even to the faithful, it must have seemed a tall story.

The Ashraf uprising of 1891, the only one that Slatin witnessed, had an immediate effect on his position. Though he, a *mulazem* forced to dance attendance on the Kahalifa throughout the emergency, had no chance to escape, some of the other European captives in Omdurman did. Father Ohrwalder, the Catholic priest whose eyewitness accounts of the Mahdi's campaigns have been quoted above, had long been preparing to flee across the desert to Egypt, together with two nuns from his missionary order who had been captured with him nine years before. On Sunday, 29 November, before the crisis in the capital had died down, this resolute trio took their courage and their crucifixes in their hands and made a moonlight dash on camels out of Omdurman. After ten days' adventurous flight, they reached the Egyptian fort of Murat some four hundred miles to the north, and freedom.

The escape of 'Joseph the priest', as he was known in Omdurman, meant two things for Slatin. First, he had to endure the wrath of the Khalifa, who suspected him of conniving in the affair. And even though Slatin, with his usual brand of obsequious eloquence, managed to turn aside the charge, he knew that some suspicion, as well as a closer watch over his own movements, would remain. Perhaps worse, he had lost almost the only congenial spirit incarcerated with him in this open-air desert prison of Omdurman. Father Ohrwalder was an Austrian like himself and a man of some culture and education. As Slatin wrote:

> I now felt completely deserted. He was the only man with whom I was intellectually on a par and with whom, however rarely, I could exchange a few words in my mother tongue.

The wretched little band of European prisoners was indeed dwindling. One of the other nuns of Ohrwalder's mission had died of typhus six weeks before the escape attempt. Frank Lupton, the Englishman who had shared Slatin's prison ordeal in chains during the siege of Khartoum, had been carried away by the same disease over two years before, in May of 1888. Ohrwalder and Slatin (who had never ceased, from his own precarious position 'at court', to do all in his power for his English friend) buried him themselves in the city cemetery after a Moslem funeral service in the mosque to which the Austrians must certainly have added some private prayers of their own. Gustav Klootz, the Prussian batman who had deserted to the Mahdi's lines from the ill-fated army of Hicks Pasha in 1883, had died only three years afterwards. He had met his end by sheer exhaustion when trying to escape on foot all the way from Omdurman south-east to the Abyssinian mountains (a warning to all his fellow-captives to go by camel, and to go north). So by the end of 1891, though there were still some Greeks, Italians and Syrians left, the only other German-speaking prisoner remaining was a 45-year-old merchant from Prussia called Karl Neufeld.* And he was of little practical value to Slatin because, ever since his capture in 1887 whilst on a foolhardy gum-buying expedition, he had almost obliged the Khalifa to keep him in chains.

Neufeld's defiance of his captors and the terrible punishment it brought him must have often caused the pliable Slatin pangs of conscience. Should he congratulate himself or reproach himself for the contrasting ease and comfort which he had purchased with that all-purpose silver tongue of his? If Slatin sometimes felt uneasy about the contrast, at least he could console himself with the thought that, from his privileged position

---

* The Egyptian Army Headquarters Intelligence report for November 1894 lists only two Italian captives still thought to be alive at Omdurman as well as 'upwards of 20 male Greeks' and eight male Syrians. There were also about eight assorted women and some twenty children.

at the Khalifa's court, he had probably helped to save Neufeld's life.

It was one day in May 1887 when Slatin saw the German being led into the camp. Rumour had it that he was the 'Pasha of Wadi Halfa' and an English spy. The truth was in the papers captured on his person and Slatin was duly summoned to the Khalifa to translate them. He read out all the letters which proclaimed Neufeld to be a German merchant engaged on a normal commercial expedition, but omitted to translate a request from the British General Stephenson in Cairo to Neufeld to bring back with him a full report on the situation in the Sudan.

Slatin then had to watch while the Khalifa, in the open square outside his house, played cat and mouse with his new captive's life. Neufeld, however, turned out to be anything but a mouse. Forced to his knees, deafened by two *ombeiya* horns blown at full blast into his ears, prodded with spears and swords, he still had the courage to reply, when told that the Khalifa was going to have him beheaded: 'Go back to your Khalifa and tell him that neither he nor fifty like him may remove so much as a hair from my head without God's permission.'

His tormentor, on hearing this astonishing message, sent back orders that Neufeld was to be crucified instead, 'like his prophet Jesus'. An hour later, Neufeld was loaded in his chains on to a donkey and led to a set of gallows. Here, with the noose dangling over his head, he was asked: 'As you will be dead in a few minutes, how do you wish to die, as a Moslem or as a Christian?' The German, who, in his own words, was determined 'that this horde should respect me even in my death', shouted back in Arabic at the top of his voice: 'Religion is not a dress to be put on today and thrown off tomorrow'. His courage and his white skin, even more than any special pleading Slatin made on his behalf, saved Neufeld's life. Instead, he was thrown for four years into the notorious *Saier*. In this, the common prison of Omdurman, he was to endure ordeals that must have made him wish the gallows had been allowed to do their work.

In these two men, Slatin and Neufeld, brought together in the unlikely setting of the Khalifa's capital, were the two opposite poles of the German race: the Prussian oak, whose defiance of the elements rested on deep roots of principle and faith; and the Viennese willow, whose supple bending before any breath of wind sprang from his supreme instinct for survival. There is room for them both in most forests. Even here in the desert, each found his appointed place.

For Slatin, however, survival meant much more than simply enduring captivity and easing it with the maximum comfort he could contrive. It meant, above all, escape at the right time and by the safest route. After November 1891, that camel track that led out of Omdurman to the north must have looked doubly tempting. Surely, what an Austrian priest and two nuns had achieved ought not to be beyond the range of one of Gordon's Governors?

The Sudan of Rudolf Slatin, his escape route marked by broken line.

Chapter Seven

ESCAPE

The escape of Slatin Pasha the Sudan warrior has its origin in the links which Rudolf Slatin the stranded Austrian managed to establish with his distant homeland. His longing for freedom was in turn intensified by these contacts, some intended and some accidental, which the Monarchy made with its lost son.

The first direct news that his family heard of his plight was late in 1884. A letter he had written them from El Fasher in February of that year – two months, that is, after his surrender – finally reached Austria after a roundabout journey via Egyptian-held Dongola on the Nile, the Red Sea, and the Austrian consular authorities in Cairo. The original is still in the possession of his great-nephew in Vienna.

Beginning 'Dearest Mama and brothers and sisters', it is essentially an apologia rather than an appeal. Like the letters he was soon to write to General Gordon, his Commander-in-Chief, it sets out to explain why he had had no other choice than to surrender. Of the five thousand troops under his command at Darfur, he tells them, 'more than three thousand had been killed in various engagements and most of the survivors were wounded'. He mentions the disaster of the Hicks relief expedition which had destroyed his last hope of military success and goes on, in a rather elegiac tone:

With God's help I strove always to do honourably by my country and my rank as an officer and to justify the confidence which the

97

Viceroy placed in me. But my efforts were unfortunately unsuccessful. The soldiers under my command, though largely natives, fought bravely even against their own fellow tribesmen and, had General Hicks been victorious, Darfur would have been preserved for Egypt.

There is no suggestion of panic or hardship in this first letter. It was indeed written when Slatin was a captive in name only. 'The enemy', he reassures his family, 'has treated me with respect and I have no ground for complaint. I receive from the Treasury all the money necessary to maintain my household.' He goes on to talk calmly of making his way to Kordofan in the near future, 'to make the necessary plans for rejoining you'. To some extent, this letter may have been a deliberate attempt to reassure his anxious relatives. Yet it also reflected the comparative freedom and optimism of these first months after his surrender, before the Mahdi had sealed Slatin's fate, and that of the Sudan, by the capture of Khartoum.

More than four long years of silence passed before Slatin received the first message back from his family. Late one evening in July 1888, in the middle of the Khalifa's campaigns against Abyssinia, the Mahdist commander at Kassala, on the Abyssinian border, arrived at Omdurman to report. At the end of his audience, he handed his master a letter addressed to Slatin which was said to have come from his relatives in Europe. It had taken no fewer than twenty months to make the journey from Vienna, and had entered the Khalifa's realm via the British-held port of Suakin, on the Red Sea. The Governor of this littoral province at that time was none other than Kitchener, the English officer who was eventually destined to avenge Gordon's death. He had passed the letter inland to the redoubtable Osman Digna, the commander of the Khalifa's forces in the Red Sea hills.

Slatin was now summoned in to read it. It was a brief and sad message, written by his distressed brothers and sister in Vienna in November 1886, to tell him that their mother had died. They sent him the dying woman's last words: 'I am ready to die; but I should have loved to have seen my Rudolf again and to have embraced him once more. It is harder for me to leave this world when I think that he is in the hands of his enemies.'

For Slatin, the news lost none of its pain for being already twenty months old. All that longing for home which his mother had prophesied he would feel when she had said goodbye to him in Austria ten years before must have overcome him in his grief. When the suspicious Khalifa ordered him to translate the letter into Arabic and read it out, it was as much as Slatin could do to struggle through the words.

The Khalifa's suspicions melted, but not his heart. He curtly forbade Slatin to mourn for his mother because she had died 'an unbeliever in the Prophet and the Mahdi and cannot therefore expect God's mercy'. As for the relatives, he ordered Slatin to reply by inviting 'at least one' of his brothers to come and join him in his 'honoured state' at Omdurman.

The next morning, the hapless Slatin, who had wept for most of the night, was summoned again to the presence and told to write the necessary message there and then. The long letter which Slatin now composed in German demonstrates that his gift for improvisation never left him and that even the sharpest grief could not dull that native guile of his. His letter read, for the most part, quite satisfactorily from his captor's point of view. But an unusual number of passages were enclosed between brackets and even more were put in inverted commas. Two of the bracketed passages gave the key. In the first of these, Slatin instructed his family to interpret everything in inverted commas in exactly the opposite sense to what was written. In the second, he explained that there were two other fellow Europeans held prisoner in Omdurman who knew German and who might be ordered by the Khalifa as a security measure to translate the letter again for him. In case this happened he, Slatin, would warn them in advance to read straight through the document without hesitation, making no change of tone when they came to the inverted commas but simply omitting all the bracketed parts which contained the secret messages.

When, many months later in Vienna, his relatives read their brother's reply, written under the Khalifa's stern eye in far-off Omdurman, they must have been grateful for these elaborate instructions. Slatin had penned them a masterpiece of Austro-oriental double-talk.

After briefly summing up what had happened to him since his

last message to them from El Fasher four years before, he plunged straight into his code:

Although I have here my own living accommodation, women and servants etc., I am practically the whole day and night with the Khalifa (more or less under detention) and it is he who provides me with all necessities so that I 'miss nothing' except your presence ...

A message from the Khalifa will accompany this letter of mine in which he invites you to come here in order to see for yourselves 'what a splendid situation I am in and how happy I am'. ...

Find a capable orientalist who knows the Arab language and reply to the Khalifa's message as soon as possible in Arabic. (In your reply you must butter up the Khalifa as much as possible, praising him, wishing him perpetual good health and victories over his enemies as well as thanking him for the gracious kindness with which he treats me. Then you must make all manner of excuses as to why you can't come here at the moment—sickness, family problems and so on—while indicating that of course you will make the journey though it will be a long time ahead.)

Mention in your letter that you are trying to purchase my liberty, though this (an escape I mean) is impossible under present conditions. Indeed the Khalifa, 'because of his love for me' is not willing to part with me at any price. As for me, now that I 'have enjoyed the happiness of being with him, I also, am not prepared to leave him'.

Slatin then tackles some practical and material matters, and here nothing is in inverted commas. The Egyptian Government, he claims, must now owe him at least £1,000 (Egyptian) for back pay during his captivity and he requests his family to secure this sum for him through the Austrian Consul-General in Cairo. Next follows a long list of things that he requests them to send him via the Cairo-Suakin-Osman Digna route. These include £100 in English money; the finest bound version of the Koran in German that they can find; a German-Arabic dictionary; a dozen pocket watches and a dozen razors for him to distribute in Omdurman as gifts; also some recent newspapers and newspaper clippings referring to the Sudan.

But the last and most important item on his shopping list comes again in brackets:

(Send me also a travelling case with mirror, shaving kit and so on inside, the whole thing elegantly but elaborately finished. I want to hand this to the Khalifa as a present from you. Don't mention in

your reply to the Khalifa that I suggested this but simply ask me to
hand it to him as a gift from you.)

And then he rounds off:

As I have already mentioned, the Khalifa invites you to visit me
here, so drop all your fears and let one of you (not) come here ...
Let us pray to God for a happy reunion. How hard life would be
to bear if we did not have hope ...

In true love

Your brother

Abdel Kader (Rudolf)

If Slatin's memory is correct (and, inevitably, when writing
his account of these years later on without any of these documents to guide him it often played him tricks) the family's return package arrived in Omdurman in the autumn or early
winter that year. For he places its arrival after one of the
bloodiest examples of the Khalifa's 'justice' that even the hardened *mulazemin* had ever witnessed – the public slaughter in
Omdurman of the *Batahin*. These were a tribe who in 1888
had rebelled against the Khalifa's orders to advance on Egypt.
Sixty-seven of the deserters were caught and taken in chains
to the capital with their wives and children. The Khalifa had
the men brought before him and summarily sentenced them to
death. Slatin describes what happened next:

After a delay of a quarter of an hour, the Khalifa got up and we
all walked behind him. A terrible scene met our eyes when we got
to the market place. The unfortunate Batahin had been split into
three groups. All of one group had been hanged. All of the second
had been decapitated. All of the third had had their right hand and
their left foot chopped off. The Khalifa stopped in front of the three
scaffolds, which were almost breaking under the weight of the
bodies, while all around lay the heaps of the mutilated victims, their
dismembered hands and feet scattered on the ground. It was a
dreadful sight ...

It was one morning after witnessing this horror that Slatin
saw a camel come in from Berber laden with two boxes. It
passed his house and was led to the Khalifa. His master kept
him waiting, wild with impatience, until after sunset before
confirming the rumour that the boxes contained gifts and messages from Europe for Abdel Kader. Slatin's brothers and sis-

101

ters had carried out his instructions meticulously. The first of the letters sent with the consignment, addressed in Arabic to the Khalifa, was couched in such flattering terms that the boxes, which had been placed temporarily in the *Beit et mal* or Common Treasury, were promptly released and handed over to Slatin. Their contents were exactly as requested. The next day, the special travel case was presented by him to the Khalifa, who called in his *kadis* to admire the silver-topped bottles, the crystal containers, and the fitted brushes and scissors. A second invitation to Slatin's family to come to Omdurman was dictated on the spot, and Slatin wrote it in the same private code as his earlier message.

The next weeks and months he spent poring over the other things from home. Almost the most precious items in the collection were those that had cost the least, a few numbers of the Vienna paper *Neue Freie Presse* for 1888. Slatin tells us he read them so often that he practically learnt them off by heart, everything from the political leading articles down to the private advertisements in which elderly Viennese spinsters sought their 'kindred spirits with view to matrimony'. There must have been times since his surrender in 1884 when he half-wondered whether anything else existed outside this remote desert prison of his at Omdurman, and whether Vienna and all that had gone before was not just a fevered dream of the Khalifa's servant, Abdel Kader. The watches, the razor blades, and above all the newspapers, were proof that the real world of Rudolf Slatin was still there. It was a decisive moment in his personal struggle both to survive, and preserve his true identity.

From now on, quite apart from Slatin's own increased efforts to keep open these links with home, periodic contacts came about by accident. One day, for example, a merchant from Darfur who had just returned from a visit to Cairo approached him in the mosque and hurriedly slipped into his hands a weeks-old copy of an Egyptian paper, saying it contained news about his Austrian homeland. Slatin hurried home and opened it. The news was of the mysterious death at Mayerling on 30 January 1889, of Archduke Rudolf, Crown Prince of his Empire and Colonel-in-Chief of the 19th Austro-Hungarian Infantry Regiment in which Slatin himself had served. It was a strange way for the lieutenant of the Reserve to hear of his august Commander's death.

Later that year, Slatin passed to his family in Austria another of his elaborate coded epistles which, after some harmless chit-chat about the Khalifa, managed to transmit a detailed military account both of the latest dervish campaign against Abyssinia and of the suppression of an anti-Mahdist revolt in Darfur. He also sent them the Khalifa's formal invitation to come to Omdurman and visit their brother 'Abdel Kader Saltian (*sic*) . . . who now lives with us as one of our trusted and honoured advisers, in complete contentment, gay and happy'.

Though not exactly 'gay and happy', Slatin at least sounds fairly brisk and confident at this period. Then comes a sudden collapse. It was probably only one of many he experienced but it is the only one of which we have such plain written evidence. A letter to his 'Dear Brothers and Sisters', dated simply 'November 1890', strikes the doom-laden tone not only of a despairing prisoner but of a captured officer resentful that his true worth is not appreciated:

My fate is hard . . . clad in rags, my feet bare, deprived sometimes of the simple necessities. I suffer, year in year out, my life, often subjected to the humiliations of brutal fanatics. The fact that my former superiors and friends do not know what I have achieved, what I have suffered and still suffer makes everything twice as hard for me. God knows that I never acted against my honour and that, in the most difficult situations, I maintained the standard of my class . . .

It is the letter to General Gordon all over again but, this time, a *De Profundis* in body and spirit.

There was a bizarre incident in December 1892. Slatin, summoned peremptorily to the presence, found a very stern-looking Khalifa seated with his judges. 'Take this thing', he ordered, 'and see what it contains.' Slatin was handed a small brass ring to which was attached a metal cylinder about the size of a revolver cartridge. His heart sank when he discovered two strips of paper rolled up inside. Fearing they were incriminating messages from Cairo, his mind was already racing over possible 'explanations' as he slowly flattened them out and read them. But on this occasion his inventive talents were not required. The strips of paper contained the following message in German, French, English and Russian:

This crane has been bred and reared on my estate at Ascania Nova in the province of Tauride in South Russia: Whosoever catches or kills this bird is requested to communicate with me and inform me where it occurred.

(signed) F. R. FALZ-FEIN

September, 1892.

The Khalifa already knew that the bird had been killed by one of his tribesmen near Dongola, four hundred miles northwards down the Nile. What intrigued him were the papers it carried. He shook his head in bewilderment when Slatin translated and explained their innocent texts. Finally he exclaimed: 'This is one of the many devilries of those unbelievers who waste their time with such useless nonsense. No Mohammedan would ever have thought of doing such a thing.'

A much-relieved Slatin was then allowed to withdraw, but not before he had memorized the name and address of the crane's owner so that one day he might tell the man what had happened to his bird. It was a resolve he was to keep.

The decisive event which brought Slatin's freedom slowly but surely nearer was not however the establishment of tenuous links with his family in Austria, and much less the appearance of flying cranes from Russia. It was something in which Slatin played absolutely no part, and of which indeed he had absolutely no knowledge. This event was the arrival in Cairo in May 1886 of a promising young British officer named Francis Reginald Wingate and, more particularly, his subsequent appointment to be Director of Military Intelligence to the Anglo-Egyptian Army.

Wingate was to be pre-eminent among that handful of Englishmen who re-fashioned the Mahdi's Sudan into something approaching a civilized modern state. In fashioning the international career of Rudolf Slatin, his role was not merely pre-eminent; it was total and unique. Everything that Slatin owed to England, or England to him, was owed by both to Wingate first of all. Wingate was to be his military saviour, his political chief, his social patron and his closest personal friend. The saga of 'Rex' and 'Rowdy', as they came to call each other, became the central thread of Slatin's life, a thread which held firm through nearly forty years of fame and obscurity, of war and peace. Such an overwhelming influence needs some introduction.

Reginald Wingate was of Scottish Lowland stock – small landowners who turned merchants in the early nineteenth century. No boy could have had a gloomier start in life. In 1862, a year after his birth, the family textile business collapsed and his own father died of pneumonia. The widow migrated with her ten children to the milder and cheaper surroundings of Jersey. Here young Reginald, like all his brothers and sisters, was brought up with much love but very little money.

It was, in fact, lack of money that was to bring him, however indirectly, into Slatin's life. He had entered the British Army as a second-lieutenant in the Royal Artillery in 1880, and then, after service in India and Aden, was posted to the Egyptian Army in 1883 with the rank of major. From Cairo, Wingate watched the rise of the Mahdi and watched also the dithering indecision with which this challenge was handled in London. He saw General Gordon arrive and depart on his ill-defined, ill-fated mission to Khartoum. Then, in 1884–5, Wingate himself served on the staff of the abortive relief expedition belatedly dispatched to the Sudan in the vain attempt to save Gordon. That wretched episode over, he was posted back to England and eventually got the same job, ADC, to the same General, Sir Evelyn Wood, with whom he had recently campaigned up and down the Nile.

Had young Wingate been a man of means, or had he found himself a rich wife, that might have been the last that Egypt and the Sudan would ever have seen of him. But he had no private income; and the young lady he now fell in love with was an orphan, as poor as she was pretty. Indeed, the couple could not afford even to marry unless he first got himself promotion and a less expensive post. There was only one thing for it: back to Egypt. On 1 May 1886, Wingate resigned from the costly life of an ADC in England. By the end of the month he was in Cairo again, to take up the more rewarding post of Assistant Military Secretary to the Commander-in-Chief.

Wingate's story over the next few years, years during which Slatin was sweating it out in Omdurman, is the story of the slow sea-change which was coming about in the official British attitude to the Sudan. Though no re-conquest campaign was yet contemplated, certain pre-conditions for such a campaign were established. One of the most important of these preparations was to make the Khalifa and his ramshackle kingdom a priority intelligence target. At the beginning of 1889, Wingate was ordered to drop all other duties in order to concentrate on this intelligence work. Three years later, his Department of Military Intelligence was formally constituted in Cairo. Its tasks included the obvious ones of gathering information about the strength, dispositions and intentions of the Khalifa's forces, as well as making assessments of the political and economic situation in the Sudan and such relations as she had with her neighbours. But one task had a much narrower target. Indeed, it concerned only a handful of people. It was to liberate the Europeans held captive by the Khalifa in advance of any general action against him. The paths of Reginald Wingate and Rudolf Slatin were thus coming together. How they crossed for the first time to enable Slatin to escape from Omdurman can be reconstructed through Slatin's own account in *Fire and Sword,* supplemented by the official English and Austrian documents of the time, which he does not quote, and may not have seen.

In his own story, Slatin tells how, after exchanging the first messages with his family in 1888, he himself got the feeling that, thanks to their efforts and to those of Wingate, escape was slowly becoming a practical possibility. His first task was to devise a safe way of receiving and sending messages apart from the channel officially sanctioned by the Khalifa. This had its limitations, even with the use of the simple codes he had devised. His master's fondness for watches and clocks gave him one secret outlet. Slatin was made responsible for keeping all the Khalifa's time-pieces in order and this provided the excuse to visit an Armenian watchmaker named Artin, whose house was near the market-place. Though Slatin was too shrewd to confide in any Armenian, he occasionally used the man's shop as a rendezvous where he could exchange a few hurried words with any of his trusted contacts.

But, inevitably, the mosque was the prinicipal meeting-place. Slatin had to be there five times a day for every day of his life in Omdurman and so did all the notables of the city and all important visitors to it. Despite the presence of spies at everyone's elbow, and the Khalifa himself peering suspiciously through his private stone grille, it was the only place where Slatin could guarantee to be present without arousing comment or curiosity. It was here, early in February 1892 – only a month after the creation in Cairo of Wingate's special department – that the first escape contact was made. As the crowd was leaving the mosque, an Arab nudged Slatin and whispered: 'I have come for you. When can we meet?' Slatin whispered back: 'Here, after evening prayers tomorrow.'

The next evening, the stranger managed to slip Slatin his 'credentials', which were hidden in the false bottom of a flat tin box smelling strongly of coffee. There followed an agonizing supper with the Khalifa, during which Slatin had to conceal the box under his flowing *jibba*. By feigning sudden illness, he managed to cut the ordeal short. Then, clutching the incriminating object tightly to his stomach, he hurried home, lit his small oil lamp, and prised open the box. A scrap of paper fell out of the secret compartment. On it were written half a dozen words in French, addressed to nobody but signed by a Colonel on the staff of the Austro-Hungarian Mission in Cairo. The text merely vouched for the trustworthiness of the bearer. It was not much, but it was a start.

The messenger, Babakr by name, had in fact been expressly sent by Wingate to prepare the ground for Slatin's escape. During the next eighteen months, he proved trustworthy enough, in the sense that he never betrayed his mission, but inadequate in the sense that he never quite managed to fulfil it. (This was not, to do him justice, entirely his fault. On at least one occasion, Slatin himself suggested postponement to avoid making a dash for it in midsummer, when the heat was too great and the nights too short for their camels to give them the start they needed.) Yet though Babakr never seemed to Slatin resolute enough as an escape partner, he did provide, with his twice-yearly journeys between Omdurman and Cairo, the prisoner's first secure and secret link with the outside world.

Thus in the summer of 1892, after Babakr's second trip to Omdurman, Slatin sent back the first of his many messages to the men who were trying to free him. This one was written, like several of them, in invisible ink and was addressed to Father

Ohrwalder, the priest who had made good his escape to Cairo seven months before. It contained a few intelligence titbits as well as a great deal about Slatin's own escape. He wrote:

Dear Friend,

I feel utterly alone since you left me but I draw consolation from the knowledge that you are free. One day, I too will try to escape ... But we must wait until winter for now the nights are too short ... What can I expect from the Government? How do my financial affairs stand? Mahmoud is due to arrive here from Dongola in the next few days with 6–7,000 rifles. General state of morale as before ... Send me medicine, ether pills to give me strength on the journey. The Big One has been ill but is recovered again now ... My relations with him are the same. He gets steadily more mistrustful ...

Even the meagre scraps of information in this first unsigned message must have made Wingate hungry for more. But how to get at the captive himself and replace such furtive messages with hours of steady interrogation? In 1894, when Wingate was detached for a few months from Cairo and sent down to Suakin as temporary Governor of the Red Sea littoral, he had the opportunity of studying the escape project from much closer quarters.

By now Babakr had dropped out of the game, complaining that Slatin 'persistently refused to risk the flight'. Wingate engaged a new man for the job, a local Arab from Suakin named Onur Isa. Curiously, Slatin in his own book makes absolutely no mention of this man, though Isa's secret mission to Omdurman in the summer of 1894 was a prolonged affair which nearly proved disastrous for them both. All that Slatin knew in advance of his arrival was that the next envoy from Wingate would identify himself by a needle held in his right hand. Onur Isa's own report describes what happened:

I left Suakin with a firm resolve to release Slaten (sic) Bey at all costs; when I arrived at Omdurman I remained 18 days before being able to speak to him (Slaten) although I saw him five times every day in the mosque.

On the 18th day, forty of Osman Digna's Mulazimin arrived at Omdurman with the object of renewing their 'Beia' (oath of allegiance).

After prayers in the mosque Slaten Bey greeted Osman's men and while he was shaking hands with them, I drew near him & held the needle in my right hand. Slaten at once observed the sign & greeted me, asking me in a whisper if I carried any letters. I answered him in the affirmative, & then he turned to Osman's men saying: 'I am quite sure that you are weary & hungry owing to the long distance you have travelled over plain and desert, therefore, I hope that you will take supper with me so that God may bestow his benediction on me & my family.'

I was amongst those who were invited; & when I entered Slaten's house, he asked me my name & said aloud; 'You, the former friend of the "Mahdi" and the faithful "Ansari" of the Khalifa, you must wait on your weary & distressed brethren who are preparing to fight against the infidels.'

I complied with Slaten's request, entered the kitchen with his servants & served his guests. I took this opportunity to hand over the letters to him, he read them with great interest, & told me to return after two days & stop at his door, begging for alms.

I came on the third day, in the guise of a beggar. Slaten, on hearing my voice, called me in & ordered me to hire a camel & go as far as Goz Regeb and inspect the various posts on the road.

I purchased a camel for 95 dollars & left Omdurman via Wad Hasuna & Abu Deleig for Asubri and Goz Regeb. I remained at Goz Regeb six days, then returned to Omdurman. It took me 27 days to make this tour of inspection.

I then saw Slaten & he asked me about the posts & whether the roads were very crowded. I told him that all the posts were occupied by Dervishes, that the roads were watched, & that Sayed Hamed's men were spread out along the roads in bands under different Emirs.

Slaten then told me that he knew previously all I had told him, but that he only meant, by sending me to personally see the state of the roads, to put me in the position of testifying to the Governor of Suakin the difficulties that exist & the dangers that stared him in the face; & thus convince him he was not a coward.

While I was talking with Slaten, the servant entered & told him that Sheikh ed Din had come to pay him a visit. Slaten at once concealed me in a cupboard & went out to receive Sheikh ed Din, who invited him to supper. Slaten went off with him and left me inside the cupboard, but after a short time his servant (who was an Abyssinian) came and opened the cupboard & let me out.

I remained in his house two days & on the third Slaten returned & handed me two letters & told me to inform Wingate Bey, that the presence of the Dervishes on the main roads & the successive reinforcements sent out from Omdurman, made his flight at present very dangerous; & that it is not want of courage, which prevented him from coming with me.

Slaten moreover asked me to remain two or three months longer & await a favourable opportunity when the Kassala campaign was taking place; but I told him that the circumstances & want of money would not allow me to remain any longer. I left on the following day.

That account gives a vivid picture of the finely-spun web in which the Khalifa held Slatin like a fly, and of the difficulties of struggling free. But it is also interesting for the note of self-justification which the prisoner strikes – the same plaintive strain he had struck earlier in his letters to Gordon about his becoming a Moslem. He had not yet heard of the jibes Babakr had made about him in Cairo. But he had surely sensed already, by the efforts that Wingate was making to release him, that his future lay with the English – as indeed had his meteoric career up to his capture – and he was anxious to preserve his 'image' with his patrons.

Towards the end of that same year, however, another of Slatin's fellow-captives managed to escape to Cairo through Wingate's ingenious chain of agents. He was an Italian, Father Rossignoli, like Ohrwalder another priest. Though not as closely watched as Slatin in Omdurman itself, once away from the city he had faced that same series of desert patrols which Slatin claimed to be almost impassable, and had eluded them. The fact that Gordon's renowned warrior was still sweating it out in Omdurman whereas two priests and two nuns had braved the dash to freedom, did nothing to help Slatin's reputation. Indeed, at this point, a faintly ironic strain creeps into the reports of his own Austro-Hungarian mission in Cairo.

Thus a telegram which Baron Heidler, the head of that mission, sent to Vienna on 4 March 1895, describes the latest arrangements for Slatin's flight and then comments: 'Whether this time Slatin will really steel himself to an escape attempt, which he has often prepared for already, depends on circumstances which this mission can, in the nature of things, neither influence nor judge.'

Yet, paradoxically, if Rossignoli's flight had made some people in Cairo a little sceptical about Slatin's excessive caution it had, at the same time, made escape for him genuinely more lifficult. Wingate's monthly Intelligence Department report for December 1894 describes how the watch over the captives had been tightened even further after the Italian priest's escape. The emirs in charge of the remaining European prisoners were held esponsible for reporting personally to the Khalifa each day that all were present. As for Slatin, Wingate reported in the same month that an agent sent to him from Suakin with letters had returned there on 30 November saying that the Austrian was so closely watched he had been unable, during a stay of several weeks in Omdurman, to find a chance of slipping him the messages.

There is a story, an account of which is preserved in the Sudan Archives at Durham, that the Khalifa once called upon all his advisers to describe the strength of their support for him. One by one, the emirs boasted how many enemies they would slaughter for their master in battle. Then the Khalifa turned to Slatin and asked him too for a pledge. Slatin is said to have replied:

> I am bound by a single hair
> But when I break that hair
> Then comes your downfall.

The tale was probably apocryphal, yet it contained both truth and prophecy. For more than ten years, Slatin Bey, the former Governor of Darfur, had been the Khalifa's proudest trophy. Now, the trophy had become a symbol as well. If Slatin too managed to escape this would do more than betray his master's closest secrets. It could also herald the Khalifa's end.

In fact, that Christmas of 1894 was the last that Slatin was to spend in captivity. After the various false alarms and false hopes of the summer, Wingate's unremitting ingenuity, added to the tireless efforts of Slatin's own family, were opening the door at last. From his relatives in Austria he had received special ether pills, prepared in Vienna by one Professor Chiari, to combat fatigue during his flight. Slatin buried the small bottle which held them safely in the ground. Further messages of encouragement came from Suakin with the names of fresh agents appointed by Wingate in Isa's place. By now, the planning had reached a detailed stage. In one of his invisible ink messages smuggled out of Omdurman on 10 January 1895, for example, Slatin commits himself, at least on paper, to th latest plan and describes his own 'cover story'. He writes t Father Ohrwalder:

> Before undertaking the flight I will leave behind me a letter t the Khalifa, in which I will thank him for all the good he did m so that he will not vent his rage on my companions remaining. will also tell him that my patriotism and the love of my brethre induced me to flee . . .

A few days after that message was sent, a stranger brushe against Slatin in the streets of Omdurman. He identified him self with Wingate's secret sign of the needle; indeed, th particular envoy produced three of them for good measure. Bu his message did not live up to his credentials. He had hoped, h said, to take Slatin out due east to Kassala, but as new militar posts had just been set up along that route, it was now to dangerous to try. Instead, the messenger promised to com again in two months' time, and asked Slatin for a letter to Majo Wingate to produce more money. Slatin handed it to him th following night and turned back, sick at heart, to his own house

Consolation was nearer at hand than he knew. Several week before, Slatin had managed to establish yet another link witl Cairo in the person of an Omdurman merchant who travelle between the two capitals. Wingate and the Austrian Missio had offered this man the handsome sum of £1,000 to effec Slatin's escape, and had advanced him £200 for his expenses Now, at the very moment when Slatin was walking sadly hom in the darkness, this other link made contact with him. One o the merchant's cousins named Mohammed, whom Slatin recog nized, suddenly appeared at his side and whispered: 'We ar ready. The camels have been bought and the guides are hired Next month during the moon's last quarter is the time. B ready!'

Slatin describes how, as he watched the man melt away with out another word, he somehow knew that this was the real thing He was right. A fortnight of anguished waiting followed, durin which time yet another escape envoy from Cairo turned up i Omdurman. With so many of Wingate's crusaders now dodging about the city, whispering their messages in the mosque or i some secluded side-street, Slatin became quite panic-stricken hat the Khalifa would learn what was going on. But both Vingate's organization and Slatin's luck held out. During the wenty-four hours' notice he was given of the final rendezvous, .e laid as long and as plausible a trail of confusion as he could o delay his pursuers. To his servants, he spun a tale that he vould be away the following day for a secret meeting with a nessenger bringing him more gifts and money from his home- and. He knew that their anxiety to get a share of the non- :xistent valuables would keep their mouths shut for a while. As or the Khalifa, all Slatin could do on the eve of his flight was o feign oncoming sickness and get himself excused from prayers he following day 'to take a dose of senna tea and tamarind, and 'est quietly at home'. Having secured permission, he then at- :ended evening service with the Khalifa that same night, as hough to show that, as long as he could walk, he would be at nis master's side.

It was four hours after sunset, and the Khalifa had retired :o rest. Slatin, carrying only his prayer-rug, and the *farda* or light woollen cloth for protection against the cold, walked up the road that led northwards from the mosque. Happily for him, it was a dark night and blowing a bitter northerly wind that had driven everyone into their huts and houses. The Khalifa's capital was still as a graveyard. After a while Slatin heard the pre-arranged signal – a low cough. He stopped and Mohammed appeared out of the shadows leading a donkey. They rode together on the beast through the deserted streets to a point at the edge of the city where a small ruined house stood just off the road. There another man was waiting with one saddled camel. 'This is your guide, Zeki Behal', Mohammed explained. 'He will take you to the riding camels concealed out in the desert. Make haste and God protect you.'

Slatin needed no encouragement. As Mohammed turned back, he jumped up behind his guide. After about an hour's ride they stopped at a low clump of trees, where yet another man was waiting for them with three fresh camels. These were the animals that were to take them on the first 200-mile stage of their journey, a zigzag route north-west to Al Karaba, where they planned to cross the Nile and put the great river between them and their pursuers.

Slatin had one question. Had Mohammed handed over his

'medicine', the famous ether pills from Vienna that were to ward off sleep? Zeki knew nothing of them and only laughed. 'Do not worry on that score. Fear will keep sleep from our eyes.' No more words were wasted. They mounted and were off, riding northwards, as fast as they could in the blackness, through an expanse of halfa grass studded with mimosa trees which led to the open desert. It was the night of 20/21 February 1895. After twelve years and two months as a prisoner of the Mahdist state, Slatin had begun his dash for freedom at last.

He knew that the Khalifa's suspicions would be aroused when he was found missing from dawn prayers. But suspicion was unlikely to harden into certainty until Omdurman had been combed in vain for him, and that was likely to take all morning. A little more time would then elapse before a pursuit party, mounted on the right camels, could be organized. All that, however, only meant fourteen hours' start at the most. Every minute counted.

They rode without a pause all through the night and throughout the following day. When they made their first halt, in open country due north of Omdurman, they had been going twenty-one hours, with only one drink of water and no food, and had put some 130 miles between them and the Khalifa's city. There had been only one incident, but that was disturbing enough. Near midday, a rider from a passing caravan picked out Slatin's paler features from a distance of two thousand yards, and galloped over on his horse to see who the 'white Egyptian' was. Fortunately he was a sheikh out on a harmless expedition to Dongola to collect dates, and a friend of one of Slatin's guides into the bargain. For a bribe of twenty Maria Theresa dollars he promised to keep his mouth shut. Yet the secret was already out.

Slatin had no complaint with his guides. Both the young Zeki Behal and an older man, Hamed Ibn Hussein, looked and proved loyal and resourceful. The camels, two stallions of the Anafi breed and a Bisharin mare, presented a less satisfactory picture that first evening. Though they had allegedly been hand-picked for strength and swiftness, they were already exhausted and could no longer manage even a trot. They even refused the food placed before them. Fearing that the animals had been bewitched by the Khalifa's holy men, Hamed made a little fire, sprinkled some resin on it, and then walked round the three camels, muttering incantations to give them strength. Slatin, more prosaically, allowed them an extra half hour's rest. He was convinced they were only second-rate stock from the Omdurman camel market.

There was nothing for it but to tighten the saddle-girths again and push on. With the comment: 'In Europe we say that time is money. Here time is life', Slatin drove the mounts as hard as he could throughout that second night. But the best they could manage was a fairly brisk walk. When the sun came up again they were only as far as the high ground north-west of Metemmeh, having added less than thirty miles to their journey. The first change of camel was to have been a day's ride north of Berber, and even that town still lay another hundred miles to the north-east. It was clear that, with these winded beasts, they would never make it. The whole plan had to be changed. They agreed to alter course instead to the north-west and make for the Gilif range of largely uninhabited hills nearby. Here Slatin could hide while his companions searched for fresh camels. The fact that both guides came from this area and knew every sheikh and every rocky path in it was to prove their salvation.

Soon after sunrise they reached the foot of the mountain. Dismounting and driving the camels before them, the guides led Slatin to his hiding-place, after a stiff three hours' climb. It was up a valley hemmed in by sheer rock walls with a spring of pure mountain water in a cleft of the stones. They unsaddled their mounts and hid the saddles among the boulders. Then the older man, Hamed, led the camels themselves into conceal-ment, in case vultures should circle overhead and betray their presence to someone on the plains below.

Despite a meal of bread and dates and the delicious water, Slatin was depressed. He had hoped to make a continuous run for it across the desert to the Egyptian border, always a few hours ahead of the Khalifa's vengeance. But now, though safe for the moment, his precious lead was gone. The mere search for fresh mounts was dangerous, yet unless they could be found no bribe was large enough and no cave dark enough to protect him in the long run.

Slatin had to spend six days and nights in the Gilif mountains with Hamed to keep him company, while Zeki rode out on their freshest camel to seek new animals. For all Slatin's native optimism and his acquired gifts of patience, it was a tense time. Once they were actually discovered in their rocky lair by a herdsman seeking water for his cattle. Again, it was Slatin's skin that had given them away: the white soles of his feet, sticking out as he slept, were visible a mile off. But the man turned out to be one of Hamed's numerous local relatives. So far from betraying them, he brought milk and millet cakes and led them to an even better hiding-place. This was a little grotto formed of rock slabs with a little shade from one parched tree which sprouted out above.

With this as a base, they passed the last three days of waiting and watching. The hours crawled by so slowly that Slatin found himself longing for any happening – even another danger alarm – to enliven them. Then, at noon on the sixth day, a figure was sighted running towards their old camp. Hamed went down to challenge him. It was Zeki, back at last with fresh camels. They could now begin the second stage of their flight which was to take them to the pre-arranged crossing-point on the Nile, where more of Wingate's agents were waiting to ferry them across.

The point chosen lay in the Bayuda desert, almost half-way between Berber and Abu Hamed, in a huge loop of the river close to the Fifth Cataract. To reach it, they had to traverse the Gilif mountains by the north-east from their hide-out, and then, once down in the plain, cross the broad grey band of the great caravan trail from Berber without being seen. This, the most dangerous single manoeuvre of their journey, went off without a hitch. Once safely across, only the Kerraba plateau stood between them and the Nile. For the fugitives, the plateau was so isolated and bleak as to be almost a sanctuary. It was a belt of sandy soil without vegetation and without inhabitants, a wilderness whose only feature was the countless black stones, ranging in size from a tennis-ball to a football, which covered its surface. Throughout the following day their mounts picked a way slowly over this rock-strewn ground. Then, towards evening, Slatin saw the Nile in the far far distance, gleaming 'like a silver streak across the landscape'. He was, it seemed, safe at

ast. They descended to the valley and as the two guides went
on ahead to arrange for the crossing, Slatin dozed off happily
by himself, dreaming already of his family and of the woods and
lakes of Austria.

He had a rude awakening. Two hours before dawn Hamed
reappeared with the ugly news that there was no sign whatever
of their friends. Something had gone wrong. Slatin could
evidently not cross the river that night. Neither could he remain
where he was, in the open valley so close to inhabited villages.
There was nothing for it but an hour's hard march back to the
Kerraba. Hamed went with him and, soon after nightfall,
picked a spot in the plateau for Slatin to sleep. Then the guide
made off for the river again to join Zeki in the frantic search for
their men. Slatin was once more left alone in the black night,
with a bag of dates, a water-skin, a rifle and his own anguished
thoughts.

His immediate problem was concealment. On Hamed's advice, he set about building a ring of stones around himself, as the
camel-herds did to protect them from the winter cold. He
piled the rocks on top of each other to form a circular wall
some eighteen inches high and scooped up some sandy soil to
fill in the cracks. He then lay down exhausted on his back to
await events, dozing fitfully in the freezing night, the woollen
farda pulled up over his face to hide that tell-tale skin in case
he should still be asleep at daybreak.

Again, the midday sun brought release. He heard a low
whistle, and peeped cautiously over his low wall of stones to see
Hamed approaching him with a broad smile. The men for the
river crossing had been found and all was prepared. One
sombre note came with this good news: reports of 'Abdel
Kader's' escape from the Khalifa had reached the Berber district
three days ago. All roads and all ferry points were being
closely watched. They would have to move like cats.

That night, Slatin bade farewell to the two guides who had
brought him so bravely and resourcefully thus far from
Omdurman, and whose work was now done. With two new
guides he rode off on the same north-easterly course towards the
river, his white man's face covered up despite the darkness. After
two hours they heard the low grinding of a water-wheel and

the splashes and cries of women at work. They had reached the left bank of the Nile.

Here, yet another relay of agents was ready. Slatin waited an hour in a clump of bushes – making his camel kneel very slowly so that it would not even utter one tell-tale grunt – and was duly presented to a group of four men whose sole business was to get him to the other bank. It was a business they evidently knew. Their leader, Ahmed Abdalla, ordered the saddles to be taken from the camels' backs and told two of his companions to swim with the animals across the river at different spots, filling their water-skins full of air and fastening them round the camels' necks for buoyancy. He then motioned to the third man and Slatin to follow him on foot, carrying the saddles with them. All five were to meet tomorrow beyond the right bank 'near the stones of the Fighting Bull'.

A few minutes' walk took them to a spot on the shore where a tiny home-made boat was moored in a hollow smoothed out by the current. It was barely big enough to hold the three passengers, and it was over an hour after they had pushed off in the darkness before they reached the other side of the great stream. While Ahmed scrambled out with Slatin, the third man guided the boat some distance back into the river, then bored a hole and scuttled it, swimming back himself to rejoin the others. All trace of Slatin's crossing had literally been sunk behind him.

With the river behind him, and curving back on its great sweep towards Merawi and Dongola, Slatin was almost out of danger. Another hundred miles further to the north-east and he would be on the outer fringe of the Mahdist state. Once that invisible boundary was reached, there were only three hundred more miles of Egyptian-held desert to cross before reaching safety and civilization. But dangerous or safe, the miles all had to be travelled, and sheer exhaustion was becoming a bigger enemy than the dervishes. There was a long walk over stony ground in the blackness to reach the appointed rendezvous. By the time they got there Slatin, in his own words, was 'dead-beat, staggering to left and right as though I were drunk'. Here, however, he had an enforced rest of two days before Ahmed appeared at last with three fresh camels and two new guides. They had just had a lucky escape back on the left bank of the

Nile. The Khalifa's local commander, fearing that an Egyptian attack was imminent along the northern border, had rushed up reinforcements. Sixty dervishes had swept through Ahmed's village on horseback twelve hours before, looting everything in sight. The food meant for Slatin had been devoured but the three precious camels had been hidden in time.

Yet another leave-taking and another remounting. Three more days of almost non-stop riding, tiring but uneventful, past the so-called Vale of Asses and over the hills of Nuranai, brought them to Bir Nauarik and the last boundary of the Khalifa's zone of influence. North of here, the Mahdist patrols rarely ventured, though the first Egyptian garrisons were still far distant. For this final leg, Slatin was handed over to an aged Arab of precarious health named Hamed Garhosh, with one camel between the two of them. It was now only a case of holding out physically, though this proved no easy matter.

After two days, the fragile guide collapsed with hunger, fatigue and cold. In order to keep going, Slatin first handed his own *jibba* over to the old man, then mounted him alone on the camel and, for the next four days and nights, walked barefoot behind him over the stones. (The previous pair of guides had lost Slatin's sandals.) To cap everything, the camel itself went lame with a pointed stone driven into one of its fore-feet and Slatin had to bandage the animal up every day with strips torn from his clothing, a trick he had remembered from the camel-herds of Darfur. This was the tattered trio that, at sunrise on Saturday, 16 March 1895, saw the Nile curving in again from the south-west, and on its shore, the Anglo-Egyptian base of Assuan. After twenty-four days of flight, Slatin had reached sanctuary. After eleven years of captivity, he was entering the houses of his own people again.

As to what happened next, Slatin merely records in his book that he was 'received in the most friendly manner' at the Mess of the British officers serving with the Egyptian garrison in the town. In all the lectures and newspaper interviews he subsequently gave throughout Europe, there is hardly any elaboration of this bare description. But the five British officers who happened to be in the mess that day told a much more colourful story.

It was shortly after noon and they were waiting for their

lunch when a mess waiter approached the Commanding Officer and Governor of the frontier area, Colonel Hunter Pasha, to say that a man was outside asking to see him. The Colonel sent a brusque message back telling him to wait till after lunch. Back came the waiter in a few minutes' time to say that the man was insisting and begged 'in God's name' to be admitted.

'I'm damned if he can't wait!' retorted the exasperated Colonel, who was evidently thinking both of his position and of his meal. But he was curious enough to inquire who the man was and what he wanted.

The servant reappeared to say that the mysterious visitor refused to say anything. He just went on squatting outside.

At this, Major Jackson, another of the officers present, became so curious that he persuaded his colonel to let the fellow in. The Major's story goes on:

A dirty little Arab with bare feet and a soiled skull cap entered. He stood bowed, with his hands on his breast and his eyes downcast.

'Who are you?' I asked him in Arabic.

'I am Abdel Kader', he whispered without lifting his eyes, and that was all I could get out of him.

But presently Archibald Hunter, who so far had taken no interest in the proceedings, got up and joined me. He gazed at the little Arab and asked in Arabic:

'Have you no other name?'

No reply.

Suddenly Hunter lit up. 'Good God above!' he shouted, and then, in Arabic: 'Are you Salatin?' A pause, and then the little Arab, still in a whisper, replied, 'Yes, I am Salatin.'

The tale belongs to the category of *Si non è vero, e ben trovato*. But indeed there is no reason to doubt it. Slatin could have been so overwhelmed by the freedom he was feeling again as to have been incapable of making a normal approach; (and we know, from later accounts, that it was some time before he could get used to looking people squarely in the face again and so abandon the downcast mien he had been forced to adopt for eleven years in the Khalifa's presence). Alternatively, Slatin, who all his life had a great sense of theatre, may have been adding a deliberate touch of stage drama to his return to civilization.

If that was his intention, it certainly succeeded. The small and tranquil British officers' mess at Assuan was galvanized into life. A bottle of beer was poured down the traveller's throat. The black bandmaster of the garrison was summoned and somehow managed to learn that lovely tune from a Haydn String Quartet that had become the anthem of Austria-Hungary – *Gott erhalte unsern Kaiser*. Slatin was given a meal, a bath, a shave, a haircut and a sleep. Everyone meanwhile searched their wardrobes for items of clothing which, put together, made up a passable imitation of an Austrian officer's uniform. When Slatin re-entered the mess as the guest of honour for dinner that evening (to the strains of his own Imperial anthem) he began by weeping. 'But,' notes Jackson, 'as the evening wore on, he might have been an ordinary foreign attaché.'

In fact, Rudolf Slatin had just become something very much more than that.

Part Two

Chapter Eight

THE QUEEN'S DARLING

When Salatin, the bedraggled Arab, came into the British officers' mess at Assuan, Baron Sir Rudolf Slatin, the bemedalled darling of Victorian and Edwardian Europe, was born. Behind him, across those hundreds of miles of Nubian desert, lay twelve lost years. They had been sometimes painful; often dangerous; more often boring and always humiliating. Yet, for him, they had spelt obscurity above all. Ahead now lay the fame, the distinction and the glittering society that the ambitious young Viennese nobody had first come to the Sudan to seek. Paradoxically, he had found it not so much in battle as in flight.

Slatin's escape from Omdurman stirred all hearts and opened all doors. Without it, he would have been for the English merely a useful, if controversial, survivor from the vanished era of Gordon Pasha. He would have been liberated, in due course, from the Khalifa's camp, and then, if he was lucky, given some temporary employment by the Khalifa's conquerors. After that, they would have finished with him. He would have had to choose between a continued search for adventure, perhaps elsewhere in an unsettled Africa; or else a return to cosy oblivion in his native Austria.

But the escape, coming at the time it did, transformed his whole life. It not only gave him new goals, hitherto undreamt of. It also put into his hands the means to achieve those goals. His services at this stage of the Sudan game were vital, and not merely useful, to those who were now preparing to crush his jailer, and to avenge the memory of Khartoum. And the manner in which he had suddenly appeared to present those services, an apparition from the sands who had battled his way from the Khalifa's couch to a British mess tent, made him, overnight, a figure of romance as well as a man of military importance. Everything that came to Slatin from now on, all the triumphs and the honours (but also the torment and sadness) came from those twenty-four days of flight and the twelve years of endurance that had gone before. He would have been the first to admit, at least during the golden time that now lay ahead, that it had all been worth it.

The gleams of this golden age shone straight away in the shape of congratulatory telegrams from official Cairo. In the capital, they had been on tenterhooks about him for a fortnight, ever since, on 10 March, the Governor of Suakin cabled an exciting report from a travelling merchant (who had allegedly got it from a Mahdist patrol). According to this, Slatin had slipped out of Omdurman fourteen days before and was on the run across the desert with three days' start on his pursuers. Baron Heidler, the head of the Austrian mission in Cairo, who had been so closely involved in all the escape attempts, was told of the report, but wisely decided on caution. The telegram he sent back to Vienna about it on 11 March ended with the words:

Say nothing to the family for the time being. If report true and flight successful confirmation probable within five days.

On the morning of 16 March, he was able to send that confirmation:

Slatin Bey arrived safe and sound in Assouan. Please inform family.

A note made by a Foreign Office clerk on the copy of the telegram in the Vienna archives records that, by 2 p.m. that same day, Slatin's relatives had been told the joyful news.

Meanwhile, however, the large and international body of press representatives in Cairo had themselves been buzzing with excitement over the Suakin rumours, which promised them a human adventure story of the highest calibre. They were also in that state of anguish unique to their profession, worrying whether any one colleague would beat all the rest of them with the news. Reuter's correspondent in Cairo at the time, David Rees, who was on close terms with Wingate, wrote to him anxiously: 'It would be awful for me if I got forestalled by any other Johnny'.

As it was, Wingate let all the 'Johnnys' into the secret at once. He issued a brief but vivid communiqué on Slatin's escape on 17 March, and followed it up, a week later, with the full details. Thus the world press correspondents were fed, in two well-spaced courses, with the meal they had rightly been hungering after for ten days. They now did it full justice. The saga of Rudolf Slatin became an international sensation. The story was, after all, the equivalent, in modern terms, of an American agent escaping from a Communist jail in Mongolia and walking across the Gobi Desert to freedom.

Of the English and Austrian papers of 18 March 1895, all of which gave the story coverage, the *Westminster Gazette* seized most precisely on Slatin's value in the impending campaign against the Khalifa. It described his escape as 'the most important haul from the military point of view', and added: 'He will be of the greatest service when the move south is made.' The *Manchester Courier*, on the other hand, stressed the dramatic side of the story: 'Though Burke may have been right in holding the age of chivalry to be dead, yet the age of romance still lives.' This aspect of the affair was also later seized on by *Le Temps* in Paris, which, in a long front-page article published on 29 March under the heading 'Le Roman de l'Afrique', declared: 'The last vestiges of romance, long since vanished from Europe, are still to be found in Africa.' Slatin simply could not lose. At one bound he had become a target for every General Staff interested in Central Africa (as most were) and a trophy for every European hostess interested in her drawing-room (as all were). It was a combination of opportunities which the little Viennese seized with both hands and feet and made the most of for twenty glorious years.

While the world press was resounding with his name, Slatin was travelling on a Nile postal steamer back to Cairo. The journey was a miniature triumphal procession in itself. At Assuan he was escorted aboard by all the officers, English and Egyptian, of the

127

garrison. The Austrian National Anthem *à la soudanaise* was played again, and Slatin duly wept again. Tourists of all nations assembled on the bank to cheer him as he went up the gang-plank. Similar demonstrations awaited him at Luxor the following evening, and also another shower of personal telegrams, including two very precious ones from his sisters and from the Vienna municipality. His family and his native city. 'How sweet', he remarked, 'those words sound.'

But all this was nothing to the reception which met the escaped hero in Cairo, which he reached by rail (having left the steamer at Girga) at six o'clock in the morning of Tuesday, 19 March. Baron Heidler and his staff were there to greet him; so was Father Rossignoli, who had helped to blaze the trail of escape from the Khalifa's clutches. Photographers as well as newspaper correspondents were among the crowd, and here, on the station platform, Slatin first saw and shook the hand of Major Reginald Wingate Bey – the man to whom he already owed his liberty and to whom he would soon owe his career.

According to one eyewitness account Slatin, 'dressed in a discarded karkee (sic) suit and a dilapidated pair of tennis shoes', seemed at first confused by the hearty welcome given to him in his native tongue. But he managed not only the replies in German, but also a speech of thanks to Wingate in English, a language of which he had only the barest knowledge, and that very rusty. Then off he drove as Heidler's guest of honour to the Austrian Mission, where, according to the same account, 'the Baron had been hard at work since well before sunrise, decorating the balcony with garlands and affixing a welcome in his own tongue over the room he was to occupy'.

A day or two later, seated on Heidler's balcony and relishing every leaf and bloom in the garden fresh with spring, Slatin saw a tame heron stalking across the flower beds. Instantly, he thought of that crane released in Southern Russia in 1892, which had been shot down in the Mahdist Sudan and its identity ring cut off and pushed under his nose by a suspicious Khalifa. This bird in the Cairo garden was like another, and very special, welcome committee. Slatin hurried to his room and wrote immediately to the crane's owner, Falz-Fein, whose name and address he had successfully memorized.

Then came the first crop of honours, and with them the first complications. On 21 March, only two days after his arrival in Cairo, Slatin was received by the Khedive and made a Pasha of Egypt. This rolled splendidly off the tongue and became, indeed, the title by which Slatin was always to be best remembered. But it created a thorny problem over his military promotion at the time. He had held the grade of Bey ever since his appointment as Governor-General of Darfur in 1881, and that grade had matched his military rank of lieutenant-colonel. But if the new Pasha was to continue as an officer in the Egyptian Army he could not, in the Khedive's eyes, be anything less than a major-general, which was the minimum compatible with his civil promotion.

To General Kitchener, however, the Sirdar, or Commander-in-Chief of the Khedive's army, and to the other English officers who ran it under him, this was plainly unacceptable. The little Austrian who had suddenly popped up in their midst in Cairo was an invaluable intelligence prize and he seemed a nice enough chap. But he could hardly be given a rank which would make him senior to nearly all of them, including the Army's English Chief of Staff. The most they could contemplate was promotion to full colonel; and even that was hard enough to absorb. The alternative was for Slatin to become a purely civilian adviser, and the hero of the hour dug his toes in at that.

In a series of dispatches to Vienna, Baron Heidler describes the tug-of-war that went on over this throughout the early spring of 1895. But as the English were the real heavyweights in the contest, and as they were anxious to bind Slatin firmly to them, the outcome was inevitable. He was duly promoted colonel, at a salary of £E800 (that is, 800 Egyptian pounds) a year, and was given, in addition, the handsome sum of £E16,500 for all the back pay due to him.

Baron Heidler reported with pride that Slatin had now become the first exception to the rule that, in practice, only British officers held senior rank in the Egyptian Army. In return for this distinction Slatin, he claims, had had to give a secret written undertaking that, even if he got further promotion, he would never ask for the post of Chief of Staff nor for an actual field command, such as the Frontier Province or Suakin. This secret personal undertaking had yet another secret qualification attached to it. All rights, military as well as civil, were to be left open for Slatin in certain eventualities 'as in the case of the reconquest of the Sudan'. In fact, though the English, who already ran Egypt, and who would soon be running the Sudan, quickly learnt to love Slatin and were always ready to listen to him, they never let him command as much as a platoon of their soldiers. As this tussle over his very first promotion showed, he could never really become one of them in this new post-Gordon era. In the official world at least, there was always to be this glass wall between Slatin's titles and his real power. It was a blessing for him that, of the two, the titles always interested him more.

Such was the byzantine way in which Colonel Slatin Pasha was reinstated in the Egyptian army and posted for special duties to the Intelligence Department of Major Wingate Bey. But Slatin had other honours in store, and perhaps already in mind. It was Wingate, his rescuer – now his chief, his mentor and his friend – who helped him towards them. First, there were literary laurels to be won, for publishers in all the major European countries were keen to produce his stirring tale in book form. Second, and closely intertwined with the first, were the social laurels. So far, the only palace Slatin had entered except as a tourist was that of His Highness the Khedive of Egypt. Now, the gates of other and far more illustrious courts were swinging open for him.

Fire and Sword in the Sudan was Slatin's only book, and the only account existing of his adventures. The process by which it was created was as cumbersome as the end product itself. Many stories circulated about its exact literary parenthood. But the authentic version must surely be that given in a letter which Wingate himself wrote afterwards to Sir Arthur Bigge – a friend, a brother-officer, and the Private Secretary to his Queen:

> You ask me who wrote the book—it was Slatin. We lived together for most of the time it was being written and I was able to guide him as to dates etc., and the general outline. As he wrote (in German) it was translated into 'English as she is spoke' by a Syrian. I then re-wrote it in its present form and it was then reconstructed back into German. Such was the somewhat elaborate process.

What this amounted to was that while Slatin provided the raw material of the tale – and much of it was very raw, for though he was a great talker he was never much of a hand at writing – Wingate did the editing as well as the final English translation and much of the factual research. Also, and this is perhaps most important, he set the general tone of the work. He soon grew very fond of Slatin, so in one sense this was a labour of love. But there were good practical reasons behind all the hard work as well, work which had to be fitted in somehow amidst all his intelligence duties and the remorseless pressure of the Cairo social round. This remarkable young British officer was, in fact, one of the first exponents of what later came to be styled Psychological Warfare. It was, for him, a plain matter of logic. He had decided to make his career on the Nile. The overthrow of the Mahdist Sudan seemed to him a compelling duty for England as well as the next stage in that career. A reluctant government in London (as well as its cautious representative, Lord Cromer, in Cairo) was the main obstacle in the way of a re-conquest campaign. English public opinion had to be stirred to prod that government. The best spoons to do the stirring were authentic tales about the Mahdist realm. The more harrowing these were the better. It was all so effective because it was all so clear-cut.

Apart from his own work on Mahdism, which had been published in 1891, virtually as an official history, Wingate had already broken the popular sentimental ground he was after in England with Father Ohrwalder's book, which came out in London the following year. It was Wingate who translated the good Father's *Ten Years of Captivity in the Mahdi's Camp* and it was Wingate who organized its publication. Its success outshone his brightest dreams. Seven editions had appeared even before Christmas of 1896. All England shuddered at the dervish barbarities recounted by this impeccable priestly source. Queen Victoria devoured it and Lord Rosebery, then Foreign Secretary in Gladstone's Cabinet, began from that time onwards to take a keen interest in Sudanese affairs.

But Ohrwalder the priest was nothing as an escapee compared with Slatin the warrior and ex-Governor of Gordon's. Nor, for that matter, was that other priest who had got away from Omdurman ahead of Slatin, the Italian Father Rossignoli. Wingate had, in fact, already started on the manuscript of Rossignoli's story when Slatin turned up. The Italian was promptly left to his own devices and Wingate – quite rightly from his point of view – switched all his literary energies over to the Austrian.

Slatin started scribbling almost as soon as he had shaken the Khalifa's sand off his fingers. For the next four months Wingate kept him hard at it in Cairo, despite the steadily mounting heat and the steadily mounting pile of invitation cards. In April, two of Slatin's sisters, Maria (or Marie as she was called) and Leopoldine, arrived in Cairo to visit their famous brother. Their letters sent during the ensuing six weeks to the other proud members of the family at home give many intimate glimpses of Slatin as the budding author and Slatin as the budding courtier of many courts. As their artless, excited reports to Vienna show, both roles were soon presenting him with problems.

Thus, in her first letter home, dated 26 April, Marie writes about the book: 'Unfortunately Rudolf has to work terribly hard. He so much wants to rest yet has to write so much which tires him because he has never written a great deal all his life.' And in another 'undated' April letter: 'Alas, Rudolf's book is making far from brisk progress. He doesn't on any account want to put it off and of course nobody can do it for him. It's a real nuisance as he really is quite longing for home and for some peace.' On 8 May, writing to her brother Heinrich, Marie gives her own rather puzzled version of the Slatin-Wingate co-operation, though she does not mention the Englishman by name:

As the book apparently includes a lot of politics and is under English supervision, the German edition won't be printed from Rudolf's draft but will be translated from the English into German by someone trustworthy; this complicates everything, and means the whole work has to be finished here ...

And in a letter to the same Heinrich dated 10 June 1895, Slatin himself lets out a groan of despair over his literary labours:

I write away at my book from morn till night but despite that progress is slow because I have to drag everything out of a brain which has been half dried up by the African heat ...

And now come the earliest signs, reflected in these family letters written during the very first weeks of his fame and freedom, of that emotional tug-of-war between London and Vienna which was to endure for the rest of Slatin's life – often dormant, at times agonizing, but always there. Thus Marie begins her letter of 5 May with a thorny protocol problem for Heinrich to ponder over, a problem which she is expressly presenting on the busy Rudolf's behalf:

He doesn't imagine there are going to be any complications over service in various (sic) armies because, in view of his age, he feels sure he will no longer be eligible for military call-ups or manoeuvres. He is mainly concerned to be an Austrian officer and, at all events, to be allowed to appear in audience before our dear Emperor as such, as he could not possibly wear English or Egyptian uniform for that. The alternative would to be appear in civilian clothes which on the one hand he wouldn't mind too much as he doesn't even possess a uniform any more; but, on the other hand, he feels that our sovereign has a very high regard for him and would rather see him as an officer...

And Rudolf, in his own letter to Heinrich about his eagerly-awaited and much-postponed return to Vienna, writes:

Perhaps you might find it a good idea to inform one of the newspapers that I am *forced* to go on to England—so that I shan't be accused of lack of patriotism...

It was strangely prophetic, this anxiousness of the hero who had yet to present himself to the two Empires with claims upon him. He had patriotism enough, and to spare, for each and either of them separately. The question eventually was: could he, or anyone, have patriotism enough for both of them together?

But all this lay far ahead. In that first hectic spring and summer of his freedom, Slatin's only thoughts were of perquisites and not of politics. To have a foot in two mighty camps at one and the same time was a splendid way to climb the ladder, provided one kept a fastidious balance. Of the forthcoming honours themselves, he was quite confident. Marie, in another letter sent to brother Heinrich on his behalf from Cairo on 24 April, writes:

Rudolf says could you send him the full-sized war medal as well as the miniature of the same he has already asked for? In the new uniform—which incidentally isn't yet quite ready—his breast is so naked that he wants to cover it up a bit while awaiting further and similar decorations . . .

On 22 May, the sisters wrote their last letters from Cairo. Twittering with excitement, they were now preparing to sail for home. The most precious item of clothing they were packing was also the roughest – the Arab cloak in which Rudolf had made his flight. They were taking it to Vienna as an advance token of the great man himself, whose arrival in Austria they announced for early July.

According to the family letters, Rudolf duly arrived in Vienna after nearly seventeen years' absence on Sunday 7 July. He had a rapturous welcome from the government, the municipality, the learned societies and the press. There was the expected cascade of invitations to attend dinner parties and address meetings. But he could only spare a fortnight for this reunion with his native city. By the 23rd at the latest, he had to leave for London, where the Geographical Society was giving a reception in his honour and where Edward Arnold, his principal publisher, was awaiting him for discussions.

Ludicrous though it sounded, it was almost a question on this occasion, of fitting the Emperor Franz Joseph in. At all events, Slatin had written, three weeks ahead of his arrival, another of his anxious queries to brother Heinrich on this topic: might it be possible, as it was his duty to present himself to the Emperor, for him to be received between 8 July and 20 July or, if not, would there be remonstrations if he left Vienna without seeing the Emperor? Indeed, could he leave at all without doing so?

There is no record in this particular correspondence as to whether the Emperor did receive him during this fortnight. One would like to think that he did. Even more one would like to believe that it was on this occasion that Slatin remarked to his nephew while nervously dressing to go to the Imperial palace:

How frightened I am about this audience—more than on my escape. You're too young to realize what it means to appear in front of the Emperor Franz Joseph!

Brother Rudolf's next letter to his family that year, though it also came from an Imperial house, sounded much more cosy and relaxed. It was dated 20 August 1895 from Osborne on the

Isle of Wight. It was evidently written just after breakfast and began:

As the Queen's guest, I sit here in my elegant sleeping quarters, next to the splendid bed I have just got out of and have to report to you that both the dinner and the audience went off very well ...

The tone of complacent bliss which this letter sounded was understandable. For Slatin's main target in hurrying to England was not the Geographical Society with its fulsome compliments, nor even Edward Arnold with his fat contracts. It was old Queen Victoria herself. He had begun his long-range courtship of her from Cairo, only a few weeks after his escape. Its spectacular success, when they met was, for her, one of the last charms of a life that was now ending. For him, it was the foundation stone of the life that was just beginning.

Slatin himself did not describe these events, nor indeed any others after his flight. *Fire and Sword* ends abruptly in March 1895. It is true that, from then on right down until his death, he kept diaries, which have all survived. But the later diaries have long gaps in them, often of several weeks at a time, and at one juncture of several years. Even when the pages are consecutively filled, they are basically factual records of his travels while on duty, and bare, incomplete lists of his social engagements while on leave. Only rarely does a comment or an opinion appear; never emotion or anything approaching a philosophy.

Much more of himself comes out in his letters to his family and his closest friends. But, for the next twenty-five years at any rate, even these give an incomplete picture of his activities, let alone his thoughts. The family letters are jovial and affectionate but mostly superficial. The occasional guarded references in them to really serious issues make it clear that, rather than correspond about these, the brothers and sisters preferred to save them up to discuss in private at their annual reunions. As for the English friends that now began to come into his life, there was no need to write to them because, at this stage, they were always with him. It is in their letters however – and above all in the papers of the Royal Archives at Windsor – that Slatin's meteoric progress is mirrored.

It was Wingate who established Slatin's first indirect contact with Queen Victoria. The English officer had been made a

Companion of the Bath (CB) in the Birthday Honours List for 1895* and, on 27 May of that year, he wrote to the Queen's Secretary, Colonel Bigge, to express his gratitude at this 'most delightful surprise'. Then came the following passage:

Should Her Majesty be interested in Slatin Pasha's flight, perhaps she would deign to accept the enclosed small souvenir of a very eventful period of his life. The apparently blank and rather soiled paper is Slatin's last letter dated a month before he escaped from Omdurman; he wrote it in the invisible ink which we managed to send him by trusted Arabs who took it openly in a small bottle with a chemist's label marked in Arabic, 'Medicine for fever, to be taken three times a day'. The letter was written in German and if the paper is exposed over a fire it will become legible—I enclose a rough translation . . .

Then, after a glowing personal tribute to Slatin who had 'borne all his hardships wonderfully well' and who was now 'an absolutely invaluable addition' to the Intelligence Department, Wingate adds simply that the Austrian 'will probably be in London in July. . . .'

It was an irresistible morsel for that most august and jaded of palates. One can imagine the old lady holding up Slatin's scrap of paper herself to a lamp or a candle and watching the words appear. The sovereign's appetite had been whetted; and that, almost certainly, was the object of Wingate's letter.

When the two friends duly met up in London in July, there was an almost immediate invitation from Edward Prince of Wales for Slatin to come to Marlborough House 'to have some conversation with him'. But the Queen, then at Osborne on the Isle of Wight, was proving more elusive, as a letter written there by Bigge to Wingate on 25 July shows. (It also suggests incidentally that Wingate had been prodding the Queen's Secretary as hard as he decently could on Slatin's behalf.) Bigge writes:

Possibly the Queen may ask to see Slatin later on. Her Majesty has had such a busy tiring season that she does not feel inclined at present to see anyone unless it is absolutely necessary. But I shall remind H.M. again. Pray understand it is not from any failure to appreciate Slatin's most marvellous experiences and his wonderful

---

* The Queen's birthday was on 24 May.

escape ... Selfishly speaking I would give anything to see and hear him and yourself. I note your address after the 3rd.

The message the pair were waiting so eagerly for must have just caught Wingate before he moved to that new address. On 1 August Bigge wrote again from Osborne saying that the Queen 'would much like' to receive them there 'some day after the 13th of this month'. The Queen's curiosity, stimulated perhaps by reports that her son had sent her about this intriguing Austrian, had overcome her fatigue.

The next fortnight was filled for Slatin and Wingate with excited preparations. These were quite a task in themselves, as the further detailed instructions from Bigge showed. They were to bring, apart from ordinary suits 'of any sort you like', frock coats or a black morning coat 'in case the Queen wishes to see either of you by day'; for dinner, an evening coat and waistcoat with knee breeches, black stockings and pumps were required, 'with all the decorations you possess'. Realizing that they might not have all these items, the worthy Bigge sends the name of his London tailor, 'who knows all about them' and even offers to help out with pairs of tights and stockings from his own wardrobe.

The great occasion came on Monday, 19 August 1895, when, according to the splendid card which Slatin preserved – with many such others – until the end of his life, he was invited 'to dine at Osborne ... and remain until the following day'.

Apart from that brief note, already mentioned, to his brother, Slatin seems to have written nothing about these twenty-four hours which launched him on his social career (though he must have talked of nothing else for weeks). Fortunately Queen Victoria was a more conscientious diarist. She helps to fill the gap with her entry for that day:

After dinner, I decorated Major Wingate with the C.B. Had a great deal of conversation with him and Slatin Pasha, which was most interesting. The latter is a charming and modest little man, whom no-one could think had gone through such vicissitudes; but there are lines in his face which betoken mental suffering. His final escape was quite miraculous ...

Slatin Pasha gave me a small private account of his escape. Major Wingate is a very clever distinguished officer and his great friend.

They generally speak Arabic together as Slatin knows no English and very little French, whilst Major Wingate cannot speak German...

The Queen's reference to the language is a little puzzling. Slatin certainly knew basic conversational English by this time, and Wingate knew some German (he was, after all, supposed to be translating *Fire and Sword* into English from that language, though this may well have been essentially a cover for his editorial function). However the Queen spoke in private audience with Slatin, the table talk was presumably in English. For the two men to speak Arabic at any length in front of her would have been an unpardonable blunder. But perhaps a few words mumbled apologetically in that tongue, to clear up some abstruse point, and immediately translated for her benefit, might have added to that 'mystique' on which the success of the meeting so depended.

That it was a great success is clear, not only from the Queen's own account, but from the message which Bigge sent on her behalf to the departed guests almost as soon as they reached the mainland. On 20 August, the day they left Osborne, he wrote to Wingate:

The Queen was delighted and much interested in your and Slatin's visit, and H.M. wishes to see the latter again before he leaves England. This will necessitate his going to Balmoral...

Then comes the real measure of Slatin's first impact on the English court. Bigge goes on:

Her Majesty, Princess Louise and Princess Beatrice would much like to have a photograph of Slatin—please ask him to send these...

And another message to Wingate, sent three weeks later by the hand of Sir Fleetwood Edwards* from Balmoral, takes the matter much further. By this time Slatin appears to have returned for a few weeks to Austria, for Wingate is asked to telegraph him and say 'that the Queen is anxious that he should have his portrait painted for H.M. while he is at Vienna by the well-known painter, Herr Angeli, or, failing him by Herr Sohn'. Wingate was told that the Queen's German Secretary was communicating direct with Herr Angeli to get in touch with Slatin

---

* Lt. Col. the Rt. Hon. Sir Fleetwood Edwards, Keeper of the Privy Purse.

on the matter, as Her Majesty wanted a start made 'as soon as possible'. She had even made up her mind how she would like Slatin to sit. The portrait was to be 'life size, head and shoulders and in his Dervish dress'.

Why had the old Queen, then in her seventy-sixth year, taken such a romantic fancy to this Viennese lieutenant of General Gordon's? The reasons lay partly with the late lamented General Gordon, but largely with the Viennese lieutenant himself.

As already described, nobody in England had been more shocked and outraged by the defeat and death of Gordon than England's sovereign. It was to her not merely an almost unendurable slight on England's prestige, of which Gordon had made himself the potent if unofficial symbol. As the savage Mahdi had been his conqueror and killer, the Khartoum disaster had also been a betrayal of what, in her eyes, was England's sacred mission in the world: 'to protect the poor natives and advance civilization'. However naïve and sanctimonious such sentiments may seem today, they were passionately and sincerely held by most of Victoria's own Victorians, and especially those who administered her great Empire for her. So deep indeed had the humiliation of Khartoum burned in the Queen's breast that even after the campaign to avenge it had been successfully launched and Gladstone himself had died, she still could not bring herself to forgive him. Her own private epitaph on her late Prime Minister accepted that he had been 'a clever man, full of talent'. But then came the failing which, for the Queen, barred any claim to his being called a great Englishman: 'He never tried to keep up the honour and prestige of Gt Britain.' And, as a prime example of this, the three stinging words: 'He abandoned Gordon.'

If that was the old Queen's mood in 1898, when vengeance in the Sudan was already in sight, how much fiercer must it have been three years earlier, when she first gave her gloved hand to Slatin Pasha. And how welcome then must he and his gallant deliverer, Major Wingate, have appeared in her eyes. They were, after all, the first living proof she had seen of a blow that England had managed to strike back at the tyrant of Omdurman, the first sweet harbingers of revenge. Even had Slatin been dumb, *gauche* and repulsive, Osborne would have accorded him a civil welcome.

He was, of course, the very opposite of all these things; and here, in his own natural talents, lies the other half of his success story. The sense of humour that had somehow spluttered on through twelve years of desert captivity fairly crackled in the gracious freedom of the Isle of Wight. And if his native wit and his silver tongue could charm even the sullen and suspicious Khalifa, what could they not achieve with this kindly old English lady who was all agog to hear his adventures? Slatin – like Disraeli, a fellow-Jew – knew how to flatter women. And, like the staunch Austrian monarchist he was, he simply adored sovereigns.

There must have also been a strong personal, as well as political, element in the Queen's attachment to Slatin. Pressed hard down under her crown, fluttering somewhere among all those widow's veils, was a suppressed love of the exotic. The extraordinary career at her court of Abdel Karim, one of the two Indian servants presented to her at her Jubilee eight years before, testified to that. When Slatin first arrived at Osborne, this wily young man was approaching the zenith of his influence, having graduated from teaching the Queen how to speak Hindustani to suggesting to her how to rule India. There was about the Queen's 'Munshi', as he was eventually styled, that same mysterious east-of-Suez whiff that Slatin brought with him from the Nubian desert. Just as with Slatin, Victoria had also commissioned von Angeli to paint her a special portrait of her precious little Indian retainer.

The fact that Slatin, in addition to being of Jewish blood, was also of relatively humble birth was certainly no handicap in the sovereign's eyes. Indeed, this could, at her court, be a distinct advantage, as the career of her Highland servant, the imperious and controversial John Brown, had shown. Brown had died only three years before Slatin's arrival on the scene and the Queen's deep anguish and her tribute, 'He became my best and truest friend, as I was his', proved that one did not have to possess blue blood to capture the sovereign's confidence or her affection. As her life without Albert dragged on and on, through decades that were half gold and half lead, she seems to have become acutely bored with courtiers as such and especially with some of the stuffier examples supplied by the aristocratic 'inner circle'. Some impish Till Eulenspiegel like Slatin, who could make merry circles around them all, ripping some of their stuffing out as he went along, was a gift from heaven. And, unlike poor Eulenspiegel, who played one trick too many, Slatin never went too far.

This was the condition which the Queen demanded without ever stating, and which he fulfilled without even trying. Slatin was impish without impiety. His native sense of fun and sheer animal high spirits were both contained, however convulsively, by his worship of monarchs and monarchy as such. Yet though he respected etiquette and protocol and understood their deeper meaning, he was always capable of seizing them suddenly by the waist and waltzing away with them. (He was, incidentally, a superb dancer.)

Off the dance floor as well as on it, Slatin never in fact seems to have put a foot wrong. He was totally unpredictable yet totally safe. With him the old Queen soon felt at ease, yet never stopped being curious. To cap it all (and this was where Slatin went one better than the Munshi, John Brown and even Disraeli) she could talk to him and write to him in dear Albert's German, which was also his native tongue. What more could the ageing matriarch of Windsor, Balmoral and Osborne want, this matriarch who still had in her something of the romantic maiden of Kensington Palace?

There were some weeks to spare before Slatin could expect the summons to Balmoral, and his letters suggest that he left for Vienna towards the end of August and spent most of September 1895 back in Austria. He was certainly there on 3 September, for a little poem of his has survived which he personally handed over that day to his brother Heinrich together with a long-delayed wedding present. The thirty-line colloquial jingle is untranslatable and not worth the labour anyway, for both the style and the sentiments are almost embarrassingly sticky. It was typical of a man who was nine parts heart and one part intellect. This is not, perhaps, the ideal blend but a far better mixture than the other way round.

Slatin's more serious literary efforts during these weeks at home were devoted to finishing his book. He seems to have written the final chapter, describing his flight, in Vienna, so that when he set out for England again at the end of September the whole manuscript of *Fire and Sword* was off his hands at last. That one book was as far as he was ever prepared to go towards putting some literary laurels on his brow. A more pressing problem – and one he was to pursue with unflagging gusto for the next twenty years – was how to get some decorations pinned on his chest. This, as he had pointed out to his brother in that message from Cairo five months earlier, looked painfully naked for a hero.

The forthcoming visit to Balmoral was the obvious occasion to get something done about it, and again it is the faithful Wingate who starts the ball rolling. On 30 September 1895, the Queen received a letter from Lord Wolseley enclosing a recommendation to him from Major Wingate that Slatin Pasha might receive 'some English decoration or medal'. In terms of services already rendered by Slatin, it was perhaps a bit early for this, since the campaign to reconquer the Sudan with him as an adviser had not even been launched, let alone won. But we know from the reports to Vienna of the Austrian mission in Cairo that Slatin, soon after his escape, had turned down an offer to enter the Khedive's service in order to take up his intelligence post with the English. This may well have been why Wolseley felt justified in supporting the proposal. (In view of the success Slatin was known to have had with the Queen, it might anyway have been imprudent as well as useless to object.)

At all events, ten days after the Queen received Wolseley's recommendation, Slatin and Wingate arrived at Balmoral 'to stay for 2 or 3 days'. Within a few hours Slatin was personally invested by the sovereign with the Military CB. He had brought something for her as well, 'a chronometer watch which really is the only object of value and interest which has been recovered from the Mahdi'. Having sought permission to do so the previous day, he presented the Mahdi's watch to her on 12 October, and, as the Queen recorded in her Journal, stayed for 'some very interesting conversation ... which unfortunately I have not the time to write down'. It was the mixture as at Osborne – a souvenir of his adventures in the Sudan and some vivid talk about the situation there. Only this time, Slatin had handed over his souvenir in person and the talk appears to have been more private. The Queen already had an unofficial 'Indian Secretary' in the Munshi. In Slatin she was now acquiring an unofficial Sudan Secretary as well. The first link in this chain was forged by the Balmoral visit of October 1895.

Balmoral was to become from now on the principal stage for Slatin's appearances at the English court. For the next twenty years, so long as Queen Victoria lived and then in the reigns of her son and grandson, Slatin's visits there became almost annual events. He soon came to regard them as the climax to his social calendar; and when, in the dust and heat of a Sudan summer, he thought of his adopted English sovereign and his adopted English homeland, it was the picture of this royal castle sprawling across the green valley of the Dee that he conjured up first of all.

But however much he mused about it, he never wrote about it. All his diary references over the years to his stays at Balmoral are in his usual style of terse factual entries enlivened only by bouts of comic spelling. Fortunately, it is possible to recreate the atmosphere of the Balmoral life that Slatin was introduced to in the autumn of 1895 from several contemporary English accounts.

Queen Victoria had purchased the castle early in her reign from the Scottish landowner, Sir Richard Gordon, and the Balmoral which Slatin saw had been totally rebuilt and refurnished by her forty years before, while her beloved Prince Albert was still alive. It could scarcely be called a dream castle, even by the most loyal of courtiers. The exterior was impressive rather than beautiful; the interior uncomfortable as well as plain. Lord Rosebery, for example, once declared that though he had always believed the drawing-room at Osborne to be the ugliest in the whole world, he had promptly changed his mind on seeing the drawing-room at Balmoral. The furniture throughout the house was of the heavily-ornamented mid-Victorian style with splashes of tartan decoration struggling here and there to relieve the gloom of these dark mahogany jungles.

Unlike other jungles, this one was freezing cold as well. The Queen positively hated fires, declaring that 'heat is unwholesome'. Even the hardened regular members of her Household got blue with cold during their stays at this icy Highland palace, whose different wings were separated by such enormous corridors that the inhabitants used to communicate with each other by letter. What Slatin must have felt, his blood thinned by nearly twenty years of African sun, can only be imagined. Doubtless he protected himself as best he could by following Disraeli's well-known advice to all Balmoral guests: 'Never miss a chance to sit down or to close a door.'

Fatigue was in fact as big an enemy as the draughts. There was interminable standing about, especially after dinner when waiting for the Queen to retire. One Balmoral guest of the Slatin era, the physician Sir Douglas Powell, fainted clean away under the strain and had to be carried from the drawing-room. The Queen's only remark, on being told the reason for the commotion, was a scornful: 'And a doctor too!' (She was never quite convinced that doctors were gentlemen, and it was not until the 1880s that her Resident Physician at Balmoral was allowed to dine with the Household.)

Nor was there any free-and-easy holiday atmosphere to compensate for all these trials. Balmoral, though a horribly inconvenient six hundred miles from London, was very much a working court. During the long weeks and months that the Queen spent there each year, it became the remote centre of the Empire, with the dispatch-boxes constantly being loaded and unloaded off the trains at near-by Ballater Station, with ministers, generals, ambassadors and archbishops coming and going amidst the flux of the Queen's personal guests, and with the royal telegraph wires to Westminster and the overseas dominions humming non-stop.

The Queen's daily routine set the life of the whole castle like some imperial metronome whose tick was heard and obeyed from the stables to the highest turret. It rarely varied. She took breakfast in her apartments at 9.45 a.m. and then worked on official documents until noon. She then went out to take the air for a while, and only after she had left the castle dare anyone else show their nose out of doors. Lunch was at two, followed by coffee in the Billiard Room. The Queen rested, and the castle around her, until three-thirty when she would again drive out, usually in her pony cart. Slatin would have found an invitation to accompany her on foot on one of these excursions almost as exhausting as trotting behind the Khalifa's horse. The royal cart did a steady four m.p.h. up and down moorland and mountains. It was not easy, trying to keep up with it, to save any breath for conversation.

Tea was served on the Queen's return to the castle at five-thirty, and from six until dinner was served at nine in the evening, the guests, at any rate, were left to their own devices. At her own dinner table (there were three others: the Household's, the upper servants' and the lower servants') the menus on all normal occasions were as regular as the rest of the routine. It was always boiled beef as the main dish on Thursday, for example, and a pineapple pudding to end up with on Friday. All the menus at all the tables were decided by the Queen, just as she regulated every other minute detail of the castle's life. Even the eighteen ponies of Balmoral were divided by her into five categories, and a pony in each category allotted every day to its user.

Apart from amateur theatricals (with the Queen not only supervising production but even rewriting the play if it annoyed her) and occasional concerts and musical entertainments arranged by Signor (later Sir) Paolo Tosti, there was not much in the way of indoor distractions to enliven the tedium. The men could smoke, but only well out of the Queen's sight, and provided the smell never reached the royal nostrils. The Billiard Room, where Slatin would light his cigar with the others after the Queen had retired, was regarded by her as little better than a late night opium den.

There were state balls, of course, when special guests like visiting royalty were present. But only once a year did Balmoral under Queen Victoria really burst into life. This was for the annual Ghillies Ball which was a riotous, almost a bacchanalian affair compared with the normally leaden atmosphere of the castle. She never missed one, even if it meant ignoring a frantic appeal from her ministers to return to London. Furthermore, until a few years before Slatin's arrival on the scene, she was still dancing reels at them (there is a record of her joining in an informal dance at the castle as late as 1891, when she was seventy-two). She would dance with factors and servants as well as with courtiers and guests. The whisky drinking, especially after she had happily retired, was prodigious. It was her annual concession to that animal frenzy which lay beneath the dour surface of the Highlands.

Slatin would have found the outdoor attractions of Balmoral much more varied. Some he would have to learn, like the reels. The newfangled sport of bicycling could easily be tried out, for the roads in the valley were as flat as plates. Then there was golf, another unfamiliar sport. Boating could be had in fine weather and salmon fishing in any weather. Then there was riding; and the Queen herself had ridden as late as 1890, mounting a docile beast twenty-six years old by means of a long ladder. But the chief sport of the castle was deer-stalking, with the ghillies dancing around the carcases by torchlight in the evening. Both the stalking and these dervish-like celebrations over the prey afterwards were closer to Slatin's Sudan experience – though not the full bottle of whisky handed to each guest as he set out.

Such was Victorian Balmoral in the 1890s. Slatin would still have loved it had icicles formed on the mantelpieces, and had there been not an ounce of gaiety to lighten the stuffiness and not a moment of excitement to relieve the monotony. Unlike the Household, he was only there for a few days at a time. During these short spells, the mere presence of the Queen of England in the same bleak building was drama and warmth enough for him. And, as he well knew, the mere fact of his own presence there was credential enough for the rest of Europe.

The visit of October 1895, for example, had an immediately gratifying effect a thousand miles away.

One thing leads to another in the way of medals, especially when, though serving one Empire, you are in fact the citizen of another. The court at Vienna could not now very well sit back and do nothing after the Queen of England had personally invested one of its loyal subjects, more or less over her Balmoral tea-table, with a coveted decoration. A letter Wingate wrote to Bigge a few weeks later, when he was back in Khartoum with Slatin, takes up the story:

Slatin is very well ... You know he has been decorated with the Franz Joseph Order with Star, which I believe is a great honour. He fully realizes that it was the Queen's most gracious act in giving him the C.B. which has brought him the second honour and he is I know most truly grateful; he never ceases to talk with the deepest gratification of his visits to Balmoral and Osborne ...

Then comes a glimpse of Slatin settling into his new life:

He has taken a little house close to mine with stables, garden etc. and he is much occupied in furnishing and arranging and I think I never saw a man happier; after all his hard life a good time has come at last. He will be most useful in the office and is now taking lessons in English ...

And the happy Slatin himself, in a letter written the following day to his 'dear, fat, sister-in-law' in Vienna describes his daily routine as follows:

In the early morning, practise in English letter writing and a few private letters. Then, from 9 a.m. until about 2 p.m. at the War Ministry. From 2-3 at the club for lunch; then home where I throw myself into civilian clothes. As I have nothing particular to do in the afternoons, I'm free until 5 o'clock. At 5.30 my English teacher comes and stays till around 7. Then I slip back into uniform and either eat dinner in the club or attend some invitation ... and with a life like this one is supposed to look fit!

Even that final mock complaint radiates contentment, as well it might. When the New Year of 1895 had dawned, it had found him in his twelfth year of captivity in Omdurman, his escape looming nearer yet still not within grasp. And outside a handful of modest friends and relatives in his native Austria and an even smaller handful of officials in Cairo, Rudolf Slatin was unknown in the world. By Christmas of that same year, his name was known in every civilized capital and his face was familiar in at least two of the grandest of European courts. Abdel Kader, that tattered survivor of Gordon's vanished world, a captive whose neck could be stretched at any moment by the Khalifa's command, had become Colonel Slatin Pasha, CB, guest of Queen Victoria and a key adviser to her Commander-in-Chief in the campaign of revenge that was now approaching. It was a fairy-tale transformation for a mere twelve months to have brought about, almost dream-like in its completeness. The new year of 1896 was to show that, for the courtier, the warrior and the author, the dream was a durable reality.

Chapter Nine

THE QUEEN'S SOLDIER

Nothing was more typical of England's crab-like approach towards the conquest of the Sudan than the event which finally prodded her across the frontier. The impetus came as much from big-power diplomacy in Europe as from big-power rivalry in Africa. The Khalifa became its target only by accident.

For some years past, Italy had been pressing inland from her Red Sea colony of Eritrea and, by 1896, was at war with Abyssinia, who barred her westward thrust. On 1 March of that year, the Emperor Menelik routed the Italian army as it made a rash and premature attack on Adowa. This defeat was serious enough in itself; but disaster threatened if the Mahdist forces in the Sudan were to choose this moment to go to the aid of the Abyssinians and strike at the reeling flank of the Italian army at Kassala. The Italian Government therefore made an urgent appeal in London to strike instantly at the Khalifa from Egypt and so pin him down. England was not allied with Italy (who was indeed a member of what was soon to become the rival grouping, the so-called Triple Alliance with Germany and Austria-Hungary). But the British Prime Minister, Lord Salisbury, wished at the time to conciliate both Rome and Berlin and so sponsored the Italian request. He had anyway been veering slowly for the past few years towards the idea of a more active policy throughout the Nile valley.

Diplomacy, not normally the speediest of machines, worked on this occasion with lightning rapidity. What Queen Victoria and the mass of her subjects had been demanding for years now happened in a matter of days. On 12 March, less than a fortnight after the battle of Adowa, the British Cabinet decided on an expedition to re-occupy at least Dongola, the northern province of the Sudan. Ten days later, Major-General Sir Herbert Kitchener, the Sirdar (Commander-in-Chief) of the Egyptian Army, left Cairo for his operational headquarters at Wadi Halfa. With him went that Sudan 'duo' of Osborne and Balmoral, Colonel Slatin Pasha and Major Wingate Bey; and two very excited and jubilant men they must have been. They would certainly have been too busy, as they rode off southwards, to reflect on the historical irony of the situation. Eleven years before, when the clamour to avenge General Gordon's death was raging in England, an event far removed from the Sudan had been one of the main factors in preventing any punitive campain being mounted against the Mahdi. The threat of a third Afghan War had suddenly blown up, bringing with it the possibility of trouble with Russia. Black fanatics on the Upper Nile had to take second place to that. Now this same game of European power politics which had held the Anglo-Egyptian army back in 1885 was propelling it forward in 1896.

The re-conquest of the Sudan was accomplished in two separate phases, with a lengthy gap between. The first stage, the recapture of the northern province of Dongola, was over in six months. It did more than just ease the pressure on the beleaguered Italian army in Abyssinia. It committed the British Government irrevocably to the annihilation of the Khalifa's army, the destruction of his Mahdist state and the total occupation of the Sudan. Though there was to be a long interval before this second stage began, it followed as inevitably from the first as night follows day. Public opinion in Britain had accepted only with reluctance the eleven-year postponement of this campaign of retribution. But once battle with the dervishes had been joined, no British Government which did not finish it off triumphantly could have survived in office.

This battle can be viewed afresh, after more than seventy years, in dozens of unpublished private letters written from the Sudan battlefield by Slatin and Wingate respectively to Queen Victoria and to her secretary, Sir Arthur Bigge.

It is important that the two lots of letters should be taken together, both as regards their eyewitness accounts of the campaign and their comments on it. Slatin who, throughout his whole career, took no major step without consulting his mentor, would obviously have submitted these very first ventures of his into high politics for Wingate's approval. (Wingate was in any case his immediate chief, despite the topsy-turvyness of their relative ranks when the expedition began.) It seems likely that, for his part, Wingate either showed Slatin what he was writing to Bigge or at least informed him of the gist of it. The whole correspondence was in fact a continuation of that combined propaganda campaign which the two men had launched on British public opinion with *Fire and Sword* and on the British sovereign with their visits at court. Now, however, this pressure was strictly secret, strictly personal and concentrated entirely on Queen Victoria and her entourage.

Amidst the wealth of diverting anecdotes and chit-chat which these letters contain, the authors develop at least three very serious themes as well. The first is the need to free the whole Sudan from the Khalifa's grip, not merely as an act of retribution for Gordon's death but as a mission of civilization against what they believed to be barbarism personified. The second is the plea for more and more English troops, as opposed to merely officers, to accomplish this mission. The third is to present the Sudan in its wider strategic context which, the writers feared, may have been underestimated at home – its vital importance as the cross-roads of Central Africa, a cross-roads that England must reach and occupy before any of her European rivals (above all France) get there before her. It is easy today to smile at the way in which, nearly a century ago, officers of Wingate's stamp could so fervently sing the praises of civilization to the strains of 'Rule Britannia'. But to them the song made sense. In the secure and self-satisfied world of the Pax Britannica, it was indeed the only song which did make sense.

Slatin's battlefield reports to the Queen are all in German and all but the first are written in the old German Gothic *Schrift* (a beautiful and easily readable copperplate *Schrift* however, and quite unlike the tiny scrawl of his diaries). They begin out of the blue on 12 May 1896, with a flourish of Central European trumpets:

Your Majesty!
Following the All-highest sympathy which Your Majesty has
deigned to take in my fate, I make so bold, in deepest homage, to
present these lines for your gracious consideration ...

As his later correspondence makes quite clear, Slatin had not
yet received formal approval from the Queen to report directly
to her. It can only be assumed that he had been informally
encouraged to do so during that triumphant visit to Balmoral
the previous autumn. An opening sentence of that sonorous-
ness was, in any case, almost a credential in itself.

There are a few details in this first letter about military
skirmishes, but most of it is politics. Slatin reports to the Queen,
for example, on the mood of the army:

The troops' morale is in general quite good. One or two Arab
publications are trying, for political motives, to stir up feeling against
England and the English officers in the expedition. They try to make
out that the soldiers are victims of an English policy which only
aims at sacrificing them on behalf of Christians (this in view of the
fact that the reason for the expedition was to ease the position of the
Italians at Kassala). But most of our Egyptian officers see these
articles as being inspired, not by patriotic feeling but by agitation
financed by France ... However, the postal authorities have been
forbidden to forward any of the journals concerned to these officers.

France is thus identified from the start as England's arch-
enemy. A little lower down comes the strategic calculation:

What will happen after the occupation of Dongola depends on
God and Your Majesty's Government. However, I permit myself
to hope that the whole Sudan will be snatched from the Mahdists
before the European powers (France or the Belgian Congo state)
succeed in establishing a foothold in the south of the country.

And then the first gentle hints as to what the Queen should
do about it: there is great stress laid on the fact that the
expedition is only supposed 'for the time being' to be a purely
Egyptian one, and orders are thus being issued 'for the moment
only' in the name of the Khedive. The assumption, no less loud
for being unspoken, is that England must soon take over
formally.

Though the writer would not want to be anywhere else in
the world at that moment than riding south in the Khalifa's

domains, the occasion is also not neglected to stir up a little compassion in the old monarch's breast:

I was planning to spend this summer in Europe, to enjoy those blessings of civilization of which I was so long deprived. God's will has decreed however that instead of northwards I go southwards back into the land where I have suffered so much...

An appeal to the same deity 'to give Your Majesty and Your illustrious family long life and health' concludes Slatin's first royal epistle.

There could not have been much doubt as to how this mixture of adulation and information would go down. Any uncertainty Slatin may have felt was dispelled by a hand-written personal reply which the Queen wrote him (also in German) from Balmoral on 5 June 1896. In this she thanks him 'most warmly' for his report. She goes on:

I hope that the campaign will go well and that you will remain in good health and unharmed. I have read your letter with tremendous (*ungeheuer*) interest and am horrified to see what you have been through.

And the Queen signs herself: 'Ever your well-wisher Victoria R. I.' It was a capital start to the Slatin-Wingate operation.

Wingate himself, writing to Bigge from Wadi Halfa at the end of May, is more down to earth, explaining the two basic communications problems of the campaign: the state of the railway being built specially to supply the expedition and the state of the Nile, on which the progress of this army, like all who had crossed these deserts before it, had to depend. He points out that, for the final advance on Dongola, the railway must be pushed down at least as far as Firket for it was there the new stern-wheeler vessels were being put together.

Ten days later, he is already writing to Bigge from Firket. The place had been taken from the Khalifa's troops forty-eight hours before in an easy operation 'which resembled rather a field day than the stern reality'. One of the reasons for this had been the 'indefatigable' intelligence work of Slatin who was now interrogating the prisoners, 'deep in conversation with some of his old friends, picking up the threads, so to speak, since his departure 1½ years ago. . . .'

From Wingate as well comes a touch of nostalgia at the end:

I see that you are at Balmoral again. The mere thought of those lovely mountains seems to cool and refresh one, and Slatin and I often talk of you . . .

On 20 June, the two friends fired off a real combined salvo towards those far-distant 'lovely mountains'. First, Wingate gave Bigge a fuller account of the victory. After telling him that fifty-six of the ninety enemy emirs had been killed and another six had been captured wounded, Wingate went on to estimate the importance of the battle for the campaign in general:

From the scanty information which has reached us from Dongola, the effect there is great and Wad Bishara, the emir, is anxiously awaiting the Khalifa's instructions. If the latter can send him reinforcements (which is doubtful) he will probably make an attempt to remain until we drive him out when the river rises and we have our steamers; but if no reinforcements can be sent from Omdurman, I do not think they will be strong enough to face us, and they may go. You can imagine therefore with what anxiety we watch the river which is now rising about 1 or 2 inches a day. It is still very low and I think at least a month must pass before we can expect to get our steamers up . . .

Slatin's report to the Queen, written the same day, (and probably in the same tent) supplies the human touches to go with this strategic stuff. He tells her how, immediately after the fight, he had ridden out over the battlefield, looking down on the dead bodies of so many of the Khalifa's emirs.

I was moved by strange feelings. I had known many of these men personally during my captivity, and though one or two of them had been friendly, even sympathetic towards me, most had been intent only upon humiliating or annihilating the white race. Now they lay dead before me with shattered limbs—justly punished for their fanaticism in defending an evil cause . . .

And Her Majesty's Austrian officer goes on to assure the Queen that all her English officers had 'fulfilled their duties most thoroughly and, by their excellent behaviour, helped to strengthen the confidence and the goodwill of the native officers and men towards their superiors. . . .'

153

Not content with a long letter each, the two comrades-in-arms, on this same 20 June 1896, also teamed up to send a special joint message to Queen Victoria, and a special memento as well. This was the *jibba* of the Emir Yusef Angar, removed from his body as it lay dead on the battlefield of Firket. The blood and dust of a desert cavalry charge must have entered Balmoral with the emir's cloak when Bigge read Wingate's accompanying words:

You will see from the holes that he must have been killed many times over.

Wingate adds that he and Slatin are making 'this little offer quite privately and personally' as a token of thanks for all the Queen's kindnesses towards them. This was all highly unorthodox, as Wingate himself appreciated when asking Bigge at the end of his letter to keep the whole thing quiet. But it was no less effective for that. One can well imagine, as the old Queen handled this blood-stained dervish garment and counted the lance thrusts in it, how her heart must have warmed to the romance of the Sudan campaign and particularly to her two very personal representatives fighting in it.

Just before getting this grim souvenir of battle, she had already shown personal concern for Slatin's welfare. A private cipher telegram from her secretary to Lord Cromer read:

Suppose all reasonable precautions taken for Slatin's safety, especially as regards possibility of assassination by an emissary of Khalifa under guise of a deserter.

Lord Cromer replied that he would 'draw the Sirdar's special attention to the subject'. The next day, 21 June 1896, he relays General Kitchener's reply:

I don't think there is any cause for alarm as to Slatin's safety. All arrivals from the enemy are carefully examined before entering the camp and kept under guard until the object of their coming is quite clear.

One would not go far wrong in detecting a somewhat astringent note in this assurance. Not only did the Commander-in-Chief quite naturally feel that he could look after the security of his own field headquarters without advice, which was as remote as it was august, from an old lady in Balmoral. The truth was

that, while appreciating Slatin's value in the intelligence sphere,
Kitchener never went overboard for the little Austrian as
Wingate and the Queen had done; indeed, one sometimes gets
the feeling that the general never quite trusted him. Charm was,
to put it mildly, not Kitchener's strong point. Perhaps he was
already a little envious at seeing what it could achieve, when
laid on as thick as Viennese whipped cream in the highest places.

Professional jealousy over their already very privileged position was a problem both Wingate and Slatin now had to face.
In addition, Slatin had to keep the lines clear with his own
government and his own sovereign in Vienna. Franz Joseph was
the Emperor of punctiliousness as well as the Emperor of
Austria-Hungary. He would never have dreamt of asking any
officer of his to report out of proper channels, and would have
dealt a withering rebuke to any officer who had tried. Slatin,
even as a mere Austrian lieutenant of the reserve, was well
aware of this. So he also found time during the first weeks of
this campaign to write to his good friend Baron Heidler, the
head of the Austrian mission in Cairo, with some explanations
clearly intended for Vienna. Heidler did not fail him. On
11 July 1896, the diplomat reported to his Foreign Minister,
Count Goluchowski that, since the beginning of the Sudan
campaign, Queen Victoria had been conducting a regular correspondence with Slatin. Slatin, he adds, had been instructed
by the Queen of England 'to report to her regularly and
personally and with complete frankness about the progress of
the campaign and about events in the military camp. . . .'

And after giving full details about the Queen's concern for
Slatin's safety, and General Kitchener's 'reassuring explanations', Heidler went on:

I gather from hints in Slatin's letter that this royal command
to submit direct reports—which he couldn't very well ignore—has
caused him great embarrassment. Clearly he needs quite a bit of
diplomatic skill to allay and overcome the jealousy of his English
comrades over this pronounced personal regard and concern of the
Queen for him, the only non-English (sic) officer in the Egyptian
army.

The idea of Slatin being forced, almost against his will, to
correspond personally with Queen Victoria, is, of course,

hilarious. But there was no harm at all in Vienna getting that impression.

Meanwhile, the campaign went on. Mile after mile of rail track was driven into the Nubian Desert, and, ahead of this iron supply line, Kitchener's troops probed ever deeper up the Nile towards Dongola. After the victory of Firket, Wingate had urged the abandonment of this cautious 'little by little' strategy and had called for a quick strike at Dongola before the Khalifa could reinforce it. Rightly or wrongly, this advice was not taken. The army moved south only as far as Kosheh. There it sat for some two months, waiting for the famous new gunboats to get this far up-river and join the troops for the final advance.

The long wait at Kosheh produced some of the most delightful of all the many letters that Slatin and Wingate sent back to court. In a twelve-page report to the Queen written in July, for example, Slatin starts off with the military situation and with his own role in undermining the morale of the Khalifa's forces. He tells her how he selected four of the prisoners taken at Firket whom he believed to be genuinely anti-Mahdist and sent them secretly down to Dongola with greetings and promises of pardon to various of the Khalifa's emirs whom he personally knew. The black native troops conscripted into the Khalifa's army were another of Slatin's special propaganda targets. The word was to be spread around in Dongola that their comrades captured at Firkes were being well treated and well fed by the English and had even been given gold for joining up with the victorious expedition.

Then Slatin, knowing that the Queen would anyway get the general military picture from Kitchener's official reports, a picture supplemented by Wingate's private letters to Bigge, produced another string of those human anecdotes which he knew she delighted in. There was first the tale of the four-year-old native girl Kalduma, who had been brought in to Slatin to be re-united with her mother waiting back at Wadi Halfa:

The merry little thing chattered away without a trace of shyness to Wingate and myself, happy at the thought of seeing her mother again. But when I gave her a piece of sugar to eat, she found this so wonderfully sweet and then declared my old and somewhat damaged tent to be so beautiful that she had decided to stay with me. Only after I had assured her that her mother had plenty of sugar and had given her a few pieces more for the journey anyway could the little thing be persuaded to put herself under the charge of a transport officer and leave. Poor ignorant child who, in her ignorance, would have abandoned her own mother for a lump of sugar.

After this came another very pungent whiff of Slatin's own homesickness, a longing, in this case, for England. He told the Queen that he had just received, in Kosheh of all places, a copy of the London *Ladies' Pictorial*. In it he had seen pictures of many members of the English aristocracy ('among them the Countess of Kintor and her two daughters') who, like himself, had also had 'the honour of being received in Your Majesty's drawing room'. And then off he went, on a strain that could never fail to appeal:

What a difference between the sandy hills of Dongola and that capital, the centre of civilization, where Your Majesty resides. May all peoples learn to appreciate the blessings of a well-ordered society!

To top it all off, he ends this particular report from the battlefield by telling the Queen about his very first race bet. Wagers had been laid at Wadi Halfa on that year's English Derby. Though, Slatin explains, he had never in his life been a betting man, he couldn't resist a wager on Persimmon because he had noticed that it was the Prince of Wales's horse. And now, in Kosheh, he had learned that Persimmon had won, and had brought him in 150 guineas in winnings.* It wasn't the money that had made him so happy, Slatin emphasizes, 'but the thought that the owner of the horse is Your Majesty's son'. As the Queen violently disapproved of betting and of the entire English 'racing set', Slatin's explanation was either lucky or nicely calculated.

The stranded little Kalduma, the *Ladies' Pictorial* and the Ascot triumph of Persimmon. It all made a wonderful change from the usual military stuff, which was either grim or grey. And it all helped to establish Slatin's own position with the old Queen as being, in his own eyes at any rate, almost 'one of the family'.

Not that there was any lack of grim things to write about.

---

* As Persimmon won at 5–1, Slatin's bet must have been twenty-five guineas, a very considerable wager for a man of his means.

Slatin had only touched on the cholera menace in this letter of 22 July. Wingate, writing to Bigge five days later, filled in the details:

It gradually crept up, station after station becoming infected, and Halfa worst of all, but fortunately there were not many troops there and civilians and the wives of the black soldiers suffered the most . . . Soon it attacked this camp and for the first few days it looked as though we were going to have a very bad time, but we all moved away from the river and camped in the desert . . .

On Saturday, cholera broke out among the troops working at railhead which has now reached the scene of the Firket fight (7 miles from here) . . . The troops whilst working in the desert were wonderfully well but so delighted were they to arrive at the river again that they had a great plunge into the water which was no doubt infected at that spot. Six cases occurred almost immediately and poor Fenwick and Trask were attacked; they were both at work in the morning and were both dead before 5 o'clock and buried an hour or two later . . .

There was another month of this grim game of hide-and-seek with cholera before the Nile at last rose high enough for the steamers to reach them. On 25 August Wingate writes again to Bigge describing the joy with which, two days previously, they had watched six steamers gaily decked with flags steaming up the broad Kosheh reach, somewhat battered in the cataracts but otherwise sound. As for the new stern-wheeler they were building at Kosheh, with 12-pounder and 6-pounder guns 'to startle the dervishes at Dongola', it towered like a leviathan over the armada of little gunboats.

Wingate was just going on to discuss the strategic question of how hard the Khalifa's garrison at Dongola would fight and whether he would reinforce it, when a violent storm struck the camp. The squall plucked at the office tent where he, Slatin and the Italian Military Attaché, Count Trombi, were 'all scribbling together' and abruptly ended work for the night. As Wingate described it when he returned to his letter the following morning:

All hands turned out to seize the ropes and keep it from blowing away, but whilst doing this Slatin and I had the mortification of seeing the wind lift our large sleeping tent and dash it to the ground, scattering our effects in all directions. After half an hour, the violence

abated and ... we walked down to the river bank to see how the
steamers had fared. Scarcely had we got there than the wind, which
had been blowing from the West, suddenly veered round to the
North and brought upon us the most awful sandstorm I have ever
seen. We tried to make our way back to where we believed our camp
was, but the clouds of sand made the atmosphere almost as black as
night and we were obliged to stand for half an hour exposed to all
its fury; then came a moment's cessation and we found that the
Headquarters tents were scarcely ten yards from where we were
standing. We had just time to rush to them when the hurricane
blew fiercer than ever; the rain poured down in sheets and the
thunder and lightning was incessant. All we could do was to hang
on to the tent ropes drenched to the skin. At length, the wind dropped a little and enabled us to get back to the Intelligence Camp,
which is pitched on a slight eminence. Here we found the office
tent had blown down and the papers and maps were blowing away
to Dongola. We saved what we could and then collected our dripping
employees, gave them some quinine, food and drink, and spent the
night as best we could.

This wild, wet and sleepless night may have caused havoc
among the intelligence records but it did not dull Wingate's
mind. Lucid and industrious as ever, he goes on in his inter-
rupted letter to deal with the other topics of the day. The first
was an extraordinary message which had just been delivered at
the camp addressed to 'Abel Kader Slatin' and sent by none
other than his former master in Omdurman, the Khalifa. It was
a very belated response to the letter Slatin had written to him
a few days after escaping to Cairo sixteen months before. In
this, Slatin, trying if possible to save his servants from the
Khalifa's wrath, had solemnly explained that the only reason for
his sudden departure from Omdurman had been the need to
visit his relatives, a favour which had been persistently refused.
However, Slatin had added, putting his tongue further in his
cheek, he was still a loyal adherent of the Khalifa's and of the
Islamic faith.

Referring to this last pledge, the Khalifa now replied:

As you have come with the infidels, make the necessary stratagem
which will enable us to take them at a disadvantage. The Moslem
armies are at this time advancing against them. All that I wish to
tell you now is to take the necessary steps in deep secrecy...

Whereas Slatin's words had been entirely bogus, it is just possible that the Khalifa meant what he wrote, even if he placed little hope in it. At all events, whatever was in the Khalifa's mind, there was already evidence that several of his lieutenants were beginning to hedge their bets. Wingate goes on to report that one of his agents who had recently done a spell in Omdurman prison had been visited privately there by some of the Khalifa's most trusted emirs. They had asked: 'How is Slatin; is he well and strong?' And on being assured that he was, had added: 'We hope he will soon come with the army to release us.'

Finally in this long report to Bigge, Wingate indulges in a little more of his unofficial but very persuasive international diplomacy. Noting that Bigge is about to go up to Balmoral with the Queen; that the Czar and Czarina of Russia are due there soon on a visit; and that Lord Cromer, on leave from Cairo, may also be among the party, he returns again to the danger of England being outpaced by the other European powers in their march towards the Sudan. He stresses in particular the likelihood of the Belgians moving north from the Congo into the Upper Nile, where the French were already active. If France and Belgium were to be 'at one in that undertaking', it would deal a blow to England. Perhaps, Wingate ends artlessly, 'this might be warded off diplomatically?' It was not a bad independent effort for a mere major (he was not promoted until later that year) on General Kitchener's staff. But then Wingate, like Slatin, was no ordinary intelligence officer.

At last, on 11 September, the whole force moved out of Kosheh for the final drive down to Dongola. It was a difficult march. Even Slatin, writing to the Queen from Fereg on 15 September found little to be chirpy or chatty about this time. The expedition had just gone through some very hard days, he tells her, after the briefest of protocol greetings. Cholera, the slow rising of the Nile and finally the destruction of more than twelve miles of the railway line by thunderstorms had all contributed to hold up the advance.

Even that giant stern-wheeler gunboat on which Wingate had pinned such hopes for the assault had let them down. On a trial run the day they had left Kosheh, the boiler had burst before the leviathan had even got under way, and there seemed little hope of getting it in action again for weeks.

The big gunboat would doubtless have come in very useful to silence some enemy cannon that gave the steamers trouble at Hafir, thirty miles north of Dongola, where tough opposition was met. But once the dervishes had been silenced there, Dongola itself fell with relative ease. Kitchener launched his attack on the town at dawn on 23 September 1896. By 10.30 a.m., after barely five hours' fighting, it was entirely in his hands. Wingate telegraphed that morning to Bigge (this time officially and in Kitchener's name) that the dervishes were in full retreat. Many important emirs had surrendered; several guns, quantities of ammunition and loot of all sorts had been captured; and hundreds of prisoners had been taken.

There was some mopping up to do in the weeks that followed, and Kitchener, pushing on a hundred miles southeast to the opposite loop of the Nile, set up an advance post at Merawi, close to the Fourth Cataract. But that, for the time being, was all. The expedition now rested in Dongola and waited for elaborate supply lines to be built up before venturing deeper into the heart of the Mahdist state. Wingate's personal irritation at this delay was doubtless mollified a little by his promotion to Colonel, which came through after the battle of Dongola. As for Slatin, General Kitchener, returning to the Sudan at the end of November after a visit to London and to Windsor Castle, brought back for him something even more precious than promotion: the medal of the Queen's own Victorian Order, accompanied by a five-page personal letter from her. In this letter she tells Slatin she is awarding him the decoration 'in recognition of the splendid services' he had rendered in the campaign to date.

The Queen ended by thanking Slatin for his 'exceptionally informative' letters and his 'interesting gifts' and by saying she hoped to hear soon again. In fact, she heard from him by the Sudan equivalent of the return of post.

'My pen is too weak', Slatin writes, 'to express the grateful feelings which I feel in reverence for Your Majesty.' But the weak pen then goes on at considerable length to try.

Wingate also wrote to Bigge describing Slatin's delight at this personal honour: 'I do not think it amiss to tell you privately that had it not been for the Queen's deep interest in and kindness to Slatin, he would not, in all probability, have remained in Egypt. . . .'

This was overdoing it a bit. Certainly, Wingate was right in saying that one part of Slatin 'rather longs for the rest and quiet of home life in Austria'. But that was not the more important part of the man, at least the man of 1896. The other part of him, the adventurous, ambitious part, knew full well that his bread was being buttered for life with the sands of the Sudan. That being so, there was no point in complaining of the gritty taste.

The long pause that now comes over the battlefield provides a good moment to look back at Slatin's other success in 1896, his emergence as a widely-read author. *Fire and Sword in the Sudan, A Personal Narrative of Fighting and Serving the Dervishes,* appeared almost as Slatin rode out of Wadi Halfa with the expedition. His publisher, Edward Arnold, brought out simultaneous English editions in London and New York. Brockhaus of Leipzig produced, also in 1896, the first of several German editions. French and Italian translations, both taken from the Brockhaus edition, appeared two years later.

Its appearance could not have been better timed. At the very moment when the Sudan leapt into the headlines again, with an English-led army marching at last against the Khalifa, here was a first-hand account of that dervish leader and his realm, written by his former captive who was now riding south at Kitchener's side to take revenge. For Arnold, the coincidence was a publisher's dream. For Wingate, whose vital role in the preparation of the book has already been described, it was a propaganda bull's-eye. That both the Mahdi and the Khalifa were remarkable leaders of men Slatin never sought to deny. But Queen Victoria, her ministers and her subjects were all concerned more with other aspects. This darker side – their barbaric cruelty, their sworn hatred of the white man, and their personal corruption – Slatin could now convincingly display. It matters here not a scrap that in the long sweep of history these men, good or evil, were among the first of modern Africa's independence fighters. We are dealing with England and the English of the 1890s. Whether it was self-deception or not, they truly believed that a spiritual banner should now fly alongside the colours of the Empire's regiments in action. More than anything else, *Fire and Sword* provided that banner.

It was this hunger for the noble cause, combined with the topicality of the book and the romantic figure of its author, which guaranteed the enthusiastic reviews and the swift sales. As a literary work it is unimpressive. Had Slatin possessed one-tenth of that gift of words with which those other soldier-authors of these same deserts, T. E. Lawrence and Winston Churchill, had been blessed, then *Fire and Sword* would have been at least a minor masterpiece. But the Austrian could only be himself: a talker but not a writer; a pragmatist but no intellectual; a man for the saddle and not for the ink-well.

His book reflects something of the wit, much of the charm and all of the sentimentality of the author. His courage, tolerance and ingenuity are also displayed to the full. Yet despite all he went through for twelve years in that agonizing limbo between two faiths and two civilizations, one can search the pages in vain for one memorable descriptive passage or one profound or original reflection. Even the pressure under which the book was produced does not quite excuse its appalling untidiness. The long digressions and the many repetitions constantly throw the narrative off its balance – until, that is, he jumps on his camel to escape. Then, in the book as in the desert, all he had to do was to stop thinking and ride it out to the end. Yet these very faults gave the book that air of spontaneity and homespun sincerity which was its greatest virtue. As for the general reader, he was propelled through its 630 pages (or 596 in the very turgid German version) by the very theme of the Mahdist Sudan itself, a theme so exotic and remote yet now, suddenly, on everyone's lips again.

Slatin was of course interested in the general reader, since, like all authors, he wanted to be known and, like most authors, he needed the royalties. But it was a small handful of selected readers he was particularly concerned with, and these were royalties of quite a different sort. Put plainly, Slatin treated his book as another rope with which to climb the social and professional ladder, and he pulled on it for all it was worth.

The English version (the Wingate-Slatin basic text) was 'by permission humbly dedicated' to Queen Victoria. The Emperor Franz Joseph accepted the dedication of the German edition, and thus the author's two essential loyalties were kept in balance. But Slatin reached much further out than London and Vienna. As his family correspondence shows, he was out to get at every crowned head in Europe. There is a letter to his brother Heinrich dated as early as 16 March 1896, in which the German Ambassador in Vienna, Count zu Eulenberg, acknowledges the special copies of *Fire and Sword* which Slatin had dispatched to the German Emperor and to Prince Henry of Prussia. William II, the envoy added, 'had been pleased to receive the book with particular interest', and wished to thank the author for his friendly courtesy in sending it.

While the expedition waited at Kosheh, Slatin found time amidst all the cholera alarms, sandstorms, special reports to Balmoral and normal intelligence duties, to return to his august readership again. A letter written to Heinrich on 27 July 1896, reveals that, apart from Queen Victoria and the Emperor Franz Joseph, the King of the Belgians and the King of Italy had already accepted copies of the book. The aim of this letter was to rope in another royal couple, the Czar and Czarina of Russia.

He writes:

I hear that the Emperor of Russia is coming to Vienna. If you can manage it, arrange for a copy of my book (the *de luxe* binding) to be presented to him through his ambassador. The sole purpose of this would be to persuade him to take a personal stand against the dervishes . . . Should it look as though I'm only after a decoration, then I'm ready to refuse one because, as I say, the only purpose is to inform His Majesty about conditions in the Sudan . . .

But with all their love and respect for Rudolf, the family came to the conclusion that, this time, he was going a bit too far. Brother Adolf writes on 12 August to brother Heinrich, from a wet holiday near Salzburg :

I absolutely agree with you that it is much better we drop the idea of presenting the book to the Czar. There is in fact just one *de luxe* copy left in our bookcase which is really only suited to some such purpose as this. But that in itself is no reason for such an act of presumption. The political aim that Rudolf imagines could obviously never be achieved, and it could for certain only be interpreted as an attempt to collect another decoration. So write to Rudolf and tell him it makes more sense to forget the whole idea . . .

There is no record of Rudolf's reply to this, but he seems to have taken his brothers' sound advice. St Petersburg and the Romanovs were never, in fact, to figure on his long list of welcoming courts and friendly sovereigns. In view of the social schedule he eventually faced each summer, it was perhaps just as well, for one wonders how he could ever have fitted them in.

There were a few weeks of small-scale social whirl to come now, for once Dongola province had been secured, Slatin and Wingate went back for a spell to Cairo. Rudolf described the life there in an entertaining letter to his sister-in-law. As Slatin always loved parties, and was the life and soul of most of them, some of his grumbles must be taken with a pinch of salt. But the dance he complains of here does sound something of an ordeal, even to the jolliest of men:

We are having a terrible time here. Dinners and invitations every day, never a let-up. A few days ago the *Cercle Khedivale* in Alexandria gave a dinner for the Sirdar and his staff, with a ball to follow. After the feeding—which went on for $2\frac{1}{2}$ hours—and all the inevitable toasts, we were dragged into the ball-room. Compared with this entertainment, a spell in a torture-chamber could only be described as paradise. For the most part there were only old Levantine ladies in the room, whose daughters were probably still in Europe or Constantinople or somewhere, or who hadn't been brought along for other reasons. The Sirdar had cunningly slipped away early. I was left behind and everyone wanted to do me full honour as the curiosity of the evening. I was towed around to introduce myself to one old lady after another and every one of these freshly painted graces smiled and said: 'Oh, we have heard so much about you' or 'read of you in the papers' or 'seen your picture' etc. etc. ... The whole lot together looked like the furnishings in some newly-decorated apartment. I was furious, and wanted to bite in front of me and kick out behind, but was forced to behave myself (and you know how hard I find that!).

But as I'm used to escapes, I suddenly disappeared from the scene of my sufferings and, bathed in perspiration, reached my hotel, where I sank down in a chair thanking God for my liberation from the clutches of these eager old hags ...

Now you have some idea of how your poor brother-in-law is faring. I was bored in Dongola but this is like coming from the frying-pan into the fire ...

In another letter, also from Cairo and addressed a few weeks later to his brother Heinrich, Slatin returns to what was already the familiar problem of keeping the balance between Vienna and London – that meticulous manoeuvre on which his whole future was poised. He had sent a batch of mail-vests, turbans and other dervish battle souvenirs to Vienna. Now the question was: how should they be distributed? If anything were handed over officially to the imperial collection this might get into the papers and cause resentment in England, because in that country Slatin had only sent things 'purely privately to the Queen'. But if he now tried the same private approach with his own Emperor there might be difficulties and it would look as though he were simply interested in 'getting noticed again'. It was all very difficult and delicate and complicated.

Finally, in a letter three weeks later, Rudolf left it all to his brother: 'Do with it what you will.' It was the first time in his career, and almost the last, that Slatin had to confess himself defeated by his own balancing act between the two courts.

Chapter Ten

RETURN TO OMDURMAN

By midsummer of 1897, it was at last time for Slatin to march south again, to collect more battle souvenirs, and much else besides. The all-important desert railway from Wadi Halfa had now been pushed down far enough for an attack to be mounted against Abu Hamed. On 7 August the town was taken, after fierce resistance by the Mahdist garrison. By 31 August Kitchener's troops had already reached the provincial centre of Berber. This second advance meant that the expeditionary force had fought its way another 150 miles up the Nile in only twenty-one days. This was brisk going indeed, for Khartoum and the Khalifa himself were now only some 250 miles upstream to the south-west. But despite the military need to hit the enemy while he was reeling and despite the political urge to reach the strategic heart of the Sudan before the French or the Belgians beat them to it, could the Anglo-Egyptian forces risk pushing on for the final clash as they were?

In another of his battlefield dispatches to Queen Victoria, written from Merawi that autumn, Slatin sets out Kitchener's problem. It will be almost impossible, he tells her, to capture Omdurman without reinforcements of European troops, and such support could hardly be expected that winter. Morale in the Egyptian army was in general still good, but there were signs of a certain war-weariness, induced by the great length of the campaign. All eyes were on the French and the Belgians,

167

in case they should exploit the slow advance of the expedition to creep further down the Nile valley themselves.

There is not much chit-chat in this letter of Slatin's, apart from descriptions of reunions with old friends, including a chance meeting with one of the guides who had piloted him safely across the desert in his escape. But this is good enough for another pluck at the old Queen's heart-strings:

> How well I recall all those events, down to the last detail as those days of peril unfold themselves again before my mind's eye. I give thanks to God, who has safely delivered me from all dangers; and I pray for His further protection now. For the times are again not without peril and this life in the Sudan—far removed from family, friends and homeland—cannot be called a pleasant one. We all feel this and I, who have been forced to spend the best years of my life here, perhaps feel it most of all. Yet all of us, whatever their station may be, fulfil their duty and will hold out until the end.

By the time he wrote that letter, Slatin seems to have received some further confirmation from the Queen that she really did desire him to report to her directly and personally in this unorthodox manner. Certainly, in the preceding weeks, he had been anxiously seeking such assurances through third parties. Thus we find Wingate raising the matter in a letter that he wrote to Bigge from Merawi on 17 September 1897. Could Sir James Reid, the Queen's personal physician, whom Slatin had met at court, perhaps secure these assurances for him?

The following day, Slatin wrote his own letter to Sir James, raising two delicate personal matters. The first is cash. The expedition, he points out, is proving very costly for him as all the old friends and helpers he keeps meeting again are now destitute and ask him for money which he cannot very well refuse. 'I'm not bankrupt yet' he adds, 'but it can happen in the future.'

The second ticklish question is this matter of his personal reports to the Queen. Is it really all right, he asks Reid, for him to write directly to Her Majesty? After all, he doesn't want to infringe English court etiquette. If it is in order, will Reid send a cable, signed with his name and with the one word 'Yes', addressed to 'Slatin, War Office, Cairo'?

The idea of pumping the Queen of England for money

through her private physician was startling enough. But the pantomime over the cable was even more bizarre. By now Slatin had already been writing his reports regularly to Queen Victoria for nearly eighteen months and had received several warm personal acknowledgments from her in return. It was a little late in the day to think about 'infringing English court etiquette'. It was also surely superfluous, if the Queen, who was the arbiter of such etiquette, so obviously approved of the arrangement herself. Rumours of the Slatin-Wingate special link with the Queen had doubtless spread around, of course, causing increasing resentment among the ambitious young British officers on Kitchener's staff. Possibly Slatin was seeking some formal royal command in writing to quell such murmurings. On the other hand, that extraordinary roundabout approach via Sir James Reid may have been just another example of Slatin following that native Viennese bent which his own countrymen summarized as : *Warum einfach wenn es compliziert geht?* or 'Why do anything simply if there is a complicated way?'

Whatever the explanation for Slatin's sudden anxiety, he duly received the reassurance he was after. This is made clear by a guarded reference in a letter Wingate wrote to Bigge from Berber on 11 November:

Slatin told me of his telegram from Reid and I am glad I was not mistaken in correctly construing your wishes to him ...

And so, from the autumn of 1897 onwards, the flow of special reports in German to Balmoral, Osborne and Windsor is resumed without any further agonizing over the author's credentials.

In that same letter from Berber, Wingate spelt out much more clearly the Intelligence Department's misgivings which Slatin had already voiced to the Queen about the expedition's vulnerability and the urgent need of European (i.e. British) reinforcements.

Had it been decided [he writes] earlier in the Season to send out British troops we might have been in Omdurman now ...

Strategically speaking and with the foreknowledge that the finale could not be this year, I think we should have done better to have maintained our frontier back at Abu Hamed. It is possible that the Dervishes may remain quiescent in their present positions, but if they could rouse up sufficient enthusiasm to assume the offensive our present advanced posts would certainly become a source of anxiety...

The Second Act may now be said to be over and the next time the curtain rises it will be to enact the final scene of the Sudan drama, but I should not be surprised if, behind the curtain, a certain amount of disturbance arose; and then the scene-shifting may possibly expose our French friends somewhere in the Nile Valley—which would mean all sorts of complications...*

Wingate's other nightmare of an over-extended expeditionary force being attacked before proper reinforcements could arrive looked like becoming reality within a few weeks of being voiced. Throughout December, as reconnaissance patrols and agents brought in their reports, the signs mounted that the Khalifa was gathering all his forces at Omdurman to sweep down the Nile and dislodge the invaders from Berber before the winter was out. The moment had come for that military decision for which both Wingate and Slatin – in their letters to Queen Victoria, to her Private Secretary and to anyone else of influence who would listen – had long been preparing the political ground.

On the last day of the year, Wingate arrived back at Main Headquarters at Wadi Halfa and urged Kitchener to call at once for British troops to stiffen his Egyptian Army force. He found the Sirdar 'suffering from a heavy cold and in a state of considerable perplexity'. But after a long discussion Kitchener agreed and the momentous telegram was dispatched to Cairo and London. The response was positive; and action, on this occasion, was immediate. By the end of January 1898 a brigade of British troops had passed through Wadi Halfa on its way to railhead and 'the front'. They were soon to be reinforced by a second brigade. Though they marched with an Egyptian Army expedition, the Union Jack fluttered everywhere, visibly or invisibly, between their regimental colours. England's commitment was now absolute.

On 2 February 1898, just after he had watched the last of the British brigade go through, Slatin wrote another of his ten-

---

* It was a prophetic dispatch. Within nine months the 'French friends' duly did loom up in the Nile Valley. Captain Jean-Baptiste Marchand, after a heroic 3,000 mile march across Africa, arrived with his tiny force at Fashoda in July of 1898 to try and claim the whole of the upper riverain region for France. The 'all sorts of complications' arising from that head-on confrontation of the two colonial powers (in which Wingate himself took part) almost led to an Anglo-French war, in Europe as well as in Africa. After six tense months, the French resentfully withdrew.

page letters to the Queen. It vibrates with the new mood of
confidence that had seized the entire expeditionary force, and
the conviction that, with British troops now marching steadily
southwards up the Nile, England in this campaign would have
to extend her gaze even beyond a reconquered Sudan.

But Her Majesty should not imagine that those troops she
had sent would be entering Khartoum straight away. Though
the question of an immediate offensive had been examined as
soon as the first British brigade arrived, the idea had been
dropped 'due to the enormous transport difficulties and the im-
possibility of assembling our new steamers and getting them over
the 5th and 6th cataracts'. Slatin prophesied (accurately as it
turned out) that the reinforced expedition would not resume its
advance 'until the next Nile flood, sometime in August'. Then,
however, nothing would stand in their way until 'by the capture
of Omdurman and the dispersal of the Mahdists, the heroic
General Gordon will be avenged and an old debt repaid'.

As well as beating the drum, Slatin sounded a quiet trumpet
note of alarm. Menelek, the Abyssinian king, whose victory over
the Italians had set the whole campaign in motion two years
before, had for months, he told the Queen, been contemplating
a thrust into the southern Sudan. Its aim would be to seize not
only the Gallabat area near his frontier but also the whole
wedge of Sudanese territory between the Blue and the White
Niles. One can imagine how Slatin and Wingate had discussed
this threat to all their (and England's) hopes in their tents at
Halfa. It is certainly no coincidence, but rather another example
of their joint approach technique, that on the day before Slatin
sent this letter to the Queen, Wingate wrote to Bigge, and
paraded the identical Abyssinian bogy. This time, however, he
had left it to his friend to paint the new peril in its full strategic
colours.

Now the King [Slatin writes] urged on by French influence . . .
seems as though he really intends to turn his plans into action and
occupy these areas. Should he succeed, then the French would be
able to link hands with their expedition which is supposed to be near
Fashoda, and thus the dream of the French colonialist party of
having a direct link right across Africa from West to East would
become reality.

This is a big-scale canvas indeed. But Slatin (probably at this point voicing Wingate's thoughts for him) has an equally ambitious counter-plan to unroll before the old Queen's eyes. He goes on:

I allow myself however the bold hope that we shall be able to put difficulties in the path of both the French and the Abyssinians. Once we succeed in taking Omdurman we can, with our steamers, push right on south to the Ugandan border at Dufile and so frustrate these gentlemen by creating our own link through Africa from north to south.

The little Austrian's dream for the England he was serving was to come true sooner than he imagined. First however there were six months of boredom and frustration to be got through as the army sat on its haunches and waited for the river to rise. It is during these impatient months that Slatin, for the first time, starts complaining about his role in the expedition. He himself put nothing down on paper. The documentary evidence is Wingate's own repeated attempts to soothe the ruffled feathers of his Austrian friend. This was no easy task, for it was General Kitchener who was doing the ruffling.

Early in the New Year Wingate had moved up again with Kitchener to the 'front line' at Berber but, try as he would, Slatin could not get permission to go forward as well. Instead he was obliged to spend the first few months of 1898 back at Main Headquarters at Halfa, some four hundred miles from the scene of action, doing the routine administrative work that he hated. He fairly bombarded Wingate with pleas to release him from his office desk or, failing that, for assurances that he really *was* wanted and that there was no hidden motive in his being kept back. On 14 March, his long-suffering friend finds time to send Slatin a telegram, a long semi-official letter and a shorter private note on the subject, all on the same day. The semi-official letter which begins (very artificially for these two friends) 'My dear Slatin', was evidently intended to boost the Austrian's morale by confirming as formally as was possible on paper what a valuable fellow he was. Wingate says he has 'spoken fully' to the Sirdar about the matter. But the Commander-in-Chief, 'while fully concurring in the value of your presence when the final advance on Omdurman takes place', thought

Slatin had better stay where he was for the time being, in case
he were killed by a stray bullet in a skirmish, 'a result which
could not fail to encourage the Khalifa and be a source of
rejoicing to him and his followers'.

Wingate's private note of the same date can be found copied
out in minute handwriting by Slatin in his diary for 1898. It
tries to reinforce the same reassurance by repeating it as between
close friends:

My dear old Rowdy,
    I know you will understand the species of semi-official letters
which I have written to you. No one wishes more devoutly than I do
that you were here, but I believe the Sirdar to be quite genuine in
the views he expressed . . .
                Best love my dear old chap,
                Ever your affect.

The episode is notable for two things. The first is its demonstration of the insecurity that Slatin felt, his craving to be accepted as an absolute equal by his new-found English comrades
and friends. (The reverse of this craving was of course as acute :
touchiness at being 'neglected', and this was to have much more
serious consequences for Slatin before long.) The second aspect
is the quite remarkable kindness and loyalty of the greatest of
these new friends, Reginald Wingate. Like that feeling of inner
insecurity which it helped to balance, it was to become a feature
of Slatin's whole life.

Wingate's insistence that Kitchener was only keeping Slatin
back to keep him safe is too emphatic to be really convincing.
Indeed, in letters to Bigge a month or two later, Wingate himself gives a broad enough hint that this was not the whole
story. In a letter of 4 May, sent when Slatin was about to go
on leave, Wingate tells the Queen's Secretary that the explanation 'did not act as a salve to Slatin's wounded feelings'. And
in another letter a month later he comes out with it:

I wish our Chief [Kitchener] appreciated his [Slatin's] sterling
qualities more than he does; but of that more when we meet.

It is easy to see why, by the spring, Slatin's feelings were
particularly sensitive. Sitting back at Halfa, he had missed the
exciting and critical battle with the dervishes fought along the

Atbara River, on Good Friday, 8 April. In this clash Kitchener
routed and destroyed the combined forces of two of the Khalifa's
most redoubtable commanders, Mahmoud Ahmed and Osman
Digna, who were converging on Berber from the south-east.
The Mahdist troops may well have been tired and hungry and
their two commanders were always at each other's throats. But
their joint camp was strongly protected by trenches and a giant-
size *zariba* or stockade of thorns, and it was steel against steel
before Kitchener's men could break through.

For the first time in the history of the Sudan, British regiments (from the newly-arrived brigade) went into action, and
played a decisive part in the victory. But on this momentous
occasion, the wretched Slatin was not on the scene to write another of his battlefield reports to Queen Victoria. Back at Headquarters he had to content himself with a second-hand account
of the engagement entered in his diary.

Wingate, writing from the battlefield to Bigge, laconically
described the victory as 'a good business from beginning to end'.
He was annoyed that almost the only people to escape in the
dense bushes were the redoubtable Baggara tribesmen on their
horses whereas their black Sudanese slaves, whom the English
had been doing so much to win over, died almost to a man in
the trenches. They had fought for their Baggara masters whom
they hated 'with a tenacity which is surprising'. And Englishman comments to Englishman on this riddle of Africa: 'It is
rather a conundrum, is it not?'

The 'conundrum' was as bloody as it was puzzling. Seven
thousand of the Khalifa's black troops were left killed or
wounded on the field. Kitchener's casualties were barely five
hundred, of whom four officers and 104 men were from the
British brigade. The road to Omdurman and to the Khalifa's own
camp was now open. Slatin, back from a visit to England, was
eventually allowed to join it. In a letter dated 21 August 1898
and written from a British gunboat on the Nile – its deck
crowded with staff officers, foreign military attachés and press
correspondents 'scribbling for all they are worth' – Wingate tells
Bigge that Slatin is with him again at last and had 'never
looked fitter or in better spirits'.

Wingate then discusses the crunch of the whole campaign, the

1 A 'beau sabreur' already, when barely six years old. Rudolf
(left) with his two brothers, Adolf and Heinrich.

2 Mohammed Ahmed—
The Mahdi (a contem-
porary sketch).

3 Gordon's head broug[ht]
to Slatin Pasha: 'Is this
the head of your uncle,
unbeliever?'

4 The Khalifa's house in Omdurman. The corner where Slatin Pasha sat when a syce prisoner of the Khalifa.

5 The Khalifa's harem (the only two-storied building in Omdurman), in which one of his wives was killed by a shell.

6 'The Prussian Oak' that never bent—the German Charles Neufeld (fellow-prisoner of Slatin's), with his wife and children.

7 General Charles William Gordon (Pasha)—Slatin's first British hero and commander.

8 The Gallows: A crowd gathers round the body of the last man hanged by the Khalifa.

9 The victorious General Kitchener leaves the field after the Battle of Omdurman.

10 The Union Jack being hoisted again over the ruins of General Gordon's Palace in Khartoum, after the victory at Omdurman.

11 The Mahdi's banner, captured at McNeill's Zeriba and presented to Queen Victoria.

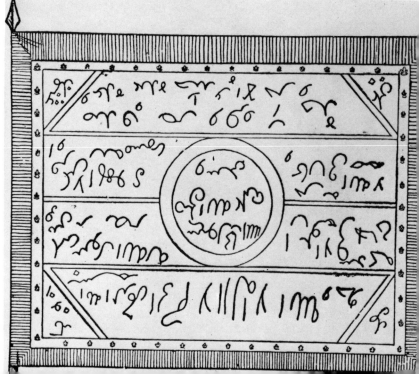

12 Kitchener as Sirdar (Commander-in-Chief) in Egypt at the turn of the century.

13 Slatin and Theodore Roosevelt on camels, during the former President's visit, March 1910.

14 'Rowdy House', Slatin's official residence in Khartoum.

15 The picture post-card hero.

16 The 'Sudan Twins':
Slatin (left) with Wingate
(probably taken shortly
before 1900).

17 Slatin on tour (among
the black beauties of the
Sudan).

18 Slatin and his lion cub in the garden of Rowdy House.

19 The Emperor Franz Joseph and King Edward VII at Bad Ischl, 1908.

20 Rudolf Slatin and Reginald Wingate at Balmoral.

21 Slatin nurses a royal infant, 1912. Left to right: Prince Alvaro of Orleans, Prince Alonso of Orleans, Princess Ileana of Roumania, Princess Marie of Roumania (kneeling).

22 Slatin with his 'Praetorian Guard' at Knockenhair, the Wingate house in Scotland. From left to right: General the Hon. Milo Talbot, Slatin, Sir Edgar Bonham-Carter, Wingate.

23 Baron Sir Rudolf von Slatin Pasha in full plumage, at his prime.

24 (Left) Slatin's wife, Alice, with Anna Marie.
25 (Right) Alice (née von Ramberg) Slatin.

26 Slatin with Alice (seated beside him) and his sisters and friend at Traunkirchen, Austria.

27 Slatin (left) on holiday
back in his native Austrian
alps. The sign reads : 'The
Gate to Heaven'.

28 Slatin Pasha with Anna
Marie, his only child
(taken June 1927).

29 Lord Curzon, Slatin's most powerful opponent.

imminent battle with the Khalifa which they were all steaming
steadily towards:

Almost all troops and supplies have now left the Atbara and
unless some unforeseen circumstance happens, the final event should
come off before September is many days old ... Our information
points to the Khalifa fighting either in Omdurman or at Kerreri ...
For the sake of the speedy settlement of the country it would be
very much better if they would stand and get smashed.

Get smashed the dervishes did; where and when Wingate
had prophesied. On 2 September 1898 their great white-clad
army, between 50,000 and 60,000 strong, faced up to
Kitchener's 25,000 men on the sandy plain between Omdurman
and the Kerreri Hills. Allah sided not with the bigger battalions
of his faithful, but with the Maxim guns and artillery of the
infidels. In the sense that it was now the Khalifa's army which
tried to storm the British lines, it was Atbara in reverse. But,
for the dervishes, the ultimate disaster was the same, only
now multiplied fourfold in slaughter, and magnified beyond
comparison in its effect.

Slatin almost certainly wrote the Queen an account of this
great day. At all events, a letter exists sent to him five days after
the victory in which Sir James Reid conveys to Slatin her desire
to receive from him 'a full account of the battle of Omdurman',
together with his own experiences and views of the situation.
Sir James added, significantly, that this royal command was not
being telegraphed because 'it might cause jealousy and un-
pleasantness' if news of it spread among the other officers in the
English camp. Though it is inconceivable that Slatin did not
jump to obey the Queen's request, no personal Omdurman
narrative of his seems to have survived.

This is less of a loss than it appears. The battle can be reconstructed, in more authoritative detail than Slatin could ever
have provided, from the official reports of General Kitchener.
As for the atmosphere that day on the shimmering stony plain
outside the Khalifa's capital, this is preserved for all time, and
with a vividness that Slatin's scratchy pen could never have
hoped to rival, in accounts such as Winston Churchill's classic
eyewitness story.*

* Churchill rode with the 21st Lancers in the action.

The day before the battle, the Anglo-Egyptian army had pushed far enough up the left bank of the river to be able to glimpse the brown pointed dome of the Mahdi's tomb towering above the mud houses of Omdurman only a few miles away. From the same rise, they had also glimpsed the dervish army streaming out of the city to do battle with them in the open desert: a black pulsating mass of sixty thousand warriors which blotted out the sands like a huge swarm of locusts for four miles from end to end. Hundreds of differently coloured banners waved in the air and the sun added to this impression of confusion by picking out at random clusters of spear-points that sparkled, now here and now there, in the plain. But such confused appearances deceived. The advance was, in fact, disciplined and precise.

The Khalifa had grouped his army into five principal divisions. On the left of his line marched 5,000 men under the bright green flag. The main assault force in the centre numbered 12,000 riflemen and 13,000 spearmen fighting under the dark green flag. The right wing was held by a small force of 2,000 tribesmen under the broad red flag. Behind the main assault force came the Khalifa himself, with his picked bodyguard of a further 2,000 warriors. Behind him, marching at the rear of the whole army, came a reserve force of 13,000 under the Black Flag. The Khalifa's aim was as clear-cut as his battle-line. It was to abandon all thought of a defensive action and fulfil the Mahdi's prophecy by sweeping 'the Turks' into the river.

The commander of those 'Turks' was, however, quite unperturbed at having his back to the Nile. For one thing, it meant that his naval gunboats could scurry up and down the river behind him with complete freedom, lobbing their shells over the heads of his soldiers towards any point of the dervish onslaught that looked menacing. He set great store on the surprise value of this mobile supporting fire from the river, and he was to prove right. Furthermore, Kitchener was convinced that, gunboats or no gunboats, the Khalifa's army could never get close enough to his lines to make their sheer weight of numbers tell and push his men even one yard back towards the water.

So, ignoring the shelter of a chain of houses scattered along the bank, he formed the bulk of his army into a thin curve nearly three miles long, only two men deep where it faced the enemy outwards and resting at the rear for its whole length on the river. This open deployment would give him the broadest arc of fire in the dawn battle he was expecting. Had the Khalifa attacked under cover of night, this Anglo-Egyptian encampment might have proved too sprawling and too lightly protected for comfort.

But the Khalifa did not attack at night. Instead, those dark hours of waiting produced only a strange spectacle that was to be symbolic of the battle to come. Kitchener's gunboats, having battered Omdurman and the dervish lines throughout the day of 1 September, anchored on the bank behind Kitchener's camp as night fell. Then, to make sure that the enemy was up to no tricks, they switched on their searchlights and swept the black plain ahead. Dervish prisoners taken the next day told how the sudden appearance of these great inexplicable shafts of light, probing their *zariba* in the darkness, struck a chill in the bravest hearts. The men covered their faces, in case the gaze of this demon eye should blind them. Even the Khalifa had his tent hurriedly pulled down after the mysterious white rays had swept across it. He was to feel more of the power of modern science before long.

The battle began at first light shortly before 6 a.m. on 2 September, as all the divisions of the Khalifa's army broke camp four miles away and wheeled forward towards Kitchener's line. It was a suicidal operation to attack, across open country, an enemy so vastly superior in fire-power. Unknowingly, the Khalifa only underlined its futility by opening the action with the one arm in which he was most inferior of all to 'the Turks', artillery. Two shells fired from the centre of the dervish lines fell harmlessly short of the Anglo-Egyptian camp. Kitchener waited for the steadily advancing dervish mass to top a ridge and come into full view some three thousand yards away before replying with every available gun he had. Then the British Field Battery, the Egyptian artillery and the gunboats from the river all opened up at once. Churchill, out with his cavalry patrol between the two converging armies, climbed up on a pile of biscuit-boxes to observe the scene. As the shells struck home, he saw the white banners of the dervishes tossing and collapsing and the warriors themselves falling by the dozen in the hail of shrapnel, 'about five men on an average to each shell'.

As though they were brushing away flies, the Khalifa's army moved on, climbing the only two heights out in the plain, the so-called Surgham Ridge and the Kerreri Hills, and pouring into the flat ground between them that led directly to Kitchener's lines. Before long, those advancing down in the open came within range of the defenders' rifles. One by one these battalions opened fire until, by 6.45 a.m., some twelve thousand Anglo-Egyptian infantrymen were pouring bullets at ranges of less than two thousand yards into the dervish mass, which was the assault division of the bright green flag. The rifles of the British brigade grew so hot that they had to be changed for the weapons of the reserve companies. Water bottles borrowed from soldiers of the Cameron Highlanders had to be emptied over the Maxim guns to cool them down. At eight hundred yards range the attacking wave was finally broken and the survivors of the assault force scattered among the litter of corpses. Only at one point, where the defenders had antiquated short-range rifles, did the Khalifa's men get to within three hundred yards. One solitary old dervish was shot at 150 yards from Kitchener's lines, brandishing a flag as he fell.

There were awkward moments among Kitchener's cavalry pushed out on the flanks. On the left, Churchill's 21st Lancers made a gallant but very costly charge below Surgham Ridge. On the right flank, the Camel Corps was enfiladed by the enemy and ordered to pull back. It was only thanks to the protecting fire of a gunboat that it managed to lumber back to the safety of the camp, pursued by several thousand dervish riflemen who could run faster than the laden camels.

There was an even tenser situation towards 10 a.m. when Kitchener, having smashed the Khalifa's first frontal assault, left camp himself and led his brigades upstream towards the empty city of Omdurman, planning to seize the enemy capital before the Khalifa could hurry back with his surviving forces to defend it. The Khalifa's army, though reeling, still had some thirty-five thousand men left on the field. The élite of this surviving force (and of the entire army, for that matter), were the fifteen thousand men of the Black Flag reserve. They now pounced on one British brigade which had straggled into isola-

tion at the rear of Kitchener's sortie. Only some quick thinking
by the Commander-in-Chief, who began 'to throw his brigades
about like companies', and the invaluable support fire of the
river gunboats prevented heavy British casualties.

But once the British line had re-formed and all three brigades
had moved in unison against the Black Flag division, it was
the story of the dawn assault all over again, though this time
with Kitchener on the offensive. No primitive weight of numbers and no dervish fanaticism could withstand this advancing
torrent of shrapnel and Maxim gun-fire. The whole of the
Khalifa's reserve eventually perished where it stood on the flank
of Surgham Ridge. Yakub, the Black Flag commander, died
under his leader's dark banner.

One last sharp dervish attack was launched out on the right
flank, where the last unbroken units of the Khalifa's army, the men
of the Green Flag, had to be repulsed and dispersed. After that,
it was all over. At 11.30 a.m., Kitchener shut up his field-
glasses, with his famous laconic remark that the enemy appeared
to have been given 'a good dusting'. Then he led his brigades
into Omdurman across a desert on which the white-clad corpses
lay strewn like crumpled newspaper.

Left behind on the plain after their 'good dusting' were the
bodies of twelve thousand dervishes. The number of enemy
wounded counted afterwards in only one of their hospitals was
four thousand. In addition Kitchener took about eight thousand
prisoners.* So the Mahdia in the Sudan, which had sprouted
from the mud of Abba Island in 1881, was crushed in the sands
of Omdurman seventeen years later.

Slatin was with Wingate and the Intelligence Staff throughout the engagement. We get only occasional glimpses of him
through the accounts of other participants. Winston Churchill,
for example, describes how, on the eve of the battle, when he
himself was excitedly awaiting a dervish onslaught at any
moment, he found Slatin with Wingate in the Intelligence tent
quietly enjoying a good meal, which looked like 'a race lunch
before the big event'. Wingate, writing to his wife four days
after the victory, tells how, once the final rout of the Khalifa's

---

* All these figures were those given by Kitchener himself when reporting on the victory to Queen
Victoria at Balmoral two months later.

army started, Slatin had ridden forward with Kitchener's cavalry 'in the hope of catching his old friend'.

But Slatin was riding the wrong way on that noon, for the Khalifa had not yet taken to his heels. This remarkable man is nowhere more impressive than in the hour of his defeat. While his conquerors were scouring the battlefield for him among the piles of dead and in the open plain beyond, he had quietly slipped back into Omdurman with a small bodyguard. There he rested, meditated, and prayed for two hours at the tomb of the Mahdi whose banner he had taken up, and had now lost. As Kitchener, carrying that same Black Flag, entered Omdurman from the west, the Khalifa rode out of the city to the south, making for the Baggara tribal stronghold of his native Kordofan, five hundred miles away up the Blue Nile. British cavalry chased him for part of the way and then gave it up, leaving him for the moment to his own devices.

Back in the Khalifa's former capital, Kitchener set about destroying one legend and refurbishing another. The great mosque was fired and the Mahdi's body was removed from its tomb, decapitated, and flung into the Nile. (Kitchener originally wanted to keep the skull as a grisly memento for himself but it was eventually sent for burial in the Moslem cemetery at Wadi Halfa.) Then, thirteen years and eight months late, came a funeral service for Gordon, held before the ruins of his palace in Khartoum. Four chaplains led the prayers and thousands of English voices sang 'Abide with Me', his favourite hymn. From the river, the successors of those British gunboats who in January 1895 had arrived just too late to help him, now fired salvoes which must have sounded somewhat poignant with repentance. But as Queen Victoria wrote in her Journal on hearing of all this: 'Surely he is avenged.'

From her faithful Slatin, the monarch received the following telegram sent from Khartoum via Cairo on 11 September:

To: The Queen, Balmoral

Slatin returns respectful thanks to Your Majesty. His return to the scene of his long imprisonment at the head (sic!) of Your Majesty's victorious troops and their Egyptian comrades has fulfilled all his hopes.

The ultimate fulfilment of Slatin's hopes was of course to capture the Khalifa himself and so turn his gaoler of old into his prisoner. Not only was this sweet dream of revenge to be denied to him. He was destined to be thousands of miles away on leave in his native Austria when the slates were finally wiped clean for him in the Sudan. He could however draw much consolation from the fact that it was his good friend Wingate who did the wiping. The Khalifa's tale may as well be concluded here.

Some twelve months after the victory of Omdurman, at the end of a summer during which the elusive dervish leader had shown great energy and even signs of a reviving strength down in Kordofan, Wingate was sent down with a flying column and orders to kill the old fox once and for all.

Wingate's letters to Bigge, now resumed again, tell the brief dramatic story. On 29 October 1899, he describes how he has been playing a long and exhausting game of hide-and-seek around Gerada, Funfur and Gedir in the Kordofan district, trying to flush the Khalifa out of his hiding-place in the thick bush and the plains of tall grass which cover the area. All in vain.

Then, on 23 November, he stumbled by chance on his quarry when his scouts discovered the enemy camp in a forest clearing at a place called Om Debrikat. It was a well-earned stroke of luck. Wingate wrote afterwards:

The way the whole of the Dervishes fell into our hands makes one feel, as the Arabs say, that their day had come and that it was arranged by Higher Powers than us poor mortals.

The 'whole of the Dervishes' was the Khalifa, two of his brothers, one of the Mahdi's sons, a number of other well-known Mahdist figures and something like five thousand fighting men: the last of the hunted, guarded by the last of the faithful. Wingate had some 3,700 men under him, including two battalions of regular Sudanese troops and some light artillery. They now cut their way in the moonlight through the bush, and by dawn were entrenched on high ground overlooking the enemy camp.

It was Omdurman once more, though this time on a smaller

181

scale. It was again the dervishes who, at dawn, launched the first attack. Again they were mown down by the Maxim guns and again their camp was overrun in a swift counter-attack. But this time the Khalifa also lay dead on the field with his warriors. How he died is a matter of some mystery. To this day, his descendants in Khartoum maintain that, realizing all was lost and that further flight was as pointless as further resistance, the Khalifa dismounted from his horse, seated himself on his *furwa* sheepskin with his emirs around him, and then drove a knife into his body. Wingate's own description of the gruesome scene, which he reached soon after 6 a.m., says that the bodies of the Khalifa and his principal emirs were found huddled together in a comparatively small space. Survivors confirmed to him that the Khalifa had indeed seated himself in a circle with his principal leaders just before the camp was overrun. Wingate, in his official report, cryptically adds: 'In this position they had unflinchingly met their death.' He does not specify whether it came to them with machine-gun bullets or at the point of their own daggers. But, one way or the other, the Khalifa Abdallahi was dead, and his end was, by any warrior's standards, a noble one.

The next day, 25 November, Slatin in far-away Austria opened a telegram that had been addressed by one of Kitchener's staff officers simply to 'Slatin Vienna', and which had reached him at Heizingerstrasse 30. The text was as sparse as the address. It read: 'Killed Khalifa today. Watson.'

The Khalifa's most famous prisoner must have also received a message of some sort from the English court, for on 26 November he dispatched the following telegram in German to the Queen at Windsor:

Most joyfully moved by the victory of my friend Wingate I humbly thank Your Majesty for the gracious remembrance. God bless Your Majesty and England's soldiers!

It was the best Slatin could do. But it must have been a bit of an anti-climax to have to hand in that telegram at a Vienna post office, a thousand miles away from his beloved London and many thousands further from the body of his late tormentor. This remoteness was not inappropriate. The truth was that, long before the end of 1898, the Queen's Darling and the Queen's Soldier had got heartily fed up with the Queen's Government. Slatin not only felt right out of it. For the moment he *was* right out of it.

Part Three

Chapter Eleven

THE INSPECTOR-GENERAL

Rudolf Slatin was indeed crossing a patch of very choppy seas before settling down to ride that long wave of success which bore him throughout his middle years of life. This uneasy passage in his fortunes had begun soon after the triumphant return to Omdurman and Khartoum in September 1898.

In the first weeks of occupation, while order was being restored to the cities which had been Gordon's graveyard and the Mahdi's capital, even Kitchener would have admitted that this Viennese protégé of Wingate's was invaluable. Slatin was quite simply the only officer in the expedition who knew the twin capitals inside out. He alone could separate the big fish from the small fry among the captives, identify the trustworthy and expose the treacherous. Spite was no part of Slatin's nature, and there is no evidence that he ever used his position to persecute, on personal grounds, any of his former tormentors. Gratitude and generosity were however a big part of his make-up, and there is plenty of evidence that he went out of his way to help those who had once helped him.

The following passage appears, for example, in a memorandum which Queen Victoria wrote down at Balmoral after hearing a first-hand account from General Kitchener of the victory outside Omdurman and the mopping-up process which followed in the town:

The women (of the dervishes) are not shut up at all like the other

187

Mohammedan women but go about like a herd of cattle... They
are very excitable and talk incessantly and wear very scanty clothing. Slatin Pasha had the charge of them as he could speak to them
and knew many of them. The first wife of the Khalifa whom he left
on the road during his flight was a very fine woman about 40 and
6 feet high. Slatin knew her and as she had shown him kindness
during his captivity when he was in danger from the Khalifa's
cruelty he was anxious to show her kindness in return. He got her a
home in Omdurman...

Yet it quickly became clear that though Kitchener was happy
to have Slatin as a guide to walk him through the ruins, he was
not prepared to accept the Austrian as the master-architect for
the edifice England proposed to build on those ruins. Indeed,
Slatin is soon complaining bitterly that his advice is being
persistently ignored by the new Governor-General of the Sudan.
Slatin did not confide these complaints to his annual diaries
which, here as always, are plain records of fact rather than
chronicles of his emotions. Nor does he appear to have put anything on paper to Wingate, who was still his immediate superior.
Where he did pour out his feelings was in Cairo, to his fellow-
countrymen at the Austrian mission. It is from their telegrams
to Vienna that we learn what was really going on.

As early as 28 October, less than two months after the capture
of Omdurman, the Austrian Minister in Cairo reports that, to
judge from what Slatin had just told him on a visit, 'any prolonged co-operation between Slatin and the English authorities ... does not appear very likely'. Slatin, he says, was urging
Kitchener to adopt a conciliatory policy towards the Sudanese
population and was arguing that the new administrative
methods of the English should be introduced only step by step,
in order to win the people's confidence. Slatin was particularly
opposed to Kitchener's policy of wholesale recruitment into the
ranks of the new Anglo-Egyptian army of all classes and types,
whether these were slaves, servants, peasants or even the sons
of influential sheikhs whom Slatin had personally tried to win
over. As a result of this undiscriminating approach, the sheikhs
were offended and the fields were left uncultivated. It was all,
in Slatin's eyes, far too sudden and far too drastic. But, as the
Austrian diplomat reports, basing all his information on his
recent lengthy talk with Slatin: 'Slatin's advice is either ig-

nored completely, or else only taken into account too late, when the effects of the controversial measures have already been felt.'

Three weeks after that telegram was sent, there was balm for Slatin's wounded feelings when the honours and promotions lists for the Omdurman victory were published in London. A cascade of medals and titles was poured out over the expedition by a grateful English sovereign and nation. Kitchener naturally came off best, with a peerage, the GCB, promotion to Lieutenant-General and a cash award of £25,000. Wingate got his thoroughly-deserved further promotion to full colonel and a knighthood into the bargain. As for Slatin, the Austrian Minister in Cairo was now able to report:

Slatin Pasha, who already possesses two English orders, has been given the Commander's Cross (sic) with star of St Michael and St George which, as is known, brings with it for British citizens the title of Sir and, for their wives, that of Lady.

But Slatin, as yet, was laying no great store by the title and it was to be many years before he acquired a wife to share it with him. The KCMG, in these circumstances, was just a magnificent addition to that *Wappenbrust*, or chestful of medals, he had set out to fill two years before; and the growing uncertainty over his whole future cast a shadow even on all that glitter.

This is graphically shown by the draft of a letter of thanks to Lord Cromer which the ever-helpful Wingate wrote out for him in reply to the great man's congratulations. After the ritual phrases, there comes a passage in which Slatin talks of 'quitting the Egyptian service' now that his task was over.

Then Wingate must have thought better of allowing Slatin to put that drastic statement on paper at this early stage, though he well knew his friend's problems. So he struck the words through and ended his draft instead:

As I am soon going to Europe and the Queen has expressed a wish to see me in Scotland, I hope to have the great honour of thanking Her Majesty in person for this very high distinction.

It was not, of course, to Balmoral that Slatin was going in an English mid-winter, but Windsor. He had prepared the ground by writing again to his unofficial intermediary at court, Sir James Reid, asking whether he might bring with him some more campaign mementoes for the Queen, and present them to her personally. (He was assured he could.) He also made what must have been received as a most embarrassing attempt to get the Queen to increase his pension, in the event of his early retirement. Slatin already worshipped the English too intensely ever to understand them properly and this was the sort of *faux pas* he went on making all his life. One can only compliment Reid on the urbane way he side-stepped it. He wrote back:

I am very sorry that the authorities are behaving so shabbily about your pension, but I hope they will yet make it all right. It is a shame that you should not be treated handsomely after all that you have come through. But I am sure the Queen recognizes your services and that she will be very gracious to you when you come here.

'Colonel Slatin Pacha (sic) KCMG, CB' was duly invited to dinner with the Queen at Windsor on 28 February 1899, and was asked on the card 'to remain until Friday 3 March'. He had a long talk with the Queen after tea on the day of his arrival and in her Journal she describes the gifts he had brought her. They were more evocations of that tragedy he had helped to avenge: 'a piece of stone from the step on which General Gordon was killed at Khartoum and a frame containing dried roses from the garden of Gordon's Palace'.

It was another highly successful visit which ended with an exchange of photographs between Slatin and the Queen. Yet this, Slatin's first visit to Windsor, must have had for him a truly *fin de siècle* feel about it, quite apart from the date, for he was no longer properly in the Queen's service any more. On the other hand, he was not completely out of it. Before leaving Egypt a fortnight before, he had struck an ingenious compromise about his future. It was so typically Viennese in the elaborate way it kept all the options open that only his countryman in Cairo, Baron Heidler, could spell it out properly. Well in advance of the final decision, the Austrian diplomat reports that Slatin would remain on active service until the end of January (1899), when he would apply for his pension, to be based on his newly-increased salary. But, as Heidler makes clear, this was to be no irrevocable retirement:

His return to service is provided for and will be given effect by periodic recalls for duty and temporary reactivation. Slatin Pasha himself chose this method in preference to any other arrangement because it will give him greater freedom of movement. It will also enable those senior to him to be given their proper precedence in the top posts.

This last point was the critical one. Slatin had now been promoted brigadier-general in the Egyptian Army. Not even Wingate would have dreamt of suggesting that he should command a division in the field, especially as British troops were now so numerous in the Sudan. Yet if Slatin, holding that rank, were to be given a desk job it could hardly be less than that of Chief of Staff. As he himself had long realized, this was an impossible thought. There was enough jealousy already between the Regular Army officers out from England and their higher-ranking countrymen in the Khedive's service without putting an Austrian intelligence expert above all their heads. So, quite apart from the strained situation where Kitchener was no admirer of Slatin's whereas Slatin could not go along with Kitchener's policies, the plain fact was, for the time being at any rate, that Slatin had promoted himself out of a job. The difficulties over finding work to match his ranks and titles, which had been tricky enough in 1896, now seemed insuperable.

There were, however, no immediate money problems, though he never had been, and never would be, a rich man. Thanks largely to Wingate's efforts, his pension, based on the promotion he had only just received, was finally fixed at £E600 or 15,600 gold francs a year. This, together with the royalties from his book and fees for articles and lectures, would have been ample to ensure a comfortable retirement. The trouble was, of course, that Slatin, still only forty-one, could not contemplate withdrawing from the world, whereas the world in which he now moved was costly as well as glittering. He had climbed to dizzy social heights for which nothing in his family background or early life had equipped him. From now on, his clothes had to be from the very best tailors and there had to be plenty of them. He had to buy guns to shoot with, horses to ride and golf clubs to swing. He had to pay for constant first-class travel across Europe. He had to fit in as a guest at royal palaces or noble homes, and he was not the first to discover that staying in these can cost more in presents and tips than a suite in the best hotel.

One wonders, for example, whether the whole of his first year's pension met his social expenses for 1899. This was his first year of complete freedom in every sense of the word since his boyhood, and he naturally enjoyed it to the full, moving like a shuttlecock between Austria and England. He returns to Vienna ('Wien' and the *fesche Mädel* as Reid archly puts it) after that winter visit to Windsor. But after spending part of the summer in Austria, the Queen's Journal shows that he is back in England and at Osborne again with Wingate on 19 August, and up at Balmoral again on 11 October. (On this occasion, the Queen records, he swore that he 'was ready at any time to shed his blood in my service'.) November finds him back for the second time in Vienna, and, as we have seen, very much out of it when he hears that Wingate has polished off the Khalifa for him. It was vital to do something, not merely to fill his energies, but to fill his purse. Prudently, he had been preparing for this for nearly a year and the time had come to act.

Early in 1900, Slatin arrived back in Egypt *en route* for the Sudan. Of the fame and fortune he had first sought there as a boy, the fame was assured. Now he had come back for the fortune. Slatin was heading for the Nuba mountains in the far south of Kordofan, there to search for gold, silver, oil, coal and anything else they might conceal.

This bizarre little chapter in Slatin's life had begun almost exactly a year before, just as he was preparing to leave Cairo on his indefinite *congé*. An international consortium of financiers, headed by the redoubtable Sir Ernest Cassel, had been lured by the legends of rich mineral deposits in the Southern Sudan into floating a special company to locate and exploit its natural resources. They were looking for someone who could first negotiate the prospecting agreement with the civil authorities and then guide the expedition on its journey. There was no need, in the Cairo of 1898, to look beyond Slatin Pasha for either task. As Slatin, for his part, was looking for fresh fields to conquer, especially if they should turn out to be gold-fields, a deal was soon arranged. He was to receive no salary or fee beyond his personal expenses for the expedition, but he was guaranteed a massive reward should they actually strike it rich. This inducement took the form of £1,000 worth of shares in the new company, made over free of charge to Slatin at their nominal value. It would have been enough to have made him a wealthy man for life, had the Nuba mountains only yielded up their elusive gold.

Unhappily for him, however, they did not. His little caravan of prospectors, after a grand send-off from Cairo on 10 February 1899, and a stop-over in Khartoum, spent three months scratching away in the desolate hills south of El Obeid. This was the very ground from where, sixteen years before, the Mahdi had gathered together the forces that had crushed Slatin on their triumphant march towards the capital. Every peak and every dried-out gulley produced its memories. But they produced nothing more. The two mineralogists with the party could find nothing but sand and rock. By the middle of May, when the thermometer in these latitudes was beginning to rise uncomfortably again, Slatin decided he had had enough. They rode off eastwards to the White Nile and a steamer was sent down from Khartoum to collect the band of exhausted and disenchanted explorers.

Passing through Cairo on his way back to Europe, Slatin told his friends at the Austrian mission there in confidence all about the fiasco. Again, it is their reports to Vienna which, at second-hand, give his frankest account of events. According to these telegrams, Slatin was still convinced that there was gold to be found in the Nuba mountains. But, he had explained, the unruly conditions down there made any systematic prospecting impossible. The writ of the Anglo-Egyptian army did not extend far beyond El Obeid, the provincial capital, where a garrison of some one thousand was maintained. In southern Kordofan, all was still in chaos, with tribal warfare raging unchecked.

There had been other distractions. No one had believed that the famous Slatin Pasha was now simply an Austrian civilian out to make money with a shovel. To the local sheikhs, he was still the embodiment of authority. This was particularly true of Darfur, the province he had once governed himself in Gordon's name. The Sultan of Darfur, Ali Dinar, who, a mere boy in those days, had been a great admirer of Slatin's, had approached him now for advice. The Sultan declared himself ready to submit to the new powers in the land; how should he go about it? Slatin told him either to go to Khartoum himself or to ask for a Commission to come out to Darfur and raise the English and Egyptian flags over his citadel.

Slatin's own diary for these months also contains several examples of him being forced, one suspects not unwillingly, to play the government official in word and deed. The local people were only proving to him what he already knew in his heart. He was nothing in the Sudan out of uniform. He was nobody in the world at large once divorced from the Sudan. Summing all this up, the Austrian Minister in Cairo reported:

It is not therefore surprising that, as Slatin himself tells me in confidence, leading British circles here have approached him to ask whether he would accept the next post which is about to be created of General Adviser for the Sudan.

That telegram was written on 15 June 1900. It did not mention the one event that made the suggestion plausible. Six months before, Kitchener had been suddenly switched to South Africa, where the Boer War had erupted, and on 21 December 1899, the freshly-knighted Sir Reginald Wingate had been appointed Sirdar of the Egyptian Army and Governor-General of the Sudan in his place. This was the decisive factor in putting the amateur gold prospector back into official uniform. Slatin's dearest friend and most enthusiastic sponsor was now to rule the land that had brought them together. Their stars had always been linked and it was inconceivable – unless Slatin had found a mountain of pure gold shining in the desert – that they should not rise again together now.

Wingate had not been in Khartoum when Slatin passed through, but it made little difference. The Austrian knew that they would meet up in Scotland that summer, and that it was here, against the background of their joint visits to Balmoral, that the decision would be taken. He was right. The few details were worked out in August at the Wingates' home near Dunbar and on 25 September 1900, Rudolf Slatin was appointed Inspector-General of the Sudan. The Queen was, of course, delighted. As for the Foreign Office in London, they raised no objections once they knew that Lord Cromer in Cairo had none. It could all be so quickly settled because the power to settle lay in so few hands. By the autumn, the old team was back in Khartoum again and officially back in harness together.

The job which Slatin held for the next fourteen years had no precedents before it and it set none after it. It was tailor-made for him, and only he could have fitted it. Moreover, it could only have worked with his friend, the infinitely patient and infinitely tolerant Wingate, as ruler of the new Sudan. And it could only have worked in the new Sudan itself which, at the turn of the century, was virgin territory in the administrative as well as the political sense, a territory where improvisation and experiment had to be the order of the day. Even the special status which Cromer had just devised for the country – an Anglo-Egyptian 'Condominium' in law but a British protectorate in fact – imposed the pragmatic approach on those who now governed it under him. At least in the early years, Wingate's Sudan was like a bizarre musical instrument that the English tuned and played entirely by ear.

Slatin's own position echoed this perfectly. How *could* one define the duties of an Austrian official who had survived from the slapdash multinational Gordon era into a regime run first by British army officers and later by British civil servants? As early as 1 October 1900, his Austrian countrymen in Cairo reported to Vienna a detailed list of the new Inspector-General's responsibilities. According to this version he was to supervise the Sudanese taxation system, including the 'levies to be raised on ostrich feathers, gum and ivory'; approve the issue of licences for industrial and mining operations; see to the expulsion of 'suspicious or condemned persons'; regulate disputes between the Anglo-Egyptian authorities and the religious leaders of the Sudan; and finally, to make proposals about any necessary military expeditions and about frontier delimitations.

The Austrian mission clearly was not inventing this strange assortment of tasks. Yet there is no evidence that they were ever officially circulated in the Sudan to launch Slatin on his career. Indeed, a paper entitled 'Duties of Inspector-General Sudan' which was distributed for comment in draft form only two years later differs in every single item. In this later list, there is no mention of Slatin actually *doing* anything, whether about ostrich feathers or manufacturing permits. He is merely to give his opinion on matters of taxation, and simply to report complaints by the religious leaders. As for his over-all task, this is expressed in words so sweeping as to be meaningless: 'To lay before the Governor-General any proposal which in his opinion would improve the state of affairs in the Sudan.'

The most specific, and significant, item in the whole draft says what he should *not* do. He is forbidden to issue direct orders to any employee under a *Mudir* (Provincial Governor) 'except in cases of absolute urgency when the Mudir is too far away to issue the orders in time'. The fact that this draft originated in Slatin's own handwriting, with marginal comments added in Wingate's hand, shows that as early as 1902, the Inspector-General was being compelled to clip his own wings. The truth was, of course, that none of these formal lists of duties made any sense. The only task Slatin had would have looked as ridiculous on paper as it was logical in reality. It was to be Wingate's eyes and ears in the Sudan, but never his voice.

Thus, though the Inspector-General technically came second in the order of precedence, Slatin never once deputized for Wingate except in ceremonial or representational matters. He had no executive power and indeed no real position in the ruling pyramid. If Wingate was absent from the Sudan, a Chief Justice or a senior provincial Governor (someone like Jackson Pasha of Fashoda Province) would take his place, and these acting Governor-Generals were always as British as Wingate himself. For a while, Slatin functioned as Chairman of the Governor-General's Council, as though to give some outward recognition to his exalted rank and title. But it was no good. He had no proper authority; he understood nothing of the English committee system; and he probably chattered too much to be an efficient Chairman anyway. He had the common sense to resign.

Slatin was excluded even more firmly from the military hierarchy on which Wingate's power rested, and which, for the first few years, also provided his chief administrators. Though now a Major-General in the Anglo-Egyptian Army, Slatin could not issue a direct order to the smallest of its desert patrols in the Sudan. Nor did the former Deputy-Director of Intelligence have any say in these secret matters now. The Army built up its own security network, run by English officers, a network which reported direct to Wingate as Commander-in-Chief. One reason for this – a reason which, in the new Sudan, it became increasingly impossible to ignore – was that Slatin, though the Inspector-General, was not an Englishman.

Yet though he had no power, he did have tremendous influence. For if he could never speak in Wingate's name, he could get Wingate to speak for him; and Wingate, under Almighty God and Lord Cromer, was absolute ruler of the Sudan. This influence was at its peak in the first years of the Condominium. Slatin's role then for Wingate in the whole of the Sudan was what it had been for Kitchener in the freshly-recaptured cities of Omdurman and Khartoum. Whereas they all knew the country from the outside looking in, he alone also knew it from the inside looking out. He could interpret almost any complicated native problem for Wingate in terms of the rivalries between the individuals, families or tribes that lay behind it. He could identify the flagrantly dishonest merchants and the bad hats in what was left of the Khalifa's administration. He could fit names to faces and match boasts against facts. He was, in short, a one-man transmission belt between the Sudan of the Mahdi and the Sudan of Whitehall.

Inevitably, this unique value of his declined as the new Sudan got under way. The turning-point was 1904, when the first batch of recruits into the newly-formed 'Sudan Civil Service' arrived from England to take up their duties. These men were a totally different breed from the Slatins and Luptons of Gordon's day; different even from that small band of English officers who had carried the main political load during the first years of Wingate's regime. These civilians from England had been hand-picked and specially trained to administer the Sudan. They were part of the golden youth of Edwardian England, assured and self-centred. Almost all held good or reasonable Honours degrees from Oxford or Cambridge. Many were in addition university 'blues' in sport. (Slatin, never quite at home in these arcane English matters, once introduced one of them as 'the man who had rowed the fastest in the Oxford boat'.) They thus had an intellectual and social background which Slatin lacked. More important perhaps, they operated within a tight career structure which Slatin stood outside. In a word, they were the first of the new professionals whereas he, for all his greater knowledge, was the last of the old amateurs.

What Slatin had to give them, apart from that greater

```

knowledge of his, was the advantage of amateurs in any walk of life, namely the broader horizon. Many of these middle to upper-middle class young Englishmen knew only the England of their public schools and universities and they tended to base their life in the Sudan on this rigid native mould. But this legendary little Austrian in their midst, who had first come to the Sudan on nothing more than a bookseller's advertisement in Vienna, had a foot in the Habsburg Empire as well as the British. He was a European figure rather than a national one, and what he lacked in brains he more than made up for in wisdom.

Though he was generally liked and respected by the new caste of Sudan civil servants, they could never as a group fully identify themselves with him. Most of his life-long friendships were formed with the first generation of administrators, soldiers or civilians, whom Wingate selected himself on taking office. Sir James Currie, Wingate's Director of Education in Khartoum, and Colonel Milo Talbot, who deputized for Wingate in 1903, are two examples whose names crop up repeatedly in Slatin's letters and diaries over the years. But even with them, the sources of friction were always latent under a smooth surface, and occasionally they broke through. One such occasion was in January 1902, when the same Jackson Pasha who later served ably as Acting Governor-General was abruptly dismissed by Wingate from the post of Civil Secretary. The reason seems to have been that Colonel Jackson had been poking fun, in club armchairs and even in official telegrams, about the Austrian Inspector-General, whose influence with Wingate he probably resented. Everything was patched up, thanks largely to Cromer's personal intervention from Cairo. Yet the incident showed what Slatin was up against, especially after the young professionals from England began to arrive in force.

Indeed, only two things, apart from Wingate's patronage, made his work possible at all. The first was that Slatin was in a cul-de-sac, however elevated, which lay off the high road of the Sudan Government as a career. Everyone knew this and he himself accepted it. Nobody could aspire to his peculiar job and he could not be after anyone else's. The second and more important reason lay in Slatin's own character. Though touchy, because he was at heart insecure, he was never vindictive and
```

he was never an intriguer. Indeed, being a kindly and easy-going fellow, he was much more likely to put in a good word for someone than a bad word whenever he had Wingate's ear. Had it been otherwise, he could never have lasted fourteen months, let alone fourteen years.

But what exactly *did* Slatin do in all those years? As with the various lists of duties drawn up for him, it is easier to see what he did not do. He is not remembered in the Sudan today, and was not noted in his own time, for any single great reform or project. He founded no college, he launched no dam or railway, he signed no treaty, he drafted no law and he inspired no social or economic programme which bore his name or even his imprint. The drinking fountain that, years later, was erected to his memory in Khartoum was a fitting symbol – anonymous but precious water, dispensed free in a million sips to all and sundry, just as his own advice had been.

This minute, painstaking, and almost humble work is recorded in his own annual diaries. These begin in German with hardly a word of English. By 1904, the languages are half and half, often switching in mid-sentence. In the later years it is mostly in English that he writes and thinks, though never without Teutonisms in phrasing or endearing schoolboy howlers in spelling. One could fill a whole chapter with extracts from these journals and the Intelligence Summaries to which they contributed. A page or two will do, for though the details always change, the picture they give is nearly always the same. The Inspector-General on his constant travels is simply engaged in generally inspecting. He is Wingate's itinerant man with the stethoscope, the oil-can and the spanner.

1902 is as good a year to take as any as an example of Slatin at his busiest. From a tour of Kordofan, he notes a list of twenty-six points to settle or discuss when back in Khartoum. He suggests prices for government corn contracts. A man called Wright has apparently 'found gold' (this written in German; it must have stirred uneasy memories of his own prospecting fiasco in these parts). What should the camel transport tariff be from El Obeid back to Omdurman and the opposite way to Duem? There are 'bad reports' about a man called Hanafi, while someone called Hassan 'has to be fired – confidential report!' A lot needs to be done about gum tree cultivation and (this underlined in English) 'Should be allowed that every gum merchant proceeds straight to his destination'. There are other entries about the telegraph line at Kawa; the pay of mounted police in the area and plans to cut them down in size; the granting of agricultural loans; problems with cattle thieves, giraffe hunters and 'horses going to the West'.

A trip to Bahr Al-Ghazal, the province south of Kordofan, produces another list of points. The ivory trade has now been re-routed; prices are given, part cash, part barter; and 'small female calfs should be sent to change them for ivory'. Many villages are evacuated which 'prouves that inhabitants don't like to be in tutch with soldiers'. In one place the Shilluk tribesmen ask to be independent and not under the Dinkas. There is much, inevitably, about wells. They must be improved all round and rewards should be given to some well-owners to keep them open. The station at Chak Chak should have bulls for corn transport; each sheikh should be allotted 2–3 police; someone unnamed is to get a 'tusk as reward'.

February of the same year finds him in the Fashoda District and here, of course, the Nile claims most of his attention. At Tewfikieh, he records in tiny German scribble, there ought to be a steamer station, summer and winter, and possibly a hospital as well. All merchants ought to report to the *Mudir* and travelling pedlar licences should be issued together with 'a special pass from the Intelligence Department'. He suggests (this time in English) that a mail boat should leave Khartoum on the first of each month, passing through Fashoda to Kenissa where, on the 15th of each month, it would meet up with a boat coming from Lado in the far south of Equatoria and exchange passengers and cargo. He adds: 'Arrangements necessary for Congo and Uganda officials and traders.' (Here Slatin was helping to put into effect that British-controlled north-south African axis about which he had written from the battlefield to Queen Victoria.)

But even at Fashoda, it is not all the great river. Plenty of personnel problems also crop up that he will have to raise with Wingate. There is the case of Wilson, an Inspector who has now passed his Arabic examination. An entry in French refers cryptically to *l'affaire Angelo Capito*. Blewitt (presumably the local District Officer) has a number of points to raise. He wants permission to send any bad characters he finds in his police force back to the army battalions from which they were recruited; he wants a new trading post; transport for sending out patrols; and permission for a working party because 'police and sailors object to carry goods'. But the English District Officer's most pressing question concerns himself. Slatin notes: 'About Blewitt's future position (private explaining to Sirdar)'.

'Private explaining to Sirdar.' That, as always, was the nub of it. The vast majority of these minutely detailed matters could be put before the relevant official or department in Khartoum and left to them to dispose of. But there were other questions arising out of these trips which Slatin always saved for his 'private explaining to Sirdar'. This, in effect, meant two wicker armchairs and two whisky glasses on the balcony of the Governor-General's spanking white new palace in Khartoum, or on the verandah of Slatin's much smaller but still spacious house nearby. These tête-à-tête discussions would cover all strategic matters, like that steamer link with Uganda; all religious and tribal matters, like the Shilluks' request for independence; and everything that English officials such as Blewitt chose to raise about themselves – whether it was pay, promotion, leave, transfer or retirement. In such matters and to such officials, the Austrian Inspector-General of the Sudan was, at the very least, an influential curiosity.

Slatin would also save up for discussion with Wingate anything relating to the general philosophy of English rule, about which the two friends would talk endlessly. Those same 1902 'Notes re Bahr al Ghazal' contain two such examples. In one, Slatin writes: 'It is to much interfering in local questions and habits from part of our officials'. This was something about which Slatin, who knew the Sudan from the grass roots level (where grass grew, that is) always felt passionately. Though he hated Mahdism and most of what it had brought in its train, those eleven years he had spent as its antagonist and then as its captive had taught him that the tribal roots and customs of the Sudan were too deep and too varied to be disentangled in the space of a few years by a benevolent but alien bureaucracy. He was always pleading for less regimentation and less speed, and for the hundred primitive peoples of the country to be given more of a chance to catch their breath under these new efficient white masters with all their stupefying mechanisms of war and peace. But the spirit of the age, as well as the science of the age, was against him. A perfect example of this comes, by an odd coincidence, in the very next note made on this same journey. 'Re. "freedom" – runaway men and womans should be send back to their master if not special reason prevent so; certainly only if masters possess them before occupation.... Re. 4 woman of Sultan Nassr Audal.'

The problem of slavery in Africa generally had become particularly acute since its abolition in America forty years earlier. American liberals, churchmen (especially Quakers) and other reformers had banded together in the British and Foreign Anti-Slavery Society and had directed their revulsion and wrath like a burning-glass on to the dark continent. Gordon, of course, had tried unsuccessfully to stamp it out in the Sudan of his day. But officially Gordon had been acting only as the agent of the Egyptian Khedive. Now, England shared the full responsibility with Egypt for Sudanese affairs and, in effect, ran them. In the climate of the age, there was no keeping the reformers out. Indeed a special department for the repression of slavery was soon set up in Cairo, with its own inspection officers in Khartoum and the Sudanese provinces and its own force of special police to watch the Red Sea ports for slave-runners.

Slatin's attitude to abolition was like that of the young St Augustine to virtue. He wanted it, but not yet. Unlike these reformers, he had owned slaves as domestic servants himself even as a mere captive of the Khalifa's. He knew how much the economy, social structure and military system depended on slavery. He knew too that if one tried now to cut it out of the Sudanese body at one stroke, like some malignant cancer, the body itself might lose too much blood. As to female slaves, it was not just Sultan Nassr Audal who had his '4 woman'. Practically everyone who was someone had them as well, and the habit died hard, even among the local officials who were supposed to be stamping it out. Slatin often told the story of the Slavery-Repression outpost set up in the Nuba mountains in 1907. A native policeman was attached to the post and the first thing he did was to claim, as his personal property, the woman who had been his father's slave.

Where Slatin was entirely at one, both with Wingate and

with the Anglo-American reformers, was in agreeing that slave-trading in or through the Sudan should be put down. According to Wingate's own estimate, put down it was – at least on any appreciable scale – by about 1912. By that time also the Slavery Repression Department had been dissolved as a separate organization and placed where it really belonged, under the Sudan Police. But, as Slatin had foreseen, slaves continued as household chattels in the Sudan long after they ceased to be profitable merchandise. Domestic slavery not only outlived Slatin's long term of office in the Sudan; it outlasted his own life.

The Inspector-General was not always preoccupied with details like steamer schedules at one end of the scale and theoretical issues like the ethics of slavery at the other. There were occasions, though they were fairly rare, when Wingate allotted him political tasks which were both concrete and important. Through no fault of Slatin's, these missions did develop a depressing habit of never really getting off the ground, or else fizzling out once they did.

In January 1901, for example, only four months after his appointment, Slatin was dispatched to his old province of Darfur, for which he had been given a special advisory duty. His task was to talk its unconquered Sultan, Ali Dinar, into some recognition of the new regime in Khartoum. But the same ruler who, the year before, had pestered Slatin, the gold prospector, for advice on the subject, now turned his back on Slatin the Inspector-General. Ali Dinar not only refused to see Wingate's envoy. He refused even to admit him to his capital. Slatin used up all the pleas and arguments he could think of; it was no use. The man who had once ruled Darfur himself in Gordon's name could not now as much as cross its borders in Wingate's. After much inconclusive parley on the frontier, Slatin had to swallow his pride (and a small piece of his reputation) and return to Khartoum empty-handed.

Ali Dinar was not totally defiant. The sum of £500 tribute money was eventually fixed for him to render to Khartoum in token acknowledgment and, according to Slatin, this was paid or at least promised for the first time in 1902. But though the Sultan opened his coffers a little, he kept his borders tightly closed. Throughout Slatin's fourteen years as Inspector-General, neither he nor any other senior Sudan Government official was ever allowed inside Darfur.

Naturally, there were those in both Cairo and Khartoum who pressed for the forcible subjection of the sultanate. Slatin always argued against this, pointing out that as long as Ali Dinar did not actually betray the central government or take the field against it, a military expedition to subdue him would only be a costly and unnecessary indulgence. Slatin even stuck to his guns in 1909, when the French, striking from Lake Tchad, occupied the vast barren sultanate of Wadai, which bordered directly on Darfur to the west. Despite Ali Dinar's sudden appeals for military aid, Slatin was convinced it was all a subtle French plot to get England to overreach herself on the fringes of the Sahara.

Weary diplomatic negotiations with the French were begun instead, to try and fix a desert frontier between the two powers. Slatin was full of ideas about 'influencing French opinion privately' on this, and eventually got himself appointed to represent the Sudan Government in any forthcoming conference in London or Paris. But this proved another of those missions which trickled away in the sands. The negotiation that finally settled the dispute was so long in forthcoming that it was not begun until 1919 and not concluded until 1924, ten years after Slatin had quitted the Sudan as an official for good. The problem of Ali Dinar was also disposed of after Slatin's departure. The maverick Sultan could be left to his own devices in peacetime, but not in war, especially after he opened up secret contacts with the nationalist movement of the Young Turks. In 1916, Wingate, then still in control of the Sudan, sent out a force to subdue Darfur at long last. In May of that year, the provincial capital of El Fasher was taken. Six months later, Ali Dinar himself, who had fled from Wingate's column, was tracked down and killed.

In all Slatin's fourteen years in office there was only one really important occasion when, though not deputizing for Wingate as Governor-General, he represented him as Number Two in protocol. That was in March 1910, when the former American President Theodore Roosevelt, who was on an African safari holiday with his family, passed through Khartoum. Roosevelt was an immensely influential figure. He was also outspoken, and did not see eye to eye with all aspects of British colonial policy. It was vital, therefore, both for the prestige of the Sudan and for the good name of England in the Sudan that the ex-President got the right picture and the right briefing. Normally, Wingate would have been there to give it. But he was ill in Cairo, *en route* to London for a serious operation. Slatin, who had shown his ability to charm the hind legs even off the Khalifa's donkey, was now given the job of entertaining the great American in Wingate's stead. He made a superb job of it, treating Roosevelt and his family with that same brand of effervescent and highly unorthodox deference which had already won the heart of Queen Victoria.

Slatin's diary for these days is packed full of scribbled notes and underlinings, a return after long blanks to the busy entries of the early years. He really did have the whole show to himself. On the 14th, he proceeded up the White Nile on the official launch to meet the former President and his party on their steamer. He conducted him to Wingate's palace, introduced to him all the heads of the government departments, and then presided at a small dinner party for him. The next two days, accompanied by a swarm of press photographers and correspondents, they went on tours of Khartoum, Omdurman and the surrounding countryside, seeing romantic relics of the past, like Slatin's old house in the Khalifa's city, and impressive monuments of the present, like the Civil Hospital, the American mission, and the Military College which bore Gordon's name.

On the third night, Slatin proposed a toast to the distinguished visitor at a formal dinner in Roosevelt's honour. As this was, in fact, a delicate political speech, Slatin wrote it all down in advance, and the text has survived on another sheet of his diary. It is worth reproducing in full, for the flavour it gives of the occasion and of the writer:

Gentlemen : I have first to express my personal regret that I have to rise instead of H.E. The Governor-General and Sirdar who on account of ill health had to leave for Cairo, and from whom we got happily the best news. He is a good speaker and can express his thoughts in an eloquent way.

I am not. The little ability I had in this way was vigorously suppressed during my stay with dear old Khalifa. I had always to shut up. The root was cut and never grew again.

But even the best orateur (sic) would not be able to describe all the high qualities of character of our illustrious guests. I cannot— but every one of you knows

> what a great statesman
> what a gallant warrior
> what a good sportsman
> what a noble friend

and what a feared opponent he is.

Therefore it is only left for me to express how proud we are that he has honoured us with his presence and how delighted we are to see him amongst us.

Gentlemen: May he live long in good health, may providence keep away from him grief trouble and sorrow and may all his wishes be realized. This, I am sure, is the heartiest wish of every one of us.

The diary entry ends: 'After this we sung: He is a jolly good fellow.'

There is so much of Slatin in those few lines: the spontaneity, which bubbles through even in a prepared speech; the modesty, both genuine and contrived (Khalifa or no Khalifa, Slatin went on talking irrepressibly all his life); and the very un-English sentimentality of those closing lines. Yet, because it was the whole man, it carries conviction, and seems to have had its effect on the day. Slatin as tourist dragoman and public relations officer combined had indeed no equal in the Sudan. Even the hardbitten ex-President was delighted and impressed when he left the following day.

The dividend came two and a half months later, when Roosevelt, now in England, delivered his famous Guildhall speech of 31 May 1910. In a long passage devoted to his stay in Khartoum, he said:

The Sudan is peculiarly interesting because it affords the best possible example of the wisdom of disregarding the well-meaning but unwise sentimentalists who object to the spread of civilization at the expense of savagery. I do not believe that in the whole world there is to be found any nook of territory which has shown such astonishing progress from the most hideous misery to well-being and prosperity as the Sudan has showed during the last twelve years while it has been under British rule . . .

During a decade and a half, while Mahdism controlled the country, there flourished a tyranny which for cruelty, bloodthirstiness, unintelligence and wanton destructiveness surpassed anything which civilized people can even imagine . . . Then the English came in, put an end to the independence and self-government, which had wrought this hideous evil, restored order, kept the peace, and gave to each individual a liberty which during the evil days of self-government not one human being possessed, save only the blood-stained tyrant who at the moment was ruler . . .

In administration, in education, in police work, the Sirdar and his lieutenants, great and small, have performed to perfection a task equally important and difficult. The Government officials . . . who are responsible for this task . . . have a claim on civilized mankind which should be heartily admitted.

Hyperbole apart, there was nothing in this tribute that the facts did not justify. The Sudan was, for example, almost solvent at the time Roosevelt was speaking, its revenue having increased nearly tenfold from a mere £E156,888 in 1900 to £E1,171,007 in 1910. But the great thing was to get an influential and searching observer like the ex-President of the United States himself to pay such a glowing public tribute. For Wingate, reading reports of the speech the next day in his London hospital, it was better than any convalescent medicine. Dear old Rowdy, one of those lieutenants Roosevelt had spoken of, had certainly 'performed to perfection' his task.

There were, of course, rough patches in Slatin's official career to be set against such personal triumphs; and these rough patches sometimes involved the ordinary natives of the Sudan as well as his own colleagues in the English ruling hierarchy. From the first, Wingate relied heavily on Slatin for advice on Islamic affairs. The Inspector-General had, after all, worshipped in Arab mosques for twelve years and had learned all the ritual of Moslem prayer literally the hard way, his knees pressed for hours against the stone. True, Slatin's theology, like his Arabic, was all of the impure Sudanese variety and he never seems to have had the time or the intellectual curiosity to try and purify either. Still, one would have thought that precisely because he spoke the dialects of the Sudan and had shared in its homespun brand of the true faith, he would always be accepted by the common people with whom he had such links.

Yet the exact opposite could be the case. There were times when the links became barriers. One old Sudan hand* re-

* Major Alec Wise, Commanding Officer of the Sudan Camel Corps in Kordofan 1904–1911, and ninety-two years old at the time of writing.

members more than one occasion on which the native troops he commanded spat in the dust at the mere mention of Slatin's name. For them (as for General Gordon) there was 'no honour in a man who would change his religion just to save his life'. With the learned religious scholars of Khartoum, Slatin seems to have got on better. At any rate it was at his suggestion that a permanent committee of such so-called *ulemas* was set up in 1901 to advise Wingate on all Islamic questions.

The importance of this was obvious. Religion had fired the Mahdist revolt and the embers from that great blaze, though scattered, were still smouldering. There were periodic scares when it seemed that the embers might even catch light again. A petty self-styled successor to the Mahdi was hanged in Kordofan in 1903. A year later a Prophet Jesus, always an alternate manifestation of Mahdism, proclaimed himself at Sinja on the Blue Nile and had to be suppressed. But the most serious trouble broke out in the Blue Nile province of Gezira in 1908. It brought with it also Slatin's one and only public quarrel with Wingate in all their years together.

A deposed Mahdist notable, Wad Habuba, whose brother had been given by the government the lands that had once been his, raised a revolt in the local village after years of unsuccessful intrigues. The Inspector of the area, one C. C. Scott-Moncrieff, was a young man newly recruited from England into the Sudan Service, and he seems to have been suffused with that splendid Edwardian conviction that a white face and a uniform were enough to settle any native discontent. Ignoring the warnings of the loyal sheikhs, the Englishman entered Wad Habuba's compound escorted by only one Egyptian official, intending to talk the rebel into submission. He knew too little of the Mahdist fanaticism that had once swept this land and soon paid the full price for his folly. The two men were set upon in the courtyard by an armed band, murdered, and their bodies tossed contemptuously into the village street outside. The challenge had to be crushed before it could take root as an example. Yet it was only after a fierce skirmish, with losses on both sides, that, on 1 May 1908, the insurgents were subdued by a company of regular army infantry under British command.

The case of Wad Habuba himself, who was hunted down and captured after the fight was clear enough. He had killed two government officials and for this, and other charges of in-surgency, he was tried, sentenced to death and executed. But what of the twenty-five rebels captured with him? A special tribunal, convened under the Chief Justice of the Sudan, Wasey Sterrey, recommended the death penalty for all of them too, on the grounds that they had raised the Mahdist banner of revolt, which was now treason and heresy combined. But Wingate felt that to execute twenty-five more captives at one go would look too much like the old blood-baths the Sudan was trying to forget. After consulting with London, he commuted all the sentences to terms of imprisonment, acting without, it appears, consulting any of his local advisers.

Partly because they had been left out of it but partly because they genuinely felt that, in this emergency, a mass execution was needed as a deterrent, there was a great commotion among Wingate's senior staff. Even Edgar Bonham-Carter, his Legal Secretary, who was normally the most loyal and placid of men, threatened his resignation. Slatin, always sensitive about being bypassed, and swept along now by the general wave of pique, went one further and actually offered his. He was up in Cairo at the time, for discussions with Sir Eldon Gorst, who had succeeded the great Cromer as British Agent two years before. Slatin's diary, with its characteristic flavour and mis-spelling, gives the story:

May 31: Lunch with Gorst who informs me that Sirdar has com-mutated death sentences—at one without appeal ...
June 1: As I consider I would not be able to fulfill my duty in a satisfactory way and to keep peace in the Sudan after all death sentences wer (sic) commuted and as Sirdar did not consult neither me nor Bonham or Phipps before answering the F.O. telegram— *I give my resignation!*

Other correspondence suggests that Slatin, who had a native caution built in even with his impulsiveness, was thinking here only of resigning from the Governor-General's Council. Yet that diary entry, and the resignation telegram to Khartoum which preceded it, were quite unqualified. Had Wingate been a lesser man, and a lesser friend, Slatin would have been out of a job that same day, at his own formal request. But though he could not see Slatin's diary, with the critical sentence written in large letters, heavily underlined and followed by an exclamation mark, Wingate knew this was just a bit of Viennese comic opera. His concern was not merely to save Slatin in his job (which he knew he could do) but to save his friend's wounded pride in the process. He wired back to his resentful Inspector-General claiming that in fact he agreed with his views but had been forced by London into clemency – none of which was strictly true. Then, imploring his friend not to resign, he hoisted the one flag that would always bring Slatin to attention, the royal standard of England. Among those, he said, who 'require our loyalty in a matter of this sort' was King Edward vii.

That august name already carried an overwhelming weight with Slatin in all the walks of his life. The next words in his 1908 diary show how it disposed of the immediate crisis.

June 4: I withdraw my resignation at
       Wingate's urgent request.

No underlinings or exclamation marks here; and the writing so far from being florid, looks hasty and even a little shamefaced. It had indeed all been a nonsense. Slatin was never so addicted to principle in anything – religion, politics, or personal conduct – that he would instinctively sacrifice career or survival for them. And to be Inspector-General of the Sudan was, for him, both career and survival. Not so much in Khartoum, where he had reached the height of his career and already passed the zenith of his influence, but in his real homelands of Europe. Here Lieutenant-General Baron Sir Rudolf von Slatin Pasha was still going from court to court, spa to spa, and from strength to strength.

Chapter Twelve

CREST OF THE WAVE

What was it that the sovereigns and princes of the old Europe saw in Slatin? Some of his characteristics have come through already: the tenacity matched with pliability, and the quick tongue coupled with the slow patience. But perhaps this is the time, at the turn of the century and the turn of Slatin's own fortunes, to take a closer look at him as his contemporaries saw him.

He was a fairly small man, only 1m. 70cm. or 5 ft 7 ins in height, and slenderly built. By 1900, when he was forty-three years old, his full dark hair and generous moustache were both tinged with grey. But there was nothing middle-aged about the lively blue eyes and the magnificent set of teeth which were always lighting up his face. (The quality of the latter was probably an unintentional gift from the Khalifa. For twelve years as his captive he had used only sugar cane, the healthiest of natural tooth-brushes.) Slatin moved gracefully yet always held himself bolt upright, thus getting the most out of his height and his richly decorated uniforms. He was exceptionally light on his feet and the ladies noticed not only that he was one of the nimblest ballroom dancers of his time but that he had as beautiful a pair of calves as you would see anywhere in Europe – no mean attribute in those days of knee-breeches.

The flashing eyes and the flashing teeth were also the keys to his personality. As Sir Ronald Wingate, the son of his greatest friend, remembers him:

Intense vitality was the first thing that struck you about him. He positively radiated health and energy whenever he came into a room, and he always bubbled over with good spirits and a sense of fun. But it never seemed contrived or put on. Everything he did and said looked and sounded spontaneous. The tremendous charm came out quite naturally and it went in all directions—to men or women, to white or black, to young or old and to the humble as well as the mighty. There was no trace of pomposity about him. He wanted so much to enjoy life and he was determined that everyone should enjoy it with him. He was a great raconteur, but rarely put himself in the middle of his tales; and he had that real sense of humour which he was always prepared to turn against himself. When it was turned against others, this was always done in the gentlest way. I grew up with him and in the forty odd years, as boy and man, that I knew him, I never heard a spiteful word about anyone or anything from his lips.

Slatin was no intellectual, as all his own writings, as well as his surviving friends, would testify. Yet though he rarely read a book, he gave the impression of being well read. He had a feel for culture without having much of an appetite for it. In high-powered conversation his wit and experience of life usually made up for what he lacked in conventional brain-power and learning. He was sentimental and, unlike his English colleagues, was always extrovert enough to show it. This sentimentality led him often into nostalgia and sometimes into self-pity. He was the true Viennese, with 'one laughing and one weeping eye'. The outside world saw the laughter. The sighs he kept for his family and his closest friends.

Above all, he was a great romantic. Romance had first lured him to the Sudan as an obscure Austrian youth. In the long run, it would probably have kept him there even if the Khalifa had not. And when Slatin became a well-known European figure it was still the romance of that old order that attracted him, even more than its glitter (though he was very partial to that as well). This romanticism shone through everything, including his snobbery. He was, of course, an incurable snob in the sense that his life became one long and dedicated pursuit of royalty and the grand families grouped around their thrones. Yet, for Slatin, the monarchy was more than that coloured fountain from which all worthwhile titles and decorations flowed. He really believed in the divine right of kings and in that deceptive social stability which still seemed to go with it in the early twentieth century.

This romanticism was one element which took any jagged edges off his snobbery. His own kindly humanity was another. Though automatically deferential to those above him on the social scale, Slatin was never arrogant to those below. That he flattered the great, whose favours or company he sought, was to be expected. What was more unusual was that he was kind to the humble, without any hint of patronizing. His hands were always fluttering upwards; but his heel never came down.

Again, this arose from his easy-going Viennese philosophy that one did not have to compete in life for happiness; there was enough to go round without that. The word genius is not one that even Slatin's most ardent admirer would normally associate with him. Yet if Rudolf Slatin was a genius in anything, it was in handling people.

Such was the Austrian Inspector-General of the Sudan who, for the first fourteen years of the twentieth century, became such an established figure of the old European scene. These years as a social lion can no more be taken in strict chronology than the parallel years as an official, or, for that matter, the years as a captive that had gone before. They are not so much a developing narrative as an ever-repeating pattern, with occasional highlights that make some patches even brighter than the others. The annual routine was always basically the same.

From mid-October to early June, Slatin would be in the Sudan, with frequent trips up to Cairo on duty or short leave. Throughout the whole of the summer and early autumn he would be on long leave in Europe. There you would find him in Vienna; at the pleasant lake-side villa at Traunkirchen in the Salzkammergut where his two unmarried sisters had settled; at the Bohemian spas; at Hungarian shooting-lodges; in Rome or Paris; at the courts of Bavaria, Saxony or any of the lesser German princelings with whom he had scraped an acquaintance; in London; in the English countryside at the houses of his Sudan Government colleagues; with Wingate at his Scottish home in Dunbar; and, above all, of course, at Windsor, Balmoral, Sandringham and wherever else the English crown which was his abiding glory had summoned him.

Socially as well as officially, the months in the Sudan and the months in Europe were closely linked. To winter in Cairo was becoming a steadily more popular fancy among rich and distinguished Europeans even before the turn of the century. After 1900, with the pacification of the Sudan and the creation of its modern capital, the romantic trip up the Nile to Khartoum was often added on as well. There was no one of note visiting Khartoum who would want to miss meeting Slatin Pasha or whom Slatin would want to miss meeting himself.

Occasionally, even crowned heads arrived as tourists and though these occasions had little of the political importance of President Roosevelt's visit, their value to the Sudan in general and to Slatin in particular was none the less considerable. Both were put further on the map by such patronage. An entry in Slatin's diary for 25 March 1911, sums up this dual aspect nicely:

Sunday last King Friederick August [of Saxony] left Khartoum and on Monday King Albert of Belgique arrived. Two kings in two days—the Sudan goes ahead! Both Majesties are very interested in the work done by us in the Sudan ... Both Kings asked me to visit them when returning to Europe.

It was the game-shooting more than the sight-seeing that had brought the 'Majesties' to the Sudan, for the sport was plentiful and varied. (Slatin's own trophies as he recorded them ranged from elephant, hippopotamus, giraffe and crocodile at the heavy end of the scale to antelopes and hartebeest at the lighter end.) Hunting was also, of course, very much the 'class-sport' in the Austrian monarchy of the time. The old Emperor was particularly devoted to the stalking of stag, deer and chamois, while his heir, Archduke Franz Ferdinand, was certainly the greediest and possibly the finest dispatcher of game-birds to be found anywhere in Europe. The landed families of the Empire needed no encouragement to follow these illustrious examples. The foxhunting of the English gentry played but a minute part in their lives;* the Englishman's passion for fly-fishing none at all. It was the shot-gun and the rifle which dominated the Austrian aristocrat's sport, and the inter-

* Almost the only hunt of consequence was at Pardubice in Bohemia, though other packs were kept in Hungary.

connecting cycle of open and close game seasons ruled his year more rigidly than any ball calendar.

Slatin, who had been born far removed from this happy breed of landed trigger-squeezers in his native Austria, now had the chance to get on terms with them in the Sudan. 'Rowdy House' in Khartoum could now be his castle and the deserts which bordered the muddy Nile his game forests. More and more, as the years go by, the names of Austria's greatest families crop up during the winter months in Slatin's diaries, private guests of the Inspector-General, and hunters one and all:

March 12, 1907:   Count Franz Kinsky arrives from the Upper Nile and stays with me.

March 29, 1908:   Prince Fritz Liechtenstein arrives for his shooting trip.

February 3, 1910:   Fürst Franz Auersperg and Prince Vincenz Auersperg arrived and are staying with me.

The Kinskys, of course, had been the august patrons of the Slatin family. It must have been delicious for Rudolf to have them now seated at his own table and with a bevy of servants to dance attendance. Quite apart from the day's sport, those evenings at Slatin's wide-verandahed house must have had a breezy charm of their own. It is well conveyed in this invitation card of his which has survived from 19 January 1905:

Please come and dance at 'Rowdy House' on Monday next at 9.30 p.m.
Opportunities will be given for:
         A great deal of dancing
         Plenty of drinks
         Some flirting
         A little food
         And no Bridge
         (Sorry, there is only one table)
                 Be good and come.

Like the foreign kings, the counts and princes of his own homeland also asked Slatin to visit them in return. His fourteen years as a British official in Khartoum thus achieved more for him socially than any forty as an Austrian official in Vienna could have done.

Yet despite the attractions of 'Rowdy House' for his illustrious visitors, the patronage which underpinned his whole career remained the crown of England. It was a highly personal patronage, however, and Slatin had to work hard to renew it with each of the three sovereigns under whom he served. When, for example, his beloved Queen Victoria finally died on 22 January 1901, Slatin feared that irreparable damage had been dealt to his prospects. He was by no means the only one who thought that the world had come to an end with the old matriarch's death. But the world not only kept turning under King Edward VII. As far as the social round was concerned, it started positively spinning, and Slatin was soon spinning happily again with it.

He had met the King several times as Prince of Wales, and seems to have scored a decisive hit with him as the new monarch during the summer of 1903. This was in fact the first of the Inspector-General's brilliant seasons. The continental part of it began with a *séjour* at St Moritz where, his diary records, he met all the visiting Archdukes and dined and danced incessantly at the Palace Hotel with international hostesses like Lady Sassoon. From St Moritz he went to Vienna to attend a dinner at the Liechtenstein Palace. This was followed by ten days of relative peace and quiet at the villa in Traunkirchen. Then, at the end of August, he returned to Vienna for the state visit of King Edward to the Emperor Franz Joseph. For the first time, Slatin was together with both the monarch whose servant he was and the monarch whose subject he was.

If the Vienna state visit was short on diplomacy (Turkish atrocities in Macedonia was the only topic discussed that could be put under this heading) it was very long on festivities. Slatin reaped the benefit of the unique position he held in the Anglo-Austrian framework. He was invited everywhere, including to the Gala Dinner which the Emperor gave for his English guest and to the splendid reception which the Vienna Jockey Club offered this royal racing enthusiast who was to saddle no fewer than three Derby Stakes winners in his life.

Remembering the great things which had sprung from that exchange of photographs with King Edward's mother, Slatin returned to the idea with her son. Earlier that summer, he had approached the King to present an official portrait of himself to hang in the Palace Reception Room at Khartoum. He now followed this up with a more personal approach. From Traunkirchen he wrote to a member of the King's personal staff:

I have from all members of the Royal family Photos with signature —from the late Maj. the Queen several, also one of the present Queen as Princess of Wales. Could you induce their Majesties to grant me theyr Photos? Certainly—I leave it to you to judge if such a demand is right and if you wont or cannot forward my request please dont think I would be hurt. Dont look on me as obtrusive— but I would consider such a gift as a special favour conferred upon me...

Is perhaps any chance to see you in Egypt or Sudan. We all would give you a jolly good time 'up the Nile'.

It was the Slatin mixture as before: so anxious to get his favours yet so anxious not to presume, like a man on tiptoe bending slightly backwards. Delicate though the balance was, he never toppled. Slatin duly got his pictures, both the official engravings for Wingate's palace and the private photographs for himself. So began Slatin's heyday with the House of Windsor, as it was later styled, a relationship with King Edward VII which was closer than that of a good acquaintance and which almost attained that of a true personal friend. We can see why Slatin welcomed this regal intimacy. The genuine pleasure which the King found in Slatin's company is also easy to understand, once we look at that monarch's temperament and tastes.

Like Slatin, King Edward was no bookish intellectual but a gregarious party-goer determined to squeeze the last drop of enjoyment out of every hour and minute of his day. Boredom was for him the one unbearable affliction, the ultimate enemy. To escape it he fled, again like Slatin, not to any consolations of the mind or spirit, but to the refined distractions of the flesh – good food and wine, elegant and beautiful women, travel, cards, horses, shooting, and the company of companions who were cheerful and witty but not too highbrow. Both men would have endorsed, even if they could not have quoted, Pope's dictum that 'the proper study of mankind is man'. Each was interested above all in personal relationships and each man in his station went to extreme lengths to preserve his friendships.

217

Indeed, one gets the feeling that had they exchanged their stations in life, each would have behaved very like the other. Slatin at Balmoral and Sandringham would have set the same relentless social pace, and he would have ruled, as King Edward tried to do, through picking men he liked and trusted, rather than through mastering every Cabinet minute and Whitehall file. And had Edward ever become Inspector-General of the Sudan, 'Rowdy House' in Khartoum would surely have been just the place it was under Rudolf Slatin.

Nor, in King Edward's case, did their very different backgrounds as regards nationality, race and birth matter one iota. As to the nationality, the King of England was the supreme European anyway, a man as much at home in Bohemia or Biarritz as he was in Birmingham (indeed, as regards that particular town, far more so). And the fact that Rudolf was of obscure Jewish origins did nothing to disqualify him in the King's eyes. At home, members of the English *haute juiverie* like Arthur, Albert and Reuben Sassoon had been admitted to King Edward's inner circle of friends long before the turn of the century when he was still Prince of Wales. Another Jewish financier, Ernest Cassel (who, by a coincidence, had backed that abortive gold-prospecting expedition of Slatin's) became perhaps the King's closest man friend as well as the shrewdest of his business managers; and Cassel's origins in the Cologne of the 1850s had been about as insignificant as Slatin's in the Vienna of the same decade, though his blazing talents were to carry him far higher.

Indeed, the fact that Slatin was born where he was and what he was may well have commended him specially for the King's patronage. As Prince of Wales, Edward had shown an open revulsion at the way the old Austrian families cold-shouldered the newly-ennobled Jews of the Empire, men who usually surpassed them in everything except the length of their pedigree. Thus, as early as 1881, when the then Prince of Wales went to Vienna to attend the wedding of Crown Prince Rudolf to Princess Stephanie of Belgium, he deliberately chose to put up at a hotel so that he could receive and entertain the Austrian Rothschilds who, for all their millions, were treated as mere commercial barons by many of the landed aristocracy.

And in 1890, when he went to Vienna again (this time to lay

a wreath on the Crown Prince Rudolf's tomb) Prince Edward
shocked the magnates even more by entertaining a Hungarian
Jewish financier who did not possess even the same international
cachet as the Rothschilds. This was Baron Maurice Hirsch, a
genial but quite remorseless social climber. Hirsch had allegedly
lent the hard-pressed Prince of Wales a great deal of money,
becoming his unofficial financial adviser before the formidable
Cassel took over. Edward liked Hirsch and he stuck to him until
his death in 1896, despite the Hungarian's increasingly tiresome demands – not for payment, which if owing would have
been made anyway – but for social preferment. And now, on
6 October of 1890, this was the 'upstart' who sat at Prince
Edward's luncheon table in Vienna's Grand Hotel, a table that
included, among the other guests, the King of Greece. What
was more, after lunch, the Prince of Wales and his party all
left for the Austro-Hungarian border, to stay for ten days as
Hirsch's guests at a shooting party. (The ten guns killed twenty
thousand partridges on that stay which, as Edward himself
wrote, 'will quite spoil me for shooting at home'.)

Slatin could never provide hospitality like that, and he had
little spare money to lend anyone. But he could supply fun and
relaxing company, and that was passport enough to the King's
affections. The important thing to note, however, is that the
Edwardian world into which that passport took Slatin was, for
all its breath-taking glitter, not entirely unfamiliar. On the
English side at any rate, there had been, and still were, other
Slatins in the landscape.

From now on until 1909, the last full year of King Edward's
life, Slatin's European seasons revolved around the English
sovereign. The King was a regular midsummer visitor to
Marienbad, where he had his own suite of rooms at the Weimar
Hotel. Though the Bohemian spa was in the middle of the
Emperor Franz Joseph's domains, once the King of England
arrived there it became the temporary capital of his own travelling European court. The Emperor called on him at Marienbad
himself in 1904, though without discussing state affairs. Statesmen and diplomatists regularly turned up there to indulge in a
little holiday politics. They were kept in their place: King
Edward saw to it that this never swamped the serious business
of enjoying oneself and indulging in that self-defeating Marien-

bad sequence of taking weight off with the famous mineral waters and putting it on again with meals prepared by equally famous chefs.

. Slatin always made this happy pilgrimage to Edwardian Marienbad, and though he only stayed for two or three days, he saw more of the King in that time than would have been possible in a month of formal court existence. From 1904 onwards, Slatin's diary entries for these visits get plastered ever more thickly with King Edward's name. The climax comes in 1908 when he spent three days there as the King's personal guest at the Hotel Weimar and was almost incessantly in his company. The first day's entry will do as a sample:

28 August: Arrived Marienbad from Vienna 6.48 a.m.
Breakfast with King at 9 a.m.
Drove with King to Mrs Waddington's lunch.
Dinner with King at 6.45, then with him in box for opera (Walzertraum) in royal party.
Supper with King at 10 p.m. after opera.

And so it went on, until a weary but glowing Slatin caught the train back to Vienna on the night of 30 August.

There was good reason for such exceptional royal favour by this time, for Slatin's King and Slatin's Emperor were developing the habit of meeting for a day or two in mid-August, first at Marienbad itself and then at Bad Ischl, Franz Joseph's beloved summer resort amid the mountains and lakes of the Austrian Salzkammergut. As Slatin was the best Anglo-Austrian that either monarch possessed, he was always in attendance. King Edward's first visit to Ischl had been in 1907, and, like the Marienbad meeting, it was a far more relaxed occasion than that initial encounter between the two rulers in Vienna four years before. Slatin never dared unbend one millimetre in the presence of his own sovereign (who was every daunting inch the Apostolic Majesty even in the green *Loden* stalking suit he wore at Ischl). But it was much easier to stay at the centre of things in the Imperial holiday villa than in any of the Imperial palaces, for there the smoking-room replaced the antechamber.

Thus Slatin notes in his diary for 15 August 1907: 'Have long talks with Emperor and King before and after dinner.' And

King Edward paid Slatin a very personal compliment, when he left by train the next morning, to have a special stop made at Traunkirchen just to meet and talk for five minutes with Slatin's two spinster sisters. ('Many spectators – but heavy rain', their brother notes of the occasion.)

Though Slatin does not reveal what was discussed at these 'long talks', we know from other evidence that King Edward was not only in Ischl to sample the shooting and the renowned pastries of the Café Zauner. Germany's naval expansion lay like a heavy cloud across England's horizon, and Edward wanted Franz Joseph to use his influence with his German ally, the Emperor William, to get that cloud diminished even though it could not be dispersed. The following August, again at Ischl on his way to Marienbad, King Edward returned to the same theme with Franz Joseph, talking this time with still greater insistence, and even hinting that Austria-Hungary might loosen her ties with Germany and move closer to England instead.

But in 1908, as in 1907, the old Austrian monarch, who clung to the sanctity of alliances and to the mythical unity of the German nation – however much he disapproved, on occasions, of the Emperor William – refused to be shifted from the Berlin axis. No one at Bad Ischl, or anywhere else for that matter, had any inkling that by that refusal he had made a European holocaust, and with it the annihilation of his own Monarchy, one degree more certain. Indeed, the two monarchs parted in the most genial of holiday spirits, King Edward noting that he had managed to persuade the Emperor to ride in an automobile for the first time in his life. It was not exactly what he had come to Ischl to achieve.

Slatin was about the last person in that illustrious company who was likely to feel any gloomy forebodings for the future. He could not imagine a world in which his English King and his Austrian Emperor could do anything except politely disagree about politics and then return to talk of stag-heads. And the more often they met, even to do that, the happier Slatin was, for he loved and revered them both. Happier, and also more favoured. This was the climate, with his two monarchs meeting almost every summer, in which honours fairly showered down upon him.

Rudolf Slatin had been made a Knight (*Ritter*) by the Emperor Franz Joseph back in March 1899. This was the lowest and newest rung on the Monarchy's great ladder of titles. It enabled him to use the predicate *von* before his surname and to ornament his writing-paper, his shirts, his luggage and whatever else he decently could with a five-pointed open crown. Now, on 24 October 1906, both Rudolf and his brother Heinrich were created Austrian barons (the nearest English equivalent of being 'raised to the *Freiherrstand*') and so blossomed out from five points to seven. This seven-pointed crown duly appears in the centre of Rudolf's new coat of arms, which was registered with his formal patent of nobility on 27 June 1907, less than two months before the first Ischl meeting. Under the crown is a tall palm tree for the Sudan, and a lion brandishing a sword and trailing a pair of broken hand-chains, to symbolize Slatin's sufferings and struggles in the Sudan. There is also a six-pointed star (not the Jewish star of David) enclosed by a pair of balanced scales whose significance is less apparent. The African symbols were taken over from his 1899 coat of arms. So was the motto: *Festina Lente* or Hasten Slowly. (It was an odd motto for the bustling Slatin. 'Strike while the iron is hot' would have been more apt.)

The next honour to come his way was a good example of this tireless opportunism. Wingate happened to be in Vienna that same June of 1907. He received an Austrian order, the Grand Cross of Franz Joseph, and dined with the Emperor on the 20th at Schönbrunn Palace. There was talk of the Sudan and Wingate did not fail to praise the great services that Slatin was rendering there for England. This was no doubt spontaneous enough. But one can discern Slatin's hand in what his ever-willing sponsor did next. Ever since the re-conquest of the Sudan, Slatin had hankered after a proper British army uniform in addition to that of the Egyptian Army which he had worn for more than ten years. This seemed the moment to go after it, with his new patent of nobility in his pocket, with his greatest English friend in Vienna receiving a high Austrian decoration and with his English King and his Austrian Emperor soon to meet on Austrian soil.

A letter Wingate wrote on his behalf to Lord Knollys, King Edward's Private Secretary, later that summer takes up the tale. After mentioning how gratified the Emperor had been about his praise of Slatin, Wingate continues:

When I was in London a few weeks ago, I was talking to Lord Camperdown about Slatin and casually said that I felt sure the appointment of Slatin as an honorary Major-General in the British Army would be taken as a great compliment not only by the Emperor but by the Austrian army and people . . .

Given the current cordial climate of Anglo-Austrian relations, nobody was going to resist that carefully placed nudge. Three days later Lord Haldane, the Secretary for War, agreed to the honorary rank being granted and on 22 August Wingate was able to write again to Knollys, expressing his delight at the decision and adding: 'Slatin's cup of joy will be full indeed.' The appointment came too late for that year's Ischl meeting. But in August 1908 Slatin was at Bad Ischl station in the full dress uniform of an English Major-General to salute King Edward on the platform.

As far as decorations were concerned, Slatin soon had to find room for one more large addition to his 'cup of joy'. During his three days at Marienbad later that same August, his host King Edward, who had already made him a CVO there in 1904, now conferred on him the KCVO, his second English knighthood. By now, though Slatin still had plenty of gratitude left for decorations, he was almost running out of room for them. King Edward, confronted with Slatin's blazing frock-coat front in which Austrian, English, Prussian, Saxon, Italian and Turkish medals struggled for anchorage on the cloth, laughingly suggested that he turned round so that this new star could be pinned on his back.

The next year, 1909, the last of these royal Marienbad summers, was not the happiest. For once, the shadow of high politics hung immovably over the promenades, the golf, the picnics and the dinner parties. It was no longer a case of England and Austria-Hungary differing about Germany but of the two monarchies being directly at odds themselves. The previous October the Emperor Franz Joseph had been persuaded by the 'activists' among his advisers to annex Bosnia and Herzegovina to his Empire. Though Austrian troops had been in occupation of the two Turkish provinces since 1878, this unilateral act of formal annexation aroused a storm of protest in every major European capital except Berlin, where the Emperor William stood by his Austrian ally. King Edward himself wrote a reproachful letter to the Emperor Franz Joseph about it all, and then pointedly refused to congratulate Aerenthal, the Emperor's Foreign Minister and one of the principal architects of the annexation, on being created a count for his zealous services. Aerenthal took his revenge by persuading his Emperor to break off his annual summer meetings with King Edward unless the English monarch formally requested their resumption, an impossible condition.

The upshot was that Franz Joseph stayed put at Ischl that August while King Edward did not stir from Marienbad. In his daily stroll across the park there, the King would pass an unhewn boulder some eight tons in weight into whose surface had been sunk bronze medallion portraits of himself and the Austrian Emperor, gazing amicably towards each other. It was a monument to their first meeting at these Bohemian waters in 1904 and had been hopefully designed on this massive scale to symbolize the solid basis on which their friendship, and the amity between their two countries, was thought to rest. Exactly five years later, the boulder had become an acute, if temporary, embarrassment. It was a sobering reflection for King Edward to take home from this, his last glimpse of Marienbad.

However, if the King had been forced to make do with only a medallion of Franz Joseph, at least Slatin was there again in the flesh as his personal guest at the Hotel Weimar. As can be imagined, it was not an easy time for the Inspector-General, whose fame, favour and happiness hung on this now-twisted thread of Anglo-Austrian friendship. The great Viennese newspaper of the day, *Neue Freie Presse,* shrewdly sent a correspondent to Marienbad to ask him how he, an Austrian subject in the service of the English, felt about things. The eloquent Pasha did his best.

'You are quite right', he replied, 'in assuming that this business has touched me very acutely. You well know that though I am a General serving England I have remained an Austrian subject, and I attach great importance to staying one. I was obviously unhappy to see public controversy between Austria-Hungary and England and particularly distressed that, in the heat of argument, King

Edward himself was attacked by name. I can only assure you, on the basis of long observation strengthened still further by my present stay here with His Majesty, that Austria-Hungary has no better friend in the world than the King of England, and that there is no one on earth with a deeper respect for our own King and Emperor, Franz Joseph I.'

Only once before had Slatin felt the two horses which normally drew him on so smoothly suddenly snap at each other in harness. This was during the Boer War, when Austrian public opinion, following the German lead, became temporarily hostile to England. Slatin, staying at Balmoral, had blandly assured Queen Victoria on that occasion that this hostility was due solely to the 'ignorance and stupidity of the (Austrian) Middle Classes, who have never left their own country'.

This second estrangement of 1908–9 was much more serious because it was much nearer home and had arisen in a political arena where there was much less room for manoeuvre: the heart of those troubled Balkans which all the European powers, England included, already saw as the greatest latent threat to world peace. Yet the threat was still only latent. Sarajevo, the capital of that annexed Bosnian province, remained for a little longer only a geographical expression. Slatin was therefore quite justified in telling that Viennese journalist who interviewed him in Marienbad that the friction caused by the annexation was 'as good as over'. The coolness between London and Vienna proved even more short-lived than in 1900 and was over by the new year.

But 1910 soon brought a far greater shock to Slatin. On 6 May, after a brief illness following a chill, King Edward died peacefully at Buckingham Palace in his sixty-ninth year. As at the death of his mother nine years before, it seemed that an era had died with the sovereign whose name it had borne. And now, as in 1901, there were few English subjects who mourned the dead monarch more deeply than the Austrian Rudolf Slatin – out of a mixture of quite genuine grief and rather more practical calculations. Two brief and agitated entries in his 1910 diary read:

May 5. The King is ill!
May 7: The King died yesterday night at 11.45 p.m. The most
      terrible loss for me!

That loss was never quite to be made up. Slatin never achieved the same degree of easy-going intimacy with the new monarch, George v, that he had established with his father. (The son was in any case much less of an extrovert in character and far less dedicated to the pursuit of fun and pleasure.) But, in some ways, George v was to prove in the end an even more wonderful friend to Slatin than King Edward had been. As for the transition between reigns, that was managed for Slatin much more quickly and smoothly than in 1901. In September 1910, when King George had been a bare six months on the throne, Slatin was up at Balmoral again with Wingate for what he quaintly describes as a 'dear (*sic*) drive'.

His diary for this weekend is more detailed than usual and has some delightful touches.

2 September (Friday): Dinner with King and Queen—sit on King's left. Play bridge with King, Asquith and Wingate and win £2.5.0

3 September (Saturday): Leave the castle at 11 a.m. with the King, Prinz of Wales, Sir Charles Frederick and Sir Harry Legge for a dear drive.
Had lunch in the woods.
At the third drive I shoot a good stack. We return at 6 p.m. Had only one shot and got one stack. Prinz of Wales missed twice. The King shot 3.

Sunday was the usual quiet Balmoral day of morning church and an afternoon excursion for tea. On Monday Slatin visited Lord Knollys (who had helped to arrange that Major-Generalship for him). The King, he records, gave him a walking-stick and showed him his bathroom in the castle, decorated with Pick's racy drawings of *Lord Humbug auf Reisen*. More notably, Mr Lloyd George arrived to stay. Slatin's visit ended in flying style:

6 September (Tuesday): When sitting at lunch next the Queen she gave me at the end of the meal light for my cigarre—and I said 'Thanks Majesty'. She said *'Sie müssen Ich küss die Hand sagen'*.*
The lunch was most animated and we were laughing the whole time.

* 'I kiss your hand' was, especially in Vienna, an ornate way of saying 'Thank you'. Queen Mary, born a Princess of Teck, spoke German as well as English.

226

To cap the day, a telegram arrived for Slatin from the Emperor Franz Joseph's Court Chamberlain in Vienna, Prince Montenuovo. It told him that an invitation to Schönbrunn from 'the All-Highest' awaited him for 12 September. As that was less than a week away, Slatin had to be off soon for London. But they had time for another light-hearted picnic the next day ('After tea we runn about – the Queen, the children, myself!'); and before he caught the night train he had another dinner seated next to the Queen and was presented with signed photographs of the royal couple as a souvenir of the stay. 'I am sorry you are going', were Queen Mary's last words, and we can believe she meant it.

The fact that, this time, Slatin had got his photographs without even asking for them showed what an established part of the English court furniture he had become. This scene indeed now moved entirely to England for him. The high jinks of Marienbad had gone for good with King Edward; so had those more stately royal encounters on Austrian soil at Ischl. But the London event for which Slatin, and indeed everyone who mattered in Europe, was now preparing more than made up for the loss of this spa diplomacy. That event, of course, was the coronation of King George and Queen Mary on 22 June 1911.

Slatin seems to have had a moment of panic that he might have been left out of it all. This is indicated by a reassuring telegram – obviously sent in reply to an anxious inquiry – which he received in Vienna from Sir Arthur Bigge on 6 June and which he entered in his diary for that day. The telegram read:

Your name was put on first list King made some months ago for one of his seats in the Abbey. Where should invitation be sent?

Nothing could have been more gratifying. A delighted Slatin set out for London with all his finery at the end of that week. He travelled via Paris where he spent a few days mixing pleasure with business – in this case, French countesses with French colonial affairs. He had what he describes as 'very satisfactory' talks with the Minister of Colonies, M. Massimy, and with several of his leading French African officials. He saw politicians and powerful journalists like the editors of the *Temps* and the *Matin*. On the social side, his most persistent pursuer was a lady he describes as 'Princess Bonoparte de Moskawa'. She asked him to luncheons on every single day of his visit and captured him twice.

But the Paris visit was merely a pleasant overture to the great spectacle which now opened in London. Though London seemed, at times, like chaos during the last days of June 1911, it was, in fact, Cosmopolis. From 17 June onward, when the King and Queen returned to Buckingham Palace from Windsor to brace themselves for this exhausting pageant of which they formed the centre, the emissaries of every acceptable state in the world began to converge on their capital. Once again, we have to go outside the terse entries in Slatin's diary to recapture that sparkling Coronation atmosphere which he so enjoyed, yet did so little to convey.

Delegations from fifty-eight states, ranging from the Argentine to Zanzibar, had been invited. London's coronation skies, which were mostly grey, were soon enlivened by many exotic touches. There were the Sultans of Perak and Kedah, for example, with magnificent head-dresses over their Western clothes, and their ladies all attired in native garb. There were the Ethiopians, headed by a cousin of that same Emperor Menelik who, at the end of the last century, had caused Slatin and Wingate so much worry in the Upper Nile Valley. Now, clad entirely in white except for the coloured silk lining of their capes, these Abyssinian warriors strolled about as peaceful guests in a friendly land.

Essentially, however, this was the last grand parade of the old European order, for those who were now united in the ball-rooms were soon to be divided on the battlefields. Even here, there was one symbol of these dark things to come. Naval rivalry between Britain and Germany was perhaps the smallest of the many factors which, but three years later, were to send the fuse of war spluttering from end to end of the Continent. Yet, both to government and public opinion in England in 1911, it was the sorest of points; and what should the German Emperor do now but send his son over from Flushing in the latest of the German Dreadnoughts. This was the *Van Der Tann,* a menacing armoured cruiser which had only been rushed into completion a month or two before – probably for this very purpose.

The capital itself was a blaze of colour and light. Street had vied with street, monument with monument, and house with house in displays of patriotic fervour. Festoons of lamps ran from one end of Piccadilly to the other; gold and blue urns lined Oxford Street; griffins, lions and angels stood guard along Whitehall. Illuminated crowns and foliage hung outside every Pall Mall club; garlands twined round every column in sight and medallions of the King and Queen gazed out from every shop window. Had a prize been offered for the most lavish decoration of all, it would probably have been won by Lord Rothschild who had submerged his house at Hyde Park Corner under two thousand electric bulbs arranged in a giant monogram of G and M.

On 22 June, the actual Coronation Day, it must have seemed as though this exotic colour, foreign and native, had been concentrated, as though through a burning glass, inside Westminster Abbey. A wonderful and specially woven carpet of Garter blue ran right up to the Choir Screen; the seats had been lined with blue and fawn brocade; Scottish tapestries hung in the annexe and suits of armour from the Tower of London watched from the walls. Deliberately, however, the designers had not overdone the decoration, knowing that the real blaze would be the audience itself.

This audience, including Slatin Pasha (who seems to have been very pleased with his good seat in the South Choir Gallery), began to take their places at 7 a.m. and did not leave them again until 3 o'clock in the afternoon, or eight hours later. All Slatin notes in his diary that day is that the spectacle was 'very impressive'.

The words do not do much to conjure up that vast cross of human colour of which he formed one tiny speck with, around him, the maroon and silver garments of the peers, the mantles of the Orders of Chivalry – blue for St Michael and George, Venetian red for the Bath, sky blue for the Star of India – the brilliant turbans of the Indian Princes themselves, the garnet robes of the judges and the spectrum of all the naval and military officers, the mayors and the aldermen, the courtiers and the prelates in their different uniforms and regalia. Nor does Slatin record (however much it must have moved his romantic royalist heart) that electrifying moment when, as the

229

King and Queen entered the Abbey doors, the cry of 'Vivat Rex Georgius, Vivat, Vivat, Vivat!' came down from the throats of the Westminster School scholars above and rang through the packed church.

He is a little more expansive about the great naval review at Spithead which followed three days later and which, indeed, struck many of the foreign guests as the most resplendent item of the entire Coronation programme. The hotels and the boarding-houses of the modest seaside towns in the area had been quite submerged under the cascade of international celebrities that had descended upon them for twenty-four hours. Wingate and Slatin were allotted overnight accommodation at Gosport which was the opposite of regal. 'Queen Street 2, very, very little rooms' Slatin recorded in his diary with just a hint of pained surprise.

But the review itself more than made up for that. The two friends were invited aboard the new British cruiser HMS *Gloucester* for the day, where a pleasant surprise awaited them: the captain was an old comrade-at-arms of the Nile campaign and they could swap memories as well as toasts. As for the display of naval might spread out in the roads around them, Slatin, ever a practical fellow, expressed his admiration in hard cash. 'The British War Ships represent a value of £82,000,000 and the foreign ships of £15,000,000.'

What Slatin was, in fact, looking at in terms of British naval power was 167 assorted ships of the Royal Navy. They included a double squadron of twelve British Dreadnoughts, the ugliest but most formidable fighting machines afloat. Facing them in the line of foreign warships also anchored in the roads was their rival the *Van Der Tann*. These long grey avenues of British sea-power represented by themselves one quarter of all the naval tonnage that floated under any flag in the world's oceans; and even this great fleet assembled at Spithead was only part of the Royal Navy's strength. Britannia had indeed got her trident firmly grasped in coronation year.

Whether or not it was a result of traditional Royal Navy hospitality, his spelling after nightfall when, on a rocket signal from the flagship, the entire fleet was lit up, got more erratic than usual:

We attend the evening illuminations from Mr May's house which is near the Pear. At 10 p.m. all ships were litten. Great vue.

And underneath, Slatin, a keen philatelist since boyhood, affixed the penny and halfpenny stamps of the new King George edition.

The next fortnight was spent in a dizzy social whirl in London, the like of which even great party-goers such as Slatin had never seen before, and were never to see again. His popularity can best be judged by the number and quality of the invitations he was forced to turn down, rather than those he accepted.

Thus, on 30 June 'R' for 'refused' appears against three different dinner invitations, including one from Countess Strafford. (He dined at Lady St Helier's instead.) The next day he had to excuse himself from luncheons given by two English peeresses and also decline a weekend invitation from a third, Countess Jersey at Osterley. A lunch and two dinners were declined on the following Monday and Tuesday and the 'R's thicken further on the pages as his stay comes to an end in July. On the 6th he declines no fewer than three lunches (including ones given by the Earl of Rosebery and the luckless Countess Strafford) and even has to turn down an invitation to dine that same evening with the Marchioness of Salisbury to meet the Duke and Duchess of Connaught because of a previous engagement at a ball. He did fit in Lady St Helier (for breakfast on the 7th) before leaving, but the Countess of Strafford never seems to have caught him. He must have been almost relieved, that year, to catch the October boat back from Europe to the Sudan.

Though neither so hectic nor so brilliant, the remaining prewar years each brought with them their separate delights. At the beginning of 1912, for example, Slatin had the pleasure of greeting King George and Queen Mary on his own home territory of the Nile Valley, as the sovereigns made their way up the Suez Canal coming home from India and the great Delhi Durbar. And that September, when they were again at Balmoral, and he was once more there as their guest, King George personally invested him at the Castle with the Grand Cross of the Victorian Order. As it replaced the insignia of the KCVO which he already possessed, there was presumably no need for King George to try and find room for the new decoration somewhere on Slatin's back, as his father had been forced to do at Marienbad four years previously.

1913 brought an honour – and with it a solace – of a very different sort. After persistent lobbying through papal officials and through the Austrian envoy to the Vatican, Slatin succeeded, on 3 June 1913, in being received in special audience by the Holy Father, and in getting his personal blessing. Slatin always confessed to wearing his Catholic faith somewhat easily. Yet to judge by some of his letters, that lightning conversion of his to Mohammedanism in 1893 when hard-pressed on the Sudan battlefield had never ceased to worry his conscience. But whatever went on afterwards in his conscience, he had been fully restored in his standing as a true Austrian Catholic by that audience of 1913. As was usual with Slatin, the matter had been dealt with at the highest level.

That September at Balmoral was another great success. Arthur Balfour and Winston Churchill (with whom Slatin could still swap yarns about Omdurman) were among the political guests. The royal family were there in force and at a ball at the Castle on 19 September Slatin noted that he had danced 'with the Princess Royal, Princess Maud, Princess Mary and Princess Victoria of Schleswig-Holstein'. As he left on 21 September 1913, he noted in his diary: 'Their Majesties expressed their hopes to see me next year at Balmoral.' Little did he dream how ironic that entry would look in twelve months' time.

As it was, 1914 dawned in its usual rosy way. Indeed, Slatin was now at the very peak. For nearly twenty years he had been swinging steadily higher on this delicious seesaw of Anglo-Austrian favours, where a new push up from London produced an automatic counter-thrust from Vienna. He now had two British knighthoods (one of them twice over), as well as the CB and the honorary Major-Generalship. He was a *Freiherr* of the Austrian monarchy and most of the other sovereigns of Europe had contributed something to enliven his uniform. He had become a Lieutenant-General of the Egyptian Army among many other favours from the Khedive. He was a member of the best clubs, including the Marlborough in London and the Jockey Club in Vienna (another example of the seesaw in action). All the hostesses of the Continent were still after him and he was physically in his mature prime.

Only one thing more was needed to complete the picture: a loving, well-born wife. And this, in 1914, he managed to get as well, just before the curtain came down on it all.

Chapter Thirteen

ALICE

The private life of Slatin Pasha is both a legend and a mystery; and the one is part of the other. The legend sprang up, instantaneous and inevitable, after the escape which brought him such romantic fame. All those beautifully-gowned princesses of Europe with whom he danced so nimbly in Berlin, Vienna, Paris, London or Balmoral knew from his own writings – let alone from other tales – that the man who now held them round the waist had not long ago been married to princesses of Africa, black ladies from the royal houses of Darfur or Abyssinia; that he had lived with them, and an unknown assortment of lower-born native women and slaves to boot, as a Moslem; and that he had sired children by several of them.

What whisperings there must have been behind the fans of those who watched him waltzing; what schemes to get him talking about those days with seemingly artless questions; what bedroom discussions afterwards between mothers all agog and their breathless daughters! Anything he said fed the legend of his past. To say nothing only nourished it more. Whether he liked it or not, Slatin was destined, all his life, to titillate as well as to charm the fair sex.

The trouble is, we do not know quite how much he did like it, much less the extent to which he took advantage of his exotic appeal during his long bachelor years. He was an immensely virile man, and presumably, therefore, had the sexual appetite which normally goes with such virility. As Inspector-

234

General of the Sudan he had, of course, to be prudent how he satisfied this appetite in Khartoum itself. The white community of the capital was too small for any affair with a European woman to be hushed up, and those who knew Slatin can recall no breath of scandal from this particular direction.

On the other hand, he does appear to have kept a miniature black harem there, as a relic, either sentimental or sexual or both, from the old Moslem days. Our witness for this is his own English friend and colleague Wheatley who recalls that, tucked away discreetly in mud houses at the back of Slatin's garden there lived 'two or three of his previous wives or women'. They were never paraded, and they never wore European clothes, but they were there just the same. As Wheatley lived for several years in the bungalow right next door to Slatin's, he ought to know.

As for romances with European women, there would, of course, be no lack of opportunity once away from Khartoum. Cairo, which Slatin visited often, was as permissive as it was cosmopolitan. Edwardian Europe, where he spent all his summers, equally so. In the first years, however, all the talk was of soberly settling down. Soon after his escape, a lady at a Cairo dinner asked him outright if he was now going to be married. Slatin set the whole table rocking with his heavily-accented reply:

'Married? What me? No, No! I haf already been prisoner fourteen year—nevare no more!'

But his letters to his family, who were already searching for a suitable bride in Austria for their famous Rudolf, show that he had by no means rejected the idea. In the first year of the re-conquest campaign, for example, he sends this breezy letter from the battlefield to his sister-in-law at home:

So you are looking for a new jailer to cast me in chains! And you want a strict one at that! On the contrary. I'll accept only a poor little thing—*verstandez vous Madama*? She doesn't need to be a poor little thing as regards cash, but poor as regards contrariness, selfishness, excessive demands and the other faults which, as you know, the ladies are so often prone to. As you, Herminka, and the sisters are all so busy in my interests, you will collect together such a mass of eligible maidens that they will have to hold a preliminary ballot among themselves . . .

But after eighteen months of desultory banter with his family about their 'marriage bureau', Slatin seems to be losing interest in matrimony. He still speaks longingly of being back in Vienna 'among the blondes and brunettes' instead of sitting eternally in the desert among the blacks ('Oh black ones, you make me shudder!'). But, as for settling down, he now writes:

Dogs that bark don't bite. At the moment, there is no serious danger of marriage; indeed that danger seems to have passed some time ago.

And that, for a long time, is the last we read or hear about the subject. In his diaries for those gay Edwardian seasons in Europe, there is only an occasional mention of a woman in any capacity but that of a titled hostess out for his social scalp. One August at Salzburg he sees a lot of a Countess Juliette Hoyos, who even comes to dine with him tête-à-tête at his hotel. But the Countess never crops up again. There is another tantalizing entry made in London on 1 July 1908. After recording a lunch with the Duke and Duchess of Connaught he writes: 'Afternoon Hull (Miss Winifred)', and he then proceeds to underline the girl's name twice with another pen in red ink. One wavy underlining with his normal pen was the maximum emphasis Slatin usually allowed himself. He used no more, for example, to chronicle that one quarrel with Wingate and his own short-lived resignation. Miss Winifred must have caused an even greater turmoil to qualify for the unique distinction of a double underlining in a different ink. But, once again, one mention is all that we are given. If Miss Winifred did not pass out of his life in July 1908, she faded abruptly from his diary.

Ladies' man though he undoubtedly was, Slatin also extended his great gift of friendship to women, and with several of them he formed affectionate, teasing relationships which lasted throughout his life, perhaps without any thought of romance. One example was 'Miss Emily', who met Slatin on a Mediterranean crossing when he was a middle-aged celebrity and she a young girl in her teens. Her parents had both great wealth and great influence and Slatin was never indifferent to either. But his hundred and fifty letters to her over the years show a tenderness which does not sound calculating. Their relationship only came to an end when the little 'niece', then a middle-aged woman herself, came to take a last leave of Slatin on his death-bed. He formed a similar friendship with a young Austrian girl, Ermina Köchert, who came from the prosperous and much-respected family of the Vienna court jewellers. Here again, their letters span the decades of peace, war, and peace again.

But though there are hints of passing affairs in Slatin's middle years and this very solid evidence of lasting friendships throughout his life, all talk of marriage dies away after the turn of the century, when he was in fact in the prime of his physical life and fame. Why was this? After all, Slatin was immensely fond of home life and he was devoted to children.

Apart from his somersaults over religion in the face of the Mahdi's cannon, money, of course, would have been one difficulty. As we have seen, the £E1,450 annual salary which he drew as Inspector-General, though enough to maintain him very comfortably in Khartoum, was hard-stretched to cover his costly social routine in Europe even living as a bachelor. Still, there were heiresses and wealthy widows enough in those salons through which Slatin skipped every summer. Even the mysterious Miss Winifred might have been not a blushing debutante, unsuitably young, but a mature spinster with plenty in the bank.

Though we can only surmise, the main reason for his long search and long hesitation probably had less to do with money and religion than with 'standing'. That word has lost much of its force today; but it was sun, moon and stars in those Victorian and Edwardian firmaments in which Slatin himself twinkled. As Sir Ronald Wingate, the son of his greatest friend, put it: 'There would doubtless have been social barriers had he ever thought of marrying one of the top-drawer Europeans he was always consorting with. The fact is that his fame and his position had put him in a European bracket far above the one he was born into.'

Whether or not this explains his unusually late marriage, it certainly touches on yet another void in Slatin's life. He was not only a man between religions and between Empires. He was also a man between classes. This did not matter one scrap so long as he was a gay bachelor moving under the regal but very cosmopolitan umbrella of King Edward's patronage. Indeed, had he found the right girl to marry, there would still have been a niche for Rudolf Slatin in contemporary *English*

237

society. This was like an open and fast-flowing river. It had a solid bed-rock of landed power for its main channel, but it was constantly being fed from the banks by fresh streams of wealth, intellect, achievement and even by sheer beauty and charm accepted in their own rights.

Admittedly, even this society, while acknowledging the place that Slatin had earned for himself in life, remained very aware of the obscurity from which he had climbed up. A totally un-selfconscious expression of this attitude comes in the diaries of a contemporary English debutante, Miss Esmé Elliott. This young girl did two seasons in Cairo from 1895 to 1897, staying with her mother and stepfather, who was Major-General Sir Charles Knowles, C-in-C of the British occupation forces in Egypt. These were the years, just after his famous escape, when Slatin was the hero of the city. Miss Elliott describes him as 'a dear little man, modest and unsophisticated'. She saw a great deal of him and says that he became a great friend of her family's.

Yet, with no trace whatsoever of malice, she records that he had started off as a nobody. Indeed, his origins had been des-cribed to her as 'a common little Austrian carpet-bagger'. She then sums up his career thus :

He was travelling in the Sudan when he was captured by the Mahdi and he was kept in prison there for twelve years. He re-nounced his religion and after a time was not treated too badly . . . His rescue was planned by Wingate and was carried out with entire success. When he arrived at Cairo a great fuss was made of him and he was sent to England where Queen Victoria received and knighted him. He then made a tour of the courts of Europe, picking up decora-tions on the way.

Miss Elliott, as her diary elsewhere records, used to bicycle with Slatin. (They actually learned to ride together, practising on the cinder track around the Cairo Race Course and at first Slatin always fell off when he greeted her by removing one of his hands from the handlebars to take off his hat.) But one feels that she would never have considered marrying him, even had he been a suitable fifteen years younger. He had apparently started life as a 'common little Austrian carpet-bagger' and that, in all probability, would have ended all thoughts of romance.

English people of Miss Elliott's stamp were however usually scrupulous, as she seems to have been, about making Slatin feel fully accepted. This was even truer of the many working colleagues who became his friends. But when Slatin looked for acceptance to his own Austria-Hungary, the picture was very different. It was not merely that, in Vienna, he did not have anything like the same professional contacts in society. Austrian society itself was much less tactful and also much more relentless about its taboos.

The Emperor Franz Joseph, like Edward VII, had no need to be a snob. But most of the court aristocracy under him were obsessed with protocol, physically inbred, and spiritually hypnotized with their ancestors. (Partly, though not wholly as a result of this, they were also politically doomed; but that is another story.) An English countess had married into one of these old Austrian families when Slatin was still a schoolboy in Vienna. Despite her rank (and wealth) she encountered fierce disdain because one of her grandparents, though titled like all the other three, had once been engaged in banking. If that could happen to a great English lady, born with a fortune and nine knobs to her crown, what was Rudolf Slatin to expect, born with nothing and earning all his seven knobs himself?

That very title of *Freiherr* which the Emperor had eventually bestowed on him was itself suspect to the landed nobility of the Monarchy. A few barons were accepted in its ranks, but only if their lineage was ancient and their acres were broad. Essentially, however, it was a society which operated 'from count upwards' as the saying went, and also from several centuries back. Those Austrian scientists, civil servants, doctors, generals, engineers, artists, and so forth who blossomed out as *Edler vons* and *Freiherr vons* in the later stages of Franz Joseph's reign were regarded by the old families as a somewhat eccentric joke of the Emperor's, or, at best, as a necessary but distasteful gesture towards 'progress'.

There could, in any event, be no question of admitting these parvenus to the closed company of the so-called 'first society'. They appeared in different social reference books and they went to different court balls. Above all, they were addressed by the formal *Sie* as opposed to the informal *Du*. This applied to Slatin along with the rest, and had a hundred English monarchs given him their friendship it would still have applied.* As far as they were concerned, Slatin had become titled without becoming noble, and there was nothing he could ever do about it. Compared with that open river valley of English society, this was a cold and motionless mountain glacier, perched high above all living vegetation, and with only its own ice to keep it company. Slatin became a member of European high society, and even an honorary member of England's 'top ten thousand', without ever penetrating the inner circle of his native Vienna. It was one of the many things which condemned him – quite happily – to cosmopolitanism.

Yet, in the end, it was in Vienna that he found his bride. His elder brother Heinrich had a bachelor colleague in the Master of Horse's Office called Baron Victor von Ramberg, and this Victor had a sister, Alice, who kept house for him. Though Rudolf had no thought of marriage in his mind when he first met Alice, or indeed for several years afterwards, she in fact met his needs admirably. Slatin would have let down his glittering position on the European stage somewhat had he married a plain *Fräulein* from Austria. On the other hand, the princess or countess who would have filled that position to perfection was quite beyond his reach, except in a Vienna ball-room.

Alice fell nicely in between. Her grandfather, a soldier, had served as Wellington's Austrian aide-de-camp at Waterloo and had been ennobled in 1849, the second year of Franz Joseph's lengthy reign. Her father was a retired cavalry general and one of her uncles a distinguished painter. Her mother, it is true, had been born a Countess of Breda; but even that wing of the family was neither too wealthy nor too resplendent to upset the balance entirely. Though a big notch above the Slatins in all particulars, the Rambergs still fell into the same broad social bracket of the Empire's new 'meritocracy'. The fact that Victor and Heinrich worked side by side in the same branch of the Imperial Household only emphasized this affinity.

Ideal though all this looked in theory, it was a long time before anything happened in practice. Alice had her brother to look after. Slatin was either immured in the Sudan or spin-

---

* Prince Alois Auersperg, a nephew of those Auerspergs whom Slatin entertained in Khartoum has confirmed that his uncles, like the contemporary Kinskys and Liechtensteins whom Slatin also counted among his friends, invariably used the formal style with him.

ning around Europe. At first the pair only met briefly and sporadically on Slatin's quick trips to Vienna. But, from the start, there was a bond of affection between them, and from 1903 onwards this was cemented by a regular correspondence. Over a hundred of her long letters to him have been preserved. They are not only a record of their own slow-flowering romance. They also form a portrait typical of a serene woman in a serene world, that pre-1914 world which was drifting all the time towards disaster, yet was still oblivious to the danger even when it had reached the very edge of the cataract.

The intimacy between them builds up slowly but steadily over the years. By 1910 one feels that, though not married, they already belong to the same family. Indeed, all her letters to him at this stage begin *Liebes Brüderl* or 'Dear little brother'. A letter characteristic of this period was the one Alice sent to him in Khartoum on 11 November 1910 from Gravosa, where she was catching the late November sunshine of the Austrian Dalmatian coast. She bemoans the fact that by the end of the year he will be down in Darfur again and she will be obliged to light a candle for her 'adopted brother' on their Christmas tree thousands of miles away in Vienna. Slatin had obviously been telling her that he was longing to give up his job if only the British Empire would relinquish him, for she goes on:

I find it terribly sad that you have to plodd (sic) on in Egypt . . . Your life must have great fascination and be a thousand times more interesting than that of a 'European', but if you are already getting tired of it . . . why *must* you stick to it . . .

You don't owe England or the Sirdar anything. Even if they have poured honours and decorations over you, that is only for the services you have given or because the egotistical John Bull needs you . . .

But if it has to be, God be with you on your ship of the desert, which all our thoughts and fondest wishes follow . . .

So far from wanting to cut loose from John Bull, Slatin was engaged at that very time, and with Alice's knowledge, in trying to get a Colonial Government post for her own brother Victor. Inevitably, Wingate was the go-between. A letter sent to him from Harcourt of the Colonial Office on 9 December 1910 reads:

My dear Sirdar,

Many thanks for sending me Sir Rudolf Slatin's letter about his friend Baron Ramberg's desire to obtain a post in the Colonial Service. Baron Ramberg's name is noted on my list of candidates for employment and I will not forget what you and Slatin say, but vacancies suitable to his age and standing are rare and are generally filled by promotion from within the service.

It was another of those amazingly inept moves that Slatin made from time to time, gaffes that showed how little he really understood his beloved English friends and masters. His own appointment had been a unique anomaly, made possible only by his own peculiar talents and Wingate's powerful sponsorship; and that had been ten years ago. By 1910, as Slatin could see for himself, Whitehall had taken over British Africa for the King. The idea of an Austrian court official transferring straight into this self-contained service was preposterous. Yet, to please Slatin, Wingate had written to London; and, out of deference to them both, the Colonial Office had sent that polite reply.

But back to Alice. There are several signs in earlier letters written by her during that same stay in Gravosa that her 'dear little brother' is already becoming something more. The subject of love is only skirted around, delicately and almost incredulously. But there is no doubt that it is now there, something that both can feel, though both hesitate to recognize.

Thus on 29 September, she writes:

Do you really think that if one turns into an old maid one does it out of passion for the calling? ... Not every girl who cannot marry the man she loves can bring herself to take someone else, and indeed I think that to marry without true love is the greatest wrong one can do both to oneself and to the man concerned. Do you remember that ball in Cairo when I didn't want to dance? I had already known then for two years (and rather sad years) that my dancing and loving days were over.

That sounded like total resignation to her fate. Yet the following month, replying tenderly to a letter of his which had just arrived, she writes:

Just one more thing I must say to you. I never believed of you that with your friendship you would seek to *buy* other feelings. I

242

always knew that you were much too noble a character for that ...

If you ask yourself why I write you all this, '*tant mieux*'. But if I have hurt you even the tiniest bit with these lines, please forgive me.

On 22 March 1914, we read in Slatin's diary: 'Tomorrow it will be twelve years that I met Alice Ramberg.' And her name has that wavy line underneath it which is the rare expression of his emotions spilling on to paper. It reads like an indication that things are moving to a climax.

Sure enough, in June of that same year, those letters of hers which, for so long, had been addressed to her 'dear little brother' suddenly begin 'My own darling' instead, and all the *Sie*s become *Du*s. At the age of 57 and 41 respectively, Rudolf and Alice had become engaged.

As far as she was concerned, the fact that the fuse had been so long burning did nothing to lessen the force of the explosion when it came. They had to part in the second week of June, and from then until their marriage she sends him one and sometimes two letters a day. No teen-age girl writing to her young Prince Charming could have shown more rapture than this middle-aged woman poured out to her elderly hero. Though publicly accessible among Slatin's papers, this side of the correspondence is still, after nearly sixty years, their private affair. The only passages it is proposed to quote from here are those which bear directly on Slatin's own character and problems. For, in these love-letters, Alice Ramberg unconsciously lays bare most of the twisted strands of her fiancé's life.

In one of the first letters after their engagement, for example, written from Golop in Hungary on 13 June 1914, Alice makes it clear that Rudolf's exotic African past is already causing certain misgivings in her family. She quotes one of her grandmothers (probably the old Countess of Breda) as being 'furious' with Slatin for planning to leave Alice behind in Europe after the wedding while he returned to the Sudan alone to wind up his existence as a gay bachelor. Alice goes on:

She says either we are to marry or not! If we do, we belong together ... I'm at least to wait in Khartoum where we can reach each other and not in Gravosa where every letter takes 14 days ... She doesn't at all approve of me being 'a meek and obedient slave'.

I think she is afraid that I won't keep you on a tight enough rein—
you know, the beautiful lady of Darfur . . .*

At another point in the letter, Alice quotes the same grandmother on the subject of Slatin's relatively humble birth. *Grossmama*, she tells him, is prepared to accept his 'bourgeois origins',
in view of the social position which he now holds. It would be
difficult to find a better illustration of the caste system Slatin
had to struggle against all his life in his native Austria. Alice
is not trying to score off him with those words nor even to
tease. She is being tender and loving, as always. Indeed, what
she was passing on was itself a benediction. For though Slatin
might have felt uncomfortable in receiving *Grossmama*'s con-
descending social blessing, he would not have felt offended. He
had entered Austrian society through the front door all right.
But he had come in walking backwards, as a British official
and an English 'Sir'. In purely Austrian terms, his marriage,
though not an outright *mésalliance,* was still a slight affront to
that principle of *Stand* which was supposed to keep the
Monarchy together. Neither Alice nor he thought there was
anything wrong in mentioning it. *Grossmama* was clearly
determined to.

Another ticklish subject that Alice felt bound to bring up
was religion. She, a devout Catholic from a strict Catholic
family background, was marrying a man who, on his own admission, had always worn that same faith lightly and had once
felt obliged to abandon it altogether. Despite that private
audience in Rome and the special Papal blessing the year before,
this still left problems between the engaged couple.

On 3 July Alice writes to him from Graz :

I think *our* religion is on the whole the same, even if I keep to
practices which you do not feel that you want for yourself. Confession
and communion have helped me in my very hard and sad times
when I had nobody else to whom I could go for help and I would
not like to give them up now that I'm happy and will perhaps feel
less in *want* of them. Dear Rudolf—you know that you'll have to
go to confession before our marriage. Would you mind, without any
sentimental fuss about it, if we went to communion together . . . I
know you don't do it as a rule, so I should like us for that once to

* Possibly a reference to the Darfurian princess whom Slatin had married by Moslem law and by
whom he had children; though she would hardly still be 'beautiful' in 1914.

receive communion together. But if you had rather not, tell me so frankly—my love, my own dear husband ...

Other little worries were caused by the mere fact that they were marrying so late, and that Rudolf (like herself, but she only thinks of him) was having to wrench himself out of such a family-settled pattern of life. There was at least one English woman friend – not mentioned in his own diaries – with whom he was now having to readjust what had obviously been a close relationship. Alice writes:

Poor Stella. But darling you must always remain her friend and adviser if she needs you. I know that, as you are *mine*, my very own, I don't grudge her your friendship if it can make her life a little happier.

And then, far more formidable than 'poor Stella', there were those twin spinster sisters of Rudolf's in their villa at Traunkirchen. For eleven years, together with the rest of his family, they had scratched together every penny they could find to send down to Cairo to help pay for all those rescue projects. And for more than twenty years after that, they had basked in the full glory of the returning hero's fame and success. They were somebodies in the life of Traunkirchen because they were Rudolf's sisters, the sisters he came to visit every year, the sisters for whom even Edward VII had been persuaded to halt his special train. The Traunkirchen villa was Rudolf's home. It was also a Rudolf shrine, where his books and clothes and photographs and souvenirs were lovingly dusted and polished by the two resident votaries against that blissful week or two each summer, the high point of each year, when their brother returned to them. Now, within a few years of his retirement – a retirement they had counted on spending all together – he was suddenly marrying away from them. There was to be another home for him after all, with another woman to cherish him. Not easy for them. Even trickier for Alice, as this letter, written by her on 9 July from Traunkirchen itself, shows:

Darling, I seem to miss you here even more than anywhere else. Your sisters are very kind to me but you know I am rather shy and afraid of them. I can't help feeling they *must* be criticizing me. I'm sure they *must* be looking at me and thinking—'So *that's* the woman Rudolf waited so long for; what a waste!'

Alice was already worried enough, without imagining things at Traunkirchen, that she might prove a little too old and unexciting for the legendary Rudolf Slatin. But he also seems to have been a little nervous that, as her real-life everyday husband, he could no longer, at fifty-seven, live up himself to the legend. There is one very moving letter of hers about all this. Unlike the others, it bears no date; nor does it seem to need one. This passage is all in English, the language she usually switched to for any very intimate exchange:

And now my own love, your last question . . . You ask me whether I could have made up my mind to marry you if I had thought your love for me was only 'platonic'? Darling, I don't think I am a sensual woman. I don't think I ever have been. Love meant to me perhaps more friendship, the wish to be a friend, a comrade, a companion. I never *wished* for the other thing—on the contrary—since the time when I *knew* about these things I rather felt that marriage must be a terrible thing. Of course I knew that in case I would marry it would have to be. I never dreamt of not being the wife of a man I would marry, but it frightened me. I tell you frankly Rudolf that even last year I shuddered at that idea.

When this winter you wrote so often about your age, your only friendly feelings, I thought you wanted me to understand your words in that [sense] of the word—to be your friend, your comrade, your keeper only. But I don't feel that 'only' stands for 'less'. Do you understand me, my own beloved Rudolf?

Slatin may not have been engaged to the most beautiful, the most wealthy or even the noblest lady of the Monarchy. Yet, had he searched for another fifty-seven years, he could scarcely have found a sweeter, gentler nature.

So her letters go on, throbbing and bubbling into midsummer. All of them carry this mixture of very private thoughts, for example, about the chances of their having children, and very humdrum matters, such as settling what little money they have to the best advantage, assembling their wedding gifts, or arranging for the ceremony itself. Yet, ironically enough, the one event of these weeks that was to shatter their whole existence was passed over by both as though it could never concern them.

On 28 June the Archduke Francis Ferdinand, heir to the Monarchy, was murdered in Sarajevo together with his morganatic wife, the Duchess of Hohenberg, as the couple drove in an open motor car through the streets of the restive Bosnian capital. In her reaction to the news, Alice showed herself the true daughter of an Austrian general of cavalry. The following day, 29 June, she writes from the depths of the Hungarian countryside to Rudolf:

Darling, isn't it terrible, this disaster in Sarajevo? We don't yet know the details. The telegraph office in Tallya has simply announced that a bomb* killed the Archduke and Hohenberg. These awful Serbs. That was certainly not simply anarchists but the Serbs... and yet the people in Vienna go on imagining that our South Slavs are loyal. We are all quite shattered and Gusti [nickname for her brother Victor] feels it especially keenly as he was on such good terms with the Archduke ... who was for him such a well-disposed patron. It's a blessing for the poor couple that she is dead as well. They say she really deeply loved the Archduke and strove so hard. The poor children—and poor Emperor, who is really spared no pain ...

I know you didn't like Archduke Francis and that he was not particularly friendly to you. Perhaps it's better like this for Austria as well, for now there won't be the problem of the succession ... If only the Emperor isn't harmed by it all ...

Then, in the very next sentence, Alice is off again telling Rudolf how much she loves him and what a terrible thing it is for him to be getting 'such an old ugly wife'. And after that, we are back to Stella once more. Would she think that their Rudolf was just *one* of the dearest and best men on earth, or *the* dearest and best? Sarajevo is already forgotten.

Rudolf got that letter in London, where he had already been for the past few days, plunged into his annual social swim. For him as well, Sarajevo seems to have been no more than a passing shock. The black crêpe may have been out in Vienna. But in London, enjoying the last of its brilliant seasons, all was still bright silks and champagne. Slatin's own Austro-Hungarian Embassy in Belgrave Square was, of course, in mourning; and, after consulting with them, Rudolf felt obliged not to attend a ball at Buckingham Palace because it was a state affair. But this was purely the protocol of mourning. It had nothing as yet to do with the international politics of the Balkans.

* The local post office got it wrong. The royal couple were, of course, killed by point-blank shots from Gavrilo Princip's revolver.

Before returning to Vienna to get married, Rudolf went the round of his private parties almost as usual. And though he and Alice had agreed, even before Sarajevo, to keep the wedding as quiet and as small as possible, it was too much to expect someone of Slatin's irrepressible nature to keep his own marriage a secret. Not only was he truly devoted to Alice; he was also proud of her and of her background. There were so many people in London who would be intrigued, and possibly impressed, by the fact that he was marrying the descendant of one of the Iron Duke's aides-de-camp. He therefore not only told his close friends about Alice but also people like Lord Kitchener, with whom he had never been on friendly terms. It was not merely that Slatin could not stop himself spreading the news. He wanted it to get out in London, in Vienna and all over Europe.

They had originally planned to marry on 24 July, a Friday. ('I am not superstitious', Alice had written to London, 'I was born on a Good Friday and if you love me darling that's luck enough for me. . . .') But they brought the ceremony forward a few days and on Tuesday 21 July, Slatin writes in his diary (duly underlining the words with his wavy lines): 'Was married to Alice today at 4 p.m. in the Votivkirche by Archdeacon Probst.' Even having regard to their mature ages and the hush of court mourning in Vienna, it was a remarkably modest affair. The only guests present at the wedding breakfast (lunch in the open-air Volksgarten restaurant just across the Ringstrasse) and afterwards in the great twin-spired church itself were Alice's mother, Baroness Ottilie von Ramberg; Alice's brother Victor, and Rudolf's younger brother, the lawyer Adolf. The twins from Traunkirchen were among the notable absentees.*

Two hours later, the bridal couple left by the night sleeper from Vienna for what was then the Austrian South Tyrol. By lunch-time on the following day, they had arrived at their honeymoon hotel at Cortina d'Ampezzo. Slatin's diary for that 22 July shows that, according to his original plans, he should have been dining in London that evening with Lord and Lady

---

* Slatin announced his own wedding to the world. Cards were distributed throughout Europe in German and English. The latter text read:
  Major General Sir Rudolf Baron von Slatin Pasha has the honour to inform you that he was married today to the Baroness Alice von Ramberg, daughter of the late General of Cavalry Victor Baron von Ramberg and of the Baroness Ottilie von Ramberg (née Countess of Breda).

Farquhar, 'To meet their Majesties the King and Queen'. Instead it was supper with Alice and their bridal night at the Pension 'Tre Croce' up in the Dolomites. But as Slatin had doubtless hoped, European royalty was with them in spirit. Telegrams of congratulation arriving at the hotel included one from King George v: 'The Queen and I wish you and Lady Slatin every good wish for your future'; one from the Emperor Franz Joseph, signed by his adjutant, Count Paar; one from Don Alfonso of Spain; one from the Duke and Duchess of Cumberland; and several more from assorted Archdukes. Slatin entered them all lovingly into his diary for Thursday, 23 July. Unbeknown to him, in Belgrade at 6 p.m. on that same day, the Austrian Minister Baron Giesl had handed the Empire's ultimatum on the Sarajevo killings to the Serbian Foreign Office.

The honeymooners stayed on another fortnight. Though Slatin devoured every newspaper he could find to follow the remorselessly mounting European crisis, he remained for days to come blithely, almost naïvely, optimistic. In a letter sent from Cortina to Wingate in Scotland he does, it is true, speculate about war, but there is no thought that it could affect him:

I wonder what the future will bring? Will it come to a European war? It would be terrible—but whatever may happen I hope that the Serbs—those murders (sic) of men and women—may get a real lesson . . .

If circumstances make it necessary to return earlier to the Sudan (I mean only through European complication) I am ready to start at a moment's notice, like an old soldier has to do . . .

And the rest of the letter is all about enlarging his bungalow in Khartoum to make room for Alice. Would his good friend, in his capacity as Governor-General, agree to sanction the £140–£180 costs from special funds?

As late as 30 July, just after Russia had taken the one fateful step – general mobilization – which military men everywhere feared could only lead to a European war, Slatin refused to see the storm clouds. He writes on that very day: 'It looks more peaceful now and as if a European complication can be avoided.'

But by 3 August, with the German ultimatum to Belgium already delivered and the German army poised to invade Belgian territory, even Slatin took fright.

They packed and left the same day by carriage and rail for

Vienna, travelling through a countryside which was draining fast of tourists and filling even faster with soldiers. When they got home to Adolf's flat on the 5th, the two sisters who had stayed away from the marriage ceremony now arrived to join the newly-weds. They had been afraid to remain alone at Traunkirchen.

Slatin's old life with England had lasted almost twenty years. His new life with Alice had lasted less than twenty days. Now both were twisted out of recognition forever.

Chapter Fourteen

AUGUST 1914: THE MAN BETWEEN

Becoming a Moslem in the deserts of Darfur in an attempt to save his soldiers and himself from the Mahdi had been the first great divide of Slatin's life. Now, thirty years later, came the second. This time it was not between two faiths but between two fatherlands that he had to choose. As on the earlier occasion, it was a case of acting in haste and repenting at leisure.

Before following the extraordinary twists and turns that Rudolf Slatin took in the late summer of 1914, it is worth looking again at the situation of this elderly and agitated bridegroom who had arrived back on 5 August at the family flat in the Reichsratstrasse with his adoring bride of a fortnight. Despite all the titles, ranks and appointments he held from the English crown, Slatin had always regarded himself an Austrian in questions of international politics. He had publicly taken this stand in 1908, when the Balkan Annexation crisis had led to a temporary cooling in relations between the English and Austrian courts. He had struck the same patriotic posture after Sarajevo, agreeing with Alice that the Serbs must be made at all costs to pay for the murder of the heir to the Imperial crown. At first it had not been too difficult to find sympathy for this point of view even in London. A wartime entry made months afterwards in the diary of the Austrian jurist and politician Josef Redlich tells us that, as late as 18 July 1914, when Slatin was discussing the crisis with King George v, the English monarch had expressed not only his deep sorrow about the Archduke's assassination but also his 'contempt' for the Serbs.

But this was not Balmoral on 18 July but Vienna on 5 August. In that short time, the world had fallen apart. By now all the European great powers except Austria-Hungary found themselves suddenly at war, with Germany in the thick of it. As the Dual Alliance with Berlin was the cornerstone (and the millstone) of Austrian policy, it was almost inconceivable that the Monarchy could stay out for long. It was just as inconceivable that it could enter in any other way but as Germany's ally and, therefore, as England's enemy. Slatin, who was at the centre of things in Vienna, sensed this as well as anybody. Yet on 6 August, the day after his return to the capital, his diary has this entry:

I am asking the Police for a Pass. President Garrupp and Reg. R. [Regierungsrat] Walderndorf are quit (sic) amiable. And still I have to go from Pontius to Pilatus. I am told that I should have a special permission too from the *Oberkommando* [Army Command].

All sorts of people were, of course, applying in Vienna at that time for all sorts of travel papers. But Slatin's reason was unique. For he was asking for his pass and 'special permission' in order to leave Austria-Hungary altogether and rejoin Wingate to continue serving the English in the Sudan. Even had the decision been taken on that day by Slatin at the Marlborough Club in London or at Wingate's own Scottish home in Dunbar, with all the English ties present and all the English pressures felt, it would still have been a remarkable step. But taken in Vienna, the capital of his native land which was about to go to war with England, it was an astounding one.

True, there were some special factors. To begin with, Wingate had officially summoned him back, doubtless in response to Slatin's own written offer, already quoted, to 'march at a moment's notice' back to the Sudan whatever complications arose in Europe. Slatin's own diary (for 3 August) merely records that he had received a telegram from Wingate that day, though without giving any indication of the contents. A special memorandum written by Wingate after the war, when he was trying to clear Slatin's name, fills the gap for us:

When war was declared with Germany on the 4th of August 1914, Slatin Pasha was on leave in Vienna. Before Lord Kitchener was appointed Secretary of State for War it was his intention to return at once to his post of Consul-General in Egypt. He and I were in London at that time and, with his concurrence, I telegraphed to Slatin Pasha to meet us at Marseilles, whence Lord Kitchener, he and I were to proceed by a British Cruiser to Alexandria ...

Slatin, in obeying the call from the man who was still his Governor-General, may well have comforted himself with the thought that, technically, he was on joint Anglo-Egyptian service in the Sudan, a condominion territory on the Nile which was safely remote from the European explosion. Wingate did indeed try to press this point of view on him though, at heart, both men must have been uneasy about the future from 4 August onwards. Uneasiness in such matters did not necessarily mean despair however. The Europe of 1914, even at war, was still a continent where courtesy and personal loyalties were allowed, on occasions, to overrule the strictly national interest.

Two such illustrations were presenting themselves those very days in Austria itself, thanks to the personal magnanimity of Franz Joseph. The Serbian Chief of Staff had, for example, been caught napping on holiday at a Styrian spa when Austria declared war on his country. Despite the general's obviously immense value as an intelligence prize, the Emperor decided that, as the luckless fellow obviously hadn't heard the whistle, it would be only fair to let him go. And go he did, the Austrian War Ministry protesting in vain. Two still more august hostages trapped in Austria by the flood of war were the Princes Sixtus and Xavier of Bourbon-Parma, brothers-in-law to the young Archduke Charles, who, since the calamity of Sarajevo, was the new Heir-Apparent to the throne. Though the two French princes inevitably became enemy aliens, the old Emperor would not hear of any harm befalling any of his family guests and, thanks to his insistence, they were allowed to leave for Switzerland and home on 20 August 1914.

But even after all these allowances have been made both for the built-in ambiguity of Slatin's personal position when war broke out, and for the relative tolerance of the age, it was demanding a lot of both to bustle around Vienna in search of official passes to go and serve under what, at any moment, might become an enemy flag. For unlike the two French princes (with whom military questions, as a matter of Habsburg family protocol, were never discussed) Slatin had moved for years in close company with the political and military leaders of the Empire. He knew most of their thoughts and quite a few of their secrets. It could not be theoretically ruled out that he might soon be employing this knowledge against them.

All this must have occurred to the Austrian authorities themselves, who, as Slatin noticed, became steadily more evasive and less 'amiable' as he plodded on through the Imperial corridors of power in pursuit of his exit permits. The anguish of the seven days that followed can be felt even in Slatin's factual jottings.

Something else is there too: just a hint that, in his subconscious mind, the Sudan is already slipping away and his native city is enveloping him again. His diary, which until 6 August has been written, as throughout the previous ten years, basically in English, suddenly, on 7 August, switches in midsentence to German. Twenty-four hours later, he takes another step into the past and starts writing in the old German *Schrift* he had learnt as a child, a style which, by now, was fast becoming archaic. It is in this, at times, almost indecipherable hand that we have to follow the story.

His plan, he says, 'is to travel via Italy as this nation is not yet engaged and maintains shipping "communications".' (There is no mention of the rendezvous in Marseilles, though we know from Wingate where he is heading.) To speed up the issue of his travel papers, he tries first a friend at court, Count Bolfras, but is told by the Count that such matters 'are not within the sphere of my authority'. All day on the 8th he bombards the Vienna military authorities. But despite the personal intervention of the Duke Elias of Parma, who goes with him to garrison headquarters, he is told that the military cannot act in such matters as they are the responsibility of the police. That evening, when he is almost in despair, it is the police who finally produce the special passes for himself and his wife.

Still Vienna clings to him. When he goes next morning to the station to catch the train to Trieste there are 'all sorts of difficulties again', and he cannot get away. He spends most of that day at the Foreign Office trying to clear up these unspecified 'difficulties'. One senior official there advises him to stay in Vienna and 'await events'. Another (whom Slatin himself says gave him 'a pretty cool reception') declines to offer any advice. Small wonder. The European war was now five days old. This English knight and honorary British major-general must have looked increasingly eccentric – and even, to some, dubious – as he strove at this late stage of the game to leave his native land for the other camp.

But like a salmon leaping doggedly home against the current, Slatin went on with it. That night, escorted by brothers and sisters, he and Alice returned to the Sudbahnhof and this time, at four minutes past midnight, their train pulled out. Alice seems to have taken it remarkably well. It was the greatest, perhaps the first adventure of her sheltered life. She was next to her beloved Rudolf and hoping to travel with him to his beloved Sudan. 'My dear little wife is brave' Slatin writes next day, as the train rattles slowly down through Styria. 'Apart from a few suppressed tears, she is almost gay. . . .'

Rudolf himself however was in a sorry state, his nerves in tatters and his stomach playing him up.

Alas, I feel very sick and am suffering from acute colic. I can't swallow anything the whole day, except a little milk produced by the conductor. Lucky that I have some Burrough and Wellcome (sic) Dover Powders with me . . . Who would have thought, even two weeks ago, that it would have turned out like this?

Fortified by his Dover Powders, Slatin reached Trieste at last on the evening of the 11th, after a journey of almost forty-eight hours. He took rooms in the Hotel Excelsior, which he must have known well from many a happy landing at the port on leave from Africa. Perhaps even this nightmare would have a bright ending? That night, at any rate, he managed a little plain food, some chicken with rice.

There was one more day of make-believe. Slatin called on the British Consul-General in Trieste, who, in contrast to those Austrian diplomats in Vienna, was 'very friendly'. Through the Consulate, Slatin had this message sent to the British Embassy in Rome: 'Slatin asks to inform Wingate that he will try and join him if he can.' He also called on the American Consul with a suggestion that he should buy or hire a Lloyd steamer to evacuate all his nationals living in Austria or Germany. Whatever was going on in his subconscious mind, Slatin was still acting as though he were entirely on the Anglo-Saxon side.

Then, at 10.15 on the morning of 13 August, while he was busy making new plans to get to Alexandria via Naples, the inevitable awakening came. The news of England's formal declaration of war on Austria-Hungary reached Trieste. Slatin makes no comment in his diary, but it is clear that he now dropped his various travel plans on the instant, like so many stones. If this was natural enough, a much more remarkable example of his flexibility followed. That very same day, with the Austrian Admiral Kudelka, he inspected the *Africa,* a passenger vessel that was being converted into a hospital ship for the Imperial Navy. 'Very good work' he notes. 'Admiral Kudelka is very satisfied.' Slatin had certainly lost no time, once forced to fold away his Union Jack, in unfurling the black double-headed eagle in its place.

That Saturday, 15 August, already on his way back to Vienna, he writes in the train:

I am convinced I have acted rightly. To begin with, I am an Austrian, and a Viennese above all. As such, it is impossible for me to serve with English who are at war with my fatherland . . .

Again, it is the swiftness and completeness of the transformation which astounds: no reservations, no regrets and no remorse from the man who, only forty-eight hours before, was still trying to report for duty with those same English. The formal declaration of war cannot entirely explain it, for Slatin, though hoping against hope, knew full well that this was only a matter of time. Perhaps, however reluctantly and however unwittingly, he had already declared war in his own heart as early as 5 August. In that case, he had been sleep-walking ever since, with all that deceptive determination which the sleep-walker has in his motions.

One would like to believe this, for what Rudolf Slatin was about to do needs a great deal of charitable explaining. To reconstruct his actions from now on, his own diary becomes a significantly poor guide. Indeed, on the critical points, it is quite silent. But the incontrovertible evidence is there – buried in the secret dispatches of his own Austrian Foreign Office for August and September 1914 and in the even more secret reports of British Intelligence at the time.

His immediate behaviour on returning to Vienna was normal

enough, and here his diary gives the essential facts. At 10 a.m. on Monday, 17 August, he presented himself in Schönbrunn Palace to his friend Count Paar, the Emperor's Adjutant-General, to inform him of his resignation from Sudan Government service and to offer the Emperor his services in any capacity. 'Though my military experience may well be of little use in Europe' he notes hopefully, 'it is not out of the question that one day they will find a special use for me.'

The following day he handed in to the American Embassy in Vienna (the Chargé d'Affaires, Frederic Penfield, was a personal friend from their Cairo days) an official letter of resignation to Wingate together with a second and private letter to him. Both were to be sent on to Khartoum via the American Embassy in Rome. Slatin gives no details of them in his diary, but the English originals of the two letters have survived. They form an eloquent contrast.

The official letter begins, in the sparsest of styles, with the one word 'Excellency' and goes on to tender Slatin's resignation as Governor-General of the Sudan 'in consequence of the political situation created by the declaration of war of Great Britain to (sic) Austria'. But when he came to writing personally, it was another story. People were always more important in Slatin's life than politics, and whatever else he faltered in, he never faltered in his friendships. He now had to take leave of the oldest and closest of those friends:

1 Reichsratstrasse 7
18.VIII.14

My dear old Rex,

It is very sad—but let us say it is fate and it had to come. I never dreamed that I should sever my connection with the Sudan on political grounds, but there is no use to regret.

I did my best to join you before the declaration of war but on account of mobilization it was impossible for me to leave this country earlier . . .

Now I think it is better so, because what is the good of being in the middle of old friends under such changed conditions? I—the Austrian as a prisoner of Britishers—with whom and for whom I spent the best part of my life!

My personal friendship to you my dear old Rex shall not suffer although I condemn the decision of your Government to fight

Austria the traditional friend of England—May the Almighty be the Judge and decide . . .

I leave it to your discretion to deal with my servants and to dispose of my private property.

With the Almighty's will we may meet once more on a neutral ground—peaceful like in olden days as good friends.

My wife sends her best love.

Good bye—

Ever yours affectionate

old

Rowdy.

And after the name comes a quixotic question mark, as though the writer is no longer sure of anything, even his own identity.

Both letters caught up with Wingate in Cairo on the last day of the month. But well before that, believing that Slatin was still staying with the Ramberg family on the Adriatic, Wingate had sent another telegram to him via the American missions in Rome and Trieste. It read: 'Please inform Sir Rudolf Slatin in Ragusa that the Sirdar wishes him to return to Egypt as soon as possible.'

A note made in Slatin's hand at the foot of the message shows that he received it in Vienna through his American friend Penfield on Sunday 23 August. By then it was too late in every sense of the word for Slatin to return to the English fold. He had not only come back to Vienna and formally resigned from Anglo-Egyptian service in the Sudan. He was already busy advising the Austrian Government how England, Egypt and the Sudan could best be undermined and attacked by the central Powers at war.

The most likely explanation for this somersault is that Slatin was being catapulted around by the emotional stress of some brainstorm. The harshest verdict of his behaviour is that it was opportunist double-dealing of the most cynical order. Perhaps he simply panicked. Whatever the interpretation, these are the facts.

At 4 a.m. in the morning of 24 August 1914, the following cipher telegram was sent by the Austrian Foreign Minister, Count Berchtold, to his Ambassador in Constantinople,

Margrave Pallavicini. The message was repeated to the Austrian envoy in Athens, Herr von Szilassy, for transmission through Greek diplomatic channels to the Austrian Minister in Cairo, Count Ludwig Szechenyi.

Strictly Confidential.

Slatin Pasha, who is here and cut off from all contact with Egypt, thinks that the news that he—Slatin—has quit English service and is not returning to the Sudan because he no longer wants to serve England ought to be spread about by the Turks in Egypt and the Sudan; Turkish relatives of Egyptian officers might be used for this purpose. He believes that this will have some effect on the Sudanese. Turkey could without any doubt bring strong influence to bear on Egypt and the Sudan. The dispatch of just a few Turkish battalions to Suez would present the English with no small difficulties as they only have a few thousand men in Egypt and only a few hundred white troops in the Sudan. The closing of the Suez Canal would be a catastrophe for England.

The word of the Caliph would carry great weight among black Moslems. A shrewd and cautious use of this influence among the Moslems of India might also be very troublesome to the English there.

Szechenyi in Cairo was instructed to try and carry out the relevant suggestions outlined, without compromising himself. Pallavicini was advised to consult with his ally, the German Ambassador at Constantinople, and then try, with German help, to persuade the Turkish Grand Vizier Said Pasha to act on some of Slatin's proposals. Berchtold did add however that he fully realized from Pallavicini's earlier reports to Vienna that, for the moment, the Grand Vizier was 'hardly to be had for any emphatic move against England'. (The powerful English fleet lying at anchor off the Dardanelles was the principal reason.)

Now it is quite wrong to suggest, as has been done, that these proposals were Berchtold's own ideas, with Slatin playing no part in them. Both the actual text and the verb tenses of the original telegrams, from which the above translation has been made, make it as plain as a pikestaff that every single suggestion had in fact originated with Slatin, and that the Foreign Minister was merely relaying them with his own approval.

Indeed, two days after those telegrams had gone out, Slatin again called on Count Berchtold to amplify his suggestions for troubling England, and to add a few new ones. In his diary, Slatin merely records of this meeting that he has 'conversed for ¾ hour about the political situation', with the Foreign Minister. Another telegram that Berchtold fired off to Pallavicini in Constantinople the following morning reveals what the conversation had been about:

Baron Slatin Pasha, who has resigned from his position in the Anglo-Sudanese (sic) service due to the outbreak of war, expressed the view, when calling on me to discuss a Turkish action against Egypt, that the Porte should harass the English by sending a Syrian division against the Suez Canal. At the same time it might be possible to block the Canal up at some points by dispatching *Hodjas* equipped with 'Ekrasit' explosive charges.

But by now, even if Count Berchtold was still avid for all Slatin's ingenious proposals, both the Austrian and German envoys to Turkey were getting a little weary and a little suspicious of this long-range guidance from the man who, until a week or two ago, had been Inspector-General of the Sudan. Pallavicini sent two telegrams back to Vienna about Slatin on 28 August. The first, replying to the initial proposals about disruptive propaganda against the English said that the Grand Vizier had been sounded out on this and had told Pallavicini that 'though there was not much to be done along these lines in Egypt, there were prospects in the Sudan and that appropriate steps had already been taken'.

That was in the morning. After lunch, on receiving Berchtold's further instructions about Slatin's more drastic proposals, the Austrian diplomat replied with a much cooler message, claiming that all Slatin's suggestions for an action against Egypt had already been considered by the Turks.

Then comes an addition, marked 'Strictly Confidential':

The Caliph has warned the German Ambassador about Slatin. It might be wise to watch him very carefully for it is not out of the question that he is playing a double game.

Count Berchtold sent back an indignant retort rejecting the Caliph's 'baseless and deliberate calumnies' against Slatin. But, whether or not the faintest of warning bells had tinkled in Berchtold's ear, he sends no more telegrams out to Constantinople with Slatin's suggestions for winning the war against England. Nor is there any record of Slatin officially putting any more ideas forward.

Such are the bare facts. On the face of it, they are ugly facts. Why on earth did Slatin do it? Less than a fortnight before he had been down in Trieste, still trying to rejoin the English with whom he had served, as a soldier and administrator, for nearly twenty years (or for more than thirty, if the Gordon era be counted). It was barely a week since he had formally resigned as Inspector-General of the Sudan. He owed everything in his life, including his Austrian titles and his position in European society, to the favour shown him by the English crown and to the devotion shown him by Reginald Wingate. With hindsight, one might say that the only sensible and decent course open to him now – especially in those first days of war, when chivalry and courtesy still prevailed over bitterness – was surely to keep quiet, to say and do nothing which might harm either the masters he had just reluctantly left or the masters he had just involuntarily rejoined. Yet here he is, the war less than a month old, going round Vienna fairly bristling with detailed and serious suggestions for attacking, not simply British interests as a whole, but the position of his own former chief and closest friend, the Governor-General of the Sudan in particular. (And no claim can be advanced that he was, in fact, playing a double game, partly in England's interest. Had that been the case, he himself, and his English friends, could not have failed to advance this in his defence in later years.)

It seems logical to take as an explanation a blend of those two possibilities mentioned above – sheer opportunism and emotional unbalance – and fairest to suggest that the latter was the greater factor. As to the former, the whole of his early life had of course been based on adventurism, ambition and on the creed of survival. At least once before, when the wind had blown too strongly for comfort, he had simply bent before it, allowing his principles to be swept away. Slatin simply could not bear to be out of things. Indeed, we shall soon find him banging on all the doors he could find in Vienna and mobilizing all his influential friends there in an attempt to secure for himself a fitting post. And in this context, his Englishness, which until now had been his strength in Vienna, became overnight his weakness. Thus he could have acted as he did partly out of opportunistic calculation, judging that the best way to get preferment in wartime Austria was to make a public bonfire of all his links with peacetime England.

That, however, is unlikely to be the whole explanation. Probably it is not even the main part of it. Rudolf Slatin was no evil man. More to the point, he was a creature of the emotions rather than of the intellect. For more than twenty years, he had performed his delicate balancing act between his two Emperors and his two Empires and, in this way, he had climbed high up the European ladder. But the latent strain of balancing these two loyalties had been there inside him all the time. On occasions, he had wobbled with the strain, whether it was to worry over offending his own sovereign by some personal service rendered to the English monarch or to fret over displeasing his English patrons by taking the Austrian side in a political argument like the 1908 crisis.

Now that ladder which, despite these strains, had borne him so high, had suddenly collapsed, and he had crashed down under it. With the fall there could well have come an emotional concussion, and in this stunned state, he would naturally have clung for comfort to what was, after all, his native land. 'I am an Austrian, and a Viennese before everything else' he had written on the way back from Trieste. That one sentence of his is perhaps the best explanation for what he did; why he did it; and how he did it.

The irony of it all was not merely that he achieved nothing for the Central Powers in Constantinople and nothing for himself in Vienna. On top of this, his own British Intelligence Department in Cairo were soon on to his new game. It must have given them quite a shock. They had rescued him from the Khalifa's clutches in the first place. He had then worked for them directly for three years and indirectly for another fourteen. Now, within a few weeks of war breaking out, the Inspector-General of the Sudan suddenly appeared on their books as a suspected enemy agent.

On 14 September, the British Foreign Secretary, Sir Edward Grey, received this telegram from his Ambassador to Petrograd, Sir George Buchanan:

I have been informed by the Russian Government on reliable authority that the Austrian Ambassador at Constantinople has received instructions to press the Porte to move a division of Turkish troops towards the Nile, in order to block that river at various points.

The instructions sent to the Austrian Ambassador are based on advice recently given to Count Berchtold by Slatin Pasha, who maintained that the action indicated above would be sufficient to effect a diversion in Egypt.

The news seemed incredible but the source was official and emphatic. The Russians, moreover, had a formidable espionage record in penetrating the highest circles of Imperial Vienna, as the great scandal over Colonel Redl, which had broken in Vienna only three years before, had shown.* The British Foreign Secretary, who knew Slatin well from his London seasons, accordingly passed the report on to the British mission in Cairo with a comment which echoed rather more outrage than disbelief:

You should, if there are means of doing so, convey to Slatin, without disclosing the source, the information that has reached us and intimate that it seems incredible that he should abuse in this way the confidence that existed so long between him and ourselves, and we find it difficult to believe the report.

To this, Mr Cheetham, the acting High Commissioner, replied merely that Slatin Pasha had not returned to his post in the Sudan and was not expected to do so. Sir Edward Grey sent back like a whiplash one sentence to Cairo: 'A replacement should be found at once.'

Slatin's friends and colleagues in Cairo found the report not merely difficult, but quite impossible to believe. It was agreed however that Slatin's chief ought to be told about it. So, on 18 September, Captain Clayton of the Intelligence Office in Cairo wrote Wingate a letter marked 'Strictly Private' giving him the text of the Petrograd telegram. He spared Wingate's feelings by not repeating a word of Sir Edward Grey's comments. Instead he added, as though to brush the whole matter aside:

I cannot quite see where the Russians could get such 'sure information' on such a subject! It is no doubt on a par with the extraordinary statements one sometimes has made to one here.

---

* The Austrian General Staff officer who had committed suicide after being exposed as a Russian spy.

Clayton was, at that time, only a junior officer writing to the great General Wingate, who, as everyone knew, was Slatin's closest friend. This may explain his cavalier dismissal of a Russian Intelligence Service that had already wrought such havoc in Vienna. No such calculations entered Wingate's mind. The Governor-General's 'dear old Rowdy' could no more have done such a thing than he himself, and that was an end to it. Wingate wrote approvingly back to Clayton, dismissing the whole affair as 'a deliberate effort on the part of our enemies to create bad blood between Slatin and the British'.

By another irony, Wingate was at that very time awaiting a response to a second, and very determined, attempt he had made to persuade Slatin to return to the Sudan – war or no war. It was again a case of the double-barrelled approach, a formal letter backed up by a very personal one. Though he had Slatin's resignation of 18 August in front of him, Wingate sat down in his Cairo office on 1 September and doggedly addressed his reply to: 'Major General Sir R. Baron von Slatin GCVO, KCMG, CB, Inspector-General of the Anglo-Egyptian Sudan.' While acknowledging receipt of the resignation letter, he pointed out that perhaps the Inspector-General was not aware of certain special rules which had been introduced concerning 'the subjects of belligerents now in the service of the Sudan Govt', rules which in fact enabled them to continue in office despite the war. In view of this he was taking no action over the resignation which he 'earnestly requested' his Inspector-General to reconsider. Indeed Slatin was informed that, in the meantime, he was being considered only 'on leave of absence pending resumption of official duties' and that even if this absence should prove 'indefinitely postponed' some 'special and equitable arrangement' would be considered regarding his pay and allowances.

Wingate's private letter, sent to Vienna the same day, hammered all the official points home again. Then, on the personal plane, it added:

... The Sudan without you is unthinkable—quite apart from the deep and real sorrow with which I should personally regard the severance of your connection with your work and with myself, your oldest and best friend in this country—and perhaps in the world.

... As soldiers you and I can afford to put aside—until the war is over—any discussions as to its merits and demerits and I am sure that I can equally guarantee that on your return to the Sudan we shall all studiously avoid referring to it. I do not think this situation would be unworkable...

So, dear old Rowdy, do think carefully over what I have said in this and my official letter. I am keeping all this quite private... so nothing is known or will be known, until I hear from you again. And of course I will still not say goodbye, for I am still hopeful that we may serve together for many a year—for the benefit of the Sudan and its people who would hate — like myself — any idea of losing their beloved 'old Slatin'.

The letter was not quite as naïvely hopeful as it sounded. Slatin, like Wingate himself, was officially in the employment of the Egyptian Government and though it was Britain in fact they both served, their pay and allowances came out of the Khedive's coffers in Cairo, not from the Treasury in London. Moreover, the war was in its early days. Many observers hoped and thought it would be over quite soon and meanwhile the Sudan seemed such a long way from the European battlefields. What poor Wingate could never have dreamt was that Slatin, torn suddenly apart between his English and his Austrian loyalties, had already made a wartime choice for the latter.

Just how much of a split personality Slatin was in these weeks is shown by the replies which he sent back to Wingate's two letters at the end of that month. His formal letter, designed to be read and placed on the official files (in Vienna perhaps even more than in Cairo) beats the drum of Austrian patriotism. After wishing again that Wingate should strike his name off the Sudan official list, Slatin goes on:

As an Austrian subject I had, after the declaration of war, to report myself to my government and, as an able-bodied man, to offer my services to my fatherland...

Holding the title of a Baron of the Austrian Empire and being a former Officer of its Army I am unable to sign the conditions governing the subjects of belligerents now in the service of the Sudan Govt.

It was all very stiff and pompous stuff for an English-style cosmopolitan like Rudolf Slatin to write. A couple of sentences reaffirming his decision with regret, though without comment, would have been far more dignified. But these were emotional times and Slatin was an emotional man. In both of the warring camps, after all, that same cry of 'fatherland' was drowning the old music of Europe. What is less easy to understand however is that having swung violently to the Austrian side – so violently that he was already hatching plots against his own Sudan and his own chief – Slatin could still sit down and write, on that same day, another private letter to Wingate as though nothing of the sort had happened.

You don't know, my dear old Rex, how sorry I am that our two beloved countries are at War and that I have to part from you, my oldest and best friend—have to part from the Sudan and its inhabitants which are to me like a part of myself . . .

But never mind—we all have to get through and we can only hope that the time isn't very far when our countries and their respective rulers will be at peace once more. If then the situation allows me to return to the Sudan and *if then I am still wanted* [writer's italics] we may meet again . . .

This letter, dripping with nostalgia and affection, was followed up with another formal note in which Slatin stated that the two English cipher books still in his posession were 'sealed and kept in my safe' and would, if necessary, be destroyed. It was a nice attempt at honourable neutrality, for Slatin was not to know that both books were, in fact, out of date. But Wingate, the Sudan and the crown of England perhaps deserved rather more than this one gesture from their Inspector-General. This was precisely the sort of yardstick that, had he been more prudent, more meticulous or more balanced, Slatin would have applied to all his actions.

The tragedy for Slatin was that all this clamorous, if confused, Austrian patriotism of his was getting him absolutely nowhere in Vienna. The files of the Imperial War Ministry from August 1914 onwards tell a pathetic tale of Slatin's repeated offers of his services in any capacity, offers which were turned aside by repeated evasiveness or polite refusals from the authorities concerned. When it came down to it, the fatherland just didn't seem prepared to take Slatin on.

He first tackled the Emperor's Adjutant-General again. In a letter sent to Count Paar on 28 August he begged his august friend for help in getting a military post and assured him that he was prepared 'to do any form of work whatever that may be desired'. Count Paar sent Slatin's request to the War Minister, Krobatin. He replied on 13 September that the Ministry had noted the offer but that the question of any operational employment for Slatin was one for the Army High Command to decide.

For the time being, therefore, Slatin had to rest content with his name appearing on the list of volunteers. He saw to it, however, that it appeared on the right lists and in the right company. Not content with 'registering' at the War Office and the High Command, he got Count Paar to include his name with a small group of individuals enrolled at the Military Chancery of the Emperor as volunteers 'for any special mission at home or abroad for the duration of the present war'. This list comprised a very assorted and highly distinguished list of frustrated officers who, for one reason or another, were denied field service. Though Slatin's military rank ('former British Major-General and Egyptian Lieutenant-General') far out-topped the others, he in turn was quite outclassed by them all socially. The names included Colonel Dom Miguel, Duke of Braganza; Major Prince Alfred zu Windisch-Graetz, and a couple of Austrian counts chafing under ceremonial duties in Vienna.

At the same time, as is made clear by cross-references in these military files, Slatin had been offering his services to the Foreign Ministry. The answer, recorded on 6 November, was the same: his name would be kept on the books, but there was no prospect of diplomatic employment at the moment. However, Count Berchtold probably felt he owed Slatin something for those intriguing and highly patriotic suggestions made at the outbreak of war.

The outcome was a memorandum which Berchtold wrote to the Prime Minister of the day, Count Stürgkh, suggesting that some sign of Imperial favour might be accorded to Slatin in view of the way he had laid down his high English offices, 'thus demonstrating in an eminently unselfish and indeed self-sacrificing fashion his loyal and patriotic feelings'. Three weeks later Count Stürgkh replied that Slatin had been granted the dignity of *Geheimrat*. This was not a job and it brought no money. But at least, it entitled Slatin to call himself, from that day forward, 'Excellency'. The award came at an appropriate juncture. It was in November 1914 that the Turkish General

Staff decided, after all, to launch an attack against the Suez Canal. And the troops they picked for it were Syrians, whom Slatin had suggested. (They were anyway, it must be added, the obvious choice for such a desert campaign.)

Berchtold made one more attempt at the end of that year to do something for Slatin. He floated the idea in Constantinople of appointing Slatin Adjutant-General to the Sultan, doubtless with the impending invasion of the Sinai in mind.* But the Sultan, never partial to Slatin, would have none of it and after this failure Berchtold gave up. Slatin could only look now to the Army again.

He had a last moment of hope in May 1915. After nine months of dithering and bargaining, Italy at last entered the war – against her Austrian and German allies. Italy had African colonies and desert armies in those colonies. Perhaps now there would be a chance for the veteran of Omdurman to put on uniform again, even if it meant fighting on the opposite side to the Union Jack. On 3 June Slatin tackled the War Minister with another personal letter. He doesn't, he begins, want to be a nuisance, but may he remind the Minister again of his existence? Perhaps in this latest situation some military post might be found for him 'either at the front or directly under the command of Your Excellency'. Any work or any position, he pleads, would 'give him the satisfaction, in these dark days, of doing something for my fatherland – to which I returned without hesitation from abroad'.

Considering that Slatin had only broken off his London season in July 1914 to get married in Vienna and that the 'return from abroad' the following month had in fact been the forced abandonment, in the Austrian port of Trieste, of an attempt to rejoin the English, this final assertion really did take several liberties with the facts.

It made no difference. There is a crisp note made on 18 June at the top of this particular file that the Army Supreme Commander Archduke Frederick 'could not consider' Slatin's request. The War Minister passed the decision back to Slatin 'with keenest regret'. General Krobatin did not even mention the other possibility Slatin had put forward, that of serving directly

---

* The attack, launched in February 1915, was mown down by British and French forces defending the east bank of the Canal. The Turks never tried again after this fiasco.

under him. In one last attempt to raise it in person, Slatin wrote, a week later, to apply for an interview. The Minister's aide-de-camp replied, somewhat remotely, that 'His Excellency holds audiences between 11 and 1 every Thursday (public holidays excepted)'. No day was suggested, and there is no record of Slatin turning up.

However, it seems to have been General Krobatin who finally found the answer for Slatin's increasingly pathetic plight. In September 1915 he was appointed Deputy Director of the Central Information Bureau for Prisoners of War and Vice-President of the War Prisoners' Welfare Committee of the Austrian Red Cross. It was the ideal solution for a man of Slatin's background and, one would have thought, a fairly obvious one. It is a pity that nobody, including Slatin, thought of it sooner.

Looking back on this sad, confused episode one can point to various purely professional reasons why Slatin failed to get any appointment in the field. Whatever rank the Sudan had brought him, he was still only a humble lieutenant on the Reserve of the Emperor's army. He had never fought in any European engagement and had never fought at all for the past twenty years. All his experience was with deserts and dervishes and, at fifty-seven, he was too old to be retrained.

Yet, having said all this, it does seem a little strange that no responsible desk job of any sort, even if not a military post, could be found for him for over a year in any of the numberless ministries, chanceries, agencies and offices of Imperial Vienna, which was itself one vast bureaucratic beehive. One cannot escape the feeling that, as on certain occasions in the past, Slatin had partly stumbled over his own eagerness. For any work where wartime secrets were being made or kept, Slatin's deep English connections were certainly no recommendation. Neither, for some people perhaps, was the lightning speed with which he had abandoned them. We shall never know the whole story. Slatin himself was mystified as well as hurt.

Early in 1915, there was a droll anti-climactic epilogue to this tragicomedy of Slatin's dual loyalties. An unsigned article printed in the English-language journal *Near East* on 8 January described the life of Slatin Pasha as 'a long career of versatility and opportunism' and went on to allege that, as the latest episode in this career, Slatin had 'renounced any and all honours conferred upon him by Great Britain'. The general proposition advanced by the anonymous writer was hostile, but at least arguable. However, the illustration he had chosen was not only false; it was ridiculous. Anybody who knew Slatin's worship of decorations was well aware that he would not willingly have returned a medal to Beelzebub, let alone to the King of England. His defenders against what was, in those days, a monstrous charge, thus had an easy field day. The editor of *Near East* not only published all their refutations but also, on 2 February 1915, added a grovelling apology of his own for ever printing the original allegation.

Wingate, of course, was among the ranks of Slatin's champions though he was after a higher target than the wretched editor. He got a message through to Slatin about the accusations and asked for a denial. This his friend promptly produced, in a letter written from Vienna on 8 February 1915:

> My decorations are all personal gifts from sovereigns, my CB and KCMG from Queen Victoria, my KCVO from King Edward VII, and my GCVO from King George V—all personal remembrances, and one does not return such. So they are still in my possession though of course I don't wear them as long as there is no peace between the two countries.

Wingate promptly forwarded this with his comments to Lord Stamfordham, for the King's eyes. On 12 April 1915 Stamfordham wrote back:

> It was a great relief to receive your letter of the 7th March enclosing a letter from our dear old friend Slatin ... Anyone who knew Slatin could never have believed the wicked stories that were spread ... as to his contemptuous treatment of his British decorations ...

Wingate did not know, and he did not ask, whether the King had learnt from his Foreign Secretary, Sir Edward Grey, about the existence of much more serious 'wicked stories' concerning Slatin's anti-English activities. For the time being, Slatin had got away with it. The London clubs and the British officers' messes rumbled with reprobation at the bounders who had attacked this loyal servant of England's. Only on certain Whitehall files did the really big question-mark about Slatin in August 1914 remain. As we shall see, it was still there when the war was over.

Part Four

Chapter Fifteen

FROM THE SHADOWS

Like so much else, the Austrian Red Cross records for the First World War did not survive, except in fragments, the collapse of the Habsburg Monarchy in 1918 and the rise and fall of Adolf Hitler's brief empire a generation later. Slatin's own diaries are of relatively little use in reconstructing this next phase of his chequered career; indeed, after 1916 they stop altogether for twelve years. There are some references to him in the various British archives and in the surviving records of the Imperial Military Chancery in Vienna; but it is his letters to his friends, and especially those to his English friends, which throw most light on these shadowy war years. They show us not only the changing scene of his actions but also the changing mood of his mind.

Perhaps it was the influence of his work, which by its very nature put the dogmas of politics below the alleviation of human suffering. Perhaps it was the simple fact that he was at work again at last, and that his resentments were no longer sharpened by the frustration of idleness. Perhaps it was a numbing realization, as the second winter of the conflict approached, that there was to be no quick end to it and that all Europe might be heading for destruction. Whatever the reasons, after twelve months of war, his attitude softens abruptly.

Those stiff patriotic 'hurrahs' he began by putting in his diary whenever an Austrian or German success was reported from the fronts fade away. So do the snide remarks he used to make about his English friends. Early in the war, for example, when the Austrian Ambassador in London, Count Mensdorff, got back to Vienna, he told Slatin how Sir Edward Grey had taken leave of him with tears in his eyes. The real Slatin, the emotional servant of England, the admirer of Grey himself, would have either made no comment, or else only a sad one in recording that item in his diary. But the prickly, artificial Slatin of August 1914 had added: 'What use is *that*?' It was a typical sign of the stress which had torn him away from his natural moorings and caused him to embark on that very questionable course of the first war weeks.

Before a year has passed, all this has gone. He even gives up claiming that the war is England's fault. It has now become nobody's fault; just an appalling, inexplicable tragedy that only a revival of the old European *camaraderie* of monarchs might settle. In one letter to his 'dear old Rex' sent from Vienna* as early as 29 July 1915, he writes: 'If you, I, and old Count Metternich would have the Kings in our hand I think we would come to a suitable agreement.' ('Doubtful!!' Wingate wrote, very sensibly, on the margin.)

Another letter to Wingate, dated 2 February 1916, shows, not the fiery would-be warrior but the anguished would-be peace-maker, a rôle Slatin was to grow into more and more:

Do you know what my ambition would be? To go to England and to have an (sic) friendly chat and to ask former friends of influence what they want—why to continue the war which brings only misery to all . . .

By May of that year Slatin is so nearly back to normal that he is already worrying about his Sudan government pension again. He had already made a point of telling Wingate that his Austrian Red Cross work was unpaid. He now writes:

I don't know what the law is about claiming pensions. As there is no official communication possible I couldn't make any representation. As you know I didn't get any pension [? pay] since May 1914 and I know I won't get it now. But I hope after peace is concluded between our two countries that the back pension [here the word 'pay' had been written first and then corrected] will be readjusted . . .

* He was able to communicate with his English friends throughout the war through neutral embassies in Vienna or through his own constant trips to neutral capitals.

This touched off, no doubt quite spontaneously, a spasm of nostalgia. Slatin had seen somewhere on his travels some old copies of the *Illustrated London News*, including one with a picture of the Prince of Wales photographed on a visit to Khartoum with the local notables. 'The old scoundrel Ibrahim – the first in the row! I wonder when the Sudan twins* will ragge (sic) each other again?'

That same summer Slatin's own diaries give one of their rare glimpses of the psychological strain that the war was imposing on this adopted Englishman in temporary exile in his native Austria. On 6 August he spent the whole day at the prisoner-of-war camps at Wieselburg and Purgstall talking to the British and French officers held there. It seems there was some pretty frank discussion about war and peace that must have cut deeply into that torment of divided loyalties that was now emerging in Slatin again. On getting back to Vienna he wrote in his diary : 'I feel so unwell after all the swapping of opinions that I'm returning to bed.' And there he remained for the next two days.

Slatin was always on the move for his Red Cross work between the neutral capitals of Europe – principally Berne, Christiania, Copenhagen and Stockholm – and it is clear both from the official documents and his private correspondence how invaluable his pre-war social contacts were proving to him on his travels. There is evidence of this in the above-quoted letter to Wingate of May 1916. Slatin describes how, after a long talk with King Haakon (sic) of Norway ('We talked a good deal about olden days when we met at Osborne and Windsor') he got one hundred and fifty thousand pairs of boots and shoes released for Austrian prisoners of war in Russia.

By the following year he is leaning above all on his English friends for help. Every request to London is based on the claims of an old friendship and every one produces a surge of longing for peace and for England, a longing that, by now, Slatin makes no attempt to subdue. In June of 1917 we find him writing direct to Lord Stamfordham (the ennobled Sir Arthur Bigge) in an attempt to bypass wartime economic sanctions. He was after a consignment of English tin sheeting which was needed in Copenhagen to make 400–500 boxes a month for sending Red Cross food to Austrian prison camps in Siberia. But he could

* As Wingate and Slatin were known in the service.

not resist a bit of royal chit-chat as well. He had met the King and Queen of Denmark, he tells Lord Stamfordham, and had been several times to Bernsdorff Castle, the birthplace of Queen Alexandra, King Edward vii's widow: 'So I am always remind of happy days gone by and realize only now how happy we were before the war.'

Stamfordham replied in the same vein: 'One looks back with pleasure to the happy days and lives in hope for the future.' But for all this fond nostalgia, he had to report failure in Whitehall about the request for tin sheets. The export restrictions simply could not be relaxed. A formal message to this effect was duly passed to Slatin via the Spanish Ambassador in Vienna, who was by this time in charge of British interests there.

By now, however, Slatin's target in London was already much more substantial than tin plates. He was after nothing less than a secret peace settlement between the two warring camps. The first official echo of this activity appears in a telegram which the British Minister in Copenhagen, Sir Robert Paget, sent to the Foreign Office on 7 May 1917:

Slatin Pasha is here staying with Prince Valdemar [of Denmark] ... He says Austria must have peace and she has no quarrel with England whilst Austrians find German tyranny intolerable ... Prince Valdemar would like to try and bring the Austrians and ourselves together but is afraid the Germans would make Denmark pay for it ...

It is perhaps only a coincidence that this move of Slatin's in Copenhagen should follow hard on the heels of the more momentous peace feelers that his own sovereign, the young Emperor Charles,* had been making to London and Paris for the past three months. It is highly unlikely that Slatin, for all his connections at court, knew about these top-level soundings, which became known as the 'Sixtus Affair' because they were made through the Emperor's two French brothers-in-law, the Princes Sixtus and Xavier of Bourbon-Parma. Indeed, we know from the Empress Zita that, apart from the Emperor, only herself and the then Foreign Minister, Count Czernin, were privy in Vienna to this highly secret and politically explosive affair –

---

* He had succeeded his great-uncle, the Emperor Franz Joseph, at the latter's death on 30 November 1916, after the longest reign in history.

the last venture in European history of the old dynastic diplomacy.

On the other hand, Slatin frequently had audiences with the Emperor Charles on prisoner-of-war problems, and his brother Heinrich was in even closer attendance as a regular court official. The passionate desire of the new ruler to end, not merely a war he had not started, but the alliance with Germany which he so feared even in peacetime was well known. Slatin, a veteran pre-war servant of the English, a European courtier with personal contacts in all of the neutral courts and capitals and now, as a Red Cross official, able to visit them as and when he pleased without arousing comment – such a man was an ideal go-between to supplement the secret missions of Prince Sixtus in the Western capitals. It is therefore quite possible that, when he made his move in Copenhagen, Slatin had been encouraged by someone of importance in Vienna to follow those missions up. The only living survivor of this 1917 Austrian peace offensive, the Empress Zita, feels personally convinced that that someone was her husband, the Emperor. But we cannot know for certain. The Emperor never said as much to his wife. The archives give us no pointer. Nor, in any of his letters or post-war memoranda, does Slatin.

In any case, by May of 1917 it was too late for anyone to save the Austrian peace bid in its original form. The English Prime Minister, Lloyd George, was the only Western leader really willing to follow it up, for he saw in it a means to break not only the long-term Austro-German alliance in politics but also the current military deadlock on the battlefield. The French, however, were undecided under a new government. The Italians, who had been promised large chunks of the Habsburg domains after Austria's defeat, were emphatically against. Barely three weeks before Slatin started his soundings in Copenhagen, the representatives of those three allied powers, in a special meeting at St Jean de Maurienne, had agreed that 'it would not be opportune' to engage in peace talks with the Austrians at this juncture. The text of this three-power decision was telegraphed by Lord Hardinge to the British envoy at Copenhagen on 11 May 1917. So that, for the moment, was that.

But Slatin soon found another peace trail to London, and this time it was one that could not be blocked by diplomatic conferences. The courier was a distinguished English prisoner of war whose release Slatin had helped to bring about, and Slatin had sent his messenger back not to the Foreign Office but to King George v himself. The officer concerned was Lieutenant-Colonel the Honourable Henry Napier, whom Slatin had met and talked with in an Allied officers' prison camp at Salzerbad as early as October 1916. By the end of 1917 he had managed to effect Napier's release for an Austrian exchange prisoner. Lord Stamfordham's papers take up the story a week or two later, in a secret memorandum to King George dated 31 January 1918:

Humbly submitted.
Today I went to see Lt. Col. Hon. Henry Napier, son of late Lord Napier of Magdala, recently released from internment in Austria chiefly through the help and influence of Sir R. Slatin.—He saw the latter when passing through Vienna and asked him to give *me* a message to the effect that he still considers himself a British General and a loyal servant to King George—and that he feels there is no reason that at the same time he should not be a loyal and faithful subject to his Emperor.—In this as it were dual position he ought to be able to help towards arriving at a peaceful settlement of the War.—Though he said a separate peace between England & Austria was out of the question he thought that the Alsace Lorraine question might admit of arrangement if they were made autonomous under as it were German protection—also we could come to an agreement about Trieste. Col. Napier said he would give me the message but said he would also like to report to Lord Hardinge what Slatin said. This he has done. I will see Lord H.

Here the echoes of the Sixtus Affair and its aftermath are heard much more strongly. Austria's support for French claims to Alsace-Lorraine had been the most substantial inducement the Emperor Charles had offered the Entente; indeed, he had gone much further the previous spring than the autonomy formula which Slatin was airing now. Moreover, without mentioning Trieste as such, the Emperor had also committed himself to ceding parts of his Italian provinces if this would help purchase a general peace settlement.

It so happened that, shortly before Colonel Napier left for England, Slatin had in fact spent a few days in the Emperor's entourage. The occasion was a tour of inspection which the

young sovereign was making of the Italian front, where he had
himself commanded an Austrian Army Corps before succeeding
to the throne. Slatin's presence in the company was revealed
by an episode so droll that it is worth describing for its own sake.
It happened when the royal party, on the way back by car on
10 November from a visit to a Divisional Headquarters, drove
along the banks of the River Torre which was swollen, though
not impassable, after heavy rain. The first automobile, carrying
the Emperor and his Chief of Staff, General Arz, slid off the
road by a damaged bridge and came to rest a few yards out in
the river. The current barely topped the wheels of the vehicle so
that its august inhabitants were not only quite safe but even
dry, provided they stayed where they were. The young Emperor,
so far from being in any panic, was seen to be grinning broadly.

His entourage, however, were quite determined to have some
heroics. After much waving and shouting, a lorry was fetched,
parked on the bank, and attempts were made to link it by a
chain to the stranded car. The first try failed because the chain
was too short. While another was being fetched, the Emperor's
personal valet decided to take the matter in his hands, or rather,
on his shoulders. Summoning one of the soldiers of the guard,
he waded into the river, and persuaded the Emperor to let them
carry him to dry land. Unfortunately, the valet was a very
small man and the guardsman a very tall one. So, after a few
stumbling yards perched on these unequal pillars of devotion,
the Emperor fell slap into the water himself. Still in the best of
spirits at the adventure, and in no mortal danger whatsoever, he
waited waist-high in the river but standing on a firm bed of
reeds, for the next bright idea.

The pandemonium on the banks knew no bounds, for this
was really no situation for an Apostolic Majesty. One courtier
hopefully flung out his coat, while holding on to one sleeve; but
it fell short. A more sensible manoeuvre was then launched by
Prince Felix of Bourbon-Parma,* who waded into the water
with a line of soldiers behind him to form a human chain.
Aided by these new helping hands, and by a piece of timber from
the broken bridge, the Emperor finally pulled himself up out of
the river. Slatin, who had been travelling in the last of the cars,

* Another brother-in-law of the Emperor's but, unlike the Princes Sixtus and Xavier, an Austrian
subject and so fighting on the Austrian side: a telling example of how the war had split dynasties as
well as families.

seems to have watched the entire proceedings from his seat. The behaviour of the Chief of Staff, General Arz, was even more phlegmatic. He just sat it out in mid-stream in the Emperor's car until, as dry as a bone, he was eventually towed clear by the lorry.

The connoisseur of Austria and things Austrian could point to a lot that was typical about this little episode. But it would never have found its way into the official war records at all had not the Emperor's press secretary, Karl Werkmann, decided that this was too good a propaganda opportunity to miss. The story was fed that evening to all the newspaper correspondents at Army Headquarters in a highly dramatized form which they duly proceeded to make even more dramatic. As a result, the loyal subjects of Austria-Hungary were horrified to learn, the following morning, that their Emperor had come within an ace of drowning just behind the Italian battle lines. The excitement and relief felt in Vienna was genuine, however uncalled for. *Te Deums* were sung in the churches and a special session of the Upper House was convened to express the loyalty and gratitude of the magnates.

There was nothing Charles could do now but go along with the charade. At a solemn ceremony held in the dining-car of his court train on 12 November (a ceremony at which the Emperor, and a lot of others present, must have had some difficulty in keeping their composure), medals were handed out all round to his 'rescuers from mortal peril'. Prince Felix got the Golden Medal of Bravery for officers. The small valet and the huge guardsman got the same decoration for soldiers, despite having tipped their sovereign into the river. And Freiherr Rudolf von Slatin Pasha received an 'honourable commendation' for his conduct, despite the fact that he never left his car throughout. It is only by this official citation, and the comedy on the banks of the River Torre which preceded it, that we know where Slatin was in the second week of November 1917. It is clear that he had other things than wet feet to discuss with his Emperor, and the impending voyage of Colonel Napier to England may well have been one of them.

Another and more straightforward purpose of Slatin's trip to the Italian front was doubtless to report to the Emperor on an important international conference he had attended on Austria's behalf the month before in Copenhagen. Though the Bolsheviks had not yet seized power in Russia, the March Revolution which had unseated the Tsar was already six months old. The will of the Provisional Russian Government to continue the struggle was in some doubt, and Berlin and Vienna were making lively efforts to probe that will and blunt it further. It was against this background that, at Copenhagen in October 1917, Russian military and Red Cross representatives sat down with those of the Allied Central Powers (Germany, Austria-Hungary, Turkey and Rumania) to discuss the welfare and possible exchange of their prisoners of war. Slatin was there to represent the Austrian Red Cross, and the archives of the Imperial Military Chancery show that he did well.

A report presented to the Emperor Charles by the War Minister in Vienna on 16 November 1917, contains the passage:

The presence of His Excellency Baron Slatin proved especially valuable for the success of the negotiations. He was repeatedly able to prevent friction as soon as it appeared from developing further and to play a conciliatory role between the delegations—all this thanks to the high esteem which he enjoys as well as to his astuteness and his experience of world affairs.

The result, later that year, was another decoration for Slatin, the Medal of Honour [German *Ehrenzeichen*] First Class. The citation praised Slatin's 'exceptionally beneficial and successful activity over the past two years on behalf of our prisoners of war and civilian internees in enemy countries'.

Meanwhile, while Wingate governed on in Khartoum and while Slatin travelled on in neutral Europe ('like the eternal Jew', as he put it in one letter to an old Austrian friend), the joys and sorrows of their personal lives came and went as well. On 12 November 1916, Alice Slatin fulfilled what was perhaps the greatest wish of her life, and presented Rudolf, in her forty-third year, with a child. Slatin had been confidently expecting 'a little Rowdy', as he told Wingate on 28 May of that year. But if he was disappointed at getting a girl, whom they called Anna Marie Helen, he did not show it. He wrote chirpily again to Wingate: 'Mother and child are doing well. The little girl looks like a monkey and everybody says she has great likeness with (sic) me.'

Wingate's own life seems to have taken a fairly even wartime course until the familiar, terrible tragedy struck the family early in February 1918. One of his two sons, Malcolm, was killed in action on the Western front. Though only twenty-four, he was already a brevet major with a DSO, MC, and Croix de Guerre. The fires of chauvinism had long been fading in Slatin's breast. This news extinguished any last embers that may have remained. Across the mounting barriers of war he wrote to Wingate the sort of letter that, apart from the spelling, any English friend sitting in England might have penned:

My dear old friend, I am more griefed than I can express. Poor Malcolm has gone for ever from us—such a good intelligent brave boy, such a good son. How I remember him; the little fair haired chap, standing on a chair preaching to us—he was then 3 or 4 years old. My deepest and truest sympathy is with you and Lady Wingate. This unfortunate war shall not interfere with our feeling of friendship, and it would take a thousand wars to make me lose one atom of affection for you and your dears...

The wheel has now turned full circle. Personal relations, always more important than anything else in Slatin's make-up, have once again swamped politics completely. It might have been his own son who had fallen in France; by whose bullet and in which line of trenches no longer mattered. The war, which Slatin, like so many others, had first taken so theatrically to heart, had become an anonymous, universal enemy which all had to endure.

Not for much longer, however. Little more than three months after Slatin wrote that letter, the complex Austro-German military edifice, which had somehow held together under so many strains and hammer-blows, began, suddenly, to crumble. Bulgaria, the smallest and weakest member of the Central Powers' alliance, collapsed on 25 September 1918, and laid bare the south-eastern flank of the Austrian Empire. The Habsburg Monarchy, which had lasted for six and a half centuries, now had little more than six and a half weeks to go. Defeated on the battlefield, it began to fall apart at home as well.

One by one, led by the Czechs, Hungarians, Croats, Slovenes, and Poles, its constituent peoples declared their independence. Ironically, their authority for this had come from the crown itself. The young Emperor, desperately trying to hold his domains together, had declared the Monarchy, in the last weeks of its life, to be a federal union of independent states. His peoples seized the independence and spurned the union. The end came at noon on 11 November, when Charles formally 'withdrew from state affairs' and a Republic was proclaimed in Vienna itself.

Slatin was in the Imperial capital when the collapse came. Like most of its inhabitants, he was no doubt dazed and frightened by this earthquake which was wiping out an entire political and social landscape around him. Though he never tells us in his letters or diaries what sort of aftermath he expected from the war, he had probably pinned his hopes on some sort of compromise between the two camps which would have enabled the Monarchy to lick its wounds and put its own house in order. That those wounds were beyond healing and that the house would come down over all their heads was something which, in their blackest dreams, Austrians of Slatin's stamp just could not envisage. This was more than defeat; it was extinction. He had been the servant of a dynasty even more than he had been the citizen of its Empire. Now, almost overnight, both Empire and dynasty had vanished. Where should he go? What should he do?

Slatin was exceptionally, almost uniquely fortunate in that he did have somewhere definite to go and something definite to do. It was, moreover, a task that he could discharge for the Republic without betraying his loyalty to the Emperor. Soon after the Armistice, he left for Berne to wind up the Red Cross work he had been doing for the past two years, work that was now reaching its climax with the impending release of hundreds of thousands of Austrian prisoners of war. He prudently took with him his wife and his two-year-old daughter (her second birthday had fallen on the day the Austrian Republic was declared). Vienna was already a freezing, starving city with a whiff of revolution in the air. As it was no longer *his* Vienna, catching that train at the Westbahnhof to neutral, warm and well-fed Switzerland probably did not even feel like desertion, except of the relatives who came to see them off.

Slatin was in any case a sick man himself. Soon after arriving in Berne he was admitted to the Sanatorium Victoria there, suffering from bronchitis and heart trouble. But the Austria he had left behind was in far more desperate straits. Vienna was now the capital only of a tiny impoverished Austrian Republic seven millions strong. The old writ of Empire no longer ran in the neighbour countries which were savouring the new independence they had just seized and were very happy to let the Austrians feel it. The only hope of the harassed men who had stepped into the Habsburgs' shoes was that the victorious Western powers would force the so-called 'successor-states' to provide Vienna with food and fuel. It was a droll situation, to call in the ex-enemies of Austria to discipline her ex-subjects. Slatin, with his unique contacts, seemed the best man to deal with it. His hospital bed in the Sanatorium Victoria thus became a diplomatic office.

It started on 9 December when Slatin received an emergency distress telegram from his native city. It was signed jointly by Dr Weiskirchner, the Mayor of Vienna, and Dr Otto Bauer, State Secretary for Foreign Affairs in the provisional government of the Socialist Chancellor Karl Renner. What follows is his own erratic English translation of the message:

Situation in Vienna disastrous owing to lack of coals. Implore Your Excellency to interfere immediately with American and British legation in order to have a pressure exercised on Tschechoslovackian government to deliver coals to Vienna. It is not a question of days but of hours. The population of a 2 million's city cannot stay in darkness with hunger and freezing. How shall I keep up order and tranquillity at Vienna under such circumstances? Food with utmost economy can last till end of this month.

Slatin may have wanted to wash his hands of these fanatical new Republicans like Otto Bauer. But he could not wash his hands of the Viennese, especially as so many of his own relatives and friends were among the sufferers. So he promptly did what he could. Inevitably, he first thought of his 'dear Lord and friend'. The following day he sent Lord Stamfordham the above translation of the Vienna telegram, begging him 'as my true friend ... to interest His Gracious Majesty and the Ministers in the sad case of my poor country and Vienna town'. And to Stamfordham he just shows the edge of the only real card the Austrian Republic had to play : 'I fear that shortely (sic) Austria will be in a state similar to that in Russia. It is impossible to rule people specially town people, if you can't offer them light, heating and food.'

Slatin had never met Colonel House, President Wilson's powerful adviser. But nothing daunted, he also wrote personally to him on 10 December, using a capital 'Y' throughout whenever addressing him as 'You', as though to suggest that the Americans were now the real Apostolic Majesties of the world. As they were a long way off, however, he thought it wise to explain a little more of the Central European background to his request for help. He also laid down that Communist bogy card fairly and squarely on the table:

Vienna got always its coals from Moravia and Bohemia . . . and these coalmines are nearly all in those parts of Bohemia which are inhabited by subjects of german abstraction (sic). Since our disastrous downbreak the Tschechoslovackian Government does not allow that coal pass to Vienna although it is there more than in abundance . . .

It is unavoidable that if assistance is not given heavy disturbances *à la bolschewiki* will take place and it will be not only fatal for the town but for the country and perhaps later for the neighbouring nations.

I implore You, Colonel House, therefore in the name of Humanity to find a way that the Tschechoslovackian Government givs the permission without any delay . . . It lays in the hands of the Allies to save us from the Bolschevism and to rebuild Austria i.e. Vienna, its old capital, or to condamn it to annihilation . . .

It was not a bad effort for a sick man in a Swiss sanatorium on behalf of a fatherland that had vanished, as he knew it and loved it. Though the Austrian authorities were at that time appealing to all the Entente powers through every channel available, Slatin's own approach seems to have had some considerable effect. His own Austrian Red Cross Society, in its Annual General Report for 1918 (one of the few records of the Society which has survived), claims indeed that it was Slatin's message to Colonel House which prompted President Wilson to intercede on Austria's behalf at the Allied Conference and 'grant help in respect of food supplies to German-Austria'. Slatin merely records, a fortnight after sending off his appeal to Washington, that 'Colonel House . . . wrote me a very nice letter assuring help for Austria and especially for Vienna'. But, at that date, he adds, no Czech coal had actually arrived in the Austrian capital.

The text of Colonel House's letter has not been traced. But that of Lord Stamfordham has. On 19 December, he wrote Slatin from Buckingham Palace:

I have ascertained that the Czecho-Slovaks have been asked to supply Vienna with all the coal they can spare.

The food question is a very pressing one and we are being urged from all quarters to help those with whom we have recently been at war. The matter is in the hands of the *Comité International de Revitaillement*. One feels very much for the sufferings, especially of the poorer classes.

And he ends on a personal note:

... we are well, but these are sad days for many of us. I look forward to the restoration of peace, and trust that the day is not far distant when we may see you again.

Slatin also was looking ahead to the post-war world and to a return to peacetime normality which, he hoped, was waiting for him at last around the corner of the new year. And the more he looked at it from his Swiss sanatorium the more it seemed that his only worthwhile future lay where his past had been, with England. Not that, in 1919, he wanted to settle there. He still found the mere thought of the climate too daunting for that. It was rather that he could not settle contentedly anywhere without the feeling that all was well with his English friends again after the bitterness of war and the spate of rumours about his own behaviour. There was also the very practical reason that he could not afford to settle anywhere without working for his living unless those same English friends helped him to get his pre-war pension rights restored.

The two problems – to get his reputation back and to get his money back – were, he knew, linked. In the closing days of 1918 he decided to tackle both problems at once. He had just written some eloquent pleas for help and sympathy on behalf of the Austrian Republic. It was now high time to perform the same services for Rudolf Slatin. The way he went about it was typical of that over-eagerness which was so much a part of his make-up. It was also, perhaps, symptomatic of both nervousness and a bad

From the Shadows

conscience over his behaviour in August 1914. Writing to his two closest and most influential English friends – neither of whom had ever dreamt of accusing him of disloyalty in wartime – he composed a memorandum in elaborate detail to prove his loyalty. A more prudent man would have been less effusive in case, under this bombardment, the thought might just flash across his friends' minds : *Qui s'excuse, s'accuse.*

The first letter, to Wingate, was posted from the Sanatorium Victoria on 21 December. That to Lord Stamfordham followed three days later on Christmas Eve. As both letters were part of the same operation and contained the same points made in virtually the same language, we can take them as one. He begins by describing his present plight and by asking whether it might be possible, though peace has not yet been concluded, to have his Sudan government pension of £50 a month paid to him already in neutral Switzerland. Then, as though to allay doubts which he imagines coming into their heads, or objections which he imagines being made to them by others, he launches out on his apologia.

First, he says, he had refused all offers of appointments, military or civilian, made to him in Vienna by his own government at the beginning of the war, and had chosen his unpaid Red Cross work instead. Then he describes offers of employment from other sources (all hostile to or enemies of England) which, over the war years, he had also refused. In December of 1914, for example, the Khedive Abbas of Egypt (by then already deposed by the British and in exile) had offered him a post on his personal staff when on a visit to Vienna. Slatin had declined, commenting that 'a dismissed Pasha who still has sympathy for England and a runaway Khedive would be a very bad combination'.

The remainder of Slatin's story of his war years is set out in an enclosure to both letters consisting of these numbered paragraphs :

1 After declaration of war from Turkey I got the offer to take service under their Government and to act as Adviser against Egypt and Arabia, which I refused without entering negotiations.

2 After Germany had concentrated troops in Turkey and Syria I was asked by the German Ambassador at Vienna if I would take

over the post of Political Officer for the German forces and to conduct or to direct expeditions like those undertaken by Mr Frobinius, Turstig, Neufeld and others. I refused without entering negotiations.

3 Before the Reichskanzler Bethmann-Hollweg's resignation, he came end of the year 1916 to Vienna and offered me through the German Ambassador there to take service under the German Government. He declared that he had the personal order from the Kaiser to make me this offer—who knows that my abilities are not used by Austria. It was proposed to me that by entering in the German service the whole value of money and property now seized by the British Government should be paid to any bank I nominate as my unconditional property, that I should get a high Military rank and a high Decoration. I declared to enter in negotiations under following conditions:

1 I must know in details what sort of service is wanted from me to enable me to judge if it is a fairplay and to judge if my abilities enable me to carry out German demands. (I thought it would not be impossible to use me for peace negotiations as middleman between Germany and England).

2 My entering in German Government service would be only possible if my own Emperor Franz Joseph would express the wish that I should do so.

I was later by the German Ambassador informed that the Kaiser was not pleased with my answer and that he wishes only my services if unconditional. I refused and negotiations were broken off.

As this document was to be much quoted in the already bulky British files about Slatin's wartime activities, it is worth examining it point by point against what is known to us about his record. It emerges as an extraordinary pastiche of untruth, half-truth, truth and question-marks. His opening claim that he rejected all offers from his own Austrian Government at the beginning of the war is quite flatly contradicted, among other places, in his own diary. We have seen how, for more than a year from August 1914 onwards, he was pleading with everyone he knew in Vienna, at court and in the Ministries of War and Foreign Affairs, for any wartime post they cared to give him. No offer in fact came from any quarter, as he himself complained. The Red Cross post was for him very much of a second best, accepted after his renewed efforts in 1915 to get a military appointment had once again ended in failure.

As to Khedive Abbas's alleged offer in Vienna in December 1914, there is no independent confirmation of this. Speaking against its plausibility is the fact that the Khedive is known to have disliked Slatin personally from pre-war days, when he regarded him as a tool of the English. Speaking for it is the phrase that Slatin quotes himself as using when he turned the Khedive down. It is such a typical Slatin quip, full of Viennese irony and *Weltschmerz*. But as regards the plea for his pension rights – which was the immediate object of this long apologia – this episode with the Khedive, true or not in the way Slatin describes it, is really irrelevant. At that point in time, he was still hoping for a wartime post in the service of his own Emperor. To have gone around instead as the chocolate soldier of a deposed Egyptian ruler would indeed have looked ridiculous.

The next claim, the offer of a post as special adviser to the Sultan of Turkey after Turkey's entry into the war on the Austro-German side, is also suspect, at least in the categoric version that Slatin gives. The impression given in the Vienna archives of the time is that it was the Austrian Foreign Minister, Count Berchtold, who floated the idea of a Turkish post for Slatin. What is missing is any reaction from Constantinople, any evidence that the Grand Vizier wanted Slatin. One way or the other, the affair was all very much in the twilight, and does not appear to match up to the clear-cut tale that Slatin produced for his English readers exactly four years later.

Slatin's last claim, to have received a pressing offer from the Emperor Wilhelm to enter German Government service, is the most detailed and most interesting part of his story. Unfortunately nothing has been discovered relating to such an offer in the Austrian diplomatic archives, nor is there any enlightenment about it in the memoirs of the German Chancellor Bethmann-Hollweg, whose name he quotes. This does not, of course, mean that the offer was never made. It was not necessarily the sort of matter which, having ended nowhere, would have been put on paper. For Bethmann-Hollweg, it would have anyway been a relatively minor episode of the war years. However, there are still one or two strange things about Slatin's version. The Germans could be pretty high-handed allies, as the Austrians discovered towards the end of the war. But it would have been outrageous behaviour on their part, in the relatively harmonious mid-war period of 1916, to have approached Slatin, an Austrian subject, directly and not through the Austrian court or the Austrian Government.

The most suspect circumstance about the whole of this 1918 apologia, however, the Bethmann-Hollweg episode included, is that, three years later, Slatin himself started to back-pedal on it. In the summer of 1921 he appears to have been engaged in bringing up to date the passage about him in the pre-war *Encyclopaedia Britannica*. As usual, Wingate was the intermediary and he had sent the *Encyclopaedia* the details of Slatin's wartime activities as provided by the good Pasha himself in his own memorandum.

Suddenly, writing 'in great haste' from Territet in 1921, Slatin urges his friend to see that the reference to his having refused all appointments in Vienna in 1914 is cut out and also all mention of the Bethmann-Hollweg offer. The reason Slatin gives is that these references sound like 'only boasting to publish an attitude taken by me which is only natural . . . and was dictated by correctness and loyalty'. This really does not sound at all convincing. In fact, whatever the *Encyclopaedia* did about it, Slatin's apologia remained unamended on the British official files.

The immediate purpose of Slatin's Christmas campaign was achieved. Within nine months, as we see by a later letter of his to Wingate, the ex-Inspector-General was getting his £50 a month pension sent to Switzerland. Indeed, this followed him from now on wherever he moved and was to be his principal source of income for the rest of his life. Neither Lord Stamfordham nor General Wingate made any specific comment on the detailed apologia Slatin had sent them about his wartime activities. Both men, however, were soothing and reassuring in general terms.

Stamfordham's reply has a bizarre touch to it. The letter is addressed in the first place to 'Baron Rudolph von Slatin GCVO, KCMG, CB'. But then, at least in the top copy which was preserved in England, someone had struck out all the English decorations with double lines. Even if, as is probable with the eminently tactful Stamfordham, the original was not sent off that way, it was all too symbolic of the uncomfortable limbo Slatin was to find himself in for the next year or two. Fortunately for him, there was one more prestigious job to be done for Austria in the meantime.

Chapter Sixteen

CLAMBERING BACK

The most unpleasant thing the little Republic of 'German-Austria' (as it at first tried to style itself) had inherited from the vanished Monarchy was defeat in war. It was also the most unavoidable. Imperial or Republican, the Austrians were in the camp of the conquered. They now had to appoint plenipotentiaries to negotiate peace terms with their conquerors.

It was only natural, when they came to select a team of experts on prisoner-of-war questions, that they should put Slatin on the list. He had already been doing this work in practice for more than three years and, as he had just demonstrated over Vienna's fuel and food emergency, his personal contacts with the victorious Entente powers stretched much further than the purely Red Cross domain. If England's retired Inspector-General, from his bedroom in a Swiss sanatorium, could stir up so much sympathy for Austria's plight with a couple of letters to a King's Private Secretary and a President's adviser, what might he not achieve in the flesh, bustling amiably around the corridors of the Paris peace conference? But the problem, quite apart from his health, was whether Freiherr von Slatin would be willing to represent the new Austria in any formal capacity. The leaders of the new Socialist Republic in Vienna were not always finding it easy to recruit the specialists they needed from the ranks of the capital's embittered monarchists. The appeal that Dr Otto Bauer, State Secretary for Foreign Affairs in the Renner

Government, sent off to Slatin on 3 May 1919, had therefore to be persuasively but tactfully worded:

I would value it most highly if you would declare yourself willing to join the peace talks delegation which is due in Paris on 12 May as spokesman for prisoner of war questions. I know of nobody in German-Austria so well suited as you are to take charge of these negotiations. I well understand your stand-point that you do not want to undertake a political mission ... If you do assume direction of the talks, your task will be purely a humanitarian one. Naturally, however, it would be extremely useful to me if you could use your extensive contacts not simply for this purpose but also to facilitate the task of our delegation in general ...

That last sentence of Bauer's telegram, of course, directly contradicted what had gone before. It was a typical example of that true Viennese reluctance (whether Imperial or Republican) to hit any nail fairly and squarely on the head and then lay the hammer aside. Slatin's reply was in exactly the same ambivalent vein. After beginning by saying that, to his great regret, his state of health simply did not allow him to accept the post, he added:

But if in the course of the negotiations it should transpire that my presence would be desired by both sides to mediate over some disputed points, then I would be prepared, if my condition permits, to go to Paris for a short while.

Just in case the State Secretary did not take the hint properly, Slatin even requested that he should be specially informed 'if the departure of the delegation is delayed for a few days'. But Otto Bauer, who was very far indeed from being a fool, had got the point all right. He immediately returned to the attack with another telegram to Berne sent from Vienna on 5 May appealing to Slatin to 'think it over once again'. Bauer emphasized that he would not dream of burdening the sick man with exhausting detailed negotiations. It was simply a question of Slatin using his unique influence in Entente circles to settle matters of principle. There was no need for Slatin to come to Vienna. He could join up with the Austrian delegation when it passed through Switzerland at the end of the week on its way to the French capital.

That, of course, did the trick. Slatin replied the very same day that, though his doctor didn't like the idea, he was now prepared 'to show his good will' by joining the mission as a special adviser. He even suggested that, on prisoner-of-war questions, he might function as Deputy to the head of the entire delegation. For good measure, Slatin also nominated two people to go with him, one as his personal secretary and the second as his expert on the Siberian prison camps. Then, at the end of the typed copy of his telegram, Slatin scrawled an afterthought in his Gothic German hand: 'I request however that my services are only called upon when they are urgently necessary.' That old yearning of his to be really wanted, and to be told so in writing, even by a Republican State Secretary, had surfaced again.

Slatin's requests were evidently met, at least as regards his personal staff, for he duly turned up with the Austrian delegation in Paris, and remained in Paris until August while the Peace Treaty of St Germain was drawn up between his country and the Entente powers. He has left us no connected account of his time there and we find only occasional references to his activities at the conference in the official papers of the period. It is clear even from these that his designated task was not easy going. At the beginning of June, Bauer instructed him from Vienna that his main object must be to secure the early release of all Austrian war prisoners from the Italian and above all from the Siberian camps – where thousands were moving towards their sixth winter of captivity. In case Slatin was in any doubt as to the urgency of the problem, Chancellor Renner also wrote to him later that summer describing how screaming relatives of Austrian prisoners still held in Siberia had besieged the Chancellery in Vienna, pinning Renner to his office for more than two hours with an angry demonstration.

These prisoners were released in the end; but not as quickly nor as smoothly as Slatin had hoped. He wrote to his wife from St Germain in July, for example:

Untill (sic) now I have no success whatever and if relatives and friends get unpatient and angry I don't wonder . . . I am not in a happy mood . . . There are so many petty intrigues in the prisoner of war department . . .

And the following month, a letter he sent to Wingate from St Germain also suggests a feeling of bitter frustration:

I am sorry to say that my demands about repatriation of prisoners was (sic) refused and the request that I may be allowed to send 3 or 4 Red Cross men to Siberia to comfort the mind of those unfortunates was 'not approved'.

Slatin was, of course, exploiting his old English contacts for all they were worth. But to judge from the few references to his conference activities in the Foreign Office documents of the time, these contacts were not worth all that much in the summer of 1919, when peace terms were being virtually dictated to the defeated little country that was his homeland. Admittedly Slatin, who was never much good at paperwork and hated all bureaucratic machines, did not help his own cause by sometimes acting completely 'outside the proper channels'. One of the first things he had done, for example, before setting out for Paris was to write to an acquaintance at the British Legation in Berne, Lord Acton, asking him to intercede with the Swiss authorities to get a Red Cross mission sent out to the Siberian camps. The correspondence on this then continued while Slatin was at St Germain as an official member of the Austrian peace delegation, an indiscretion which provoked a great rumpus in London. Slatin got nowhere with his request, while Lord Acton got a personal rebuke from the Foreign Secretary, Lord Curzon, for breaking regulations by 'communicating with an enemy subject direct'.

Nothing daunted, in July Slatin tried another of his personal initiatives by writing direct to Lord Newton, this time about the release of Austrian civilian prisoners still held by the British at Malta. Some of Slatin's old Sudan friends had clearly been getting at him, for the list of Austrians he was interested in included 'Mr Dittrich, former photographer of Cairo and Mr Mossig, electrician of Khartoum'. Though this was none of Lord Newton's business, at least he was with the British delegation at St Germain and not sitting in some unconnected legation. Yet the outcome for Slatin was just as negative. Lord Newton was told to fob Slatin off and keep out of it.

However, the important thing from the Austrian Republic's point of view was that Slatin did know all these high-sounding people and could write to them personally. It is possible that he approached such contacts informally on matters of high diplomacy as well. Though he was ranked as an expert adviser and not as a *conseiller politique*, it is clear from the private diary of one Austrian delegate* which has survived that Slatin was often present when political questions, as opposed to repatriation problems, were being discussed within the delegation. At all events, as he prepared to leave St Germain and return to Switzerland at the conclusion of the peace talks, Slatin's reputation with his republican masters was as high as ever. In one of his letters written from Paris to Wingate, he had mused idly as to what he might do when the conference was over, wondering if he would be allowed to visit London. Unbeknown to Slatin, Chancellor Renner had been pondering precisely the same problems for him in Vienna. The result of his pondering was a startling suggestion: would Slatin like to be the first envoy of the Austrian Republic to the Court of St James?

Again, it was State Secretary Bauer who made the approach:

Vienna, 11 July 1919

Dear General,

Now that peace negotiations have been concluded, diplomatic relations may consequently be resumed with the Entente powers and I must already therefore start looking out for those men who appear suitable to head the missions which our young state will send to represent it in hitherto enemy countries. For the post in London, which is of particular importance, I can think of no better choice than yourself. I do not ignore the fact that to accept at your advanced age means a sacrifice on your behalf, but I am equally convinced that you will bring yourself to bear this sacrifice in the knowledge that, because of your personal contacts, you are better placed than anyone ... to prepare the way for that good relationship with England which is so desirable ...

The text of Slatin's reply, which was sent to Vienna on 16 July, has not survived. But a second letter to Slatin, written by a disappointed Dr Bauer four days later, is in the Austrian archives. It shows that Slatin, in hesitating to accept the offer, had given the most unexpected of reasons. This legendary servant of the English crown and one-time darling of London society now appeared to doubt whether the Court of St James would even be willing to receive him. But, in typical fashion, Slatin had evidently tried to keep the options open. Bauer writes:

* Dr Kamniker of Graz. I am indebted to his son, Herr Primarius Dr Kurt Kamniker, for providing me with his father's St Germain diary.

I would have preferred a firm acceptance from you as I am absolutely convinced that you would be more acceptable in England than anybody. But if you stand by your opinion then perhaps I may interpret your letter in this way. I will for the time being appoint a Chargé d'Affaires in London who will take the opportunity as soon as possible of sounding out the English Government about your appointment. When, as I do not doubt, it becomes clear that the English Government is agreeable, then I hope you will follow our call and put at our disposal those services of yours from which I expect so much . . .

This, however, is the last thing we hear officially from the Austrian, as opposed to the English, side about the idea. If Dr Bauer did what he said he was going to do, one can only assume that the Austrian soundings in London turned out much as Slatin had feared. This can only be an assumption; nothing is known for certain. What is more intriguing is why Slatin gave Bauer that reply in the first place. A possible explanation will emerge soon. Meanwhile he was giving his friends a rather different version of the episode.

To 'Miss Emily', for example, (with whom he had corresponded throughout the war) he wrote from Switzerland on 27 October of that year:

It is true that, already in St Germain, they offered me the post of Austrian Minister to England. But I refused with thanks. I was never a diplomat or a politician. My state of health doesn't allow me to discharge the social obligations, and I have no money for representation anyway. So even now I would say 'No Thank-you' to the honour offered me . . .

Three weeks earlier, prompted by rumours that had appeared in the British press about the London appointment, Slatin had also written to Wingate about it. With his old friend he is a little more forthcoming. After declaring that he had refused Chancellor Renner's offer outright because of his health, lack of money and lack of interest in politics (the same reasons he was to give to 'Miss Emily'), Slatin went on:

And last but not least I don't think that the British Govt would specially like my nomination even if the agreement [*agrément*] would be given, and that Austria would benefit at all by sending me officially to England . . .

There were, as a matter of fact, two other circumstances which, by now, were turning Slatin's nervousness about his reception in England into acute anxiety. He mentions them both in that same letter to Wingate. His first concern is that though Lord Stamfordham had sent him 'the most friendly letters' at the beginning of 1919, there had been 'never one since again'. 'Do you think,' Slatin asks, 'that he has anything against me, or is his silence due to his position and situation only?'

There were no question-marks about the other problem. The evidence was there on his desk as he wrote. On 10 September he had sent a formal application to London to be allowed to visit England, not as an official, much less as an envoy, but as an ordinary ex-enemy alien wanting only to see old friends and sort out his private affairs. He had renewed his campaign of lobbying in high places to prepare the way for his application before he sent it off. But this time it was no good. The Austrian Peace Treaty had not yet been ratified and though some ex-enemy aliens were being allowed to come to England on compassionate grounds in advance of ratification, Slatin, for all his unique pre-war connections, was not included among them. Indeed, the day before he finally posted his request from Switzerland, it had been virtually rejected in London. A curt memorandum by a Foreign Office official on Slatin's preliminary feelers dated 9 September 1919, read:

I see no object in making any exception in Slatin Pasha's request —as far as I know there is nothing to be gained by his coming to England.

What Slatin now beheld in his Swiss hotel room was the formal outcome of that ruling. It was a horrid slip of paper, unsigned and unadorned, from the Home Office in Whitehall, dated 29 September 1919:

The Under Secretary has to inform Mr Slatin in reply to his letter of the 10th instant that permission for him to return to the United Kingdom cannot be granted.

'Mr Slatin' had been typed in on what was otherwise a standard printed form of rejection. Those two words must have caused this twice-dubbed English knight, Austrian baron, and Egyptian Lieutenant-General as much pain as the refusal itself.

After sixty-two years of struggle and glory he was for the moment back to that naked social status into which he had been born in Ober Sankt Veit in 1857.

Slatin was plunged into the deepest gloom by it all. As he wrote to 'Miss Emily' at this time:

These perpetual worries and upsets give my old heart no respite, and my nerves are pretty shattered. Who would have imagined this happening to me? I, who was always the merriest of the merry now get fits of despondency where everything around me seems grey, grey, grey, so that I almost get to avoiding people altogether.

It is not surprising that he should feel so lost. Suddenly, this European and man of two homelands found himself with no homeland at all. England had, for the moment, rejected him and about Austria, he could not make up his own mind. In that same letter to 'Miss Emily' he talks of perhaps returning after all to Austria just to be with his own relatives and friends again, for in Switzerland he has 'nobody apart from my wife and child to whom I mean anything'. Yet he had written to Wingate earlier that year:

I think I have done with Austria for ever. Young people may adapt themselves to the new regime and new ideas but for an old bird like myself it is too difficult... My longing is to find a sunny spot, warm enough that one doesn't feel the want for coal and to live quiet with the family as long as God will choose...

This gloomy autumn of 1919 brought two more blows. Barely had his own health picked up again than his wife fell seriously ill. She had awoken one morning with such terrible pains, he tells 'Miss Emily', that she had nearly fainted. Doctors had been summoned and a blockage of the intestines was diagnosed. Alice had been hurried for X-rays to Lausanne where, soon afterwards, an emergency operation was performed. More worry and more expense.

The second blow was just as severe in a different way. Slatin learned from the newspapers at the end of October that Wingate was not returning to Africa at all. Despite the fact that Wingate had been dead right in his warnings to London that serious trouble would break out in Egypt if concessions were not made to the Nationalists, it had been decided to appoint a new man to implement new post-war policies. The famous Lord Allenby was accordingly named High Commissioner to Egypt (Wingate's wartime post) in his place. As soon as he read the news in Switzerland, Slatin sat down to write to his old friend. As usual, when he is agitated, Slatin's English grammar and spelling become more erratic than ever:

> It is a sever blow to me to see in newspaper that you have resigned and that Lord Allenby is nominated H.C. for Egypt. It is too sad for words and deny that it is the right politic for England to take you away from Egypt which you know better than anyone else ... Is this Curzon's* first decision? There is also selfishness in my sorrow. As long as you were in Egypt I had always a connecting link. Now is only the younger generation there with whom I am out of contact ...

Though this hardly seemed the right moment to bother his friend with his own personal problems again, Slatin was desperate about the future and could not resist the temptation, feeling perhaps that Wingate would soon have lost all direct influence. So while gratefully acknowledging again the monthly pension payments he is now being paid, he asks for 'advice' about getting the cash still left from pre-war days on his Cairo bank account. Letters he had written to the financial authorities there had simply been ignored. He had even, in despair, sent a copy of them to 'Jimmy Watson, who was the first who met me at Assouan on the 13th of March, 1895, and who, I suppose, hasn't altered his feelings towards me. . . .' And then, of course, there was this terrible business of being refused a permit to come to London. If only the Home Office had added 'as yet', or 'for the moment' to that dreadful printed rejection slip they sent him. However, he tells Wingate in conclusion, the British Legation in Berne are now holding out some hope for him along these lines, if he will only be patient.

Slatin's desperation was understandable. With Wingate's resignation, the old Cairo and the old Khartoum had suddenly vanished, as well as the old London and the old Vienna. The second of the 'Sudanese twins' was now pensioned off as well. They would never 'ragge each other' down the Nile again. Was

---

* The Marquess of Curzon had been appointed Foreign Secretary in October of 1919.

nothing at all left, nothing anywhere, of that blissful pre-1914 world?

One piece of good news was on the way at last. In mid-December, with his wife still recovering in the clinic from the severe operation she had undergone the previous month, and little Anna Marie also in bed, at the Hotel d'Angleterre, with 'a fairly high temperature which the doctor can't explain', Slatin nonetheless writes in jubilation to Wingate. His permit to visit London had finally come through, for a 'preliminary stay 6 weeks'.

What a sigh of relief Wingate must have uttered! Not merely because he was going to see his 'dear old Rowdy' again after more than four and a half years of separation, but because by now he knew what Slatin feared – namely that there were some influential people in London who were not at all sure whether the former Inspector-General deserved to be let back into England at all. Without telling Slatin, Wingate had sounded out the ground in Whitehall three months before about the prospects for an entry permit. This he did by sending an unofficial exploratory letter to Lord Hardinge at the Foreign Office, asking for guidance. The reply he received from Hardinge must have confirmed his worst premonitions:

My dear General,
   I have thought carefully over your letter of the 20th and my advice to you is to do nothing to facilitate Slatin's journey . . .
   If you tried to obtain permission for him you might possibly meet with a rebuff and be exposed to criticism, but once he is over he must have been to a certain extent whitewashed by the Authorities . . .

Needless to say, Wingate had kept this ominous communication from Slatin, hoping that time and patience would bring a solution. It was not the only thing he had kept from his old friend. Indeed, the reason why Wingate had moved so gingerly on Slatin's behalf in September 1919 was an official inquiry he had already received in the spring about his former lieutenant. The Foreign Office records show that barely had Slatin arrived in Paris as a member of the Austrian peace delegation than the wires had started to hum about him. On 13 May 1919, the

British mission to the conference sent back the following cipher telegram to London:

Please send by bag all available information regarding proceedings and attitude of Slatin Pasha since the beginning of the war, more particularly towards England, consulting Cairo if necessary.

Wingate was up at his Scottish home at Dunbar at the time and was the first person the Foreign Office approached for guidance. The request to Wingate made no mention of any specific charges against Slatin that called for comment. In particular it did not mention the files for August and September 1914 which contained the fairly accurate if incomplete British official version of Slatin's behaviour. Wingate did not refer to that episode by name either. His reply, dated 18 May 1919, enclosed a two-page memorandum entitled 'Note on Slatin Pasha' and gave this verdict in the covering letter:

I am under the impression that Slatin Pasha behaved as loyally as he possibly could to England in spite of the fact that, being an Austrian and at war with this country, he had to be loyal to his own Government as well. I am well aware there have been many rumours to the contrary but I think they usually spring from ignorant and prejudiced persons.

The memorandum, a copy of which was sent to the Palace, began by mentioning Slatin's efforts to secure the release of various British subjects captured by the Austrians such as Dr Christopherson, a former Sudan Government colleague who had been taken prisoner with a Red Cross unit in Serbia. For the rest, it merely repeated verbatim that long apologia which Wingate had received from Slatin early in the year.

Wingate had done as much as he dared for his friend (though probably no less than he himself believed to be justified) and does not appear to have been approached again. Yet Lord Hardinge's letter to him four months later proved that the authorities were still far from being universally and unreservedly happy about Slatin's wartime record. However, the fact that, at the end of the year, Slatin had finally got his visitor's permit showed at least that, as Hardinge had put it, 'he must have been to a certain extent whitewashed by the Authorities'. Now 'dear old Rowdy' was coming to London. The rest was up to Providence, and to Slatin himself.

In blissful ignorance of the Hardinge-Wingate exchange, Slatin was meanwhile busy preparing in advance the best reception he could arrange for himself in London. As a letter he wrote off to his 'Dear Lord and Friend' on 15 December showed, it was his social position as well as his finances that he hoped to restore by the trip. After describing in detail again all the health problems of himself and family, he goes on:

I don't expect to stay long time in London and have not the intention to bother my friends. I know that, as an Austrian subject I have forfeited the titles and honours I received once by your Gracious King—may God bless him and his family for all he has done for me...
I will not be obtrusive but behave as a 'conquered Austrian'. Nevertheless I hope that I may be allowed to see you, if your official position permits you to receive what is called 'an enemy alien' – but which, God knows, I never have been!

It was an extraordinary epistle: somewhat devious if one knew the facts; somewhat cringing even if one didn't. Lord Stamfordham replied with impeccable dignity and tact, expressing the hope that they would be able to meet as old friends but warning Slatin:

You probably do not realize how strongly the feeling is in this Country and in my position my own personal feelings must be subordinated to the exigencies of the political situation.

Slatin's departure was delayed for a week. This time it was the French who were holding up his clearance, for he wanted to stop in Paris on the way. But by 12 January 1920, all his permits and visas had come and he finally set off on this journey into his past.

The only connected account which Slatin ever gave of his visit (and this only describes some of his movements and none of his thoughts) was never seen by British eyes at all. It was indeed never intended for them, and there was good reason for this. Slatin had been bombarding Whitehall for months for permission to come to London purely on compassionate grounds in order to settle his private affairs. Yet so far as the Austrian authorities were concerned, he was in effect going to England on their official business. This, at any rate, is the clear impression he gives in a letter which he sent to Chancellor Renner after his return to Switzerland from his travels. Indeed, he enclosed with it a formal six-page report on his official activities in Paris and London on behalf of the Austrian Prisoners of War Commission. In view of all that we know (and even of all that Slatin himself knew) about the shaky way in which the whole trip was launched, the opening paragraph of this report to Vienna is worth savouring:

With the object of utilizing my personal links with leading English statesmen in the interests of our prisoners of war and of the Austrian state, I applied last December for permission to visit England, which was granted. As my friends advised me to wait until after the Christmas and New Year holiday period before coming I did not apply for my Swiss and French visas until the beginning of January . . .

That version was, of course, some way from the truth. However, no one in Vienna reading Slatin's report would have suspected it. The rest of his memorandum is an impressive catalogue of contacts with Western leaders. During his four days in Paris he was received, he says, by both the British Prime Minister Mr Lloyd George and by Mr Bonar Law, both of whom promised help over the repatriation of the Austrian prisoners in Siberia. He also appealed in the same sense to prominent French officials such as M. Alphand of the Quai d'Orsay.

Then follows a long list of English personalities he called on during his stay of nearly two months in London to discuss the prisoner-of-war problem. They included the War Minister Winston Churchill, 'who greeted me warmly as an old comrade-in-arms in Africa'; the Archbishop of Canterbury; Sir Arthur Stanley, the President of the British Red Cross; and an imposing array of senior military and civilian officials connected wih the British operations then in progress against Bolshevik troops in Russia.

Slatin claims, and here we have no reason to doubt his word, that he achieved one or two concrete successes at these talks. Though, for example, the main military clothing depots in Russia had been overrun by the Bolsheviks, quantities of medical supplies had been preserved at Vladivostok by the British expeditionary forces and Slatin was promised that these would be made available for the Austrian prisoner-of-war camps. He concludes his report by quoting a decision just made (on 23 March) by the Entente Powers in Paris to the effect that the Austrian Republic was now formally authorized to repatriate all her prisoners from Siberia, provided she produced the necessary money. Though Slatin does not claim that this was the direct outcome of his journey, it is reasonable to suppose that his latest efforts had helped.

In his covering letter to Renner, Slatin touches on these technical problems, but puts high politics in the foreground. With all the Entente leaders he had met, he tells the Chancellor, he had stressed how important it was for their countries 'to get a firm foothold in Austria'. He had also pleaded with them to secure Austria's earliest possible admission into the League of Nations. Slatin in turn had been given a message for Renner which he now passed on. The Austrian Chancellor should stabilize the government in Vienna at all costs, and suppress violent opposition from any quarter. (In this, Slatin was almost certainly referring to the dangers of a Communist *putsch*. That the Austrian monarchists might rise up to restore their Emperor had not occurred to anybody – least of all to those monarchists themselves.)

So much for Slatin's official 'mission', which the English only learned about after his arrival. But what of the more interesting, and, for him, the more important side of his visit – the personal reception that awaited him in London from all his pre-war friends there? Here the mixture was bitter-sweet, though in his own letters sent abroad Slatin is careful to dwell only on the sweetness. His claim to 'Miss Emily', for example, that everyone in England 'from the highest to the lowest have received me not just in a friendly way but in the warmest fashion', is something of an exaggeration. A more accurate summing-up of his reception was the one he had given to his wife a few weeks before:

Everybody is very nice and until now I didn't feel that I am treated as a foreigner; of course I go only to those who wish to see me . . .

('*Vederemo* how London people will be with me', he had written to her on arrival in England after 'a ruff passage and a cold wind that made shiver everybody'.)

Certainly all his closest friends from the old days in Khartoum stuck to him with wonderful loyalty and tried to behave as though nothing had happened. They also opened their houses to him, which was no mean consideration in view of the fact that he had landed in England on 16 January with very little money to hand. He seems to have gone straight to the Talbots at Hartham Park in Wiltshire and it was evidently here, a day or two later, that the reunion with Wingate took place. If the meeting was not exactly an anticlimax, there were one or two clouds that needed dispersing between the two men. Slatin stayed on at the house after Wingate had left, and wrote to him from there on 22 January. The beginning is all that it should be:

My dear old Rex, you don't know what it meant to me to see you again—the dearest and truest friend since 25 years!

It is clear from the rest of the letter, however, that Slatin had been very worried about the cool attitude of Wingate's wife, who had never acknowledged any of Slatin's good wishes throughout the war, let alone sending him any in return. Wingate had now done his utmost to persuade Slatin that there had been no personal reasons behind this, but that, inevitably, the war and the loss of her son on the battlefield had produced a strain. Slatin seized on this explanation gratefully and tells his friend: 'I shall dismiss those thoughts to which I gave expression when we met.'*

The same letter shows that, at their meeting, Slatin had been anxiously sounding Wingate out as to which of their mutual social friends of pre-war days he might now safely approach without fear of a rebuff. Lord Stamfordham seems to have sent a verbal message through Wingate that he would be glad to see Slatin privately again, and that news, of course, was greeted with delight. But what of all the others last seen in the glittering summer of 1914, which seemed an eternity away in this grey January of 1919? Wingate had evidently picked one or two names as being quite 'safe', for, after their meeting, Slatin writes:

* In fact, as so often, Wingate had been trying to spare his friend's feelings. Sir Ronald Wingate recalls that his father and mother had always 'agreed to differ' on the subject of Rudolf Slatin. Lady Wingate had never really warmed to the Austrian and never wholly trusted him, even before the war.

At your advice, I will certainly ask Lady St Helier and the Midletons (*sic*) when they will receive me and it is very comforting to know that their feeling for me has not changed.

Slatin was duly asked to lunch with Lady St Helier and with many another as well. Indeed, he had soon accumulated enough invitations to move his base from Wiltshire to London. He arrived there on 26 January and was put up at 17 St James's Court, the flat of another great Khartoum friend, Lieutenant-Colonel R. P. Phipps. He seems to have stayed there until returning to Switzerland on 15 March and, as Phipps wrote to Wingate, Slatin was soon 'doing a London season of his own'. For this he had not just the loyalty of so many of his old English friends to thank but also all those great human qualities of his own, qualities which, in the last resort, could always be counted on to fill over any cracks in his character.

He was now an enemy alien, without money or position or good health, and with a social and political standing still so precarious that it had to be clawed back inch by cardboard inch as one invitation card followed another. Yet his cheerfulness, his kindliness, his modesty and his charm (which could now be used to pluck at all receptive heart-strings over his plight) worked their old wonders. As each new door is opened to him in London one feels his spirits reviving like an August rose garden after rain.

By the first week of February he is able to send a report to Wingate on his progress which almost recaptures the breathless chirpiness of his pre-war seasons:

I met Sir Maurice de Bunsen and had long chats with him. He left the diplomat (*sic*) service but is a man of influence. He talked very nice about you and your work in Egypt. Tomorrow I lunch with Churchill; on Friday with Sir Ernest Cassel and Friday evening I dine with Haldane.

Then comes something typically Slatin. Barely has he got a toe-hold again himself on the slippery ledge of London society than he starts exerting all the leverage he can to help Wingate back to office, or else secure proper compensation. In the first week of February Slatin at last saw Lord Stamfordham again and immediately tackled the King's Secretary on the subject of

Wingate's enforced retirement. Afterwards he writes to his friend:

> ... St is doing his best to put it right. I understood from him that you will get a public recognition and a special pension and perhaps later on an offer for further service ... I also hear that Lord Grenfell takes great interest in your case and is ready to help but I think the best thing is for you now to wait. But please *don't say anything* about that I have written this to you as perhaps it would [be] looked on as an indiscretion on my part.

Another subject which Slatin certainly broached with Stamfordham was the possibility of being received by the King. For Slatin, this was a psychological as well as a social imperative. Just as that audience with the Pope in 1913 had finally given him spiritual absolution for his apostasy in embracing the Moslem faith, so now an audience with George v would provide the political absolution he so badly needed after his ups and downs and twists and turns during the four years of war.

There is no record of Lord Stamfordham consulting the Foreign Office about the advisability of such an audience. For Slatin, that was just as well, since some of his most implacable opponents sat in that great square-towered building. In any case, whatever Slatin was up to in reality, the fact that he had technically been admitted to England as a private person on purely compassionate grounds meant that an unofficial audience could be given without any political complications if the King was willing. As for King George himself, he may have been ready to forget and forgive. But he may not necessarily have known all there was in the way of rumours over Slatin's wartime behaviour which needed forgetting. There is at any event no reference in the Royal Archives to those damning Foreign Office telegrams of September 1914. The only papers preserved there on the subject, and quite possibly the only ones that the King ever saw, were a copy of the memorandum with appendices which Wingate, quoting Slatin's own apologia verbatim, had written in the previous spring.

Whatever the monarch may have seen or heard, he agreed to receive his one-time knight and honorary major-general. Slatin's great moment came before dinner on Friday, 20 February. Three references to it have survived, two of them from him. Back at

Colonel Phipps's flat after the audience he writes joyfully to Lord Stamfordham that he could not have wished for a better way to celebrate the day, for it had been twenty-five years ago on 20 February that he had 'left Omdurman and the Khalifa without saying goodbye'.

His account to Wingate, written four days later, is touchingly self-important, and touching also in the concern which Slatin continues to show about his old friend's downfall. As usual, the accuracy of the English is in inverse proportion to the writer's excitement.

... And now a thing throughly (sic) secretly. The King wished to see me and I was brought by Stamfordham on Friday at 6.30 to the Buckingham Palast and was with H.M. nearly an houre. He was kind as usual just like in olden days and talked quite informal about all sort of things ... I told him we were together at Horsham, about your feelings on your inforced retirement and my opinion about. He listened very sympathetic ... I made the remark that I hope you will get 'a good satisfaction' and he said he 'hopes so too', and I am told by Lord Stamfordham as I wrote you before that your friends are at work but please keep this utterly to you ...

The third reference to the meeting comes from George v himself. It consists of only two laconic sentences in his diary for the day but they probably get closer to the heart of the matter than all Slatin's accounts:

Slatin Pasha came to see me. He was miserable at everything that had happened.

Though the audience was not allowed to be recorded in the Court Circular (Lord Stamfordham, Slatin wrote to Wingate, had told him that this would 'perhaps rise (sic) questions') it *had* taken place, and word of it would go round London. Surely, Slatin must have said to himself, no doors will be barred to me now? If this was indeed what he thought, he was to be disillusioned. So far we have looked mainly on the bright side of his visit, the side he naturally showed to the outside world himself. There was a darker side as well.

His own travel papers for the trip, which he preserved to the end of his life as a rather bitter souvenir, tell the essential story of his changed fortunes. His passport, issued by the Austrian Legation at Berne, still gives him his title of *Freiherr von** and his dignity of *Geheimer Rat* on the opening page. But that which alone once gave meaning to both has gone. The printed words: 'In the name of His Majesty Charles, Emperor of Austria, King of Bohemia, etc. and Apostolic King of Hungary' have been crossed through and 'In the name of the Austrian Republic' written in ink instead.

By 1920, Slatin was perhaps slowly getting reconciled to that transformation. But the slip of paper that went inside the passport was horribly unfamiliar. It was his British Certificate of Registration No. 11703 under the Aliens Order of 1919. Though he had proudly written on it, in the space for 'Government Service', the words 'Former Inspector-General of the Anglo-Egyptian Sudan', this did not save him and his friends from the indignity of having to register all his movements with the local police. These regulations seem eventually to have been eased for him as a special concession. While they were in force, he put the best face on it, writing to Alice: 'I have to report myself now to Scotland Yard and hope they won't keep me there. . . .'

But, despite all his good humour and all the kindness of his friends, the fact remained that the grey-haired little man whom Lord Stamfordham quietly ushered into the King's presence on 20 February was technically still under the surveillance of that same King's police as an ex-enemy alien. Moreover, there were some who still treated him as such in the full sense of the words. Clayton, for example, who had handled those 1914 telegrams about him at the Intelligence Department in Cairo, apparently cut him completely. Whether any other of his former colleagues went as far as that is not known. But Slatin makes it abundantly clear himself, in a letter written months later to England, that his loyal trio of Wingate-Talbot-Phipps are rather like the Three Musketeers defending the honour of the fourth. It is also plain that they are still having plenty of parrying to do on his behalf.

I cann't thank you enough for advocating my case [he writes to Wingate] and telling people that I behaved like a gentleman, being just as loyal to England as I was to Austria. Thank heavens that I

* The use of titles was not yet officially abolished in Vienna.

didn't anything which I would have to regret or to be ashamed
about it. I wouldn't have been worthy of your, Talbot and Phippsy's
friendship . . .

Among the 'people' who needed persuading were the Committee of the Marlborough Club who refused to readmit him
despite the fact that the club's august founder, King Edward
vii, had been one of his original sponsors. Even though, as the
years went by, other distinguished Austrians were re-elected to
membership, the club still barred its doors to Slatin, thus proving
that some members were black-balling him personally.

Slatin could understand why he should not attend military
functions like the annual Egyptian Army dinner. As Jimmy
Watson, the man who had first welcomed him at Assuan when
he had staggered from the Khalifa's desert, had pointed out,
ninety members of that particular dining club had fallen in the
war against Slatin's fatherland and its allies. Not even the charm
and one-time popularity of the Inspector-General could stretch
across all those graves. But while accepting sad necessities such
as these, the snub administered by the Marlborough Club hurt
him badly. And, in true Slatin style, instead of letting the
wound heal with dignity, he only aggravated it by never leaving
it alone.

However, what Slatin wanted back above all else was not his
place at any reunion dinner nor his membership of any London
club. It was his English decorations. He would have quite liked
a higher pension as well, despite the fact that he had no earthly
claim to it. But to be able to wear his medals again was worth
far more than money, obsessed though he always was with
financial security. Quite naturally, he was intensely proud of
those three decorations, two of them knighthoods, received from
successive British sovereigns. Yet there was more to it in his case
than mere pride. The more insecure a man is at heart, the more
titles and honours mean to him. Slatin had always been mightily
insecure, and now more than ever, with one of his monarchies
gone for good and his position in the other one still uncertain.
It was not just his medals he wanted back. It was his armour.

Ironically, and quite unbeknown to him, this campaign of
Slatin's to win back the insignia of his English acceptability

only stirred up the secret mud that clung to his name in some parts of Whitehall. And with it there now surfaced the most powerful of all his antagonists.

Slatin began his campaign with a frontal attack. On 5 November 1920, he wrote to Stamfordham asking what the position was about wearing his pre-war decorations. The King's Secretary did not reply for five weeks and then told Slatin:

If there should be any restoration of titles and honours held by non-British subjects I will take care for your interests. Meanwhile I know your Orders are safe in your keeping.

That last sentence needs to be noted, for when indirect approaches were made by Slatin's friends on his behalf, the whole affair started running off the rails. More alarming for Slatin, had he only been aware of it, it also started running dangerously backwards. In April of 1921, a certain Sir Alfred Pease bestirred himself to get what he considered justice for Rudolf Slatin. His letter went first to an MP, Mr M. M. Wilson, who passed it on to a Minister at the Colonial Office, the Hon. F. L. Wood, who in turn passed it on to Mr Cecil Harmsworth at the Foreign Office. Sir Alfred began by stating, quite incorrectly as we know from the 1914 muddle, that Slatin Pasha had handed his English honours back to the King at the outbreak of war. He then goes on, this time accurately, to say that Slatin's wife is ill, and that the retired Inspector-General 'is only getting £61 per month as pension for his services in the Sudan'. Would the British Government consider returning his honours and raising his pension to £1,000 a year?

The British Government did what all governments do on such occasions. It consulted the files to refresh its memory. It is from these that we learn, for the first time, that the Foreign Office had already been consulted twice in 1920 about Slatin's decorations, and had ruled against him. A minute dated 7 May 1921, by Mr Alexander Cadogan,* says:

I have a recollection that a similar appeal was made last year but I have been unable to trace the papers. So far as I remember, it was turned down.

* Later Sir Alexander Cadogan, and Permanent Under-Secretary of the Department.

Shortly before that, Mr Winston Churchill referred a similar appeal to Lord Curzon and Mr Campbell tells me that, so far as he is aware, nothing came of it.

The fact that Lord Curzon's name had been invoked meant that Cadogan's minute, together with the draft of his reply to Sir Alfred Pease, landed on the desk of the Foreign Secretary in person. This formidable figure gave it short shrift. At the bottom of the minute Lord Curzon scrawled in his large florid hand:

This case came before me last year and in 1919. There is a file about it—perhaps in the Priv. Sec's office. I declined to move then and I decline to move now. There are certain unforgivable offences.

Fortified by that august and emphatic backing, Cadogan sent off the reply he had drafted. On the pension question, he pointed out to Sir Alfred Pease that the sum Slatin was already drawing, £732 a year, would, if he went to live in his native Austria go 'quite a long way at the present rate of exchange in providing for a modest existence, which retired government servants living on their pension are almost invariably compelled to lead'. And who, he asked, was to provide the extra money in any case? One could hardly call on the Sudan or the Egyptian Government for it, while the British Treasury were unlikely to be 'moved to compassion'.

All this was accurately stated and reasonably argued. But when he dealt with the other matter at issue, Cadogan only elaborated in good faith on the initial error made by Sir Alfred Pease, namely that Slatin had ever returned his decorations in the first place. This red herring is now dressed up and served again as follows in Cadogan's reply:

Sir Rudolf Slatin went out of his way, on the outbreak of war, to discard his British decorations and return them to the King. It was an act of deliberate and needless discourtesy, and shocked me at the time ...

And so, in successive stages over the following weeks, the rejected appeal was sent back to Sir Alfred Pease along the same tortuous route by which it had come. By now, however, (to take this particular tragicomedy to its conclusion) the subject of all these letters and minutes had himself arrived again in England

for his second post-war visit. The next document we see is a communication from Rudolf Slatin, sent from Canterbury on 27
July 1921, and addressed to Mr Harmsworth at the Foreign
Office with a copy to the then Permanent Under-Secretary, Sir
Eyre Crowe. In this, Slatin says that all these recent efforts of his
friends, 'actuated by the best intentions', had been made without
his knowledge. He recapitulates, in full summary, that same
version of his war record ('refusing all civil or military appointments and devoting myself to Red Cross work', etc.) with whose
imperfections we are already familiar.

But the lie about his British decorations he is able to nail
with a flourish:

> I never return (sic) my British decorations to H.M. The King and
> am still in proud possession of them and I informed so H.M. The
> King when I had the honour of being received in private audience
> on the 20th February, 1920, on the occasion of my first visit to
> London after the war.

One can imagine the upset this particular passage of Slatin's
letter caused at the Foreign Office (they were familiar already
with all the rest of his case). Sir Eyre Crowe wrote immediately
to Lord Stamfordham who replied on 5 August:

> It is quite untrue that Slatin Pasha returned his British decorations
> to the King. It is true that the King received him privately on the
> date named by Slatin. He is an old friend of the King's as he was of
> King Edward and used to stay every year at Balmoral.

Worse and worse, for the Foreign Office officials now realized
that, on the matter of the decorations, they had not only falsely
accused a former twofold British knight but had maligned a
personal friend of the monarch's as well. Without consulting the
Foreign Secretary again, they wrote in his name on 16 August to
Slatin at Canterbury saying that Lord Curzon 'unreservedly
accepts' the explanation about the decorations and expressing
his 'sincere regret at any pain caused to you by the mis-state-
ment'.

It was some three months before Curzon learned about this
letter. The occasion was yet another attempt by Slatin or his
friends to get the right to wear his British orders restored. Unlike

his subordinates, Lord Curzon was not impressed by anyone just because he happened to have been invited to Balmoral. The noble Lord did not get the soubriquet of 'Most Superior Person' for nothing. Moreover, he knew far more about the Slatin affair than the two officials who had handled the question for him in the summer.

On 9 November 1921, in an explosion of wrath and offended dignity, he minutes in his own hand when the weary file reaches his desk once again:

I am perfectly astounded at the treatment of this case. As recently as May 7 there is a note from me on the Slatin case into which I went exhaustively some time ago and which has nothing to do with decorations or pension.

Nevertheless the Dept. [one word illegible] without my knowledge and without any reference to me has committed me, in [the] letter from Mr Harmsworth to all sorts of statements and expressions of opinion with which I wholly disagree.

To this thunderbolt from on high, Mr Harmsworth unctuously replied that he had written the particular letter he did purely because of the decorations muddle and that he had no idea at the time that 'there was anything against Slatin not disclosed in the papers before me'. Where indeed was the special confidential file Lord Curzon was referring to containing 'the other particulars relating to Slatin's conduct'? He, Mr Harmsworth, had been searching for it in vain.

The Foreign Secretary did not enlighten his minion on this point.* 'There is nothing more to be done', he wrote back on 14 November, 'except to say that I do not think Slatin Pasha should be allowed to resume his British decorations.'

It was quite clear from this that, so long as Lord Curzon was at the head of the Foreign Office, Slatin would never be formally rehabilitated. So it proved. Yet another approach made on his behalf, and this time quite certainly prompted by Slatin himself, reached the Department the very next month. On this occasion, the intermediary was his old Khartoum friend and

* Unfortunately for the biographer. Beyond the diplomatic telegrams about Slatin's behaviour in August and September 1914, which have already been quoted, the special file on the case cannot be traced in the Foreign Office archives today. It is possible that it has been simply mislaid. It is inconceivable that it was destroyed as part of a pruning operation for space reasons, since so much trivia on Slatin has survived. Was it quietly put to death by his well-wishers after Curzon's departure?

colleague, Sir James Currie. Slatin had, on 12 December, very unwisely stirred Currie into indignant action with an emotional appeal: 'Could I go and sit between my old comrades with a bare chest, deprived of my British war medals which I earned with my own blood?' (Considering that he had been plainly advised not to go and sit between his old comrades at any function for the time being, bare chest or not, this was all rather irrelevant.) But the good Sir James, like the good Sir Alfred before him, ploughed on, only to get a very curt rejection for his pains. On 10 January 1922, he was told that similar approaches had been turned down the previous autumn and that 'there is no prospect of this decision being reconsidered'. And so matters rested for the next few years.

Looking back on this complicated and abortive manoeuvring, over an issue which was so vital to Slatin at the time (however trivial it may seem to us today), one suspects that he had some idea all along of what he was up against. There is, for example, that nervousness in July 1919 about how his proposed nomination as post-war envoy to England would be received in London (which meant received by the Foreign Office). Then, in one of his early letters to Wingate sent soon after he had arrived in England in 1920, he writes: 'I asked to be received at the F.O. and I wonder if I will be asked to come.' During the first post-war visit, though Lord Hardinge received him politely, he could never get to Lord Curzon himself. As Slatin says in his report to Chancellor Renner, which has already been mentioned in another context: 'Lord Curzon was for several weeks in the South of France and then so preoccupied by his work that he could not see me.' But whatever Slatin may have suspected, it seems unlikely that he ever learnt just how bitterly Lord Curzon felt towards him because of his wartime record and just how adamantly the great man was opposed to Slatin's formal readmission into the English fold.

One hopes, at any rate, that Slatin was left in partial ignorance of this feeling against him, for he had personal grief enough of another and deeper kind to cope with during this period. On 26 June 1921, at the height of the first decorations battle in London, his wife Alice died at Territet of cancer. He can have had no illusions, ever since that serious internal operation she had undergone in November of 1919, but that her life hung by a precarious thread. As he wrote to Wingate in June of 1920, that last operation had been her third in two years, and 'the future looks very dark for me'. But the loss, when it came, was traumatic just the same. It would have been almost impossible for him to have loved her as much as she so passionately adored him (and anyway, as the French saying goes, such feelings are never equal). Yet all his letters about her, both before and after her death, reflect a deep devotion and respect for this very remarkable woman.

His dear friend 'Miss Emily', who was then staying at St Moritz, was one to whom he wrote the sad news as soon as he got back to his lonely room at the Hotel d'Angleterre after the funeral. A few days later, after getting her letter of condolence, he sent back a fuller account of the burial:

Now she lies in an idyllic spot, on the sunny mountain slope of the little communal cemetery at La Peanche, a spot she loved dearly when she was alive . . . And so this patient creature, who had to endure such a martyrdom on this earth, has found her last rest here. May the soil rest lightly on her . . .

His main concern now, he went on, was to erect a proper tombstone for Alice and leave enough money with the municipality so that her grave would be properly tended. He had decided on something rather macabre. He had recently received, seven years after the event, a sum of money (it was £43, though he does not say so in this letter) which the English officers of the Egyptian Army had subscribed for his wedding present back in the summer of 1914. It had lain all this time in some regimental account in Cairo and had only been released and sent to him three months ago. This wedding gift he was now going to use for her funeral. 'Those officers who subscribed the money would never have thought,' he adds, 'that it would be put to this use.'

For Slatin there was not just the grief of the moment. There was sorrow for the past and anxiety for the future. As to the past what, he must have asked himself, had poor Alice had of her married life? A wedding on the eve of hostilities; a honeymoon cut short in less than a week by the European crisis; four and a half grim war years in Vienna; and finally, a bare two years of hotels and hospitals in Switzerland, plagued by illness, shortage of money and all Rudolf's own miserable doubts and uncertainties. Married at forty-one; dead at forty-seven; and never once a real home of her own.

She had never complained. Indeed, from her death-bed she had written the serenest and gentlest of letters both to him and to their daughter. One especially moving one to Anna Marie, for example, had tried to explain what it is that makes pain, 'physical or moral', easier to bear in life. First there is 'submission to God's will' and though a mother, she, the dying woman, was not so terribly stricken as the Holy Mother had been, 'because she saw Her own child suffering and that is far worse than suffering oneself'. Then there was breeding:

> We ought not to be proud of our better birth . . . if that makes us hard and unkind to those around or *under* us. But . . . for the very reason that we are better born, better educated, we must be *more brave* . . . Our pride, if pride we have must make us doubly severe with *ourselves* . . . So when you suffer try and lighten some other's burden. Don't live in and for yourself. Try always, always to think of others . . .

It would be difficult to think of a purer expression of the Christian gentility of her generation. Yet Slatin, reading these last letters of hers, must have been troubled even though he knew his wife had died at peace with herself. He could not say of himself or feel for himself the things she had written. All he knew was that, through no fault of his own, the balance sheet of her wedded bliss had been a meagre one.

The only positive thing left was their infant girl daughter, now aged four and a half. Even she was a worry as well as a joy when Slatin started thinking of the future. He was now sixty-four, and his own health was none too good (though better than he imagined it to be). He would probably be dead himself, however, before Anna Marie was a grown woman and married. How was he, still a soldier-bachelor in many of his ways, to bring up this child all alone? And even more important, how was he to provide for her future in case he should die while she was still young and single?

His worries on this score were certainly not relieved by a poignant message he received from friends in England with whom his daughter was staying when her mother had died. The little girl, they wrote, now no longer cried every time anyone mentioned her mother because they had made it clear to her that her mother was now an angel. But they had heard her say one night in her prayers: 'Please dear God don't take Daddy and my nurse away for angels as well, because you really must have enough of them.' For the rest of his life, Slatin was to be haunted by the fear that he would be 'taken away' too soon.

It is significant that, stricken by this sorrow and faced by this calamity, he took refuge not in his native Austria – where, after all, his brothers and sisters still lived, even if in reduced circumstances – but in his adopted England, the England in which he was not even certain of his standing. Perhaps a telegram from Buckingham Palace had something to do with it. At the end of June, his old friend in London, Colonel Phipps, had told Lord Stamfordham of Alice's death, and he in turn had sent a note in to the King. George v wrote on his secretary's memorandum: 'Very sorry. Please send him a message from us both', and an expression of Their Majesties' 'sincere condolence' was duly dispatched to Slatin on 1 July.

Whatever the immediate impulse, Slatin not only went back to England as soon as Alice was buried at Territet and her modest affairs sorted out. He now, for the first time, started thinking of settling in England for good. 'Home is where your heart is', and one's heart is usually where one's friends are. When Slatin thought of friendship he knew there was nobody in the wide world who could match Wingate, Talbot and Phipps, with the Curries a close fourth. And if England had an uncertain physical climate, her political complexion was reassuringly constant. The Apostolic Majesties had vanished from Vienna, but the same King-Emperor still ruled in London. The first essential, however, was to become one of his subjects.

Presumably Slatin discussed this with his closest friends while in England during that summer of 1921. All we know is that he finally took action on it early in 1922 when he was staying at Monte Carlo with his old American friends, the Penfields. It was from there that he wrote to an acquaintance at the Home Office, John Baird, and asked him outright what the chances of British naturalization were. It is clear from Baird's reply that a long delay and presumably a great deal of inquiring intervened in London before Slatin could be given an answer. When that answer was finally sent, on 2 March 1922, it was a politely worded refusal. Though the matter had been gone into 'very carefully', Baird wrote, it had been found that the regulations simply ruled out any question of British citizenship for Slatin. He had not resided in the United Kingdom for at least one year before applying, as was required, nor did his previous long residence in the Sudan qualify him because the Sudan was not legally a British dominion. For the same reason, Slatin's service there could not be technically called 'Crown Service' so he was barred from applying on that ground as well.

Slatin evidently could not believe, when he read this bitterly disappointing reply, that exceptions could not be made for someone whose career had itself been one long exception to all and any sort of rule. Surely, if the goodwill was there, and the right word was spoken in the right place, a way could be found around this tiresome thicket of regulations?

Off he wrote to the ever-faithful Wingate again, to see what he could do. But the outcome was the same. Wingate at first wrote simply to the Home Office Department concerned who told him that 'if something exceptional was required' he would have to provide full particulars of the applicant (a possible indication that exceptions to the rules were sometimes made). But when, on 7 April, Wingate got a personal reply from Baird himself, the statutes were again quoted as barring Slatin, and very convincingly quoted, for Baird added: 'I understand that the question was gone into during King Edward's lifetime and it was then found that in spite of his great services to us Slatin was not able to comply with the requirements and nothing could be done in the matter.'

On this occasion, Slatin seems to have accepted 'No' for an answer. He did not pursue any relentless campaign for naturalization through his friends* similar to that he was conducting over his decorations. Though he could never banish England from his life, he ruled it out as a place of residence. But where else to go? With his wife dead, Slatin could not face the prospect of living on in a Switzerland which was efficient and prosperous but expensive and anonymous. As for the Austria of the Republic, this

---

* There is no evidence that Slatin's application for naturalization was sponsored by anyone but Wingate.

was too full of ghosts, though all his blood relatives still lived there in the flesh.

A choice of some sort had to be made. The period of post-war temporizing was over, ended by the double blow of his wife's death and the failure of his attempts to gain British citizenship. He now had to set out alone to find that 'little place in the sun' where he had wanted to end his days with Alice.

Chapter Seventeen

THE LAST PLATEAU

Slatin finally found what he was looking for in the South Tyrol. It was a comfortable though fairly modest stone house at Obermais above Meran in the country of the Dolomites. Of course the province was now called Alto Adige, Meran was Merano and even Obermais was Maia Alta. When the defeated Austrian Empire had been dismembered a few years before, Italy, *the* Austrian enemy *par excellence*, had seized all these ancient Habsburg lands south of the Brenner for herself. It was the choicest part of the prize promised to her by the Entente powers in 1915 for denouncing her alliance with Austria and entering the war on their side.

Yet, apart from occasional awkward reminders of Italian conquest and Italian rule, Meran was an ideal spot for Slatin to unpack his bags at long last. His own Austria, or what was left of it in its shrunken republican guise, lay conveniently near across the mountain passes to the north. Southward, the land ran on down to the sea that washed the shores of Africa as well as Europe. This province, with its blend of granite peaks and lush valleys carpeted with vines, flowers and fruit, marks the point where the Alps and the Mediterranean join hands. As such, it was not a bad symbol of Slatin's own life.

The house he rented there (initially, he wrote to 'Miss Emily', for a period of five years) was called the Villa Mathilde.* He moved there in the spring of 1923 with evident relief to get

* An entry in his diary for 22 March 1928 shows the rent to have been £170 per annum.

away from hotel life but also with a feeling of finality, as though he sensed that this first real home of his would also be the last. 'May Mathilde be my last flirt', he quipped in another letter. That sudden uncharacteristic aversion to meeting new people and getting to know fresh faces which had first swept over him in the gloomy post-war months in Switzerland, now returned with redoubled force, although the gloom itself had mellowed into resignation.

An amusing example of this came on his first visit to England after moving in to the Villa Mathilde. He writes to 'Miss Emily' that he had just bought himself, at the Army and Navy Stores in London, an iron letter box for the gate of his house at Obermais. As sold in the shop, it had two spaces across the top marked 'In' and 'Out' which could be covered and uncovered by a movable slot. But he had told the shop to screw down the slot straight away so that it would always show 'Out', and he added: 'That way I won't get too many visitors... but don't let that frighten you and yours away when you are passing through Meran – for old friends I am always "In".'

Lack of money was a recurrent nightmare of Slatin's. At this stage of his life, the nightmare was far removed from the reality, but Slatin now became so obsessed by it that we must try to establish what his financial position as a pensioner really was. The exchange rate for sterling* into lire was a highly favourable one when he retired, so that his basic income of £60 a month was in itself sufficient to guarantee, under normal conditions, the comfortable if unpretentious existence of a distinguished pensioner. On top of this came the gratuity which the Sudan Government, doubtless prodded by Wingate and other old colleagues, had paid to its former Inspector-General after the war. We know from much earlier correspondence of Slatin's that this had been very generously calculated on a salary basis of £1,800 a year instead of the £1,400 a year which Slatin had actually drawn while in office. The result was a lump sum entitlement of £4,175. In 1919–20, Slatin had drawn £1,000 of this in advance of the official settlement through Wingate, and there were also some minor deductions for payments made to his former servants in Khartoum. But he was still left with

---

* The Egyptian pounds in which his pension was calculated and paid were worth slightly more than pounds sterling.

nearly £3,000 in cash from this source alone, and that was a handsome sum of money in the early 1920s.

Then there was the sale of the furniture and other effects which had remained throughout the war at 'Rowdy House' in Khartoum. A former colleague, Mervyn Wheatley, looked after the disposal for him and it realized over £1,000 gross. (The Holland and Holland guns included in the sale would have fetched far more than that by themselves today.) The English authorities were also involved over some investments he had left in Cairo and in London. The latter included 275 shares in his favourite Army and Navy Stores and were finally released in September 1922 by the Public Trustees 'as well as dividends thereon amounting to £67.7.6'. Among the other umbrellas which Slatin kept against stormy financial weather was his stamp collection, which he always regarded as an investment and a hobby combined. Like everything else, this investment was for his child. As he once wrote to his friend Grant-Smith:

I collect for my child since many years and my collection has the value of at least $2,500. So you see if you send stamps it is a pleasure for me and a good thing for my girl, who will one day inherit the whole collection.

Such reminders to his friends that he would be glad if they sent him something – be it stamps, money or food gifts – are typical of Slatin the pensioner. They inevitably raise the question: was Rudolf Slatin a *Schnorrer*, that word the Austrians felt obliged to invent for themselves to describe their own gentle but effective variety of what in other nations would be called plain scrounging? Even if he was not, he often hovered very close to the brink. He would bemoan his plight in his letters, possibly seeking, in the first place, soothing words back. His friends would offer him money or gifts as well or instead of sympathy. Then, as soon as the offer was made or the gift received, Slatin would recoil with a mixture of reproaches that anyone should have gone so far as actually to help him out, and gratitude that he had.

Dear old, loyal old Wingate was the principal partner-cum-victim in this strange Viennese waltz. He was not finding life too easy himself on the half-pay of a pensioned-off general, especially as he had rather over-stretched his income with the large house at Dunbar to which he had retired. But when 'Rowdy' let out some great wail about his own plight or even dropped only a dolorous hint, his friend always stepped forward. Even the angelic Alice had once chided her beloved Rudolf for being so tactless as to mention to Wingate the subject of a delayed wedding-present more than six years after the event. And at Christmas that same year, following Slatin's mournful talk of having to tighten the festive purse-strings, Wingate sent him no fewer than eight hampers of Christmas delicacies out to Switzerland. 'Why 8 parcels?' Slatin writes back in deliciously controlled delight. 'One or two would have been ample.'

But Slatin did nothing to inspire Wingate's most generous offer, which came in the spring of 1922. Wingate had been negotiating on both their behalves with Edward Arnold, the London publishers, for a new edition of *Fire and Sword* to be brought out. He had secured the very handsome flat-rate royalty of fifteen per cent for them and had then offered to waive his share of the profits altogether to help his friend. But this idea Slatin refused to entertain, saying that it was unthinkable 'to dissolve the old firm which is over a quarter of a century old'. To put Wingate's mind at ease he goes on to give this fairly reassuring over-all picture of his finances as he entered on complete retirement:

Of course I have to live economically (what decent person hasn't to do this nowaday?) but I am well off compared to others! I have my £600 pension and was able to put away for little Anna Marie £6,000* that she isn't in need if anything happen to me. Then I have still a certain money under my name (securities in Egypt worth £3,000 and money in Austria which isn't good for anything at the moment).

Then I have furniture, Silver, etc. of which I can sell if I am in need of money and, last but not least, you know Mrs Penfield is Roman Catholic and knew little Anna Marie when she was born at Vienna. She has sent me several times sums to aid for Anna Marie's expenses. Mrs Penfield is immensely rich and ... for her little sums means nothing but for me and Baby a lot ...

With his 'immensely rich' friends like Mrs Penfield, Slatin, at any rate in his later years, did not even prevaricate when money was handed to him. Thus his diary for 13 August 1931

* Slatin's underlining.

records that when taking the cure with her in Austria that summer, the wealthy old American lady suddenly, in the middle of reading the morning papers, broke off to write Slatin a cheque for $1,000 and handed it to him 'to help you with Anna Marie'. He simply pocketed it with thanks. Another of his wealthy American benefactors was a Mr Edward Tuck, who is recorded in Slatin's diaries for 1931 and 1932 as having sent him at least three donations, one for $1,000, one for $500 and one for $300. Considering the slump that the world markets were then undergoing, these were all generous gestures.

All his life, Slatin had enjoyed an excellent digestion. Was he merely swallowing vast doses of his own pride now, in order to stave off really pressing money problems? One would like, for his sake, to believe this. But ironically, he himself disposes of any such suggestion by various entries in his diary which record in detail how the world slump was affecting him personally. These entries show that Slatin was indeed suffering losses, like everyone else. But they also reveal that his investment capital alone was far higher than anything ever indicated in letters to any of his friends. Moreover, it appears to have shrunk far less than most portfolios.

Got today from the Nat. B. of Egypt London the valuation of all my securities in the Bank at the price of Stock Exchange of 4 March. With all the lists of my holdings everywhere on hand I calculate my present fortune compaired with last year—1929: £39,500; 1930: £36,600 (i.e. nominally less for £2,900).

On 27 February 1931 he notes that his fortune is 'now £3,400 down'. The worst point is reached on 1 March 1932 when he estimates that his investments are '25% down'. However, only a few days after writing that, a series of excited diary entries shows that Mrs Penfield, who had died at a ripe old age the month before, had left him the handsome sum of $50,000 in her will.

Thus the blunt truth, revealed by Slatin's own hand, is that he was a very well-off pensioner indeed with a basic income of £60 a month and investments never worth less than £30,000 and usually worth nearer the £40,000 mark. It was little wonder that he had told Wingate not to be worried about his finances. Slatin was probably better off in reality than this English friend who was always ready to come to the somewhat unnecessary rescue. On money matters, as on some other issues, Slatin emerges as something less than straightforward.

The only excuse for his behaviour was the gnawing concern, not for his own comfort, but for his daughter's future. Indeed the crucial problem of these last years was to give her the most expensive education and upbringing he could afford and then to provide her with a reasonable private income for life. All this, he well knew, she would need if she were ever going to move with ease in that international society he had entered by a prodigious expenditure of valour and suffering, and had then conquered by his natural wit and charm. He already knew too that the best gate for her to enter by was the English one through which he himself had entered. In his native Austria, he had virtually nothing to offer his little girl in the way of a social position or a home. Even the villa at Traunkirchen had been sold by his two sisters, whose one-time joint income of fifty thousand crowns a year had been as good as wiped out by post-war inflation. His one ambition left was that Anna Marie should settle and eventually marry well in England.*

The idea formed very early on. A letter he wrote to 'Miss Emily' from England when he was staying with Anna Marie at the Curries' and recovering from the shock of his wife's death paints the sort of idyllic English picture he was already forming for his daughter's future:

She is riding happily around with her little friend, Lady Currie's daughter, on Shetland ponies, and enjoying life to the full.

He had taken the Villa Mathilde to give his daughter a base, even if only a rented one. Yet the need to keep up regular contact with England meant that every year they moved over there for two or three months, usually from June to September. As he put in a letter to 'Miss Emily' sent from Meran in December of 1924:

If it wasn't for Anna Marie I would perhaps stay the whole year here. But the little one must get about and for her sake I must keep up the personal links with certain families who are our friends.

In addition, trips had to be fitted in to Austria so that the girl

---

* She was to over-fulfil the ambition for him by marrying there three times.

would not lose touch altogether with Slatin's brothers and sisters in Vienna or with her own maternal grandmother, the formidable old lady in Graz. Quite often, Slatin would arrive back at the Villa Mathilde in the autumn tired out.

Exhausting or not and welcome or not, these annual summer trips to England helped to give Slatin a framework to his retired life. The months from October to June, which he usually spent at Meran, together with his cures at Bad Hall, completed this pattern of regularity. His life at the Villa Mathilde, as registered factually in his diaries, is like the tick-tock of a grandfather clock – monotonous, soothing and resigned. The same entries appear time and time again: the lunches and teas with his handful of local cronies; the letters received and sent; the days he went for walks, and where to; his visits to the dentist, the bank, and to church; taking and collecting Anna Marie from the near-by school; sorting out his stamps and acquiring new ones ('bought stamps for £7 though hard up for cash'); the barometer and temperature readings and the vagaries of the South Tyrol climate. One year is usually very like the one before and very like the one to come. Slatin the pensioner, like Slatin the captive and Slatin the Inspector-General, was again moving across a plateau. This time, however, the horizon was fixed and final.

There were, of course, a few ups and downs in this last level journey of his. One of the ups, or at least one of the excitements, came in November and December of 1926 when he revisited the Sudan again for the first and last time since leaving it in 1914 (as he had then imagined just for his annual European leave and London 'season'). Once again, we have cause to regret that Slatin's many talents, natural and acquired, did not include those of the writer. Even a moderately gifted pen could have left a memorable account of the journey of this Viennese student turned Cairo book-assistant, turned Sudan warrior, turned Mahdist captive, turned avenger at Omdurman, turned Inspector-General, turned frail post-war pensioner, back to the country which had brought him fame as a young man and which was still supporting him as an old one.

There must have been hundreds of nostalgic moments as Slatin, now just a visitor, wandered around the places he had first helped to make famous and had then shown to so many others. A face from the past might pop up suddenly in any guest list at the Residency or out of any crowd in the streets. Most of these moments he kept to himself. One of the incidents he did tell his friends about afterwards happened on 24 November when he went across the Nile to Omdurman to look again at the Mahdi's capital and the Khalifa's house. The building had been converted into a museum and was a regular calling-point on the official tour of the city. A party of tourists came in as Slatin stood there silently, looking at the room where, in the century before, he had seen and endured so much. He was suddenly startled to hear his name mentioned as the guide pointed out to his flock the spot where the well-known Slatin Pasha had always stood when he attended the Khalifa's presence. But the guide had got it wrong and the Khalifa's one-time orderly, without revealing his identity, gently spoke up and corrected the official dragoman. This worthy, understandably put out, insisted that, on the contrary, Abdel Kader had stood exactly on the spot he had first indicated. There was nothing else for it. 'But I *am* Abdel Kader,' Slatin protested at last. Both guide and audience burst out in wonder and excitement. It was the sort of episode that could only happen once. But then, it was the sort of visit that could only happen once.

From Khartoum itself, only one Slatin letter has survived, a brief note to Wingate sent two days after that quixotic episode at the Khalifa's house. It is nostalgic, though in a jerky, staccato way as though the writer doesn't want to awaken too many memories either in Wingate or himself. One or two servants and members of the Sudanese bodyguard, he tells the retired Governor-General, still ask after him. His old office at the Palace is now a drawing-room. One now travels round by motor car, 'much quicker than ... on camels'. It is evidently all a bit eerie and disturbing, for Slatin ends, after giving his timetable: 'And then Home, Hurrah. Cheers for Merano and Anna M.'

As it turned out, this successful *voyage sentimental* to Cairo and Khartoum did more than provide a lasting souvenir. It was also to help Slatin win back that lost apple of his eye in London. Three months after Slatin took farewell of them, his English hosts in Africa, doubtless prompted by their departed guest, launched yet another campaign in Whitehall to restore to the

Pasha his right to his British decorations. This time, at long last, it succeeded.

This new approach came from the most natural and persuasive direction, Egypt and the Sudan itself. It arrived in a London where the resentments of the immediate post-war period were already fading. Above all, it arrived at a Foreign Office no longer ruled by Lord Curzon who had behaved rather stuffily over the whole Slatin case. Indeed, the 'Most Superior Person' was no longer alive.* His total removal from the scene is immediately apparent in the way in which his former subordinates now tackled the Slatin case.

Slatin's sponsor on this occasion was Lord Lloyd, High Commissioner in Cairo. While Slatin had been on his recent visit in Khartoum, Lloyd writes to Sir Austen Chamberlain on 16 April 1927, he had raised with Sir John Maffey, the Governor-General there, the familiar problem of his decorations. The final paragraph of Lloyd's strong letter of recommendation was the most effective. It rang true because every word of it was true:

> Slatin Pasha is now seventy years old and it is the chief ambition of his life to regain the right to wear the British decorations which he so amply earned.

The Foreign Office clerks, sniffing the way the wind was blowing up top, and doubtless glad themselves to drop anchor on this tiresome issue at last, set their sails accordingly. A minute was prepared in which all the strictures which their former master, Lord Curzon, had put down in writing over the Slatin case six years before were either glossed over or amended. The comments of an earlier Foreign Secretary, Sir Edward Grey, on the original Slatin scandal of thirteen years ago were not even mentioned. Nor were the secret telegrams – still, presumably, on the files – which had given rise to them. The new Foreign Secretary clearly needed very little encouragement to follow Lord Lloyd's advice. This little was duly provided for him by his officials.

The upshot was a letter to Sir Frederick Ponsonby, Keeper of the Privy Purse, sent from the Foreign Office on 27 May 1927. The operative paragraphs were these:

* He had left office at the end of 1924 and had died the following year.

While the Secretary of State is not anxious to raise the general question of allowing ex-enemy subjects to resume wearing their British decorations, he feels that the case of Slatin Pasha is so highly exceptional that the concession which he asks can safely be made to him without prejudice to the larger issue ...

Perhaps therefore you would kindly take the King's pleasure on the subject and let me know whether His Majesty approves of a favourable reply being returned to Lord Lloyd's enquiry.

King George, always fond of Slatin, was only waiting for his pleasure on the matter to be formally requested. On 13 June Lord Lloyd was officially informed that the King had been 'graciously pleased to accede' to Slatin's application 'and that you may notify him accordingly'. It was agreed to make no public announcement in order to hold off a flood of similar appeals.* To Slatin, that silence was perhaps the only imperfect aspect of his triumph. But all his closest friends learned of it at once and they spread the glad word around. The wider circle of his colleagues could see it for themselves when, at the next Darfur Dinner held at the Café Royal in London, the old Inspector-General could turn up in person,† his chest 'naked' no more, but blazing with those enamelled stars and crosses he had been obliged to lock away for so long.‡

The medals brought back with them something else as well, something almost equally precious. Though Slatin had been received by King George v in audience soon after the war, this was a strictly private gesture and had purposely not been recorded in the Court Circular. Since then, Slatin had sighed out loud more than once, in letters to his friends, that he was not being received officially at court again. In fact, there were to be no more of those regular pre-war stays at Windsor and Balmoral ever again for him. That intimacy was gone for good. But at least he was now allowed to rejoin the swim in public, even if it was in the largest and least selective of the royal tanks. He was in England during this happy summer of 1927 and on 7 July, only a week or two after getting the wonderful

---

* The flood came just the same until, before long, Ponsonby was authorized to deal with them as he felt fit himself.

† At least we may assume he did. It is entered in his diary for 24 July 1928, and though he had been ill, he was up and about by then.

‡ Slatin was, in fact, the very first of the 'ex-enemy nationals' to have his British decorations formally restored. Some, like the King of Bulgaria, just brazened it out by turning up at Balmoral wearing them. Others, like the former Austrian Ambassador to London, Count Mensdorff, had the tact not even to raise the issue but, after the Slatin case, were invited to wear them again.

news about his decorations, Slatin tells Wingate that he has been invited to the King's Garden Party on the 22nd, an invitation 'of which I will avail myself'. And, as he knows that his friend has two grey top hats, could Wingate please lend him one of them for the occasion?

If 1927 had been a good year for Slatin, 1928 turned out to be a bad one. To begin with, in the spring, there was a humiliating and somewhat mysterious muddle with Cambridge University. In March, a certain Professor Henry Guillemard of that ancient institution had written to Wingate, apparently out of the blue, asking him to support a proposal for conferring an honorary degree on Slatin. What prompted Mr Guillemard to do this is not clear. What is clear is that, on this particular occasion, that inveterate collector of honours, the Inspector-General himself, was not behind the move. Indeed, as an entry in his diary for 15 March shows, his own view was that it would be better to 'leave it alone'.

Slatin was right. Wingate approached Stamfordham on 10 March to ask if the King would approve of Mr Guillemard's idea and two days later was informed that 'the King would of course be very glad'. But when, next month, Cambridge bestowed degrees on two distinguished foreigners, Slatin was not among them. Considering that one of the two foreigners just honoured had been Albert Einstein, Slatin had no reason to feel insulted. Remarkable man though he was in his prime, the Pasha had never been in *that* class. But he was quite justified when he wrote sorrowfully in his diary: 'Many may think that I wished to become a DCL, that I started the idea, which is nonsense.'

The whole episode had proved an unnecessary irritant to a man who had always been hypersensitive about rebuffs, supposed or genuine, and never more so than in these delicate post-war years.

Slatin soon had worse things to worry about. A few weeks after the Cambridge degree fiasco, he left for his annual visit to England and there, on 21 June, he fell really ill, probably for the first time since that dreadful winter of 1918–19. One writes 'really ill' because it is impossible to escape the feeling that, for some years now, Slatin was becoming increasingly a hypochondriac. The man who had once shrugged off or laughed off cholera, malaria, dysentery, leprosy, and a dozen other hazards of the Sudan now saw a threat to health lurking behind every headache and every sneeze. Much of the trouble he did have was, of course, due to his nerves, and nervous imagination.

In this summer of 1928, however, without imagining anything, he had a really bad time of it, and was nearly a month in a nursing home with angina pectoris and a heart thrombosis. A 'little blood clot on the brain' but 'not really a stroke' is how he describes it. Soon after he was released, he went to Vienna to consult a specialist. Though the verdict was not alarming, it was far from enthusiastic. As he wrote to a friend that autumn:

I am much better and stronger—but at my age it is hard work to get fit again. With some luck I will be able to fiddle along for a while without being a thorough invalid.

His illness sharpened that torment that had nagged him ever since his wife's death: could he somehow 'fiddle along' until Anna Marie was grown up and settled? If not, what on earth was to happen to his child? He probably already had, in the back of his mind, one last social ambition for her which, if he could only achieve it, would set her firmly on the English road he had chosen for her. But she had to be old enough, and he had to be still alive, in order for them to fulfil it. It was a double race against time.

1929 brought little cheer. His own health held up rather better but there were several other blows. In his diary he records the death of two old Sudan hands he had once served with, and they were the first of many who were soon to go in quick succession. Even more distressing, in December, his own brother Heinrich died in Austria, aged seventy-four. They had always been close and their careers, culminating in their sumultaneous baronies in 1906 from the Emperor Franz Joseph, had to some extent run in parallel. Rudolf wrote an anguished letter of condolence to his bereaved sister-in-law. In it, one senses that something of his own being has just crumbled away too.

Anna Marie's health had given way as well. She spent several months that year in a mountain sanatorium and the doctors had now ordained that she be kept there over the winter. The height that was supposed to do her good was harmful to her father's suspect heart, and so the old man faced a lonely

Christmas Eve without her in the Villa Mathilde – 'like a poor little plucked sparrow', as he wrote to his 'Miss Emily'.

He entered dolefully in his diary on New Year's Eve:

I am glad that this year is over. It has brought me disappointment, grief and sorrow. A-M's illness, my state of health, poor Heinrich's death and the loss of money on account of the loss of my investment. *Gäbe Gott* (sic) that 1930 will be better.

It was a little better. There were no new blows in the New Year; only the mounting concern about his own frailty and his daughter's slow recovery added to his constant if somewhat needless agonizing over money. These three worries seem always to be skipping hand in hand around his brain whenever he sits down to write to friends or relations.

In a letter of 3 March 1930 to his sister-in-law, for example, there comes this brooding passage:

I'm still troubled about Anna M . . . How I wish I were younger or at least stronger! Having to travel around and make arrangements for where my child is to stay is really taking it out of me. Yes, it's as though my escape 35 years ago, with the exhausting perils it brought with it, were somehow easier to bear than all these journeys with my child; and my worry over her goes deeper than anything else. The only thing is to hold out.

There is another touching last entry in his diary for the year:

I pray that the Almighty may give Anna Marie health and joyfulness and improve my condition that I may still for a while watch [over] my dear child.

One would like to be able to record that the object of all this devotion returned the old man's love to his satisfaction in equal measure, and with the right amount of gratitude thrown in as well. Perhaps, at heart, she did. But their relationship was clearly not an easy one. Slatin, as always in his life, craved not simply for affection but for constant evidence of affection, and the moody, sickly, motherless child seemed often unable to supply it in the massive doses for which he craved. Whether he only imagined her slights and sulks is impossible to say. But he now begins to brood over them, and over her long silences when they are apart. So another torment disturbs his last years.

In June of 1930, for example, when he has to tell Anna

Marie that she cannot go to England for the summer, her reaction (on a postcard) is so fierce that even Slatin loses patience. 'Impertinent,' he writes in his diary in English, 'That is the thanks I deserve!' (By which of course, he means, '*Is* that. . .?')

Relations become even more strained the following year. By now, Phipps, who had visited him in Meran in the autumn of 1930, was choosing a school for Anna Marie in England and was also looking around for some English girls of her own age (and, of course, of good family) for her to have as companions. Anna Marie's reactions to all this tender planning for her future had been anything but amicable. Indeed, the young miss informed her father in a curt letter that she would 'choose her own future friends for herself'. 'Rather sulky, even impertinent,' Slatin feels bound to comment.

It was the long silences from his child that worried poor Slatin almost as much as the unfriendly letters that did arrive. His diary is full of pathetic lamentations. 'No letter from Anna M. I wonder if she would know that her silence hurts me if she would (sic) not write' (21 March). 'Of course if I would not be alone I would think less about A-M as I do – but she is old enough that she could understand and could drop me now and then a line' (7 October). 'I wonder if Anna M knows what an amount of pleasure a nice letter would give me. . . . Children are selfish and cruel!' (9 December). And on the apparently rare occasions when he does get what he considers a 'nice letter', he joyfully marks the event with those characteristic wavy underlinings of his.

In 1931 it was his turn for hospital again. This time, there was a new and ominous complication, an internal growth for which he had to undergo a major operation in Vienna early in September. In a shaky hand, he records the event in his diary the morning after, listing the distinguished participants as though it had been not an operating table but a luncheon table. It led him, however, to the luncheon table he was after.

A mention of his illness was carried in the English papers but in case the King had not noticed it, Wingate drew it to the Palace's attention. The result was a personal message from King George and Queen Mary to the sick man in Vienna, wishing him a speedy recovery. It probably did more good than all the medicine he was swallowing, for there was something of the old Slatin in the grateful message he sent back to Sir Clive Wigram at Buckingham Palace:

I'm still unable to keep sufficient food to get strength but I fight as good (sic) as I can ...

For the money I spend for operations, sanatorium and doctors, I would get at least three first-class funerals!

And underneath his signature the invalid wrote: 'God Bless Their Majesties!'

No one, not even the implacable Lord Curzon had he still been on the scene, could have suppressed admiration for the way the old Pasha was fighting his last battle, not only doggedly, but almost chirpily. His friends in England, sensing that, though the immediate danger was over, there was not a lot of time left, would have done anything for him. Perhaps Slatin sensed it too. The moment had come to ask his most august English friend of all to do him that final and very special favour. For the last time, the faithful Wingate would serve as his spokesman, and it was to him that Slatin now wrote from Vienna. He planned, he said, if he was fit enough, to pay one more visit to England the following summer. He wanted to be received once more at the court on which so much of his life had centred. But above all, this time, he wanted to be allowed to present his young girl to the King and Queen.

'Their Majesties' – and everyone else involved – knew exactly what this meant to him. They did not let him down. At the end of September, Wigram wrote to Wingate:

Thank you for your letter of the 24th instant and enclosure from Slatin ... When you write to him will you kindly say that of course the King and Queen hope to meet his daughter, Anna Marie, when he brings her to England.

When Slatin heard the news he must have felt, not only that he had not 'fiddled along' in vain himself for so many years, but that his brief and ill-starred marriage had not, after all, been for nothing. Anna Marie, for all the worry she caused him, was now a lively and attractive girl of 15. She would be just about mature enough to reap the full benefit socially in England from this honour. With any luck, he, though a frail and wobbly seventy-four, would last just about long enough to enjoy it with her.

338

On 7 June, he celebrated his seventy-fifth birthday. For a week or two before the event, the peace of the Villa Mathilde was shattered by a stream of well-wishers with congratulations and journalists with notebooks. One of the most impressive tributes among the piles of messages came from Dr Miklas, the Federal President of Austria. In a four-page letter, he praised the man who 'though living for decades in far-off places and making a mark in the most varied fields always remained a true son of our country'. On 21 May Slatin's diary records another honour from his homeland. Vienna, his birthplace, had bestowed on him the Freedom of the City.

But Slatin's eyes, more than ever before in his life, were now fixed, not on his native Vienna, but on London. On 8 June, as soon as the birthday festivities were over, he set out with Anna Marie on their momentous journey. On arriving at the capital they went to stay at Colonel Phipps's rooms in St James's Court, the same apartments from where he had set out for Buckingham Palace twelve years before for that first post-war audience with King George.

When that year had dawned, Slatin had told Hilda Currie that cold was his greatest enemy in old age. Now, in London in the summer, it was fatigue. After only a few days, he was so worn out that even his host and dear friend seemed to get on his nerves. 'Phipps', he writes in his diary on 13 June, 'is a very nice kind fellow but he talks such a lot and his conversation is sometimes annoying, at least to me and perhaps to Anna M.'

There had been more trouble with the daughter too. On 22 June, they tried on the new dress that had been bought for the great event. The 'very nice kind fellow' wanted to pay for it as a special present. But Anna Marie was angry at the mere suggestion. Colonel Phipps, she declared, could give her any other gifts he liked, but *not* dresses. Poor Slatin writes it all down wearily in his diary. We never learn who paid in the end.

It was on Friday the 24th of June that Slatin, in morning clothes, accompanied by a pretty Anna Marie, who looked every inch the fashionable and grown-up young English woman as she walked by his side, entered Buckingham Palace by the Privy Purse entrance a few minutes before 1.15 p.m. for their private luncheon with the King and Queen. The last link had closed in that long chain of royal favour that had started with the visit to Queen Victoria at Osborne nearly forty years before.

Slatin, as usual, committed few of his emotions to paper. His diary merely records that the King and Queen joined them ten minutes after their arrival and that, during lunch, 'we talked on all different subjects and I enjoyed the meeting thoroughly'. Of the reactions of his formidable young daughter he writes only: 'Anna Marie was pleased and interested but not amused.'

Whether the girl was 'amused' or not, she was certainly, in Slatin's eyes, now 'launched' on that upper-class English road he had chosen for her. He could breathe at last. And though the composure she showed on her very first appearance at a royal dining-table probably puzzled him, it must have made him proud as well. He wrote joyfully of the occasion to those he knew would share his joy. King George, characteristically, was more phlegmatic. The entry in his diary for that day records without comment : 'Slatin Pasha and his daughter came to luncheon.'

Slatin was only just in time. Everyone in London remarked how grey and frail he was looking. It seemed as though now he had indeed shrunk into that 'poor little plucked sparrow' he had described himself as three years before. At the end of June, leaving Anna Marie behind in England because he felt it might do them good to be separated for a while, he cut his own visit short and left for his annual cure in Austria. He still had enough energy to fly, on the way home, from Croydon to Le Bourget on the 30th; enough curiosity as well, for it is the first aeroplane flight he is recorded as having taken. In Paris, he spent a few days with Edward Tuck, the sole survivor of his band of American friends and benefactors. There was an emotional, tearful, parting.

When he got to Bad Hall however, and tried to relax at last, he seemed to sag and shrivel up instead. On 13 July his diary sounds the first cry of alarm: 'My stomach gives me pain!' Two days later he complains of sudden cramps in his calves. (He could never quite believe this English word, and writes the German *Waden* alongside it.) The following week, he lost more than two pounds in weight. It was clear that the iodized waters of Bad Hall, which he had been swallowing religiously for years past to cure all sorts of ailments, were not going to do the trick this time. The doctors at the spa examined him, shook their heads about the state of his insides, and advised him to go to Vienna for a specialist's opinion.

A sorrow sharper than any of his physical pains now struck him. On 7 August, his brother Adolf woke him with a telegram saying that Colonel Phipps had died suddenly and peacefully in London. The ailing Slatin was almost incoherent with grief as he wrote in his diary:

I can hardly believe it. Poor Phipps. Poor one. I lost my best, most unselfish friend. It is terrible to think the greater (sic) loss to me and Anna-M. England will never be to me what it was. I shall keep him a grateful memory as long as I live. How long!!?

Not much longer. On 16 August, he underwent another serious internal operation to remove the growth that was eating away his life. As with his previous operation, he tried, as soon as he was out of the anaesthetic, to record the names of the medical men in attendance in their correct order of precedence. But after 'Professor Lorenz', who was the chief surgeon, he had to give it up. Punctilious to the last about birthdays, he managed to scrawl a few lines on the 23rd to Edward Tuck, who was '90 today'.

The last weeks were spent in the so-called Cottage Clinic of Vienna, a modern hospital quietly situated in clumps of trees on the main road out to Grinzing. There is a sharp bend in the road just opposite the entrance, and among the last noises Slatin must have heard were the rasping brakes of the trams as they carried the loads of thirsty citizens out to the wine-hills early in the evening and brought them back as cheerful revellers late at night. It was not the worst music for a Viennese to die to, and by the beginning of September, he sensed that he was indeed dying.

Apart from his family, only a handful of his closest friends were allowed near the weakening patient as September moved on. One of these was 'Miss Emily', the rich, pretty, well-born girl who had adored him when he was famous and who had been devoted to him ever since. Though she was now a mature woman in her forties (she never, for some reason, married) he was still avuncular towards her. She recalls sobbing so violently at his bedside that he became both upset and embarrassed by the noise, and practically ordered her to quieten down.

As for his own beloved Anna Marie, around whom all his hopes and fears and efforts had revolved for the past ten years, the last service he could do for her now – whatever it cost him – was to spare her the sight of him dying. In this he followed the example of his wife, who had written from her own death-bed eleven years before asking him to 'keep graves and cemeteries' away from their child. But though Slatin insisted that his daughter be kept abroad, and in ignorance of his hopeless condition, she was, as usual, never far from his thoughts. Indeed, the last complete entry in his diary, for 23 September, was written after hearing that she was gaily setting off on a holiday trip. He writes weakly: 'I hope her visit will be a success and that there will be nice girls with A–M. And that she will find her friends!'

That same loving solicitude to see that his child is installed in the 'right company' before he leaves her thus continues to the very end.

It is a strange sight to see a man's death traced in his own hand. From this point onwards, Slatin's diary becomes a succession of brief convulsive scrawls, each fainter and more confused than that of the day before. The last legible words, still in English, come on 25 September: 'I didn't do anything. . . .'

The final attempt at writing that he made is a long jerky squiggle under the date for 28 September. It looks for all the world like the mark of a seismograph responding to some distant elemental call. Six days later, on 4 October 1932, Slatin Pasha was indeed dead.

He would have relished his own funeral, which was held two days later in the cemetery at Ober Sankt Veit, the same Viennese *Bezirk* where he had been born seventy-five years before. Though it was a rainy October day, a large crowd of mourners turned out. They included the highest representatives of all those elements that had made up the dead man's life.

The Federal President of Austria, Dr Miklas, who only four months before had written Slatin that long birthday letter of congratulations, headed the list. By command of King George V, the British Ambassador in Vienna, Sir Eric Phipps, represented the sovereign, and Phipps reported afterwards that Dr Miklas had begged him to convey 'an expression of his grateful thanks

... to His Majesty for having been so gracious as to be represented at the funeral of a great Austrian'.

From the distant Nile came a wreath, in the name of Sir Percy Lorraine, the High Commissioner for Egypt and the Sudan. Wingate, who probably could not have got from Scotland to Vienna in time, also sent a wreath for his 'dear old Rowdy'. High society too was represented, at least in flowers. Another large wreath came from Prince Ulrich Kinsky, the current head of the family that had done so much, materially and socially, for Slatin, for his father, and for his brothers. He was buried, as he had lived, in cosmopolitan style.

Rudolf Slatin himself lived on, of course, in the memory of old Sudan hands. Wingate, the greatest of these and the second of the 'Sudanese twins', did not die until 1953, at the ripe age of 93. A handful are still alive today. Even Whitehall, which had alternately been the boon and the bane of Slatin's life, was not quite finished with him after the official report of his funeral had been filed away in London. On 4 October 1934, two years to the day after his death, the idea was raised of making a film on the Mahdia, centred around Slatin Pasha's career. Wingate had been among the sponsors but the film company concerned were not going to proceed unless they were assured in advance of the Sudan Government's approval and backing.

This assurance Sir Stewart Symes, the Governor-General of 1934, was emphatically not prepared to give. Indeed, he warned against the project, saying he 'felt strongly that there would be a grave danger of such a film re-awakening both Mahdist feeling in the Sudan and political reactions in Egypt'. The Pasha would have snorted at that verdict, which caused the whole idea to be dropped.

In the spring of 1935, Whitehall dealt for the last time with Slatin Pasha. Appropriately, the matter at issue was a memorial which a group of nine of his old friends (including, of course, Wingate and Currie) were proposing to erect to him in Khartoum. Their letter to *The Times* in May of the previous year, which had appealed for public donations, had raised £280, but the proposed memorial would cost £400. After eight months of to-ing and fro-ing between London, Cairo and Khartoum, the Foreign Office finally approved a contribution of £25, to be drawn from the 'Unforeseen Missions and

Services' account of the Diplomatic Budget. One cannot claim they had exerted themselves unduly in His Majesty's name.

The memorial was duly erected and formally unveiled in 1936 by Sir Stewart Symes. It took the form of a drinking fountain on a raised granite platform enclosed by four hexagonal granite columns, all cut from the stone of the Sileitat quarries north of the capital. It was placed in Omdurman on the site of the Khalifa's house and the mud hut of Abdel Kader, his servant. On two sides of the memorial, inscriptions in English and Arabic commemorated the memory of 'Baron Sir Rudolf von Slatin Pasha GCVO, KCMG, CB, who alike in good and evil fortune served this country and its people'. Above the English inscription was set a bronze plaque of Slatin's head.

In 1956, only three years after the Sudan was given its independence by Britain, this was removed by the Omdurman Municipality. For good measure, they also renamed the near-by street that had been called after him. The man who took his place on the street sign was a famous emir of the Mahdi's. No one wanted to be reminded any longer of Slatin Pasha, the white imperialist lieutenant of General Gordon's day. Times were indeed changing.

Long before this however, they had changed far more rapidly and far more drastically in Slatin's native Austria. In the last spring of his life, he had already been anxiously watching the sinister convulsions of German politics. After the Presidential elections there in April 1932 he had written in his diary: 'I am glad that Hindenburg was elected against Hitler.' Yet only four months after Slatin's death, Hitler swept into power in Berlin. The year after that, Hitler's thugs had shot Engelbert Dollfuss, Austria's tiny but resolute Chancellor, dead in his Vienna office. Four years further on, and Hitler's troops had marched into Austria, greeted by a fairly weighty if extremely misguided section of its people.

For all his pliability, Rudolf Slatin would not have been among that wildly cheering crowd of two hundred thousand who crammed Vienna's Heldenplatz on 15 March 1938 to welcome the Austrian-born Führer home. Indeed it is questionable whether Slatin would have survived the Nazi era at all. He was a full Jew by blood, a passionate monarchist at heart and a notorious Anglophile by reputation and background. Not even his age and the romantic legend of his name would have weighed down the scales against those three capital crimes had he lived to fall foul of Austria's new masters.

Without realizing it, Slatin had in fact timed both his entrance and his exit on the world stage to perfection. He had been born into the new age of social freedoms (though not social equality) of an Imperial Vienna that had been shaken and almost overtoppled by the 1848 Revolution. He had arrived in the Sudan, panting for fame and adventure, in the very decade when, thanks to General Gordon and his haphazard recruitment methods, a meteoric career was still possible for an obscure young foreigner. And when fame arrived, Slatin just had time, before Queen Victoria died, to set upon it that seal of royal patronage under which he was to flourish. True, the 1914 war broke off his career at its zenith and faced him, during its first months, with the bitterest moral challenge of his life, one that he failed to master. But in the twenty years that had gone before, and above all in that blissful Edwardian decade, Slatin had been able to bask in the sunset of the old Europe, and he had savoured every golden moment of it.

His exit, too, was well taken. Slatin was above all a European, a man to whom the continent meant more than any single country in it, and for whom the concert of civilized peoples was more important than any one government among them. Hitler arrived to shatter the last faint echoes of that harmony which had lingered on after the collapse of 1918. It is only today that Slatin's Europe is re-forming again, not around dynasties, but around whole nations. Whatever he might have thought about present-day Africa, the Pasha would have liked this new Europe, and have stretched his short legs gratefully in it.

Notes

Source References

The following are the abbreviations for the principal archives consulted and quoted:

RA: Royal Archives Windsor
PRO: Public Records Office London
HHSA: Haus, Hof und Staatsarchiv Vienna
MKSM: Imperial Military Chancery Vienna
KM: Austrian War Ministry Vienna

All the Slatin papers in the Sudan Archives are at the School of Oriental Studies of Durham University. Where the source is made clear by the text (for example, all the dated extracts from Slatin's diaries) the general box reference number to the material is given only once.

The various other diaries and collections of letters relating to Slatin which are in private hands are referred to by name and date.

Chapter One: The Boy from Vienna

page 6 line 33   Baptism Register of St Augustin's, Vienna, Tome VIII, Folio 58.

p. 9 l. 3   Paul Slatin Family Papers: Rudolf Slatin to his future sister-in-law, 15 November 1881.

p. 11 l. 4   These and other details of his early life are taken, with grateful acknowledgements, from the *Mitteilungsblatt des Absolventenvereins der Handelsakademie Wien*, Nos. 17 and 18, November 1970.

p. 13 l. 5   Rudolf Slatin: *Fire and Sword in the Sudan*, London, 1896, pp. 1–2.

Chapter Three: The Mahdi

p. 33 l. 4   Reginald Wingate: *Mahdism and the Egyptian Sudan*, London, 1891, pp. 13–14.

p. 38 l. 17 Slatin: *Fire and Sword*, op. cit., p. 120.

p. 39 l. 23 Text given in P. M. Holt: *The Mahdist State in the Sudan*, Oxford 1958, p. 50.

p. 43 l. 5 J. Ohrwalder: *Ten Years' Captivity in the Mahdi's Camp*, London 1893, pp. 52 et seq.

Chapter Four: Defeat and Surrender

p. 50 l. 18 *Fire and Sword*, op. cit., pp. 215–6.

p. 52 l. 20 The German merchant-adventurer Charles Neufeld in his *Prisoner of the Khalifa*, New York 1899, pp. 203–206.

p. 56 l. 4 Quoted in Wingate, op. cit., pp. 86–87.

p. 27 l. 28 Text in *Fire and Sword*, op. cit., p. 254.

Chapter Five: Khartoum

p. 68 l. 11 Given as Appendix 'R' to C. G. Gordon: *Journals of Khartoum*, London 1885.

p. 70 l. 25 *Fire and Sword*, op. cit., pp. 330–331.

p. 73 l. 8 *Fire and Sword*, op. cit., p. 340.

p. 74 l. 3 Sir Ronald Wingate: *Wingate of the Sudan*, London 1955 pp. 70–71.

p. 77 l. 13 *Fire and Sword*, op. cit., p. 366.

p. 77 l. 23 Wingate: *Mahdism and the Egyptian Sudan*, op. cit., p. 228.

Chapter Six: The Khalifa's Captive

p. 82 l. 23 RA 023/50 Lord Wolseley to the Secretary of State for War, 5 October 1884.

p. 82 l. 33 Charles Neufeld: *A Prisoner of the Khalifa*, New York 1899 p. 203.

p. 85 l. 20 *Fire and Sword*, op. cit., p. 367.

p. 89 l. 12 *Fire and Sword*, op. cit., pp. 557–558.

p. 90 l. 33 *Fire and Sword*, op. cit., p. 454.

p. 93 l. 3 *Fire and Sword*, op. cit., p. 484.

p. 93 l. 24 7 Report passed to the Austrian authorities and preserved in HHSA PA XXXl/14.

Chapter Seven: Escape

p. 99 l. 16 The original is in the possession of Herr Paul Slatin to whom I am indebted for permission to reproduce it.

p. 101 l. 25 *Fire and Sword*, op. cit., p. 446.

p. 108 l. 4 Text in HHSA PA XXXI/14. Report of Count Wass to Count Kalnocky in Vienna dated 11 July 1892.

p. 108 l. 32 Reproduced in full in the Monthly Intelligence

Report of Egyptian Army Headquarters for November 1894.

p. 110 l. 31   HHSA PA XXXI/15 Cairo, 4 March 1895.

p. 114 l. 10   Unless otherwise indicated, the account of Slatin's escape which follows is based on his own *Fire and Sword*, op. cit. pp. 591 et seq.

Chapter Eight: The Queen's Darling

p. 126 l. 26   HHSA, PA XXXI/15.

p. 127 l. 12   Slatin Archives, Durham Box 121 for collected press material on Slatin's escape.

p. 128 l. 19   Published in the *Daily Graphic* on 28 March 1895.

p. 129 l. 24   HHSA PA XXXI/15, 22 April to 23 May 1895.

p. 130 l. 32   RA Windsor 028/262; Wingate to Bigge, 28 March 1896.

p. 132 l. 13   All from the collection of Paul Slatin, Vienna.

p. 134 l. 34   Paul Slatin, family anecdote without date.

p. 135 l. 17   Slatin Archives, Durham, Boxes 440 and 441 N.B. (This reference applies to all diary extracts quoted)

p. 136 l. 5   RA L7/127, Wingate to Bigge 27 May 1895.

p. 136 l. 33   Slatin Archives, Durham, Box 256/1, Bigge to Wingate 25 July 1895.

p. 137 l. 5   14 Bigge to Wingate August, 1895, Slatin Archives, Durham, Box 256/1.

p. 137 l. 32   RA Queen Victoria's Journal for 19 August 1895. (Letters of Queen Victoria; third series, Vol. II p. 554.)

p. 138 l. 22 Slatin Archives, Durham, Box 104/6.

p. 138   l. 26   Slatin Archives, Durham, Box 256/1; letter of Sir Fleetwood to Wingate, 11 September 1895.

p. 139 l. 24   Kronberg Letters 31 May 1898, quoted in Elisabeth Longford *Victoria R.I.* London 1964, p. 692.

p. 142 l. 10   RA L7/129, report of Sir A. Bigge.

p. 142 l. 27   RA 028/229, memorandum of Sir Arthur Bigge, 11 October 1895.

p. 143 l. 15   Most of what follows is drawn from *Henry Ponsonby* by his son Arthur Ponsonby London 1942; *Recollections of Three Reigns* by Sir Frederick Ponsonby London 1951; and *Life with Queen Victoria* (The Letters of Marie Mallet) (Boston 1968).

p. 146 l. 33   RA 028/236, Wingate to Bigge, 2 December 1895.

Chapter Nine: The Queen's Soldier

p. 151 l. 1   RA 028/273 Slatin to Queen Victoria, 12 May 1896.

p. 152 l. 14   Slatin Archives, Durham, Box 454/4.

p. 153 l. 4   RA 029/4 Wingate to Bigge, 10 June 1896.

p. 153 l. 13   RA 029/14 Wingate to Bigge, 20 June 1896.

p. 153 l. 24   RA 029/12 Slatin to Queen Victoria, 20 June 1896.

p. 154. l 24   This exchange of messages in RA Windsor 029/15 and 16.

p. 155 l20 HHSA PA XXXl/17 Heidler to Goluchowski 11 July 1890.

p. 156 l15   RA 029/21 Slatin to Queen Victoria, 22 July 1896.

p. 158 l4   RA 029/19 Wingate to Bigge, 27 July 1896.

p. 158 l. 23   RA 029/25 Wingate to Bigge, 25 August 1896.

p. 159 l. 35   The letter is dated from Omdurman 20 Safar 1314 or 31 July 1896. A Translation is in RA 029/25A.

p. 160 l. 29   RA 029/29 Slatin to Queen Victoria, 15 September 1896.

p. 161 l. 28   Slatin Archives, Durham. Box 454/4.

p. 161 l. 41   RA 029/56 Wingate to Bigge from Cairo, 30 November 1896.

p. 164 l. 4   Paul Slatin papers, Count Eulenberg to Heinrich Slatin, 16 March 1896.

p. 164 l. 15   Paul Slatin papers, Rudolf Slatin to Heinrich Slatin, 27 July 1896.

p. 165 l. 15   Paul Slatin papers, Rudolf Slatin to Frau Heinrich Slatin, 26 October 1896.

p. 166 l. 1   Paul Slatin papers, Rudolf Slatin to Heinrich Slatin, 19 December 1896.

p. 166 l. 14   Paul Slatin papers, Rudolf Slatin to Heinrich Slatin, 8 January 1897.

Chapter Ten: Return to Omdurman

p. 167 l. 17   RA 029/72   Slatin to Queen Victoria, 15 October 1897.

p. 168 l. 22   RA 029/70 Wingate to Bigge 17 September 1897.

p. 169 l. 22   RA 029/74 Wingate to Bigge 11 November 1897.

p. 170 l. 24   Wingate, op. cit. p. 114.

p. 170 l. 36   RA 029/77 Slatin to Queen Victoria 2 February 1898.

p. 172 l. 30   RA 030 1a Wingate to Slatin from Berber 14 March 1898.

p. 173 l. 30   030/1, Wingate to Bigge from Abbadia, 4 May 1898.

p. 173 l. 34   RA 030/3, Wingate to Bigge from Assuan, 4 June 1898.

p. 174 l. 18   RA 030/1 Wingate to Bigge 4 May 1898.

p. 174 l. 33   RA 030/7 Wingate to Bigge from Shabluka 21 August 1898.

Notes

p. 175 l. 38   W. L. S. Churchill; *The River War* London 1899, Volume II pp. 107–164.

p. 181 l. 16   RA 031/95 Wingate to Bigge from Cairo, 3 December 1899.

p. 182 l. 25   Slatin kept the telegram. It is among his papers in the Slatin Archives, Box 452/302.

p. 182 l. 31   RA 031/94.

Chapter Eleven: The Inspector-General

p. 187 l. 20   Memorandum of Queen Victoria, 3 November 1898 Slatin Archives, Durham.

p. 188 l. 23   HHSA, PA XXXI, Cairo to Vienna, 28 October 1898.

p. 189 l. 12   HHSA PA XXXI/19 Cairo to Vienna, 18 November 1898.

p. 189 l. 24   The pencilled draft dated 14 November 1898 has survived in the Sudan Archives, Durham, Box 452/2.

p. 190 l. 10   Slatin Archives, Durham, Box 452/302, Reid to Slatin, 16 January 1899.

p. 190 l. 19   Slatin Archives, Durham, Box 454/4.

p. 191 l. 1   HHSA PA XXXI/19, Cairo to Vienna, 23 December 1898.

p. 191 l. 27   HHSA PA XXXI/20 Cairo to Vienna, 24 March 1899. (This was worth slightly more than 600 English pounds.)

p. 194 l. 11   HHSA XXX/21 Cairo to Vienna, 15 June 1900.

p. 195 l. 20   HHSA PA XXX/21, Cairo to Vienna, 1 October 1900.

p. 195 l. 33   Slatin Archives, Durham, Box 403/6.

p. 203 l. 3   *Wingate of the Sudan,* op. cit., p. 148.

p. 203 l. 37   HHSA PA XXXI/22 Cairo to Vienna (quoting Slatin) 9 October 1902.

p. 204 l. 18   PRO 16:21544/658 of 1911.

p. 206 l. 29   Quoted in Wingate, op. cit. pp. 159–60.

Chapter Twelve: Crest of the Wave

p. 212 l. 1   Conversation with the author June 1970.

p. 217 l. 3   RA Edward VII B 1889. Slatin to Sir Arthur Davidson.

p. 221 l. 7   See E. C. Corti-Sokol, *Kaiser Franz Joseph,* Vienna 1960 pp. 384–388.

p. 223 l. 3   RA Edward VII C22593, Wingate to Lord Knollys, 9 August 1907.

p. 223 l. 11 RA Edward VII C22593, Wingate to Lord Knollys.

p. 224 l. 34   *Neue Freie Presse*, report of 23 August 1909.
p. 225 l. 13   RA Journal of Queen Victoria. 5 September 1900.

Chapter Thirteen: Alice

p. 235 l. 9   Sir Mervyn Wheatley, in a conversation with the author, 29 July 1971.
p. 235 l. 32   Paul Slatin family papers. Rudolf Slatin to his sister-in-law, from Kosheh, 3 August 1896.
p. 236 l. 37   Very generously provided by 'Miss Emily' herself, now an energetic old lady well in her eighties.
p. 237 l. 5   A selection of which has been kindly provided by Frau Köchert herself who, unlike 'Miss Emily', had no objection to her name being used.
p. 237 l. 27   In a conversation with the author (June 1970).
p. 238 l. 24   Diary of Miss Elliott (now Mrs Nicoll) kindly provided through the good offices of her son, Sir James Bowker, K.C.M.G.
p. 241 l. 13   Slatin Papers, Durham, Box 450/109. All the letters are partly in English and partly in German. The English passages have been left in their original form.
p. 241 l. 37   Slatin papers, Durham, Box 150.

Chapter Fourteen: August 1914: The Man Between

p. 252 l. 2   Josef Redlich, *Tagebuch*, 13 February 1915, recording Slatin's conversation at a Vienna dinner party.
p. 252 l. 36   RA GV 25124 'Note on Slatin Pasha' by Sir Reginald Wingate 18 May 1919.
p. 252 l. 33   See Gordon Brook-Shepherd, *The Last Habsburg* London 1968, p. 63.
p. 257 l. 15   Slatin Papers, Durham, Box 223/1.
p. 259 l. 4   HHSA Vienna, Politisches Archiv I/887, Liasse Krieg 7.
p. 259 l. 33   See Richard Hill 'Slatin Pasha' London 1965, p. 121.
p. 260 l. 6   HHSA Vienna: As above, Telegram No. 385 Vienna to Constantinople, 27 August 1914.
p. 260 l. 25   HHSA Vienna: As above, Pallavicini to Berchtold, Telegram No. 493, 28 August 1914.
p. 260 l. 31   HHSA Vienna: As above, Pallavicini to Berchtold, Telegram No. 512, 28 August 1914.
p. 263 l. 1   PRO 1914. 49402 and W 16. 50084 for this whole episode.
p. 263 l. 36   Slatin Archives, Durham, Box 233/1.

p. 264 l. 9   Slatin Archives, Durham, Box 233/1.

p. 264 l. 17   Slatin Archives, Durham, Box 223/1 (the letter is in draft form).

p. 264 l. 32   Slatin Archives, Durham, Box 223/1.

p. 265 l. 22   Slatin Archives, Durham, Box 223/1 Slatin to Wingate 30 September 1914 (both letters).

p. 266 l. 18   Slatin Archives, Durham, Box 223/1.

p. 267 l. 2   Austrian War Ministry (KM) Präs. 50 – 1/85 No. 12, 638 of 13 September 1914.

p. 267 l. 13   Austrian Imperial Military Chancery Archives (MKSM) 69 – 1/13 – 17 of 1914.

p. 267 l. 30   Austrian Foreign Ministry: F 23, 1X F – 540 Berchtold to Stürgkh, 24 November 1914.

p. 268 l. 34   KM Präs 76 – 2/1 – 78, No. 10,009 of 18 June 1915.

p. 270 l. 18   RA GV O. 1231/3.

p. 270 l. 26   RA GV P2116/8.

Chapter Fifteen: From the Shadows

p. 276 l. 16   Slatin Archives, Durham, Box 223/3.

p. 276 l. 21   Slatin Archives, Durham, Box 223/4.

p. 276 l. 30   Slatin Archives, Durham, Box 223/4.

p. 278 l. 4   RA GV 25124. Slatin to Lord Stamfordham, 25 June 1917.

p. 278 l. 5   RA GV 25124. Lord Stamfordham to Slatin, 31 July 1917.

p. 278 l. 19   P.R.O. 9398/64156/W3/17.

p. 279 l. 2   See Brook-Shepherd, op. cit., pp. 62–79.

p. 279 l. 18   The Empress Zita in a letter to the author, 12 September 1971.

p. 279 l. 36   PRO 93098/64156/W3.

p. 279 l. 10   RA GV O. 1231/3.

p. 282 l. 26   MKSM 7171, 11 November 1917.

p. 283 l. 14   MKSM 1917, No. 7632 of 17 November 1917.

p. 283 l. 24   MKSM 464/7. 9 December 1917.

p. 284 l. 11   Slatin Archives, Durham, Box 223/5. Slatin to Wingate 16 June 1918.

p. 286 l. 20   Translated text in RA GV 25124.

p. 286 l. 33   As above. Slatin to Lord Stamfordham, 10 December 1918.

p. 287 l. 12   RA GV 25124. Slatin to Colonel House, 10 December 1918.

p. 287 l. 33   *Generalbericht der Öst. Gesellschaft vom Roten Kreuze für das Jahr 1918*, p. 54.

p. 287 l. 38   RA GV 25124.

p. 288 l. 6   RA GV 25124. Lord Stamfordham to Slatin, 19 December 1918.

p. 289 l. 9   Slatin Archives, Durham, Box 223/5. (Slatin repeated this letter on 28 December, with minor variations, in case the first had gone astray.)

p. 289 l. 11   RA GV 25124.

p. 292 l. 14   Slatin Archives, Durham, Box 223/8, Slatin to Wingate, June 1921.

p. 292 l. 36   RA GV 25124. Lord Stamfordham to Slatin, 14 January 1919.

Chapter Sixteen: Clambering Back

p. 295 l. 3   Slatin Archives, Durham, Box 435/12

p. 295 l. 21   Slatin Archives, Durham, Box 435/12 Slatin to Bauer (undated, but probably 4 May 1919)

p. 295 l. 31   Slatin Archives, Durham, Box 435/12.

p. 296 l. 21   Slatin Archives, Durham, Box 435/412. Bauer to Slatin, 1 June 1919.

p. 296 l. 26   Slatin Archives, Durham, Box 435/412. Renner to Slatin, 12 August 1919.

p. 296 l. 33   Slatin Archives, Durham, Box 455/6. Slatin to his wife, 21 July 1919.

p. 297 l. 1   Slatin Archives, Durham, Box 223/6. Slatin to Wingate, 3 August 1919.

p. 297 l. 6   PRO W3/78225 and 731886 (FO 371/3542). Telegrams of 22 May 1919 to 14 June 1919.

p. 297 l. 28   PRO 1203/6364/290. 9–14 July 1919.

p. 298 l. 16   Slatin Archives, Durham, Box 435/312.

p. 298 l. 33   Slatin Archives, Durham, Box 435/312. Bauer to Slatin, 20 July 1919.

p. 299 l. 35   Slatin Archives, Durham, Box 223/6. Slatin to Wingate, 5 October 1919.

p. 300 l. 24   PRO 303/126174 (FO 372/1219). Memorandum of Eastern Department of 9 September 1919.

p. 300 l. 31   Slatin Archives, Durham, Box 435/15.

p. 301 l. 6   Slatin to 'Miss Emily', 26 October 1919.

p. 301 l. 20   Slatin Archives, Durham, Slatin to Wingate, 28 February 1919.

p. 301 l. 29   Slatin to 'Miss Emily' from Territet, 13 November 1919.

p. 302 l. 6   Slatin Archives, Durham, Slatin to Wingate, 28 October 1919.

p. 303 l. 8   Slatin Archives, Durham, Box 223/6. Slatin to Wingate, 16 December 1919.

p. 303 l. 22   Slatin Archives, Durham, Box 223/6. Lord Hardinge to Wingate, 30 September 1919.

p. 304 l. 3   PRO FO 371/3542, Paris to London, 13 May 1919.

p. 304 l. 16   PRO FO 371/73241. Wingate to L. Lloyd, 18 May 1919.

p. 304 l. 23   RA GV 25124. See pp. 289–90 above.

p. 305 l. 8   RA GV 25124.

p. 305 l. 24   RA GV 25124. Lord Stamfordham to Slatin, 23 December 1919.

p. 306 l. 2   Slatin Archives, Durham, Box 435. Slatin to Renner, 26 March 1920.

p. 307 l. 28   Slatin from London to 'Miss Emily', 27 February 1920.

p. 307 l. 33   Slatin Archives, Durham. Slatin to his wife, 25 January 1920.

p. 308 l. 12   Slatin Archives, Durham. Slatin to Wingate, 22 January 1920.

p. 308 l. 24   Slatin Archives, Durham, Box 223/7. Slatin to Wingate, 4 February 1920.

p. 309 l. 28   Slatin Archives, Durham, Box 223/7. Slatin to Wingate, 7 February 1920.

p. 309 l. 38   RA GV 25124. Slatin to Lord Stamfordham, 20 February 1920.

p. 310 l. 3   Slatin Archives, Durham. Slatin to Wingate, 24 February 1920.

p. 311 l. 5   RA Geo. V Diary. 20 February 1920.

p. 311 l. 11   Slatin Archives, Durham, Box 452/269.

p. 312 l. 36   Slatin Archives, Durham, Box 223/8. Slatin to Wingate, 30 January 1921.

p. 314 l. 8   RA Geo V 0 1231. Lord Stamfordham to Slatin, 13 December 1920.

p. 314 l. 29   All the material on this episode which follows is in PRO FO 371/5784 (April to November 1921).

p. 318 l. 16   PRO FO 371/7348 (C 160/163).

p. 318 l. 22   Slatin Archives, Durham, Box 223/7. Slatin to Wingate, 28 January 1920.

p. 318 l. 28   Slatin to Renner. Memorandum of 20 March 1920.

p. 319 l. 1   Slatin Archives, Durham, Slatin to Wingate, 8 June 1920.

p. 319 l. 15   Slatin, from Territet, to 'Miss Emily'. (undated)

p. 320 l. 12   Slatin Archives, Durham, Box 455/7/1.

Notes

p. 321 l. 16   RA GV 25124. Lord Stamfordham to Slatin, 1 July 1921.

p. 322 l. 1   Slatin Archives, Durham, Box 435/315. Baird to Slatin, 2 March 1922.

p. 322 l. 25   Slatin Archives, Durham, Box 435/315. Baird to Wingate, 7 April 1922.

Chapter Seventeen: The Last Plateau

p. 325 l. 31   Slatin Archives, Durham. Slatin to Wingate, 9 January 1920.

p. 326 l. 12   PRO FO 371/7351 (C 12581) 4–22 September 1922.

p. 327 l. 6   Slatin Archives, Durham. Slatin to Wingate, 4 December 1920.

p. 327 l. 11   Slatin Archives, Durham, Slatin to Wingate, 24 December 1920.

p. 327 l. 24   Slatin Archives, Durham. Slatin to Wingate, 30 April 1922.

p. 328 l. 22   Slatin Archives, Durham, Box 440 for this and other financial details.

p. 329 l. 16   Slatin Archives, Durham. Slatin to Wingate, 27 August 1920.

p. 331 l. 23   Slatin Archives, Durham, Box 223/11. Slatin to Wingate, 26 November 1926.

p. 332 l. 12   PRO FO 372/2306. 16 April – 3 June 1927 for this final correspondence on the Slatin case.

p. 334 l. 1   Slatin Archives, Durham, Box 223/12. Slatin to Wingate, 7 July 1927.

p. 334 l. 20   RA GV 25124. Stamfordham to Wingate, 14 March 1928.

p. 335 l. 12   Slatin to Grant-Smith, 28 September 1928.

p. 335 l. 32   Slatin Family Papers: Slatin to 'Gusti', 19 December 1929.

p. 336 l, 1   Slatin to 'Miss Emily', 15 December 1929.

p. 336 l. 14   Paul Slatin papers.

p. 338 l. 28   RA GV 25124. Wigram to Wingate, 29 September 1931.

p. 339 l. 6   Original in Slatin Archives, Durham, Box 435/323.

p. 340 l. 16   RA Geo. V Diary, 24 June 1932.

p. 342 l. 5   Slatin Archives, Durham, Box 455/7.

p. 342 l. 38   PRO FO 371/16128. Phipps to Sir John Simon, 6 October 1931.

p. 343 l. 27   PRO FO 371/18021. (The film was never made.)

p. 344 l. 1   PRO FO 371/19094, April to December 1935.

INDEX

Index